World's End

A Story in Three Books

Richard Jefferies

World's End: A Story in Three Books

The present edition is a reproduction of previous publication of this classic work. Minor typographical errors may have been corrected without note; however, for an authentic reading experience the spelling, punctuation, and capitalization have been retained from the original text.

ISBN: 978-1-64799-598-0

CONTENTS

VOLUME 1

VOLUME 2

VOLUME 3

VOLUME ONE

Chapter One

Book One

Facts

It is not generally known that the mighty city of Stirmingham owes its existence to a water-rat. Stirmingham has a population of half a million, and is the workshop of the earth. It is a proud city, and its press-men have traced its origin back into the dim vista of the past, far before Alfred the Great's time, somewhere in the days of those monarchs who came from Troy, and whose deeds Holinshed so minutely chronicles.

But this is all trash and nonsense, and is a cunning device of the able editors aforesaid, who confound—for their own purposes—the city proper with the tiny hamlet of Wolf's Glow. This little village or cluster of houses, which now forms a part, and the dirtiest part, of the city, can indeed be traced through Hundred Rolls, Domesday Book, and Saxon Charters, almost down to the time of the Romans. But Stirmingham, the prosperous and proud Stirmingham, which thinks that the world could not exist without its watches and guns, its plated goods, its monster factories and mills, which sends cargoes to Timbuctoo, and supplies Java and Malabar with idols—this vast place, whose nickname is a by-word for cheating, for fair outward show and no real solidity, owes its existence to a water-rat. This is a fact. And it happened in this way.

Once upon a time there was a wide expanse of utterly useless land, flat as this sheet of paper, without a trace of subsoil or any kind of earth in which so much as a blade of grass could grow. It was utterly dry and sterile—not a tree nor a shrub to shelter a cow or a horse, and all men avoided it as a waste and desolate place. It was the very abomination of desolation, and no one would have been surprised to have seen satyrs and other strange creatures diverting themselves thereon. Around one edge of this plain there flowed a brook, so small that one could hardly call it by that name. A dainty lady from Belgravia could have easily stepped across it without soiling the sole of her boot.

At one spot beside this brook there grew a willow tree. This tree was a picture in itself, and would have made the fortune of any artist who would have condescended to make a loving study of it. The trunk

1

had been of very large size, but now resembled a canoe standing upon end, for nearly one half had decayed, and the crumbling wood had disappeared, leaving a hollow stem. The stem was itself dead and decaying, except one thin streak of green, up which the golden sap of life still ran, and invigorated the ancient head of the tree to send forth yellow buds and pointed leaves. Up one side of the hollow trunk an ivy creeper had climbed to the top, and was fast hanging festoons from bough to bough.

In the vast mass of decaying wood at the top or head of the tree a briar had taken root—its seed no doubt dropped by some thrush—and its prickly shoots hung over and drooped to the ground in luxuriance of growth. The hardy fern had also found a lodging here, and its dull green leaves, which they say grow most by moonlight, formed a species of crown to the dying tree.

This willow was the paradise of such birds as live upon insects, for they abounded in the decaying wood; and at the top a wild pigeon had built its nest. As years went by, the willow bent more and more over the brook. The water washing the soil out from between its roots formed a hollow space, where a slight eddy scooped out a deeper hole, in which the vermillion—throated stickleback or minnow disported and watched the mouth of its nest. This eddy also weakened the tree by underlining it at its foundation. The ivy grew thicker till it formed a perfect bush upon the top, and this in the winter afforded a hold for the wind to shake the tree by. The wind would have passed harmlessly through the slender branches, but the ivy, even in winter, the season of storms, left something against which it could rage with effect. Finally came the water-rat.

If Stirmingham objects to owe its origin to a water-rat, it may at least congratulate itself upon the fact that it was a good old English rat—none of your modern parvenu, grey Hanoverian rascals. It was, in fact, before the Norwegian rat, which had been imported in the holds of vessels, had obtained undisputed sway over the country. It had, however, already driven the darker aboriginal inhabitants away from the cultivated places to take refuge in the woods and streams. It is odd that in the animal kingdom also, even in the rat economy, the darker hued race should give way to the lighter. However, as in Stirmingham the smoke is so great that the ladies when they walk abroad carry parasols up to keep the blacks from falling on and disfiguring their complexion, there can after all be no disgrace in the water-rat ancestry.

This dark coloured water-rat, finding his position less and less secure at the adjacent barn on account of the attacks of the grey invaders, one fine day migrated, with Mrs Rat and all the Master and Missy rats, down to the stream. Peeping and sniffing about for a pleasant retreat, he chose the neighbourhood of the willow tree. I cannot stay here to discuss whether or no he was led to the tree by some mystic beckoning hand—some supernatural presentiment; but to the tree he went, and Stirmingham was founded. Two or three burrows—small round holes—sufficed to house Mr Rat and his family, but these ran right under the willow, and of course still further weakened it.

In course of time the family flourished exceedingly, and Mr Rat became a great-great-great-grandpapa to ever so many minor Frisky Tails. These Frisky Tails finding the ancient quarter too much straightened for comfort, began to scratch further tunnels, and succeeded pretty well in opening additional honeycombs, till presently progress was stayed by a root of the tree. Now they had gnawed through and scratched away half a dozen other roots, and never paused to sniff more particularly at this than the others. But it so happened that this root was the one which supplied the green streak up the trunk of the tree with the golden sap of life drawn by mysterious chemical processes from the earth. Frisky Tails gnawed this root asunder, and cut off the supply of sap. The green streak up the trunk withered and died, and the last stay of the willow was gone. It only remained for the first savage south-wester of winter to finish the mischief.

The south-wester came, and over went the trunk, crash across the brook. At first this was very awkward for the rats, as thereby most of their subterranean dwellings became torn up and exposed. But very soon a geological change occurred.

The tree had fallen obliquely across the stream, and its ponderous head, or top, choked up the bed, or very nearly. The sand and small sticks, leaves, and so on, brought down by the current, filled up the crevices left by the tree, and a perfect dam was formed.

Now, as stated before, the ground thereabout was nearly level, and so worthless in character that no man ever troubled his head about it. No one came to see the dam or remove it. The result was the brook overflowed, and then finding this level plateau, instead of eating out a new channel, it spread abroad, and formed first a good-sized puddle, then a pond, then something like a flood, and, as time went by, a marsh. This marsh extended over a space of ground fully a mile long, and altogether covered some nine hundred acres.

The rats, sagacious creatures, instead of deserting their colony, showed that they possessed that species of wisdom which the Greek sage said was superior to all other knowledge—namely, the knowledge how to turn an evil to a good. Exploring this shallow lake which their carelessness had caused, they found several places still unsubmerged—islands, in fact. To one of these they swam, dug out new catacombs, and being now quite safe from interruption, and protected upon all sides, the Malthusian laws of population had full play, and soon proved its force, for the whole place swarmed with them. The axiom, however, that at the very point when empires are apparently most prosperous, their destruction is near at hand, to some extent applied even to the dominion of the water-rat. They were no longer to be the sole undisturbed possessors.

Arguing à priori, one would have concluded that if this waste land was worthless before, now it was a marsh, and miasmatic vapours arose from it, it would be still more avoided. But the facts were exactly opposite. So soon as ever the water had spread over the level plain, and had well soaked into the sterile soil, there began to spring up tough aquatic grasses, commonly called bull-polls, from a supposed resemblance between their tangled appearance and the rough hair that hangs over the poll of a bull.

These grasses are gregarious—that is to say, they prefer to grow in huge bunches. Each bunch increasing year after year, forms in time a small hillock or tuft, and, the roots spreading and spreading, these hillocks of grass almost covered the lake, leaving only narrow channels of water between. Upon these innumerable frogs and toads crawled up out of the water, and they were the chosen resorts of newts.

In summer time the blue dragon-fly wheeled in mazes over them, or, while settled on the stiff blades of grass, looked like a species of blossom. The current of the brook brought down seeds, and soon the tall reed began to rear its slender stem, and rustle its feathery head in the breeze. The sedges came also, and fringed the marsh with a border of green.

Meantime, the root which the rats had gnawed asunder beneath the ancient willow tree, felt the power of spring, and made one more effort. Freed from the incubus of the dead trunk, it threw out a shoot of its own. From this shoot there proceeded other shoots; and, in short, after a while the islands in the marsh became covered with willow trees and osier-beds. The reeds grew apace, and by the time the islands were clothed with willow, the rest of the marsh was occupied by them, saving only the fringe of sedge, and the almost immortal bull-polls, which were as tough as leather, and which nothing could kill.

Now, also, animal life began to people the once-deserted waste. With the sedges came the sedge-warblers; with the willows came the brook-sparrows; and above all, came the wild-fowl. The heron stalked to and fro between the bull-polls; the ducks swam in and out; the moor-hens took up their residence; and in winter the widgeons and snipes visited the place in myriads.

It was now time for man. And man came. He came first in the person of here and there a cotter, who cut himself a huge bundle of reeds for fuel, to mend his thatch, or litter his pig; then in the person of the poacher—if it could be called poaching to hunt where no one preserved—who, with long-barrelled gun, brass-fitted and flint-locked, brought down half a dozen ducks at once, and then waded in after them.

One day a travelling gipsy tribe came by, and encamped for the night close to the marsh. In this tribe there was a man who, in his way, possessed the genius of Alexander the Great. Alexander chancing to pass a landlocked harbour utterly neglected, saw at a glance its capabilities, and built a city which is renowned to this day.

This gipsy fellow, who was only a gipsy by marriage, saw this unoccupied marsh, with its wild-fowl, its fish, and, above all, its willows, and at once fixed upon it as a promising spot.

He was a basket-maker by trade.

He waded in to one of the islets, carrying his infant in his arms, and followed by his wife, who carried his tools. He set up his tent-pole, and in time superseded it with a cottage of sod, roofed with reeds. All day he made baskets of willow and flags, in the evening he shot ducks and widgeon. The baskets he sold in the towns, the ducks he ate. One or two others followed his example.

The gipsy tribe made it a rule to come that way twice a year to purchase the baskets and retail them all over the country. The original settlers had sons, and the sons took possession of other islets, built sod cottages, of wattle-and-daub, and married wives, till there were ten or twelve settlements upon the islands; and these ten or twelve, all in a rude sort of way, gave the chieftainship to the original basket-maker, whose name happened to be Baskette.

These people, in the heart of a midland county, lived almost exactly the life that was led at the same period by the dwellers in the fen countries to the eastward. It was a rude existence, but it was free and independent, and not without a charm to those who had been born and bred in it. Even this unenviable life was, however, to be disturbed. Two mighty giants were preparing, like the ogres in the fairy tales, to eat up the defenceless population. The lid of a certain tea-kettle had puffed up and down, and Steam had been born. The other ogre was called Legal Rights, and began to bite first.

Chapter Two

So long as this waste land was tenanted only by the "owl and the bittern," Legal Rights slumbered. The moment man put his foot upon it the ogre woke up, for it is not permitted to that miserable two-legged creature to rest in peace anywhere in this realm.

The village of Wolf's Glow was distant about a mile and a quarter from the old willow tree whose fall had dammed up the brook and caused the marsh. The brook, in fact, ran past the village, and supplied more than one farmhouse with water. These farms were of the poorest class—mere stretches of pasture-land, and such pasture which a well-fed donkey would despise!

The poorest farm, in appearance at all events, was Wick—a large but tumbledown place, roofed with grey slates, which, stood apart from the village. It was the largest house in the place, and yet seemed the most poverty-stricken. The grey slates were falling off. The roof-tree had cracked and bent, the lattice windows were broken, and the holes stuffed up with bundles of hay and straw. The garden was choked with weeds, and the very apple trees in the orchard were withering away.

Old Sibbold, the owner and occupier, was detested by the entire village, and by no one more than his two sons. He was a miser, and yet nothing seemed to prosper with, him; and pare and save as much as he would he could make no accumulation. His sons were the only labourers he employed, though his farm was the largest thereabouts, and he paid them only in lodging and food, and not much of the latter.

The eldest, Arthur, chafed bitterly under this treatment, for he appears, from the scanty records that remain of him, to have been a lad of spirit and energy.

The second son, James, was of a grosser nature, and his mind was chiefly occupied with eating and drinking. He had an implicit faith in the wealth of his father, and submitted patiently to all these hardships and rough treatment in the hope of ingratiating himself with the old man, and perhaps supplanting Arthur in his will—that is, so far as his money was concerned, for the land, as the villagers said, "went by heirship"—i.e. was entailed—but who would care for such land?

Arthur saw the game and did nothing to prevent it; on the contrary, he took a certain pleasure in irritating the savage and morose old man, whom he thoroughly despised. Perhaps what happened in the future was a punishment for this unfilial conduct, however much it was provoked.

The mother, it must be understood, had long been dead, and there was no mediator between the stern old man and his fiery-tempered son. Old Sibbold was descended of a good family—one that had once held a position, not only in the county but in the country—and he dwelt much on the past, recalling the time when a Sibbold had held a bishop a prisoner for King John.

He pored over the deeds in his old oak chest—a press, which stood on four carved legs, and was closed with a ponderous padlock. That chest, if it could be found now, would be worth its weight, not in gold merely, but in diamonds. At that time these deeds and parchments were of little value; they related mostly to by-gone days, and Arthur ridiculed his father's patient study of their crabbed handwriting.

What was the use of dwelling on the past?—up and speculate on the present!

Irritated beyond measure, old Sibbold would reply that half the county belonged to him, and he could prove it. All that they could see from that window was his.

6

"Why," said Arthur, "all we can see is the Lea, which is as barren as the crown of my hat, except in weeds and bulrushes!"

"Barren or not, they're mine," said Sibbold, closing his chest; "and I will make those squatters pay!"

For the Lea was that piece of waste ground which the brook had overflowed, and in a sense rendered fertile.

From that hour began a persecution of the basket-makers who had settled on the little islets in the marsh. Sibbold had an undoubted parchment right—whether he had a moral and true right to a place he had never touched with spade or plough is a different matter. He claimed a rent. The cotters refused to pay. Their chieftain, old Will Baskette, wanted to compromise matters, and offered a small quit-rent.

Now every one knows that quit-rent and rent are very different things in a legal point of view. A man who pays rent can be served with notice to quit. A man who pays quit-rent has a claim upon the soil, and cannot be ejected. Sibbold refused the quit-rent, and had the squatters served with a notice. They went on cutting reeds, weaving baskets, and shooting wild-fowl, just the same; till one day old Sibbold, accompanied with a posse of constables (there were no police in those days), walked into the marsh with his jack-boots on; and, while one of the cotters was absent selling his baskets, began to tear the little hut down, despite the curses of the women and the wailing of the children. But the hut, as it happened, was stronger in reality than appearance, and resisted the attack, till one of the constables suggested fire.

A burning brand from the cottage hearth was applied by old Sibbold himself to the reed thatch, and in a moment up shot a fierce blaze which left nothing but ashes, and sod walls two feet high. One can imagine the temper a man of gipsy blood would be in when, on returning home, he found his children crying and the women silent, sitting among the ruins. From that hour a spirit of revenge took possession of the dwellers in this Dismal Swamp of hostility to the village.

Hitherto these half savage people had paid of their own free will a kind of tribute to the regular house-folk of Wolf's Glow. The farmers' wives received useful presents of baskets and clothes-pegs, and every now and then half a dozen wild ducks were found on the threshold in the morning. The clergyman was treated in a similar manner; and being known to have a penchant for snipes and woodcocks, his table was well supplied in the season. Sometimes there were other things left in a mysterious way at the door—such as a bladder full of the finest brandy or Hollands gin, or a packet of tobacco or snuff.

This was generally after the visit of the gipsy tribe, who were smugglers to a considerable extent. No farmer ever missed a lamb or a horse: such property was far safer since the settlement of the Dismal Swamp.

But now the village had attacked the Swamp, the Swamp

retaliated on the village, and a regular war commenced. The farmers' sheep began to disappear—none so often as old Sibbold's. Once a valuable horse of his was lost. This drove him to the verge of frenzy. He went down to the Swamp, and presently returned swearing and vowing vengeance—he had been shot at. This aroused the clergyman into action. He went to the Swamp, and was received with respect. He talked of conciliation, and reproved them, especially speaking of the sin of murder. They listened, but utterly scouted the idea.

"We steal," they said, openly. "It is our revenge; but we do not murder. Sibbold was not fired at. One of our young men was seeking ducks—he did not know that Sibbold at the same moment was creeping noiselessly through the reeds to fire our huts. He shot at the ducks, and some of the pellets glanced off Sibbold's jack-boots. That's the truth."

And it was the truth. But Sibbold vowed vengeance, and was heard to say that he would have their blood. He refused to see the clergyman who came to mediate and explain. He accused him of complicity, and reviled him.

James, as usual, agreed with and seconded him. Arthur sided with the squatters, and said so openly. Sibbold cursed him. Arthur said pointedly that when he inherited the land the squatters should be unmolested. Sibbold struck him with an ash stick.

Arthur left the house and went to the Swamp. He called on old Will Baskette, and expressed his hatred of his father's tyranny. He asked to be taught to make baskets, and to be initiated into the gipsy mysteries. He was a quick lad, and they took an interest in teaching him. He soon knew how to make two or three kinds of baskets, learnt the gipsy language, and imbibed their singular traditions.

Meantime the war continued. At first the farmers and villagers put up with patience with their thefts, considering that it was Sibbold's fault. But repeated losses exasperated them. If one of the Dismal Swamp people was seen abroad he was set upon and maltreated, beaten black and blue. Savage dogs were hounded at them. Sibbold was encouraged to eject them. He tried to get a posse of constables to do so, but the constables hung back. They had heard the story of the shooting at Sibbold; they knew these men to be desperate characters; and most of them had had presents of brandy and tobacco, and ribbons for their wives.

They could not be got to move. That was a lawless age in outlying places. Finding this, the village began to contemplate a raid en masse upon the Swamp. Nothing was talked of in the alehouse but fighting. Men compared the length of their gun-barrels, and put up marks to prove the range of their shot. The younger men were ready for the fray, the elders hesitated. They looked at their thatched houses, at their barns and ricks. The insurance companies had not then penetrated into the most obscure nooks and corners.

After all, the Swamp people were not unsupported: they were a branch of a tribe. If they were seriously injured the tribe might return, and no one could calculate the consequences.

So the foray was put off from day to day. But the news that it was meditated soon reached the Swamp, and made the dwellers there more desperate than ever. Their thefts grew to such a height that nothing was safe. The geese and turkeys disappeared; wheat was stolen from the barns; sheep were taken by the dozen, and no trace could be found. Now and then a horse disappeared. It came to such a pitch that the very beer in the barrels, the cider in the cellar, was not safe, but was taken nightly.

Old Sibbold, of course, suffered most. Tapping a cider barrel, he found it quite empty. The old man was beside himself with rage; but he said nothing. He studied retaliation. He watched his barns—the wheat seemed to disappear under his very eyes. One night as he was returning from his barn, carrying his long-barrelled flint-lock under his arm, he fancied he saw a gleam of light in the ivy, which almost hid the cellar window. Stealthily he peeped through. There was a man stooping down, drawing off the cider from a barrel into a bucket.

Old Sibbold's lips compressed; a fire came into his eyes. He grasped his gun. Just then the thief held up the candle in his left hand, and revealed the features of old Will Baskette, the very chief of the Swamp. Sibbold hated him more particularly because he knew that Arthur frequented his hut. Up went the long gun. The gleam of light from the candle guided the aim. The muzzle was close to the lattice window. A cruel eye glanced along the barrel, a finger was on the trigger. The flint struck the steel with a sharp snick—a spark flew out— an explosion—the window-glass smashed—a cloud of smoke—one groan, and all was still.

Sibbold rushed round the house, opened the door gently, locked it behind him, and stole upstairs. On the landing he met his youngest son James. For a moment they looked at one another. The young man spoke first.

"Quick, and load your gun," he said. "Then put it in the rack and get into bed. Give me your breeches."

They wore breeches and gaiters in those days.

The old man did as he was bid. The gun was put in the rack; old Sibbold got into bed. James took his breeches, poured a bucket of water on them, and hung them up in the wide chimney—the embers still glowed on the hearth. Then he stole upstairs.

"Arthur is out," he whispered, as he passed the old man's bedroom.

Ten minutes passed. Then there arose clatter of feet and a shouting.

"Farmer! farmer! your house is a-fire. The thatch be caught alight."

James opened the window, yawned, and asked what was the matter.

9

"Father's asleep," he said, as if not comprehending them. "He got wet in the brook, and went to bed early. Can't ye come in the morning?"

But the others soon roused the house.

The thatch had indeed caught over the cellar window; but fortunately it was nearly covered with moss and weeds, and was easily put out.

Then some one noticed the smashed window. "Who was it fired?" they asked. "We heard a shot, and thought it was the swampers. We were watching our sheep and barns. Then we saw this fire in your thatch, and ran. Who was it fired? How came the window smashed like this? How came the thatch alight?" James answered, "He really did not know. He had heard no shot, he slept sound, knew nothing of the thatch being on fire, and they would have been burnt in their beds if it had not been for their kind neighbours." Old Sibbold stood and shivered in his shirt, his breeches were wet. The neighbours came in.

"I'll go upstairs and fetch father a blanket to wrap his knees in," said James. "Father, thee blow the embers up; John Andrews, thee knows where the cellar is: give 'em the key, father, and do you go, John, and draw some cider."

Away went John Andrews with the lantern, and came back with a face white as a sheet, just as James got downstairs. There was a dead man in the cellar, in a flood of gore and cider!

The result was a coroner's inquiry; the thefts and so forth might have gone on for ever, but death could not be disregarded. Even in that lawless age, death was attended to. An inquest was held, and the jury was composed of the farmers of the village. Suspicion fell very strongly upon old Sibbold. The Swamp people openly denounced him as the murderer. His neighbours, much as they hated the Swamp, believed in their hearts that they were right; and not all their class prejudice could overcome the innate horror they felt in his presence. More than one had heard him say he would have blood. Now there was blood enough.

Still there was not enough evidence to arrest Sibbold. The Swamp people said he would run away, and if he did they would watch him and bring him back. But Sibbold did nothing of the kind. He faced the inquiry with a stern dignity which imposed on some.

First came the medical evidence. The doctor proved that the shot had entered the left side, just below the heart, and had passed downwards. It had entered all together—the pellets not spread about, but close together, like a bullet, which proved that the gun had been fired very close. Death must have been absolutely instantaneous. Deceased was in a stooping posture when he received the charge.

The constable who had examined the premises, declared it as his belief—as, indeed, it was the belief of everyone present—that the shot had been fired from without the window. The shot itself could not have smashed every pane—that was the concussion. The thatch had been doubtless set on fire by a piece of the paper which had been used as wadding.

When this had been said there was nothing more to be done, at least so the jury thought. Suspect Sibbold as much as they would, they were determined to protect him if possible. This was partly class-feeling, and partly remembrance of the provocation.

But the Coroner was not to be put off so easily. He had Sibbold called, and questioned him closely. He called James also, but they both stuck to their tale; they had never heard the shot, etc. The Coroner sent for Sibbold's gun, keeping Sibbold and James at the inn where the inquest was held meantime. It was brought. It told no tales: it was loaded. Finally, the Coroner, still dissatisfied and vaguely suspicious, called Arthur Sibbold, who, white as a sheet, was sitting near on a bench watching the proceedings.

He started at his name and looked round, but finally came forward. Where had he been that night? He was at Bassett, a small town six miles distant. What was his business there? what time did he leave? and so on. Arthur answered, but not so clearly as was desired. He contradicted himself as to the time at which he left Bassett, and got confused.

The Coroner's suspicions shifted upon him. He must have arrived about the time the shot was heard, yet he did not go indoors, did not show himself till breakfast-time next morning. James vouched for that, unasked. What was he doing all night?

Suspicion fell very strong on Arthur. But at this moment the wife of the deceased started forward and declared her belief in his innocence, recounting how he had learnt basket-making, etc, of the dead man, and they had been on the most friendly terms.

Still, said the Coroner, he might have mistaken his man in the uncertain light. Had he a gun? It was shown that the three Sibbolds had but one gun; that Arthur never used a gun, being of a tender nature, and often expressing his dislike to see birds wantonly slaughtered.

The Sibbolds were then, with the other witnesses, ordered out, and the Coroner addressed the jury.

He told them plainly where his suspicions lay: one of the Sibbolds, he was certain, did the deed, but which? Two were in bed, or at least were to all appearance in bed, and one point in their favour was that the thatch was alight. Now, if they had known that, they would hardly have lain till the neighbours came up. The third was out that night, and, according to his own showing, must have returned about the time the murder was committed. But in his favour it was urged that he was on the best of terms with the deceased; that he had no gun of his own; that he disliked the use of a gun. He said much more, but these were the chief points, and particularly he laid down the law. They must not imagine because a man was stealing that thereby his life was at any one's mercy. If a struggle took place, and the thief was killed in the struggle, there were then several loopholes of escape from the penalty of the law. First, it might be called chance-medley; next, there would be a doubt whether the stab or shot was not given in self-defence, and was not intended to kill. But in this case there was every appearance of deliberate murder. The thief had been spied at the cask; the murderer had coolly aimed along his gun and fired, hitting his man in a vital part, evidently of design and aforethought.

He then left the jury to their deliberations. They talked it over half an hour in a sullen manner, and then returned an open verdict—"Found dead." The Coroner remonstrated, and recommended that at least it should be "Wilful murder against persons unknown," but they were obstinate.

That verdict stands to this day. The dread spectre of the gallows vanished from Wolf's Glow. Old Will Baskette was buried in the churchyard, and his funeral was attended by the whole of the Swamp people and half the village. And over their ale the farmers whispered that it served the old thief right, but they avoided old Sibbold. The work of the rats had already brought fruit in bloodshed.

Chapter Three

In these days such a verdict and such an ending to a tragedy would be out of the question; but there were no police in those times to take up a case if it chanced to slip by the Coroner. Once past the Coroner, and the criminal was practically safe. The county officers were never in a hurry for such prosecutions, for a gallows cost at least 300 pounds. They wanted a public prosecutor then ten times more than we do now. Sibbold was shunned by the very men who had acquitted him; but there is no reason to suppose he ever felt remorse. He was made of that kind of stuff of which the men in armour, his ancestors, were composed, who thought little or nothing of human life. But one day he met Arthur, his eldest son, face to face upon the stairs. It was the first time they had met since the inquest—Arthur had avoided the place, and wandered about a good deal by himself, till some simple folk began to think that it was he who had committed the deed, and that his conscience was troubling him.

This meeting on the stairs took place by accident one morning—Sibbold was going to pass, but Arthur put his hand on his shoulder, "I saw you do it," he said. He had just entered the rick yard when the shot was fired. He had held his peace, but his mind could not rest. "I cannot stay here," he said, "I am going. I shall never see you again."

Old Sibbold stood like a stone; but presently put his hand in his pocket and held out his purse.

"No," said Arthur; "not a penny of that, it would be blood money."

He went, and evil report went after him. Perhaps it was James who fanned the flame, but for years afterwards it was always believed that Arthur had shot the basket-maker. Only the Swamp people combated the notion. Arthur was one of them, and understood their language—it was impossible. Not to have to return to these times, it will be, perhaps, best to at once finish with old Sibbold; though the event did not really happen till some time after Arthur's departure.

Sibbold went to a fair at some twenty miles distance—a yearly custom of his; and returning home in the evening, he was met by highwaymen, it is supposed, and refusing to give up his money bag, was shot. At all events his horse came home riderless, and the body of the old man was found on the heath divested of every article of value. Suspicion at once fell on his known enemies, the Swamp people. Their cottages were searched and nothing found. Their men were interrogated, but had all been either at home or in another direction. Calm reason put down Sibbold's death to misadventure with highwaymen, common enough in those times; but there were those who always held that it was done in revenge, as it was believed that the gipsies retained the old vendetta creed.

As Arthur did not return, James took possession, and went on as usual; but he did not disturb the Swamp settlement. He avoided them, and they avoided him.

When Will Baskette was shot he left a widow and two sons, one of them was strong and hardy, the other, about sixteen, was delicate and unfit for rough outdoor life. This fact was well-known to the clergyman at Wolf's Glow, the Rev. Ralph Boteler, who was really a benevolently-minded man.

The widow and her eldest son joined the gipsy tribe and abandoned the Swamp. The Rev. Ralph Boteler took the delicate Romy Baskette into his service as man of all work, meaning to help in the garden and clean the parson's nag. Romy could not read, and the parson taught him—also to write. Being quiet and good-looking, the lad won on the vicar, who after a time found himself taking a deep interest in the friendless orphan. It ended in Romy leaving the garden and the stable, and being domiciled in the studio, where the parson filled his head with learning, not forgetting Latin and Greek.

The vicar was a single man, middle-aged, with very little thought beyond his own personal comfort, except that he liked to see the hounds throw off, being too stout to follow them. He had, however, one hobby; and, like other men who are moderate enough upon other topics, he was violence itself upon this. Of all the hobbies in the world, this parson's fancy was geology—then just beginning to emerge as a real science.

The neighbours thought the vicar was as mad as a March hare on this one point. He grubbed up the earth in forty places with a small mattock he had made on purpose at the village blacksmith's. He broke every stone in the district with a hammer which the same artisan made for him.

His craze was that the neighbourhood of Wolf's Glow was rich in the two great stores of nature which make countries powerful—i.e. in Coal and Iron. He proved it in twenty ways. First, the very taste of the water, and the colour of the earth in the streams; by the nodules of dark, heavy stone which abounded; by the oily substance often found floating on the surface of ponds—rock oil; by the strata and the character of the fossils; by actual analysis of materials picked up by himself; lastly, by archaeology.

Wolf's Glow! What was the meaning of that singular name? The only Glow in the county. Wolf was, perhaps, a man's name in the centuries since. But Glow? Glow was, without a doubt, the ancient British for coal.

The people who argued against him—and they were all he met— ridiculed the idea of the ancient Britons knowing anything of coal. Boteler produced his authorities to show that they, and their conquerors the Romans, were perfectly familiar with that mineral. Wolf's Glow was, in fact, Wolf's Coal Pit. "Very well," said the Objectors, "show us the coal pit, and we'll believe." This the vicar could not do, and was held to be mad accordingly.

But all this talking, and searching, and analysing made a deep impression upon the mind of young Romy Baskette, who was now hard upon twenty years of age. Boteler, really desirous of pushing the lad on, sent him to London, whither Arthur Sibbold had preceded him, and placed him, at a high premium, in the care of a friend of his, who was in the iron trade. Romy grew and prospered, and being of a serious disposition saved all the money he could lay hands on. Presently old Boteler died, and left him, not all, but a great share of his worldly wealth. With this he bought a share in the iron business, and became a partner. Wealth rolled in upon him, and at an early period of life he retired from active labour, married, and bought an estate a few miles from Wolf's Glow.

In his leisure hours the memory of the old days with the vicar returned. He resolved to test the vicar's theory. He purchased a small piece of land in Wolf's Glow parish, sank a shaft, and sure enough came upon coal.

This discovery revivified the whole man. He cast off sloth, forgot all about retirement, and plunged into business again. Another search, conducted by practical hands, proved the existence of iron.

There was a furore. Collieries were started; iron furnaces set going. It was just at the dawn of the great iron and coal trade. The railways had been started, and the demand was greater than the supply. Romy Baskette and Company soon employed two thousand hands coal-digging and iron-smelting. The man, in fact, wore himself out at the trade of money-making. He could not rest. Night and day his brain was at work: An accidental conversation with one of his workmen suggested to him a new idea. The smiths of the time could not make nails fast enough for all the building that was going on. This workman had been a sailor in his day, and had seen nails abroad which were made in batches by machinery, instead of slowly and laboriously, one by one, by hand.

Baskette caught at the idea. He studied and learnt what he could. He made a voyage himself abroad, and soon mastered the secret. He erected machinery, and cut nails were first made. The consumption was enormous. The business of this Baskette and Company became so large that it almost passed out of control. Meantime other firms had come and settled, bought land, dug up coal, and set up smelting furnaces. In ten years the population from being absolutely nil rose to thirty-five thousand people. By this time Romy had killed himself. But that mattered little, for he had left a son, and a son who inherited all his genius, and was—if anything still "harder in the mouth." He was named, from his mother's family, Sternhold Baskette.

Sternhold picked up the plough-handle which had dropped from his father's grasp, and continued the good work, never once looking back. But although equally clever, the bent of his genius was different from that of old Romy. Romy was at heart a speculator, and believed in personal property. Sternhold was a Conservative, and put his faith in real property, houses, and land. He kept up the old forges and collieries, but he started no new ones. He invested the money in land and houses, particularly the latter. His life may be summed up in two strokes of genius—the first was bringing the iron horse to Stirmingham, as the new town was called; the second was the building lease investment.

It is hard to give the pre-eminence to either. They were both profound schemes—neither would have been complete without the other. He did not originate the idea of the railway—that was done for him—but he put it on its legs, and he brought it to the centre of the town.

The original scheme almost omitted Stirmingham. Railways were not then fully understood; their projectors had such vast ideas in their heads, they aimed at long trunk lines, and so this railroad was to connect London, the sea, and a certain large town—larger than Stirmingham then, but now nothing beside the modern city.

Sternhold, as the largest shareholder, and as finding the capital to get through Parliament, prevailed to have the course altered so as to sweep by Stirmingham. He knew that this would improve his property there at least fifty per cent. But he had other ideas in his head. The line could not be finished under three years, and in those three years it was his intention to become possessed of the whole ground upon which the town of Stirmingham stood. He foresaw that it would become a mighty centre. He braced up his nerves, and prepared to spend his darling hoards like water.

One by one the fields, the plots, the houses, became his; and the greed growing on him, he cast longing eyes on the adjacent marsh, now called Glow's Lea.

The solicitors he employed tried to restrain his infatuation. They represented to him that even his vast wealth could not sustain this more than kingly expenditure, and as to the marsh, it was sheer madness to purchase it. In vain. Perhaps a tinge of pride had something to do with it. He would buy up the rotten old Swamp where his progenitor had dwelt, drain it, and cover it with mansions.

But now came a difficulty—the title to the ground was not all that could be wished. James had been dead some years, but it was well-known that had Arthur returned—if Arthur still lived, or his heirs—that James had no right. He had enjoyed the farm and the land, such as it was, unmolested, all his life. He had married, and had eight sons. Six of these had married since, and most of them had children.

As none could claim the property, they all found a miserable livelihood upon it, somehow or other. They had degenerated into a condition little better than that of the squatters in the Swamp.

Three families lived in the farmhouse, constantly quarrelling; two made their dwelling in the cowsheds, slightly improved; one boiled the pot in the great carthouse, and the two single men slept in the barn. Such a condition of slovenliness and dirt it would be hard to equal. And the language, the fighting, and the immorality are better left undescribed! The clergyman of Wolfs Glow wished them further.

To these wretches the offers of Sternhold Baskette came like the promised land. He held out 300 pounds apiece, on condition that they would jointly sign the deed and then go to America. They jumped at it. The solicitor warned Baskette that the contract was not sound. He asked, in reply, if any one could produce the deed under which the property descended by "heirship." No one could. Somehow or other it had been lost.

In less than a month eight Sibbolds, with their wives and families, were en route to the United States, and Sternhold took possession. Then came the Swamp settlement difficulty.

At first Baskette thought of carrying matters with a high hand. The squatters said they had lived there for two generations, or nearly so, and had paid no rent. They had a right. Sternhold remembered that they were of his clan. He gave them the same terms as the Sibbolds—

16

and they took them. Three hundred pounds to such miserable wretches seemed an El Dorado.

They signed a deed, and went to America, filling up half a vessel, for there were seventeen heads of families, and children ad libitum.

Thus Sternhold bought the farm and the Swamp for 7500 pounds. His aim in getting them to America was that no question of right might crop up—for the Cunard line was not then what it is now, and the passage was expensive and protracted. He reckoned that they would spend the money soon after landing, and never have a chance of returning.

Meantime the railway came to a standstill. There had been inflation—vast sums of promotion money had been squandered in the usual reckless manner, and ruin stared the shareholders in the face. To Sternhold it meant absolute loss of all, and above everything, of prestige.

Already the keen business men of the place began to sneer at him. At any cost the railway must be kept on its legs. He sacrificed a large share of his wealth, and the works recommenced. The old swamp, or marsh, was drained.

Sternhold had determined to make this the Belgravia of Stirmingham, and had the plans prepared accordingly. They were something gigantic in costliness and magnificence. His best friends warned and begged him to desist. No; he would go on. Stirmingham would become the finest city in England, and he should be the richest man in Europe. Up rose palatial mansions, broad streets, splendid club-houses—even the foundations of a theatre were laid. And all this was begun at once. Otherwise, Sternhold was afraid that the compass of an ordinary life would not enable him to see these vast designs finished. So that one might walk through streets with whole blocks of houses only one story high.

Everything went on swimmingly, till suddenly the mania for speculation which had taken possession of all the kingdom received a sudden check by the failure of a certain famous railway king.

As if by magic, all the mighty works at Stirmingham ceased, and Sternhold grew sombre, and wandered about with dejected step. His friends, men of business, reminded him of their former warnings. He bent his head, bit his lip, and said only, "Wait!"

Meantime the line had been constructed, but was not opened. The metals were down, but the stations were not built, and the locomotives had not arrived. Everybody was going smash. Several collieries failed; land and houses became cheap. Sternhold invested his uttermost in the same property—bought houses, till he had barely enough to keep him in bread and cheese. Still they laughed and jeered at him, and still he said only, "Wait!"

This place, this swamp, seemed to be fated to demonstrate over and over again at one time the futility of human calculation, and at

17

another what enormous things can be accomplished by the efforts of a clever man.

Chapter Four

The owner of three parts of Stirmingham—now a monstrous overgrown city, just building a cathedral—actually had nothing but a little bread and cheese for supper. There were people who condoled with him, and offered to lend him sums of money—not large, but very useful to a starving man, one would have thought. He shrugged his shoulders and said, "Thank you; I'll wait."

Certain keen speculators tried to come round him in twenty different ways. They represented that all this mass of bricks and mortar—this unfinished Belgravia—really was not worth owning; no one could ever find the coin to finish the plans, and house property had depreciated ninety per cent.

"Very true," said Sternhold. "Good morning, gentlemen."

He held on like grim death. Men of genius always do—mark Caesar, and all of them. 'Tis the bulldog that wins.

By-and-by things began to take a turn. The markets looked up. Iron and coal got brisker. The first locomotive was put on the line, then another, and another; London could be reached in two hours, goods could be transmitted in six, instead of thirty by the old canal or turnpike.

The Stock Exchange got busy again. You could hear the masons and bricklayers—chink, tink, tinkle, as their trowels chipped off the edges—singing away in chorus. The whistle of the engines was never silent. Vast clouds of smoke hung over the country from the factories and furnaces. Two or three new trades were introduced—among others, the placed goods, cheap jewellery, and idol-making businesses, and trade-guns for Africa. Rents began to rise; in two years they went up forty per cent. The place got a name throughout the length and breadth of the kingdom, and a Name is everything to a town as well as to an individual.

But by a curious contradiction, just as his property began to rise in value, and his investment looked promising, Sternhold grew melancholy and walked about more wretched than ever. The truth soon leaked out—he had no money to complete his half-finished streets and blocks of houses. Nothing could induce him to borrow; not a halfpenny would he take from any man.

There the streets and houses, the theatres, club-houses,

magnificent mansions, huge hotels, languished, half-finished, some a story, some two stories high, exposed to wind and weather. In the midst of a great city there was all this desolation, as if an enemy had wreaked his vengeance on this quarter only.

Large as were the sums derived from his other properties—houses and shops and land, which were occupied—it was all eaten up in the attempt to finish this marble Rome in the middle of a brick Babylon. Heavy amounts too had to be disbursed to keep the railway going, for it did not pay a fraction of dividend yet. Men of business pressed on Sternhold. "Let us complete the place," they said. "Sell it to us on building leases; no one man can do the whole. Then we will form three or four companies or syndicates, lease it of you, complete the buildings, and after seventy years the whole will revert to you or your heirs."

Still Sternhold hesitated. At last he did lease a street or two in this way to a company, who went to work like mad, paid the masons and bricklayers double wages, kept them at it day and night, and speedily were paying twenty per cent, dividends on their shares out of the rents of the completed buildings. This caused a rush. Company after company was formed. They gave Sternhold heavy premiums for the privilege to buy of him; even then it was difficult to get him to grant the leases. When he did accept the terms and the ready cash, every halfpenny of it went to complete streets on his own account; and so he lived, as it were, from hand to mouth.

After all this excitement and rush, after some thousands of workmen were put at it, they did not seem to make much impression upon the huge desolation of brick and mortar. Streets and squares rose up, and still there were acres upon acres of wilderness, foundations half-dug out and full of dirty water, walls three feet high, cellars extending heaven only knew where.

People came for miles to see it, and called it "Baskette's Folly." After a while, however, they carefully avoided it, and called it something worse—i.e. "The Rookery;" for all the scum and ruffianism of an exceptionally scummy and ruffianly residuum chose it as their stronghold. Thieves and worse—ill-conditioned women—crowds of lads, gipsies, pedlars—the catalogue would be as long as Homer's—took up their residence in these foundations and cellars. They seized on the planks which were lying about in enormous piles, and roofed over the low walls; and where planks would not do they got canvas.

Now, it is well-known that this class of people do not do much harm when they are scattered about and separated here, there, and everywhere over a city; but as soon as they are concentrated in one spot, then it becomes serious. Gangs are formed, they increase in boldness; the police are defied, and not a house is safe.

This place became a crying evil. The papers raved about it, the police (there were police now) complained and reported it to headquarters. There was a universal clamour. By this time Stirmingham had got a corporation, aldermen, and mayor, who met in a gorgeous Guildhall, and were all sharp men of business. Now the corporation began to move in this matter of "Baskette's Folly." Outside people gave them the credit of being good citizens, animated by patriotic motives, anxious for the honour of their town, and desirous of repressing crime. Keen thinkers knew better—the Corporation was not above a good stroke of business. However, what they did was this: After a great deal of talk and palaver, and passing resolutions, and consulting attorneys, and goodness knows what, one morning a deputation waited upon Sternhold Baskette, Esq, at his hotel (he always lived at an hotel), and laid before him a handsome proposition. It was to the effect that he should lease them the said "Folly," or incomplete embryo city, for a term of years, in consideration whereof they would pay down a certain sum, and contract to erect buildings according to plans and specifications agreed upon, the whole to revert in seventy years to Sternhold or his heirs.

Sternhold fought hard—he asked for extravagant terms, and had to be brought to reason by a threat of an appeal by the Corporation to Parliament for a private Act.

This sobered him, for he was never quite happy in his secret mind about his title. Terms were agreed upon, the earnest money paid, and the masons began to work. Then suddenly there was an uproar. The companies or syndicates who had leased portions of the estate grew alarmed lest this enormous undertaking should, when finished, depreciate their property. They cast about for means of opposing it. It is said—but I cannot believe it—that they gave secret pay to the thieves and ruffians in the cellars to fight the masons and bricklayers, and drive them off.

At all events serious collisions occurred. But the Corporation was too strong. They telegraphed to London and got reinforcements, and carried the entrenchments by storm.

Then, so goes the discreditable rumour, the companies bribed the masons and bricklayers, who built so badly that every now and then houses fell in, and there was a fine loss! Finally they got up an agitation, cried down the Corporation for wasting public funds, and, what was far more serious, brought high legal authority to prove that as a Corporation they had no power to pledge themselves to such terms as they had, or indeed to enter into such a contract without polling the whole city.

This alarmed the Corporation. There were secret meetings and long faces. But if one lawyer discovers a difficulty, another can always suggest a way round the corner. The Corporation went to Parliament, and got a private Act; but they did not go as a body. They went through Sternhold, who was persuaded; and indeed it looked plausible, that by

20

so doing, and by getting the sanction of the House of Commons, he improved his own title.

Then the Corporation smiled, and built away faster than ever. In the course of an almost incredibly short time the vast plans of Sternhold were completed by the various companies, by the Corporation, and by himself; for every penny he got as premium, every penny of ground-rent, every penny from his collieries, iron furnaces, and cut-nail factories, went in bricks and mortar. It was the most magnificent scheme, perhaps, ever started by a single man. The city was proud of it. Like Augustus, he had found it brick, and left it marble.

Yet, in reality, he was no richer. The largest owner, probably, of house property in the world, he could but just pay his way at his hotel. Although he had a fine country house (which old Romy had purchased) in the suburbs, he never used it—it was let. He preferred a hotel as a single man because there was no trouble to look after servants, etc. He lived in the most economical manner—being obliged to, in fact.

Yet this very economy increased the popular belief in his riches. He was a miser. Give a man that name, let it once stick to him, and there is no limit to the fables that will be eagerly received as truth. Give a dog a bad name and hang him. Call a man a miser, and, if he is so inclined, he can roll in borrowed money, dine every day on presents of game and fish, and marry any one he chooses. I only wish I had the reputation.

No one listened to Sternhold's constant reiteration of what was true—that he was really poor. It was looked upon as the usual stock-in-trade language of a miser. His fame spread. Popular rumour magnified and magnified the tale till it became like a chapter from the Arabian Nights.

After all, there was some grain of truth in it. If he could have grasped all that was his, he would have surpassed all that was said about his riches.

At last the Stirmingham, Daily News hit upon a good idea to out-distance its great rival the Stirmingham Daily Post. This idea was a "Life of Sternhold Baskette, the Miser of Stirmingham." After, the editor had considered a little, he struck out "miser," and wrote "capitalist"—it had a bigger sound.

The manuscript was carefully got up in secret by the able editor and two of his staff, who watched Sternhold like detectives, and noted all his peculiarities of physiognomy and manner. They knew—these able editors know everything—that the public are particularly curious how much salt and pepper their heroes use, what colour necktie they wear, and so on. As the editor said, they wanted to make Sternhold the one grand central figure—perfect, complete in every detail. And they did it.

They traced his origin and pedigree—this last was not quite accurate, but near enough. They devoted 150 pages to a mere catalogue of his houses, his streets, his squares, club-houses, theatres, hotels, railways, collieries, ironworks, nail factories, estates, country mansions, etc. They wrote 200 pages of speculations as to the actual value of this enormous property; and modestly put the total figure at "something under twenty millions, and will be worth half as much again in ten years." They did not forget the building leases; when these fell in, said the memoir, he or his heirs would have an income of 750,000 pounds per annum.

They carefully chronicled the fact that the capitalist had never married, that he had no son or daughter, that he was growing old, or, at least, past middle age, and had never been known to recognise any one as his relation (having, in fact, shipped the whole family to America). What a glorious thing this would be for some lucky fellow! They finished up with a photograph of Sternhold himself. This was difficult to obtain. He was a morose, retiring man—he had never, so far as was known, had his portrait taken. It was quite certain that no persuasion would induce him to sit for it. The able editor, however, was not to be done. On some pretext or other Sternhold was got to the office of the paper, and while he sat conversing with the editor, the photographer "took him" through a hole made for the purpose in the wooden partition between the editor's and sub-editor's room. As Sternhold was quite unconscious, the portrait was really a very good one. Suddenly the world was taken by storm with a "Life of Sternhold Baskette, the Capitalist of Stirmingham. His enormous riches, pedigree, etc, 500 pages, post octavo, illustrated, price 7 shillings 6 pence."

The able editor did not confine himself to Stirmingham. Before the book was announced he made his London arrangements, also with the lessees of the railway bookstalls. At one and the same moment of time, one morning Stirmingham woke up to find itself placarded with huge yellow bills (the News was Liberal then—it turned its coat later on—and boasted that John Bright had been to the office), boys ran about distributing handbills at every door, men stood at the street corners handing them to everybody who passed.

Flaring posters were stuck up at every railway station in the kingdom; ditto in London. The dead walls and hoardings were covered with yellow paper printed in letters a foot long. Three hundred agents, boys, girls, and men, walked all over the metropolis crying incessantly "Twenty Millions of Money," and handing bills and cards to every one. The Athenaeum, Saturday Review, Spectator, and Times; every paper, magazine, review; every large paper in the country had an advertisement. The result was something extraordinary.

The name of Sternhold Baskette was on everybody's lips. His "Twenty Millions of Money" echoed from mouth to mouth, from Land's End to John o' Groats. It crossed the Channel, it crossed the Alps, it crossed the Atlantic and the Pacific. It was heard on the Peak of Teneriffe, and in the cities of India.

The New York firms seized on it as a mine of wealth. The book, reprinted, was sold from the Hudson River to the Rocky Mountains, and to the mouth of the Mississippi for twenty cents. The circulation was even larger in the United States than in Britain, for there everybody worshipped the dollar. The able editor made his fortune. The book ran through thirty editions, and wore out two printing machines and three sets of type. The two gentlemen of the staff who had assisted in the compilation had a fair share, and speedily put on airs. They claimed the authorship, though the idea had certainly originated with the editor. There was a quarrel. They left, being offered higher salaries in this way:—The other paper, the Post, though blue in principles, grew green with envy, and tried to disparage as much as possible. They offered these respectable gentlemen large incomes to cut the book to pieces that they themselves had written. No one could do it better—no one understood the weak points, and the humbug of the thing so well. The fellows went to work with a will. The upshot was a little warfare between the Sternholders and the anti-Sternholders. The News upheld Sternhold, stuck to everything it had stated, and added more. The Post disparaged him in every possible way. This newspaper war had its results, as we shall presently see. For the present these two noble principled young men, who first wrote a book for pay and then engaged to chop it into mincemeat for pay, may be left to search and search into the Baskette by-gone history for fresh foul matter to pour forth on the hero of Stirmingham.

Chapter Five

"The Hero of Stirmingham;" so the News dubbed him; so it became the fashion, either in ridicule or in earnest, to call him. People came from all parts to see him. Every one who, on business or pleasure, came to the city, tried to lodge at the hotel where he lived, or at least called there on the chance of meeting the mortal representative of Twenty Millions Sterling. The hotel proprietor, who had previously lost money by him, and execrated his economy, now reaped a golden harvest, and found his business so large that he set about building a monster place at one side of the original premises, for he was afraid to pull it down lest the capitalist should leave.

Now a curious psychological change was wrought by all this in old Sternhold's character. Up till this period of his life he had been one of the most retiring and reserved of men, morose, self-absorbed, shrinking from observation. He now became devoured with an

23

insatiable vanity. He could not shake off the habit of economy, the frugal manner of living, which, he had so long practised; but his mind underwent a complete revolution.

It has often been observed that when a man makes one particular subject his study, in course of time that which was once clear grows obscure, and instead of acquiring extraordinary insight, he loses all method, and wanders.

Something of the kind was the case with Sternhold. All his life had been devoted to the one great object of owning a city, of being the largest proprietor of houses and streets in the world. His whole thought, energy, strength, patience—his entire being—had been concentrated upon this end. In actual fact, it was not attained yet, for he was practically only the nominal owner; but the publication of this book acted in a singular manner upon his brain. He grew to believe that he really was all that the "Life" represented him to be—i.e. the most extraordinary man the world had ever seen.

He attempted no state, he set up no carriage; he stuck to his old confined apartments at the hotel he had always frequented; but he lived in an ideal life of sovereign grandeur. He talked as though he were a monarch—an absolute autocrat—as if all the inhabitants of Stirmingham were his subjects; and boasted that he could turn two hundred thousand people out of doors by a single word.

In plain language, he lost his head; in still plainer language, he went harmlessly mad—not so mad that any one even hinted at such a thing. There was no lunacy in his appearance or daily life; but the great chords of the mind were undoubtedly at this period of his existence quite deranged.

He really was getting rich now. The houses he had himself completed, with the premiums paid for building leases, began to return a considerable profit. The income from his collieries and factories was so large, that even bricks and mortar could not altogether absorb it. Perhaps he was in receipt of three thousand pounds per annum, or more. But now, unfortunately, just as the fruits of his labour were fast ripening, this abominable book upset it all.

There can be no doubt that the editor of the Stirmingham Daily News, with the best intentions in the world, dealt his Hero two mortal wounds. In the first place, he drove him mad. Sternhold spent days and nights studying how he could exceed what he had already done.

Dressed in a workman's garb for disguise, he explored the whole neighbourhood of Stirmingham, seeking fresh land to purchase. His object was to get it cheap, for he knew that if there was the slightest suspicion that he was after it, a high price would be asked. In some instances he succeeded. One or two cases are known where he bought, with singular judgment and remarkable shrewdness, large tracts for very small sums. He paid only one-fifth on completion, leaving the remainder on mortgage. This enabled him to buy five times as much at once as would have otherwise been possible.

But there were sharp fellows in Stirmingham, who watched the capitalist like hawks, and soon spied out what was going on. Their game was to first discover in what direction Sternhold was buying in secret, then to forestall him, and nearly double the price when he arrived.

In this way Sternhold got rid of every shilling of his income. Even then he might have prospered; but, as bad luck would have it, the railway, after two millions of money had been sunk on it, actually began to pay dividends of three and a half per cent, then four, then six; for a clever fellow had got at the helm, and was forcing up the market so as to make hay while the sun shone.

Sternhold was in raptures with railways. Some sharp young men of forty-five and fifty immediately laid their heads together, and projected a second railway at almost right angles—not such a bad idea, but one likely to cause enormous outlay. They represented to Sternhold that this new line would treble the value of the property he had recently bought, extending for some miles beyond the city. He jumped at it. The Bill was got through Parliament. One half of these sharp young men were lawyers, the other half engineers and contractors.

Sternhold deposited the money, and they shared it between them. When the money was exhausted the railway languished. This exasperated old Baskette. For the first time in his life he borrowed money, and did it on a royal scale;—I am almost afraid to say how much, and certainly it seems odd how people could advance so much knowing his circumstances.

However, he got it. He bought up all the shares, and became practically owner of the new line. He completed it, and rode on the first locomotive in triumph, surrounded by his parasites. For alas! he had yielded to parasites at last, who flattered and fooled him to perfection. This was the state of affairs when the second mortal wound was given.

It happened in this way. The "Life of Sternhold Baskette, Esq," had, as was stated, got abroad, and penetrated even to the Rocky Mountains. It was quoted, and long extracts made from it in the cheap press—they had a cheap press in the United States thirty years before we had, which accounts for the larger proportion of educated or partly educated people, and the wider spread of intelligence. After a while, somehow or other, the marvellous story reached the ears of one or two persons who happened to sign their names Baskette, and they began to say to themselves, "What the deuce is this? We rather guess we come from Stirmingham or somewhere thereabouts. Now, why shouldn't we share in this mine of wealth?"

The sharp Yankee intellect began to have "idees." Most of the cotters whom Sternhold had transhipped to America thirty years or more previous, were dead and buried—that is to say, the old people were.

The air of America is too thin and fine, and the life too fast, for middle-aged men who have been accustomed to the foggy atmosphere and the slow passage of events in the Old Country. But it is a tremendous place for increase of population.

The United States are only just a century old, and they have a population larger than Great Britain, which has a history of twenty centuries, or nearly so.

So it happened that, although the old people were dead, the tribe had marvellously increased. Half who were transhipped had borne the name of Baskette. This same question was asked in forty or fifty places at once—"My name is Baskette; why should not I share?"

These people had, of course, little or no recollection of the deed signed by their forefathers: and if they had had a perfect knowledge, such a trifling difficulty as that was not one calculated to appal a Yankee's ingenuity. When once the question had been asked it was repeated, and grew and grew, and passed from man to man, made its appearance in the newspapers, who even went so far as to say that the finest city in England, the very workshop of the Britishers, belonged to United States citizens.

Some editor keener than the rest, or who had read the book more carefully, pointed out that the capitalist had no heirs living, that he had never been married, and no one knew to whom all this vast wealth would descend.

Twenty millions sterling begging a heir! This was enough to set the American mind aflame. It was just like applying a lighted match to one of their petroleum wells.

The paragraph flew from paper to paper, was quoted, conned, and talked over. Men grew excited. Presently, here and there one who considered that he had some claim began to steal off to England to make inquiries. The Cunard were running now, though they had not yet invented the "ocean highway," by keeping to a course nothing to the north or south of a certain line. Passage was very quick, and not dear. In a little time the fact that one or two had started oozed out, then others followed, and were joined by a lawyer or so, till at last fourteen or fifteen keen fellows reached Stirmingham.

Now mark the acuteness of the American mind! Instead of announcing their arrival, every one of these fellows kept quiet, and said not a word! When they met each other in the streets they only smiled. They were not going to alarm the game.

These gentlemen were not long in Stirmingham before they found out that the Stirmingham Daily Post was a deadly enemy of old Sternhold. To the office of the second able editor they tramped accordingly.

There they learnt a good deal; but in return the editor pumped something out of them, and, being well up in the matter, sniffed out their objects. He chuckled and rubbed his hands together. Here was a chance for an awful smash at the News.

26

One fine morning out came a leading article referring also to several columns of other matter on the same subject, headed "The Heirs of Stirmingham."

Being Blue, you see, the Post affected to abominate United States' Republicanism and all the American institutions. This article recounted the visit of the dozen or so of possible claimants, described them so minutely that no one could help recognising them, and wound up with a tremendous peroration calling upon all good citizens to do their best to prevent the renowned city of Stirmingham falling into the hands of the Yankees!

Such property as Sternhold's, the article argued, was of national importance; and although the individual should not be interfered with, the nation should see that its rights were not tampered with. There was danger of such tampering, for who knew what an infirm, old man like Sternhold might not be led to sign by interested parties? At his age he could not be expected to possess the decision and mental firmness of earlier years. This was a cruel hit at Sternhold's mental weakness, which had begun to grow apparent.

An endeavour should be made to find an English heir, and that there was such an heir they (the staff of the Post) firmly believed. Two gentlemen of the staff (meaning thereby the late writers for the News), who had devoted some time to the matter, had made a certain important discovery. This was nothing less than the fact that Sternhold had had an uncle! This in big capital letters.

An Uncle. Then followed a little bit of genealogy, in approved fashion, with dashes, lines, etc—the meaning of which was that Sternhold's father, old Romy Baskette, had had a brother, who, when the original Will Baskette was shot, had departed into the unknown with his mother.

What had become of Romy's brother? The probability was that by this time he was dead and buried. But there was also the probability that he had married and had children. Those children, if they existed, were undoubtedly the nearest heirs of Sternhold Baskette, Esq, now residing at Dodd's Hotel, South Street. As an earnest of the anxiety of the Post to preserve the good city of Stirmingham from Yankee contamination, they now offered three rewards:—First, fifty pounds for proof of Romy's brother's death; secondly, one hundred pounds for proof of Romy's brother's marriage, if he had married; thirdly, one hundred and fifty pounds for the identification of his child or children. This was repeated as an advertisement in the outer sheet, and was kept in type for months.

It deserves notice as being the first advertisement which appeared in the Great Baskette Claim Case—the first of a crop of advertisements which in time became a regular source of income to newspaper proprietors.

When this leading article and advertisement, supported by

several columns of descriptive matter and genealogies was laid on the breakfast tables of half Stirmingham, it caused a sensation. The city suddenly woke up to the fact that as soon as old Sternhold died half the place would have no owner.

The Yankee visitors now had no further reason for concealment. They went about openly making inquiries. They were fêted at hotel bars and in billiard rooms. They called upon Sternhold bodily—en masse—forced themselves into his apartment, though, he shut the door with his own hands in their faces, shook him by the hand, patted him on the shoulder, called him "Colonel," and asked him what he would take to drink!

They walked round him, admired him from every point of view, stuck their fingers in his ribs, and really meant no harm, though their manners were not quite of the drawing-room order.

They cut up the old man's favourite armchair, whittled it up, to carry away as souvenirs. They appropriated his books—his own particular penholder, with which he had written every letter and signed every deed for fifty years, disappeared, and was afterwards advertised as on show at Barnum's in New York City, as the Pen which could sign a cheque for Twenty Millions!

When at last they did leave, one popped back, and asked if the "Colonel" believed this story about his Uncle? He was sure he had never had an uncle, wasn't he? The old man sat silent, which the inquirer took for once as a negative, and wrote a letter to the News, denying the existence of Romy's brother.

Poor old Sternhold was found by the landlord, old Dodd, sitting in his chair, which was all cut and slashed, two hours afterwards, staring straight at the wall.

Dodd feared he had an attack of paralysis, and ran for the nearest doctor; but it was nothing but literally speechless indignation. After a while he got up and walked about the room, and took a little dry sherry—his favourite wine. But the mortal wound Number 2 had been given. Henceforth the one great question in Sternhold's mind was his heir.

Chapter Six

His heir! Sternhold seriously believed that he had no living relations. It is often said that poor people have plenty of children, while the rich, to whom they would be welcome, have few or none. This was certainly a case in point. The poor Baskettes, who had been shipped to

America, had a whole tribe of descendants. Here was a man who, nominally at least, was the largest owner of property known, who was childless, and had already reached and exceeded the allotted age of man.

Sternhold was seventy-two. He looked back and ransacked his memory. He had never heard anything of this uncle, his father's brother; his mother's friends were all dead. There was not a soul for whom he cared a snap of his fingers. Firstly, he had no relations; secondly, he had no friends, for Sternhold, wide as was his circle of acquaintances, had never been known to visit any one. His life had been solitary and self-absorbed.

Now, for the first time, he felt his loneliness, and understood that he was a solitary being. Who should be his heir? Who should succeed to that mighty edifice he had slowly built up? The architect had been obliged to be content with gazing upon the outside of his work only; but the successor, if he only lived the usual time, would revel in realised magnificence unsurpassed. The old man was quite staggered, and went about as in a dream.

The idea once started, there were plenty who improved upon it. The Corporation at their meetings incidentally alluded to the matter, and it was delicately suggested that Sternhold would crown his memory with ineffable glory if he devised his vast estate to the city. Such a bequest in a few years would make the place absolutely free from taxation. The rents would meet poor's-rates, gas-rates, water-rates, sanitary-rates, and all. One gentleman read an elaborate series of statistics, proving that the income from the property, when once the building leases fell in, would not only free the city from local, but almost, if not quite, from imperial taxation. There were many instances in history of kings, as rewards for great services, issuing an order that certain towns should be exempt from the payment of taxes for a series of years. Sternhold had it thus in his power to display really regal munificence.

Other gentlemen of more radical leanings cried "Shame!" on the mere fact of one man being permitted to attain such powers. It was absurd for one man to possess such gigantic wealth, and for several hundred thousand to live from hand to mouth. The people should share it, not as a gift, but as a right; it should be seized for the benefit of the community.

The Corporation people were much too knowing to talk like this. They went to work in a clever way. First, they contrived various great banquets, to which Sternhold was invited, and at which he was put in the seat of honour and lauded to the skies. Next, they formed a committee and erected a statue in a prominent place to the founder of Stirmingham, and unveiled it with immense ceremony. Certain funds had been previously set apart for the building of a public library; this being completed about that time, was named the Sternhold Institute.

29

An open space or "park," which the Corporation had been obliged to provide for the seething multitudes who were so closely crowded together, was called the Sternhold Public Park. Yet Sternhold never subscribed a farthing to either of these.

Nothing was left undone to turn his head. His portrait, life-size, painted in oil, was hung up in the Council-hall; medals were struck to commemorate his birthday. The Corporation were not alone in their endeavours; other disinterested parties were hard at work. Most energetic of all were the religious people. Chapel projectors, preachers, church extension societies, missionary associations, flew at his throat. His letter-box was flooded; his door was for ever resounding with knocking and ringing. The sound of the true clerical nasal twang was never silent in his anteroom. The hospitals came down on him flat in one lump, more particularly those establishments which publicly boast that they never solicit assistance, and are supported by voluntary contributions caused by prayer.

The dodge is to publish the fact as loudly as possible. To proclaim that the institution urgently wants a few thousands is not begging. A list of all the charities that recommended themselves to his notice would fill three chapters: then the patentees—the literary people who were prepared to write memoirs, biographies, etc—would have to be omitted.

Now here is a singular paradox. If a poor wretched mortal, barely clothed in rags, his shoes off his feet, starring with hunger, houseless, homeless, who hath not where to lay his head, asks you for a copper, it means seven days' imprisonment as a rogue. If all the clergymen and ministers, the secretaries, and so forth, come in crowds begging for hundreds and thousands, it is meritorious, and is applauded.

Now this is worthy of study as a phenomenon of society. But these were not all. Sternhold had another class of applicants, whom we will not call ladies, or even women, but females (what a hateful word female is), who approached him pretty much as the Shah was approached by every post while in London and Paris.

He was deluged with photographs of females. Not disreputable characters either—not of Drury Lane or Haymarket distinction, but of that class who use the columns of the newspapers to advertise their matrimonial propensities. Tall, short, dark, light, stout, thin, they poured in upon him by hundreds; all ready, willing, and waiting.

Most were "thoroughly domesticated and musical;" some were penetrated with the serious responsibilities of the position of a wife; others were filled with hopes of the life to come (having failed in this).

Some men would have enjoyed all this; some would have smiled; others would have flung the lot into the waste-basket. Sternhold was too methodical and too much imbued with business habits to take anything as a good joke. He read every letter, looked at every photograph, numbered and docketed them, and carefully put them away.

Other efforts were made to get at him. He had parasites—men who hung on him—lickspittles. To a certain extent he yielded to the titillation of incessant laudation; and, if he did not encourage, did not repel them. They never ceased to fan his now predominant vanity. They argued that the Corporation and all the rest were influenced by selfish motives (which was true). They begged him not to forget what was due to himself—not to annihilate and obliterate himself. It was true he was aged; but aged men—especially men who had led temperate lives like himself—frequently had children. In plain words, they one and all persuaded him to marry; and they one and all had a petticoated friend who would just suit him.

Sternhold seemed very impassive and immoveable; but the fact was that all this had stirred him deeply. He began to seriously contemplate marriage. He brooded over the idea. He was not a sentimental man; he had not even a spark of what is called human nature in the sense of desiring to see merry children playing around him. But he looked upon himself as a mighty monarch; and as a mighty monarch he wished more and more every day to found not only a kingdom, but a dynasty.

This appears to be a weakness from which even the greatest of men are not exempt. Napoleon the Great could not resist the idea. It is the one sole object of almost all such men whose history is recorded. Occasionally they succeed; more often it destroys them. Some say Cromwell had hopes in that direction.

So far the parasites, the photographs, the stir that was made about it, affected Sternhold. But if he was mad, he was mad in his own way. He was not to be led by the nose; but those who knew him best could see that he was meditating action.

Dodd, the landlord of the hotel, was constantly bothered and worried for his opinion on the subject. At last, said Dodd, "I think the Corporation have wasted their money." And they had.

In this unromantic country the human form divine has not that opportunity to display itself which was graciously afforded to the youth of both sexes in the classic days of Greece, when the virgins of Sparta, their lovely limbs anointed with oil, wrestled nude in the arena.

The nearest approach to those "good old times" which our modern prudery admits, is the short skirts and the "tights" of the ballet.

Sternhold, deeply pondering, arrived at the notion, true or false, that the wife for him must possess physical development.

This is a delicate subject to dwell on; but I think he was mistaken when he visited the theatres seeking such a person. He might have found ladies, not females nor women, but ladies in a rank of life nearer or above his own, who exulted in the beauty of their form, and were endowed with Nature's richest gifts of shape. But he was a child in such a search: his ideas were rude and primitive to the last degree. At all events, the fact remains.

31

It was found out afterwards that he had visited every theatre in London, but finally was suited on the boards of a fourth-rate "gaff" in Stirmingham itself.

There was a girl there—or rather a woman, for she was all five-and-twenty—who was certainly as fine a specimen of female humanity as ever walked. Tall, but not too tall, she presented a splendid development of bust, torso, and limbs. Her skin was of that peculiar dusky hue—not dark, but dusky—which gives the idea of intense vitality. Her eyes were as coals of fire—large, black, deep-set, under heavy eyebrows. Her hair at a distance was superb—like night in hue, and glossy, curling in rich masses. Examined closer it was coarse, like wire. Her nose was the worse feature; it wanted shape, definition. It was a decided retroussé, and thick; but in the flush of her brilliant colour, her really grand carriage, this was passed over. Her lips were scarlet, and pouted with a tempting impudence.

This was the very woman Sternhold sought. She was vitality itself impersonified. He saw her, offered his hand, and was instantly accepted. He wished her to keep it quiet; and notwithstanding her feminine triumph she managed to do so, and not a soul in Stirmingham guessed what was in the wind.

Sternhold went to London, got a special licence, and the pair were married in Sternhold's private apartments at his hotel in the presence of three people only, one of whom was the astounded Dodd. They left by the next train for London, where the bride went to Regent Street to choose her trousseau, with her husband at her, side.

Not a bell was rung in Stirmingham. The news spread like wildfire, and confounded the city. People gathered at the corners of the streets.

"He is certainly mad," they said. Most of them were in some way disappointed.

"He may be," said a keener one than the rest; "he may be—but she is not."

Chapter Seven

Lucia Marese, now Mrs Sternhold Baskette, was the daughter of an Italian father and an English mother, and had a tolerably accurate acquaintance with Leicester Square and Soho. She was not an absolutely bad woman in the coarsest sense of the term—at least not at that time, she had far too much ambition to destroy her chance so early in life. Physiologists may here discuss the question as to whether any latent trace of the old gipsy blood of the Baskettes had in any way influenced Sternhold in his choice. Ambitious as she was, and possessed of that species of beauty which always takes with the multitude, Lucia had hitherto been a failure. Just as in literature and in art, the greatest genius has to wait till opportunity offers, and often eats its own heart in the misery of waiting, so she had striven and fought to get to the front, and yet was still a stroller when Sternhold saw her. She knew that if only once she could have made her appearance on the London boards, with her gorgeous beauty fully displayed, and assisted by dress and music, that she should certainly triumph. But she could not get there.

Other girls less favoured by Nature, but more by circumstance, and by the fickle and unaccountable tastes of certain wealthy individuals, had forestalled her, and she stored up in her mind bitter hatred of several of these who had snubbed and sneered at her.

The fairy prince of her dream, however, came at last in the person of an old man of three score years and ten, and she snapped him up in a trice. No doubt, like all Stirmingham, she entertained the most fabulous ideas of Sternhold's wealth.

These dreams were destined to be rudely shattered. She seems to have had pretty much her own way at first. Doubtless the old man was as wax in her hands, till his former habits began to pull at him. She had one good trait at all events, if it could be called good—the first use she made of her new position was to provide for her family, or rather for the only member of it in England.

This was Aurelian Marese, her brother, who must have been a man of some talent and energy, for despite all obstacles of poverty he contrived to pass his examination and obtain a diploma from the College of Surgeons. He came to Stirmingham, and with the assistance of Sternhold's purse set up as a mad doctor, in plain parlance, or in softer language, established a private lunatic asylum. Oddly enough, it would seem that notwithstanding the immense population of the city, there was not till that time any establishment of the kind in the place, and the result was that Aurelian prospered. He certainly was a clever fellow, as will be presently seen, though some fancy he over-reached himself. When at last Sternhold, worn out with the unwonted gaieties into which Lucia plunged him, showed unmistakable signs of weariness, and desired to return to Stirmingham, she yielded with a good grace. She reckoned that he could not last long, and it was her game to keep him in good temper; for she had learnt by this time that he had the power to dispose of his property just as he chose.

We can easily imagine the restlessness of this creature confined in the dull atmosphere of three or four rooms at Dodd's Hotel, South Street. But she bore it, and to her it was a species of martyrdom—the very reverse of what she had pictured.

After a while, as time went on, whispers began to fly about—

people elevated their eyebrows and asked questions under their breath, exchanged nods and winks. The fact was apparent; Sternhold could scarce contain himself for joy. There was an undoubted prospect of The Heir. The old man got madder than ever—that is, in the sense of self-laudation. He could not admire himself sufficiently. The artful woman played upon him, you may be sure; at all events there was a deed of gift executed at this time conveying to her certain valuable estates lying outside the city, and tolerably unencumbered. Why she came to select those particular estates which were not half so valuable as others she might have had, was known only to herself then; but doubtless Aurelian had heard about the Yankee claims, and advised her to take what was safe. These estates were, in fact, bought with old Romy's money made by the nail factory, and were quite apart from the rest.

About this time, also, Sternhold left Dodd's Hotel. This was another evidence of her power over him. The best joke was, that although there was old Romy's country mansion about five miles from Stirmingham, although Sternhold had since purchased four other mansions, and had nominally street upon street of houses in the town, he had not a place to take his wife to. He was obliged to rent one of his own houses of the company who had built it on a building lease.

Mrs Sternhold now had her great wish gratified to some extent. She was the observed of all observers. They tell you tales now in Stirmingham of her extravagance, and the lengths she went. Her carriages, her horses, her servants, her dinners, parties, and what not, were the one topic of conversation. Even old-fashioned, straitlaced people found their objections overcome by curiosity, and accepted her invitations.

Old Sternhold was never visible at these gatherings; but he rejoiced in them. He was proud of his wife. He looked upon her as a prodigy. He gave her the reins. But personally he practically returned to his old habits. He still retained his old apartments at Dodd's; and there he might be found, at almost all hours, sitting at his desk, and eagerly, joyously receiving every visitor who came to tell him of some fresh extravagance, some fresh frolic of his wife's!

How was all this expenditure supported, since his actual income was so small? By a series of loans, which there were always men ready to offer, and whose terms Sternhold always signed. Once or twice he did remonstrate, but darling Lucia went into tears, and her brother Aurelian assured him that, in her state of health, any vexation was dangerous, etc. Aurelian, through the Sternhold connexion, was now a fashionable physician.

At last the event happened, and a son was born. The memory of the week succeeding that day will not soon pass away in Stirmingham.

Old Sternhold, himself a most temperate man, declared that he would make every one in the city tipsy; and he practically succeeded. He had barrels of ale and gallons of spirits and wine offered free to all comers at every public-house and tavern. He had booths erected in an open field just outside the town, for dancing and other amusements, and here refreshments of all kinds were served out gratis.

The police were in despair. The cells overflowed, and would hold no more, and the streets reeled with drunken men, and still more drunken women.

This saturnalia reigned for four days, and would soon have culminated—at least, so the police declared—in a general sack of the city by the congregated ruffians. A detachment of dragoons was actually sent for, and encamped in Saint George's Square, with their horses and arms ready at a moment's notice. But it all passed off quietly; and from that hour Sternhold, and more particularly the infant son, became the idol of the populace.

They still look back with regret to those four days of unlimited licence, and swear by the son of Sternhold.

This boy was named John Marese Baskette, but was always called Marese. Singularly enough, the birth of this child, which one would have prophesied would have completed the hold Lucia had over the father, was the beginning of the difficulties between them. It began in his very nursery. Proud of her handsome figure, and still looking forward to popular triumphs, Lucia flatly refused to nurse the infant herself.

This caused a terrible quarrel. Old Sternhold had old-fashioned ideas. But there is no need to linger on this. Lucia, of course, had her own way, and Sternhold retired to sulk at Dodd's Hotel. From that time the chink widened, and the mutual distrust strengthened.

There never was any real doubt that the boy was legitimate; but some devil whispered the question in Sternhold's mind, and, he brooded over it. I say some devil, but, in actual fact, it was one of those parasites who have been once or twice alluded to. Is there anything that class will stop at in the hope of a few formal lines in a rich man's will?

It was their game to destroy Lucia. The plan was cunningly formed. As if by accident, passages in Lucia's previous life, when she was a stroller, were alluded to in Sternhold's presence.

He grew excited, and eager to hear more; to probe her supposed dishonour. The parasites distinctly refused; it was too serious a matter. Still, if he wished to hear—it was common talk—all he had to do was to go into the billiard rooms. Some of the fellows there did not know him by sight, and they were sure to talk about it.

Sternhold went. Of all the sights in the world, to see that old man making a miserable attempt to play billiards while his ears were acutely listening to the infamous tales purposely started to inflame him, nothing could be more deplorable. The upshot was he grew downright mad, but not so mad that anything could be done with him. He watched over Lucia like a hawk. She could not move; her life became really burdensome.

35

It must be remembered that at that time she really was, though wild enough in blood, perfectly stainless in fact. The temper in the woman was long restrained. In the first place, she wanted his money; in the next place, there was her son, whom she loved with all the vigour of her nature. She bore it for a year or two, then the devil in her began to stir.

Old Sternhold, who had watched and inquired hour by hour all this time, had found nothing wrong; but this very fact was turned against her by those devils, his lickspittles. They represented that this was part of her cunning—that she had determined he should have no hold upon her, in order that her son might inherit. They reminded Sternhold that, although he could not divorce her, he could alter his will. Here they rather overshot the mark, because he began to reflect that if he cut off his son the old question would arise—To whom should he leave his city, as he called it?

The miserable dilemma haunted and worried his already weakened brain and body till he grew a shadow, and Lucia had hopes that he would die. But he did not; in a month or two the natural strength of his constitution brought him round.

All this time Lucia was in dread about his will. Aurelian astute and cunning as he was hardly knew what to advise or how to act. He had his spies—for he was wealthy now to a certain degree, and could afford it. He had his strong suspicions that some of the companies who had leased the property for building had a hand in the persecution of Lucia, and in the inflammation of Sternhold's jealousy. It was certainly their interest to get the boy disinherited. Aurelian began to grow seriously alarmed. Sternhold was stronger and better—perhaps if he had had Aurelian for physician he would not have recovered so fast; but with his distrust of Lucia, came an equal distrust of her brother, and he would not acknowledge him.

Aurelian looked at it like this: Sternhold was now about seventy-five, and had no organic disease. His father, Romy, had lived to a ripe old age; his grandfather, the basket-maker, though shot in the prime of life, came of a hardy, half-gipsy stock. The chances were that Sternhold, with all the comforts that money could buy, would live another ten years. This very worry, this jealousy, by keeping his mental faculties alive, might contribute to longevity. In ten years, in a year, in a month, what might not happen?

His greatest fear was in Lucia herself, who had shown signs of late that she must burst forth. If she did, and without his being near her, there was no knowing what indiscretion she might not commit. It was even suspicious that Sternhold had recovered. It looked as if he had made up his mind, and had signed a will averse to Lucia's interest and his son's—had settled it and dismissed it. This was a terrible thought, this last. When he suggested the possibility of it to Lucia, you should have seen her. She raved; her features swelled up and grew inflamed; her frame dilated; her blood seemed as if it would burst the veins: till at last she hissed out, "I'll kill him!" and fell fainting.

Aurelian determined one point at once. There must be no more delay; action was the order. But what? Suppose the worst. Suppose the will already made, and against Lucia's interests, what was the course to be taken? Why, to accumulate evidence to invalidate it. Prove him mad!

Chapter Eight

The idea having been once entertained, grew and grew, till it overshadowed everything else. The singular circumstance then happened of one man slowly and carefully collecting evidence during another's lifetime to prove him insane the moment he died.

Aurelian placed his principal reliance upon the violent jealousy Sternhold had exhibited. So vehement and irregulated a passion founded upon mere phantasms of the imagination, was in itself strong presumptive proof of an unsound mind. He had no difficulty in finding witnesses to Sternhold's outrageous conduct. The old man had been seen walking up and down the street, on the opposite side of the pavement to the house in which Lucia lived, for hours and hours at a time, simply watching. He had been heard to use violent and threatening language. He had made himself ill. The mind was so overwrought by excitement that it reacted upon the body, and it was some time before the balance was restored—if indeed it could ever be restored.

There were many trifling little things of manner—of fidgetiness—absurd personal habits—which, taken in conjunction with the bad temper he had displayed, went to make up the case. Aurelian added to this the vanity Sternhold had of late openly indulged in. This was notorious, and had become a by-word.

But when Aurelian had written all this out upon paper—when he had, as it were, prepared his brief—his shrewd sense told him that in truth it was very weak evidence. Any lawyer employed for the defence could easily find arguments to upset the whole.

Day by day, as he thought it over, his reliance upon the insanity resource grew less and less—and yet he could not see what else there was to do. He racked his brain. The man, like others, was in fact fascinated by the enormous property at stake: he could not get it out of his mind. It haunted him day and night. He ransacked his memory, called up all his reading, all his observation, all that he had heard—

every expedient and plan that had come under his notice for gaining an end.

For a time, however, it was in vain. It is often the case that when we seek an idea it flies from us, and will not be constrained, not even by weeks of the deeply-pondering state. Often the more we think upon a subject, the less we seem to see our way clear. And so it was with him.

Sometimes a little change of scene, even a little manual exercise, will stimulate the imagination. So it was with him.

He had an important and serious case to attend—a rich patient underwent an operation at his hands, and the physician grew so absorbed with his delicate manipulation and in genuine delight in his own skill, that Lucia and the property passed for a day or two completely out of his memory. This was followed by profound slumber, and next morning he awoke with the answer to the great question staring him in the face.

If Sternhold was not mad enough now, why not drive him mad? If he was driven frantic and shut up in an asylum, Lucia's son would to a certainty inherit the property. Possibly he (Aurelian) might be appointed trustee—he, as uncle, would be a guardian, and probably the only one. He might also have the pleasure of receiving Sternhold into his own retreat for lunatics; and so, while furthering the interests of his sister and nephew, do himself a good turn. The idea enraptured him.

Aurelian possessed the true scientific mind which is incapable of feeling. Some thinkers believe that the true artistic mind, the highest artistic mind, is also incapable of feeling. It is so absorbed in its own realisation of one idea, that it loses all consciousness of possible suffering in others. He never doubted for an instant that it was in his power to attain the proposed object—it was only to let Lucia loose. Let her loose—a little way. Let her loose under strict supervision—under the constant surveillance of himself, his son, a youth of twenty whom he was training up in the right road, and perhaps of other witnesses.

There was such a thing as divorce—this might not destroy the child's right, but it would place him out of Lucia's hands. There must be no handle for Lucia's enemies to grasp at. She must be manoeuvred so as to make Sternhold frantic without committing herself.

Lucia was aflame for such a course. She had restrained herself for years. She was burning to be free, on fire for "life" and excitement; above all, for admiration, for praise—the intoxicating breath of the multitude that cheers to the echo! The Stage! the dance—music—the fiery gaze of a thousand eyes following each motion! There must have been something of the true artist in her. The grandest position, the most unlimited wealth, would not have satisfied her without the stage.

She had married Sternhold in the hope of appearing as other women did in the theatres owned by their lovers. She had tried to broach the subject to Sternhold; he had held up his hands in horror, and she constrained herself and bided her time.

38

Nearly four years now—four years! The coarse jests, the loud laughter, the shouts and screams and cat-calls of the low threepenny gaff or music hall from which she had been snatched—even such a life as that seemed to her far, far superior to this irksome confinement, this slavery which was not even gilded. Aurelian was right in his conjecture that she could not be much longer held in—she must burst out.

Half-formed schemes had been working themselves into shape in her mind for months past. She would leave her boy with Aurelian, take her jewels and sables, sell them, borrow money upon the estate which Sternhold had made hers by deed of gift, go to London or Paris, and plunge headlong into "life," paying any price for the one grand ambition of her existence.

The craving—the fury, it might almost be called—the furious desire for admiration from men which seized upon her at times, would certainly, sooner or later, have hurled her on to a desperate step.

At this moment Aurelian came with his carefully-considered plan. She met him open-armed. With one blow she could avenge herself upon Sternhold, with one blow gratify herself and destroy him—destroy him body and soul. This moment—this hour!

But not so fast. First, Aurelian obtained the money—no small sum. Next, said he, this thing must not be done by halves. It was useless for her to appear on some small stage; she must at one bound become the talk of all the town. This required care, thought, and organisation. Those great successes that seemed so suddenly attained without an effort, as by a wave of the hand, had really been preceded by months and months of preparation, and depended in great part upon the matured judgment and clever advice of men who had watched the public for years.

Impatient as she was, Lucia again controlled herself, and did as she was bid. Aurelian made it his business first to discover where she could appear with most effect. He soon selected the place, Paris! he obtained an interview with the proper authorities, and confided to them a part of his secret. They saw their way to profit, and agreed.

The next thing was the character she should take, and the second, the season. This last the manager, or rather owner, who was in raptures with the thing, easily decided. It must be at the height of the Paris season. He was a popular man, who could gather together a mighty crowd of his own acquaintances.

If poor Sternhold, sitting in his apartment at Dodd's Hotel, could have heard these "fast" young men discussing the approaching appearance of his wife, Aurelian would have gone no further.

The choice of character Aurelian insisted upon deciding, and he chose Lady Godiva. As has been stated, Lucia had extraordinary hair, both for length and abundance, and, unlike long hair generally, it was curly. Had it been fine and delicate hair she could have boasted that few women in Europe could equal her. The coarseness of its texture would not be visible upon the stage.

She had really a magnificent figure. The character of Lady Godiva was one exactly fitted for her. It is needless to say that there was little or no acting—no study of parts, no insight into the meaning required, as in the case of Shakespeare's heroines. The piece was simply a spectacle devised to bring out one central figure into the boldest relief.

The greatest difficulty the conspirators—for so they may be fairly called—had to contend with was the necessity of keeping Sternhold completely in the dark, and yet at the same time getting together a large audience, which could only be done by advertising. But Aurelian was capable of dealing with more difficult dilemmas than this. His plan was very simple and yet effective. The manager had a piece in his répertoire which, owing to the fame or infamy of a certain fascinating lady, was the rage of the town. Suddenly this creature disappeared—went off to Vienna with a titled gentleman—and after blazing as a meteor of the first water there for a short time, as suddenly dropped out of sight altogether.

The manager, at Aurelian's suggestion, gave out that this lady had turned up, and was going to again act at his house on a certain night.

The excitement was intense. It was an awful falsehood, for the poor girl was in reality dead. (She met with her death under some strange and suspicious circumstances, which were, by influence, suppressed.) Her beauty, great as it was, had lost its charm in the tomb; yet her name, in flaring letters, was prominent all over Paris.

The deception was kept up to the very end; and the company of the theatre, by dint of double pay, were got to carry it out to perfection. An exceptional number of waiters were, however, hired, and no one but the manager and Aurelian had any idea what the object of this troop of apparently idle fellows could be.

The house filled to the last seat. The poor dead girl's name was on every lip—her frailties were discussed with horrid flippancy; the orchestra began, and Lucia Marese Baskette robed, or rather unrobed, as Lady Godiva.

The owner of the theatre was there, and with him a whole host of men about town, most of whom were partly in the secret, but not quite.

Just before the time arrived for the curtain to rise, this troop of idle waiters entered the arena, swarmed into the boxes, into the galleries and pit, distributing to every single individual who had entered a handbill, announcing that, instead of Miss, "Mrs Sternhold Baskette, the beautiful wife of Sternhold Baskette, Esq, the richest man in the world, the owner of twenty millions sterling worth of property, would appear as Lady Godiva; a part for which her splendid physique and magnificent hair peculiarly fitted her." At the same moment a large poster was put out in front of the curtain, bearing the same announcement.

The effect was singular. The house, which had been full of noise before, became as still as death. People were astounded. They could not believe it possible; yet, at the same time, they knew that the manager dared not play a trick. Theatres had been wrecked before now by indignant audiences. They waited in silence.

The curtain rose. I cannot pause to describe the gradual enthusiasm which arose, nor to draw a picture of the grand tableau. But there are many living who remember that memorable night, who declare that anything equal to it has never been seen upon the stage.

Lucia rode on a milk-white palfrey, and looked extraordinarily handsome. The house rose—the audience went mad. Recalled and recalled, again and again that white palfrey paced to and fro, and the mighty multitude would not allow the scene to pass.

The mesmeric influence of the excitement filled Lucia with a glowing beauty; with a brilliance which made her seem a goddess—of her order. No one remarked whether the piece was properly gone through after this. I think it was not. From all that I can learn, I believe the audience watched Godiva to and fro till the palfrey or its rider grew exhausted, and then left en masse.

Paris was aflame next day. The papers said nothing—they were wise. There is, however, something more powerful even than the newspaper—it is conversation. Lucia had got conversation—her name was heard everywhere. It was not only the acting, or show—it could not be called acting—it was the fact of her position as Sternhold's wife. She stood upon the pinnacle of his fame for wealth, brazen and shameless in the eyes of the world. Brazen and shameless, yet secure; for Aurelian never left her. He watched her himself. His son—his paid servants—did the same; not from fear of her indiscretion, but in order to appear as witnesses if any proceedings should take place.

Next night and next night, and again on the third night, this extraordinary spectacle was repeated. The crowds that came to the doors could not be admitted. But by this time the leading papers had felt the pulse of the people—not the excitable populace, but the steady people. With one consent they rushed at the exhibition with lance in rest. Improper was the softest insinuation. They were undoubtedly right. The moment they took this tone all the press followed, and before the week was over those who had the power had prohibited the performance.

Chapter Nine

The exhibition was stopped, but the end had been attained—Lucia was famous. The manager and Aurelian had foreseen the inevitable official veto, and had prepared for it. They had arranged for her to appear as Cleopatra; it was a part which could be made to suit her admirably by leaving Shakespeare's text out of the question, and studying spectacle instead.

It is a singular fact that Sternhold had no idea of what was going on until the fourth or fifth day. He was told that Lucia had left Stirmingham with her brother for a short visit to Paris, and paid little or no attention to it. For the first day or two the papers had been silent. At last the news reached him.

What Dodd had previously feared now happened—he was struck down with a slight attack of paralysis, which affected one side. Some persons said it was a merciful infliction, as it prevented him from witnessing his wife's disgrace with his own eyes. They were wrong. His body was bent, but his mind was torn with contending and frenzied passions. The sense of outrage—of outrage upon his dignity—was perhaps the strongest. That after all his labour and self-denial, after long, long years of slowly building up a property such as his, which rendered him in his own estimation not one whit inferior to a king; that he should be insulted, his name dragged in the dirt, his wife a spectacle for all Paris!

Sternhold had the vaguest ideas of stage proprieties and theatrical morality. He had not a doubt but that Lucia was already an abandoned woman. There were plenty who urged upon him to commence a suit for divorce, though in reality it was extremely doubtful whether there were sufficient grounds for anything beyond a judicial separation.

But Sternhold was filled with one consuming desire—to see her with his own eyes. Whether it was this passion, or whether it was the natural strength of his constitution, certain it is that in a marvellously short time after the attack, he had himself conveyed to Paris, and sat, a miserable, haggard, broken-down old man, in a box at the theatre the same night, watching his wife upon the stage. He did this night after night. A species of fascination seemed to carry him there to sit silent, brooding over the utter wreck of his great schemes.

After a while he went suddenly back to Stirmingham without a word, without so much as seeking an interview with Lucia, or issuing any instructions as to what was to be done. He went back to his old apartments at Dodd's Hotel. He shut himself up, refusing to see even the wretched parasites who had sown the seed of this mischief. It was an instinctive attempt to return to the old, old habit, the ancient self-

42

concentration, apart from the world. But it failed. So soon as ever he began to read his letters, to look into his accounts, every figure, every transaction reminded him of Lucia and her extravagance; the follies she had been guilty of, and the no less greater folly he had himself yielded to in granting her every wish, thereby involving his affairs in the most hopeless confusion. The attempt failed. He rushed again from his retreat to seek her. Then he heard that she was in Vienna performing. He got there, supported by his attendants. Doubtless the physical fatigue of the journey irritated his nerves; at all events, there seems no doubt that when he reached Vienna he was for the time absolutely mad.

He went to the theatre. He saw Lucia as Godiva, just as she had been seen in Paris. He was alone in his box. Deliberately he levelled a pistol, resting the barrel upon the edge of the balustrade. As the incense of praise and adulation rose up, as the pageant moved to and fro, the deadly weapon was aimed at the central figure. He fired, and the house was in commotion.

Those who know what happens when a full theatre is alarmed and excited will require no description; those who have not seen it cannot imagine it.

A second report, and the curling smoke caused a rush to the box, and the occupant was found upon the floor, as was thought, dead. Lucia alone was calm and cool. The bullet had not passed even near her; the distance was great and the aim unsteady; the ball had struck a screen, and did no injury. She dismounted and advanced to the footlights, extended her hands, and in a few words begged the audience to be calm. Speedily they saw her thus, as it were, in their very arms.

The theatre rang with acclamation. If it had been a scene prepared it could not have succeeded better.

There were threats and loud cries of rage against the man who had fired at her.

"Do not injure him," she said, at the top of her full, deep voice; "he is mad!" For she guessed in a moment who it was.

In a few minutes the whole thing was understood. Continental people are quick at comprehending—an old husband, a young wife—bah! An attempt first at murder, then at suicide—bah! What could he have done better calculated to put Lucia upon the pedestal of fame?

Sternhold was not dead; not even injured. The ball he had fired at himself had not touched him. He had fallen exhausted. When he became physically conscious, he was raving mad.

There was no doubt about it this time. It was a pitiable sight.

Aurelian insisted upon seeing him: even he shuddered. The old man was muttering gibberish to himself. Half his grey hair was gone, for before he could be stayed he had dragged it out. His arms and limbs were pinioned, but his body shook with a trembling convulsive movement. The deed was done.

43

Aurelian braced himself up, and hastened at once to Lucia. He knew he should have a struggle with her, and hoped that in the conflict he should forget the sight he had left. He had determined to at once withdraw her from the stage. The victory was won; there must be no more risk.

The conflict between the brother and sister was terrible. She raged, her frame swelled; she had tasted triumph, and the draught is more intoxicating even than the taste of blood. She would go on.

But he was resolute, and he won. That very day he took her to England—took is the right word, for it was necessary to use physical force at times. He got her to her house at Stirmingham, and never left her till she had grown more composed.

Sternhold was in an asylum. Aurelian thought that he would surely die; but he did not.

Aurelian then began to scheme to get him in his own "retreat." Possession was nine points of the law. He went to Vienna at once before any one guessed his object, obtained the proper permit, and in six days deposited the wretched being in his asylum in the suburbs of Stirmingham. Once there, thought Aurelian, let them get him out if they can.

The fact was soon known; and there was an excitement. The parasites, disappointed and raging, did their best to inflame the populace. There was a growl, and the police began to prepare for an attack upon the asylum; but, after all, the moment any of them reflected, they said, "Why, it's all right; the poor fellow is mad. He could not be in better hands." The plan of a popular tumult fell through.

The parasites next tried the law, but found that Aurelian had been before them: he had all the proper documents; he could not be touched.

Next the companies began to stir. They were uncertain what to do, and whether it was better for their interests that Sternhold should be in his brother-in-law's custody or not.

That astute gentleman very soon learnt what was passing in their minds, and he had a very good conception of what could be effected by powerful combination.

He opened negotiations with them. He pointed out to them privately that the real point at issue was not Sternhold, but the boy—the heir—for no one doubted the legitimacy. Who was to have the custody of the heir?

Clever Aurelian hoped that by making friends with the companies who held the building leases that there would be no opposition to his holding the boy—to his guardianship of the estate. He had strong grounds to go upon. To all intents and purposes he was the nearest relation. If the boy died, and no son of the phantom brother of Romy turned up, perhaps he might have a claim to the estate.

44

He gave the companies to understand that if he had the guardianship of the boy their interests should be most carefully studied.

They appeared favourable. The step was taken. The boy remained with his mother; his mother remained in her house, seeing Aurelian daily, and indeed watched by his employés.

No change took place. Aurelian congratulated himself that all was going on favourably. The boy, who had little or no idea of the meaning of the word "father," was constantly at Aurelian's residence—the asylum where his parent was confined—playing with Aurelian's son, who was carefully instructed to please him, and indeed was sharp enough already to require little instruction.

Sternhold lingered in his melancholy state. He was no longer violent—simply dejected. He did not seem able to answer the simplest question. If asked if he was hungry, he would stare, and say something relating to his school-days.

And this was the man who had built Stirmingham. For five years he remained in this state, and then suddenly brightened up; and it was thought and feared that he would recover the use of his faculties. It lasted but three days. In that short time he wrote three important documents.

The first was a statement to the effect that he had wronged Lucia. He now saw his folly—he had been led into his persecution of her by designing people, and blamed himself for his subsequent conduct. He earnestly entreated her forgiveness. The second was a species of family history, short but complete, refuting the claims of the American Baskettes. They were indeed of the same name, he wrote, but not of the same blood. The truth was that the cotters who had lived in the Swamp, now covered with mansions, had no name. They were half gipsies; they had no registered or baptismal name.

Will Baskette, who had been shot, was the chief man among them, and gradually they came by the country people to be called by his name. They were not blood relations in any sense of the term. This paper also gave the writer's views of his transactions with the Sibbolds and the cotters or "Baskettes," and concluded with the firmly expressed conviction—the honest statement of a man near his end—that his title was irrefutable, and he knew of no genuine claim.

The third document was his Will. For now it appeared that hitherto he had never made a will at all. It was extremely short, but terse and unmistakable. It left the whole of his property, real and personal (with the single exception of the gift to Lucia), to his son, John Marese Baskette.

The will Aurelian took care was properly attested, and by independent witnesses whom he sent for.

On the fourth day old Sternhold died, quietly and without a word. He was buried, and hardly was he in the tomb before the battle began. The companies at once cut off all connection with Aurelian.

They had reckoned upon his managing to get their terms at all events extended, as he had promised. The Corporation refused any honours to the dead king, and all eagerly sought about for the means of dividing the spoil.

After all their consultations, not all the subtlety of twenty solicitors could suggest any feasible plan—the old man had baffled them at last. It was useless to plead that he was insane, and actually in an asylum at the moment of executing the will. What was the good even if such a plea was successful—if the will was upset, the property would descend to the boy just the same. There seemed no way of getting at it.

But at last a weak point was found. It was a time when a great deal of commotion was made about the Roman Catholic question and the religious education of minors. Now Lucia was certainly half a foreigner, and it was believed she was a Catholic. Aurelian was certainly a Catholic. With all his cunning he had not foreseen this, and he had allowed himself to become a somewhat prominent member of the Catholic community in Stirmingham. He had no religion, but it paid him. Catholics are rich people, and when rich people go insane they are profitable. So he was caught in his own trap.

There was an agitation got up among the ultra-Protestant community. Funds were started to release the heir from the clasp of Rome. The companies, the Corporation, all joined in the outcry. The question was made a national one by the newspapers. But there was one difficulty: the law required that there should be a person to sue. After much trouble this person was selected in one of the Baskettes of American origin, who had settled in Stirmingham, and claimed to be a nearer relation than Aurelian.

The battle was long and furious, and cost heavy sums. No expense was spared on either side, and the estate got still further encumbered. It promised to be a drawn battle; but at last, having passed all the tribunals, it began to approach the place of power, and to be discussed in the Ministerial Cabinet. There was a man there who desired to obtain the Catholic vote of Ireland, and the Aurelian party began to boast already of success. But this very boasting spoilt their game. The Ministry lost the confidence of the people, the House followed suit, a new Ministry came into place, and the final decision was against the Catholic, or, as they termed themselves, legitimate party—for they said the uncle and the mother were the legitimate guardians.

The result was in truth disappointing to all the parties. The boy was made a ward of Chancery, proper receivers of the estate were appointed, and the companies who had begun to exult were entrapped. The lad was taken from his mother and uncle, and sent to Eton to prepare for college.

Thus a new element of complexity was added to the already chaotic state of this vast estate.

Chapter Ten

If ever there was a life that illustrated the oft-quoted phrase "poor humanity," it was that of Sternhold Baskette. But this is not the place to moralise—we must hasten on. The orchestra has nearly finished the overture; the play will soon begin.

Lucia had now no longer any reason for restraint. Her boy was safe—safe as the laws of a great country could make him—certain to inherit a property which by the time he was forty would be of value surpassing calculation. She rejoiced in it, gloried in it. To her it was more welcome than the confirmed guardianship of Aurelian would have been, because it left her free.

The lad was at Eton, and happy—far happier than he could have been elsewhere. His mother immediately commenced a course which led her by a rapid descent to the lowest degradation.

She returned to Paris. Aurelian felt it was useless now to interfere, neither could he afford more expense.

She easily got upon the stage again, and became more popular than ever. At the age of forty she was even more handsome than in her youth. Her features had been refined by the passage of time and by the restraint to which she had been subjected. Her form was more fully developed.

It is unpleasant to linger on this woman's disgrace. She formed a liaison with a rich foreign gentleman, retired with him from Paris after a time, and the Stirmingham Daily Post, which pursued the Baskettes with unmitigated hatred year after year, did not fail to chronicle the birth of a son.

Aurelian, baffled, was not beaten. He was a resolute and patient man. Like the famous Carthaginian father, he brought up his son and educated him to consider the Baskette estates as the one object of his attention—only in this case it was not for destruction, but for preservation.

When young John Marese Baskette, the heir, after distinguishing himself at Eton, was sent higher up the Thames to Oxford, Aurelian immediately placed his son, Theodore Marese, at the same college.

The result was exactly as he had foreseen. The heir formed a bond of friendship—such as it is in these days—with Theodore. Their one topic of conversation was the estate.

John was full of the most romantic notions. He was in youth a really exemplary lad—clever, hard-working, winning to himself the good will of all men. Theodore had a genuine liking for his cousin—then, at all events, though probably in after life the attachment he professed was chiefly caused by self interest.

John was full of ambitious dreams. His vivid imagination had been worked upon by the talk among his companions about the famous owner of twenty millions sterling—his father. Upon an old bookstall he obtained a copy of "The Life of Sternhold Baskette," now out of print. It inflamed him to the uttermost. There was good metal in the boy if he had only had friends and parents to put it to proper use. He formed the most extraordinary schemes as to what he would do with this wealth when he became of age, and stepped at one bound into the full enjoyment of it, as he supposed he should.

It was all to be used for the alleviation of the misery of the world, for the relief of the poor, for the succouring of the afflicted, the advancement of all means that could mitigate the penalties attaching to human existence.

As time wore on, however, these benevolent intentions received their first check.

He reached his twenty-first birthday. He claimed his birthright, and was refused. Briefly, the reason was because the companies and the American claimants had entered pleas, and because also the property was terribly encumbered, and would require long years of nursing yet before it could be cleared, and this nursing the higher Courts insisted upon.

Instead of the magnificent income he expected, the young man received two thousand pounds per annum only. It struck his nature a heavy blow, and did much to pervert it, for he looked upon it in the sense of a shameful injustice. With Theodore he left college; at all events he was now his own master, and entered "life."

Every one knows what "life" is to a young man of twenty-one with two thousand a year certain—the power of borrowing to a wide margin, and no monitor to check and retard the inevitable course.

Theodore was much older—fully thirty at this time; but he was as eager for enjoyment, and perhaps more so.

To make the story short, they ran through every species of extravagance—visited Paris, Vienna, and all the continental centres of dissipation.

Ten whole years passed away. John Marese Baskette was by this time a thorough man of the world, deeply in debt, brilliant and fascinating in manner, false and selfish to the backbone. He inherited his mother's beauty. A tall, broad, well-made man, dark curling hair, large dark eyes, and large eyelashes, bronzed complexion, which, when he was excited, glowed with almost womanly brilliance; strong as a lion, gentle in manner, and fierce as a tiger under the velvet glove. Polished and plausible, there were those who deemed him shallow and wholly concerned with the pleasure of the hour; but they were mistaken.

John Marese Baskette had rubbed off all the soft and good aspirations of his boyhood; but the ambition which was at the bottom of those schemes remained, and had intensified tenfold. He was burning with ambition. The hereditary mind of the Baskettes, their brain power, had descended to him in full vigour (though hitherto he had wasted it), and he also inherited their thirst for wealth. But his idea of obtaining it was totally opposed to the family tradition. The family tradition was a private life devoted with the patience and self-denial of a martyr to the accumulation of gold.

Marese's one absorbing idea was power. To be a ruler, a statesman, a leader, was his one consuming desire. As a ruler he thought, as a member of the Cabinet, it would be easy for him to affect the market in his favour, for Marese was a gambler already upon a gigantic scale. The Stock Exchange and the Bourse were his arena.

The intense vanity of the man, which led him to seriously hope even for the English Premiership, was, doubtless, a trait derived from his mother. "If I had my rights," he was accustomed to say to Theodore, "I should be not only the wealthiest man in England, but in Europe and America. My father's property has more than doubled in value. In England the wealthiest man at once takes a position above crowds of clever people who have nothing but their talents. Without any conceit, I can safely say that I am clever. A clever, wealthy man is so great a rarity that my elevation is a certainty. But nothing can be done without money. At present my wealth is a shadow only. The one thing, Theodore, is money. Our Stock Exchange labour is, in a sense, wasted; our operations are not large enough. What we make is barely sufficient to provide us with common luxuries (he did not pretend to say necessities) and to keep our creditors quiet. Nothing remains for bolder actions. I am thirty, and I have not yet entered the House."

This last remark was always the conclusion of his reflections. In a sense, it was like Caesar lamenting upon seeing a statue of Alexander—that he had done nothing at an age when Alexander had conquered the world. He had not even the means to fight the enemies who withheld his birthright from him. The bitterness engendered of these wrongs, the constant brooding over the career that was lost to him, obscured what little moral sense had been left in him after the course of life he had been through; and the once gentle boy was now ripe for any guilt. The verse so often upon the lips of the tyrant was for ever in his mind, and perpetually escaped him unconsciously—

> Be just, unless a kingdom tempt to break the laws,
> For sovereign power alone can justify the cause.

Like his father Sternhold, he looked upon the undisputed possession of such an estate as conferring powers and position nothing inferior to that of a monarch. His dislike to all things American—in consequence of the claims, now more loudly proclaimed than ever, of the Baskettes from the States—grew to be almost a monomania. He wished that the United States people had but one neck, that he might destroy them all at once—applying the Roman emperor's saying to his own affairs.

His especially favourite study was "The Prince" of Machiavelli, which he always carried with him. His copy was annotated with a scheme for applying the instructions therein given to modern times—the outline of the original requiring much modification to suit the changes in the constitution of society. Some day he hoped to utilise the labours of the man whose name has become the familiar soubriquet of the Devil.

Theodore, whom Aurelian had made qualify as a surgeon, was imbued with an inherited taste for recondite research. He would return from a wild scene of debauchery at early dawn, and drawing the curtains and lighting his lamp to exclude daylight, plunge into the devious paths of forbidden science. Keen and shrewd as he was, he did not disdain even alchemy, bringing to the crude ideas of the ancients all the knowledge of the moderns. Cruel by nature, he excelled in the manipulation of the dissecting knife, and in the cities upon the Continent where their wanderings led them, lost no opportunity of practising with the resident medical men, or of studying those wonderful museums which are concealed in certain places abroad. Marese was the fiery charger, ready to dash at every obstacle Theodore was the charioteer—the head which guided and suggested. Yet all their concentrated thought could not devise a method by which Marese might obtain the full enjoyment of his estate. Briefly, this was the condition of Marese's mind and his position, when the death of Aurelian took place, and a letter reached them written by him in his last hours, entreating their return to Stirmingham for reasons connected with the estate. They went, and a woman went with them as far as London—a woman whom we must meet hereafter, but who shall be avoided as much as possible.

They arrived at Stirmingham unannounced, and examined the papers which the deceased had particularly recommended to their study. Aurelian, as has been said, was baffled but not beaten. The fascination of the vast estate held his mind, as it held so many others, in an iron vice. The whole of his life was devoted to it. He had searched and searched back into the past, groping from point to point, and he had accumulated such a mass of evidence as had never been suspected.

He knew far more even than poor Sternhold, who had occupied himself exclusively with the future.

Marese and Theodore, living quietly in the residence attached to the asylum for the insane, which Aurelian had continued to keep, carefully studied these papers by the light of the lucid commentary the dead man had left. It is needless to recount the whole of the contents—most of them are known already to the reader. But the substance of it all was that three great dangers menaced the estate. The first was the claims of the Baskettes from America.

The evidence which Aurelian had collected was clear that the land they had occupied in the Swamp had been practically theirs, since they had paid no rent; but as to their power of handing it over to Sternhold, it was extremely questionable. The second great danger was the claim of a new tribe that had recently started up—the descendants of James Sibbold, who had also expatriated themselves.

It was doubtful if the transfer made by their ancestors could be maintained, and for this simple reason—it was doubtful whether James Sibbold himself had any right to the property his sons sold to Sternhold. He was not the eldest son. The eldest son, Arthur, had disappeared for a number of years; but there was not the slightest proof that he had died childless. Far from it. Aurelian, incessantly searching, had found out what no one else yet knew—that Arthur had married, had had children, and that one at least of his descendants was living but a short time since.

When Marese had read thus far his countenance turned livid, and Theodore feared he would have fallen in a fit. The savage passions inherited from his mother surged up in his frame, and overmastered him. He was ill for days, almost unconscious—the shock was so great, his passion so fierce—but presently recovering, read on.

Aurelian had traced Arthur in his wanderings, had traced his marriage—but there was one loophole. Do what he might, Aurelian could not discover where Arthur had married. It was in London, but a minute search failed to discover the church, and the register could not be found.

This fact, and the fact of the long silence, the absence of any claim being put forward, led Aurelian to believe that there really was no legal marriage—that it was only reputed. He hoped as much, at all events.

There was another loophole—the deed which old Sibbold had so treasured in his padlocked oaken chest—the deed which settled the inheritance (on the female as well as the male)—had disappeared. Sternhold had searched for it and failed. It was lost. If the marriage could not be proved, and if the deed was really lost, then there was no danger from Arthur Sibbold's descendants; but there remained those "ifs." Also, if Arthur's claim was put aside, then the succession would of course belong to his brother James Sibbold's descendants: but then again came in the question—Could these Sibbolds sign away (to Sternhold) an inheritance which at the time was entailed?

Aurelian finished with several hints and schemes which need not be gone into here, and indeed were never carried out. But his one great point throughout was a warning against the living descendant of Arthur Sibbold, whose name and present address he had discovered and left for Marese, and against the companies who held the leases. "For," said he, "these companies would foster any and every claim against the estate; anything to bar the succession of Marese, the heir, in order to obtain a grant or extension of time from the courts of law, to enable them to hold the property till the succession to the estate was established." These companies were so rich and powerful that it was difficult to contend against them. Their strength was money, their weapons were the various claimants.

"Therefore," wrote Aurelian, "the first thing is money, and I wish my property to be used freely for this end, convinced that you will do Theodore full justice; and I bid you, if possible, to take the weapons of the companies out of their hands. Without the claimants they are powerless."

These papers, and the facts and reflections they contained, made the deepest impression upon Marese and Theodore. In secret they walked through the city of Stirmingham, and marked its wealth, its vastness, its trade and population.

"And nearly all this is mine," whispered Marese, pale as death in his subdued excitement. He had to hold Theodore's arm to sustain his body, for, strong as he was, he trembled.

Next day they left for London, for Marese could not bear the Tantalus-like view of the wealth which was and was not his. In London they thought and planned as only such men seeking such an end can think and plan.

Chapter Eleven

While Marese and Theodore are maturing their plans, it will conduce to the easier comprehension of the horrible, complicated events which followed, if the past history of the estate be briefly summed up in such a manner that this chapter can be used for reference.

In the commencement, nearly a century previous to the present time, we have seen old Sibbold, the morose miser, gloating over his money, and studying his title-deeds. These gave him an unquestioned right to the farm he occupied, and to the Swamp, or waste land, which had been squatted on by Will Baskette and his companions. This right mainly depended, though not entirely, upon a certain deed of entail. Without that deed Sibbold had still sufficient evidence to prove his right to his farm, but not to the Swamp; without that deed there was no fixed succession—that is to say, he could have devised it to any one he chose.

There was, therefore, just the possibility that, hating his eldest son Arthur, he had himself destroyed this deed, in order to prepare the way for his second son, James. But against this supposition there was the known character of the man, which led one to imagine that he would rather have died than give up the smallest fraction of his possessions. At all events, this deed was missing, as were several others of little or no value, such as expired leases of fields to tenants, which had once been kept in Sibbold's oaken press, under padlock and key.

When Sibbold met with his death at the hands of highwaymen, the farm and waste lands, in the natural course of things, would have passed to his eldest son, Arthur, but he having disappeared, and not appearing to make a claim, James Sibbold, the younger son, took the property. The majority of people always thought, from the fact of Arthur's not returning to claim his birthright, that he had had a hand in the slaughter of old Will Baskette, and that his conscience drove him away.

James Sibbold, after a while, married, and had several sons. In time he died, and these sons, though married, still all remained living on the farmstead, or in the outhouses; for as it was known that James' right was doubtful, they could not agree about the succession, and preferred to live like pigs rather than go to law and have it settled, since the result was so uncertain. At the same time the squatters, basket-makers, reed-cutters, clothes-peg makers, etc, who resided in the Swamp which the rat had caused, had considerably increased in numbers, and were always called, after their former chief, by the name of Baskette.

This chief at the date of his death had two sons. The eldest went off with his mother, and joined the original gipsy tribe; the youngest, whose name or nickname was Romy, entered the service of the clergyman. The eldest was never heard of more; but Romy prospered, and in early middle age bought an estate and country mansion, not far from his birthplace.

It was he who opened up the concealed mineral wealth of coal and iron, and thus, as everything goes by contradiction in this world, it happened that the descendant of gipsies, notorious for their wandering habits and dislike of houses, was the founder of one of the largest cities in the world.

He married with every legal formality, and his son, Sternhold Baskette, imbued with the firmest convictions that in the future the young city would prosper to an unprecedented extent, employed the whole of the wealth he inherited in purchasing land and erecting houses.

In the course of his transactions he desired to purchase the Wick Farm, where old Sibbold had dwelt, and the Swamp where the Baskette tribe flourished. Finding the title of the vendors imperfect, he devised the strongest safeguard he could think of, which was to make all the Sibbolds then living or known, to sign one document, and all the reputed Baskettes to sign another. He then transhipped them all to

53

America—first, to get complete possession; secondly, in the hope that they would never return to trouble him.

He proceeded to drain the Swamp, and to convert it into the Belgravia of Stirmingham. But this project required an enormous expenditure, and just at that moment the first railway to the place, which he had largely supported, came to a standstill, and ate up all his available capital. When, therefore, a return of commercial prosperity took place, he found it impossible alone to complete the vast scheme of streets, squares, etc, which had been commenced.

Then the building lease plan was resorted to—the very keystone of all this curious history. First, the Corporation of the city took a large slice of the uncompleted property of him on a building lease for a term of years, on the expiration of which the whole reverted to him or his heirs (practically his heirs, as he was not likely to live to the age of 120 years).

After they had commenced building some uncertainty arose as to whether or no they had the power to enter into such an agreement; they could bind themselves, but could they bind their successors in office? This took place, it must be remembered, long, long before the recent sanitary legislation, which gives such extensive powers to local bodies.

In order to confirm their proceedings they obtained a private Act of Parliament, which, when it was drawn up, seemed to be worded clearly enough. But every one knows that after the lapse of thirty years or less, words in an inexplicable manner seem to lose their meaning, and to become capable of more than one interpretation. This is perhaps because the persons who read them are influenced unconsciously by a series of circumstances which did not exist at the time the document was composed.

At any rate, at the date when Marese and Theodore were thinking and scheming, there had already been a great deal of contention over the precise scope of several sentences in this Act: a part of which arose over the question of repairs to the buildings, and partly as to whether, by a little straining, the seventy years of the lease might not be construed to mean practically for ever.

This little straining was managed in this way. When did the lease commence? Had not each successive Mayor got the right to say, "This lease, as interpreted by the Private Act, means, not seventy years from the days of my predecessor, but seventy years from the commencement of my term of office." By this way of looking at it, so long as there was a Mayor the Corporation would always have seventy years to look forward to.

Of course all such reasoning was nothing but pure sophistry; but then most law is sophistry, and sophistry when supported by a rich body of men and called Vested Interest, is often much stronger than the highly belauded and really feeble truth.

Here was a tough Gordian knot, to add to the already difficult question of original title. But this was only the preface to the complications to follow. There still remained, after the Corporation had taken a part, a huge howling wilderness of streets with walls two feet high. Companies or syndicates were formed (eight companies in all)— perhaps they had better be called in modern parlance building societies—who took this howling wilderness on the same system of building leases, to fall in at a certain date.

Apparently in this case it was all plain, straightforward sailing; but not so. Sternhold Baskette got into difficulties over Railway Number 2, and had to borrow money. He also had to borrow money to complete portions of the estate which he had kept in his own hands, and to acquire lands just outside the city. Lastly, he had to borrow money to support the extravagance of his wife. In the aggregate these sums were something enormous.

At the moment of borrowing he was under the impression that he had dealt with independent persons—with financiers, in fact, of London, being so assured by his solicitors. These solicitors had had a pretty picking out of his railways and estates; they had grown fat and prosperous upon him, and might, one would have thought, have been trusted to serve him honestly.

But no—whenever was there a friendship formed in business? Ostensibly, the financiers who advanced the cash were independent; in reality, they acted for certain of these very aforesaid building societies who had taken the building leases! Four at least of them had their money thus out upon good security; and Sternhold, unknowingly at first, owed them a large fortune.

For their own interest they had proved easy creditors. They had not called in the loans; not a fraction of the original sums borrowed from them to complete Railway Number 2, to finish houses, buy fresh lands, to pay for Lucia's extravagance, had been repaid. Very little of the interest had been cleared off; none while Sternhold lived. They knew that they were safe. The railway was now paying a fair dividend, the houses and lands had trebled in value; as for Lucia's waste it was small in comparison—when they chose to call in their money they could seize upon property to twice the amount due, even with added interest.

But they did not choose to call in their money. The leases were now approaching the day of expiration. They knew that the trustees of Sternhold's estate had not one tithe of the cash required to meet their demands: they would be compelled to submit to one of two things— first, they must yield up a good part of the estate, or they must grant an extension of the leases—either of which would suit the societies exactly.

They intended to push matters in such a way as to compel the trustees to extend the term, in order to retain both halves, as it were, of the estate under their control. This was Gordian knot Number 3. How was the heir to come by his own through all this? It was impossible, unless he could scrape together sufficient money to pay off the loans which had been contracted by his father. He would then be in a position to claim the property held by the trustees at the expiration of the leases, which was now fast approaching.

The other four companies had got wind of this nice little arrangement, and it upset them extremely. They had not been half so shrewd as their fellows, and that was a bitter reflection. They foresaw their valuable properties passing away from them, while the other societies held fast to their share. It was gall and wormwood.

But they were not to be outdone in the Art of Entanglement. Sternhold was dead; they could not lend him money. But the heir, our friend Marese, was living, and living "fast;" and not only that, he was speculating heavily upon the Stock Exchange. Here was a fine opening. With careful and judicious management they bought up all Marese's debts; they lent him money to a large amount through their agents, keeping themselves in the background out of sight; and they had gentlemen always on the watch on the Exchange, whose business it was to tempt Marese into apparently good bargains with floating paper.

Not content with this, they had still further secured themselves. They had allied themselves with a certain powerful and enterprising railway company. This company had hitherto been shut out of Stirmingham, and were extremely desirous of getting access to it. These second four societies combined, and declared that in the interests of the properties committed to their charge (save the mark!) it was essential that there should be more direct railway communication with a certain district which it is immaterial to name, and that there should be a station close to their portion of the estate, the other stations being at some distance. The enterprising railway company would guarantee good terms if the trustees of the estate would enter into agreement with them.

The upshot was that another Act of Parliament was obtained by the influence of the said powerful railway company, authorising this line, station, and agreement. It was now argued that this Act and agreement would override the original building leases; especially as the railway company were prepared to prove that they had not yet reaped any reasonable benefit, and, unless the leases were extended, would be serious losers. As they had immense interest in the House, they were likely enough to gain their point. Here were two more Gordian knots, Numbers 4 and 5!

Then there was the list of claimants to the estate, which had now been swelled from all parts of the world, and the series of suits and pleas, and Heaven knows what other litigation threatened by them, making Gordian knot Number 6. Finally, the estate was in Chancery. Knot Number 7.

Here was a pleasant prospect for the heir! To put all the rest on one side, on the day that the building leases expired, and he stepped forward to claim his rights, the building societies would present him with the following neat little bill:—

"After all," said Marese to Theodore, as they planned and schemed, and smoked cigars at 120 shillings the hundred, "after all, old fellow, this is but one year's income if I could only get possession. And I believe we could finance the thing and raise the money without difficulty, if it were not for those cursed, hateful claimants from America and elsewhere. The Jews fight shy on account of the title difficulty. If we could but get rid of those claimants!"

Societies 1, 2, 3, 4 :—

To Loans advanced for completion of Railway	£123,000	0	0
To Interest on same at 4 per cent.	50,000	0	0
To Loans advanced for completion of Houses, and Purchase of Estates	240,000	0	0
To Interest on the same at 3 per cent.	38,000	0	0
To Private Loans on Bills [to Sternhold Baskette] at 5 per cent.	20,000	0	0
To Interest on the same	3,000	0	0
TOTAL	£474,000	0	0

Societies 5, 6, 7, 8 :—

To Private Loans on Bills [to Marese Baskette] at 8 and 10 per cent.	£65,000	0	0
To Interest on the same	11,000	0	0
To Paper Transactions as per Bill of Particulars, due	80,000	0	0
To Advances on Railway Extension, as per Parliamentary Act	118,000	0	0
TOTAL	£304,000	0	0

Total of Bills to meet before taking possession of property on expiration of leases, £778,000.

Chapter Twelve

There was once a very wise man who invented what was considered a saying almost inspired, which was afterwards inculcated as a most important lesson by mighty princes upon their sons, and continues to be constantly quoted in our day with approval—it is, that "Unity is strength." But the strength of the claimants to the Baskette estate consisted in the number of their scattered forces.

All that Marese, the heir, could have desired was that by some means they could be condensed into one person, and thus destroyed at a blow. They had increased as the years went by in a geometrical ratio, till the total formed a small battalion.

When the idea of making claims upon the estate first arose in America, there were already quite fifty families who in one way or another thought they had "rights." About a dozen visited Stirmingham, and all but drove poor old Sternhold frantic. That was a generation ago, and the tribe had nearly trebled. Mothers of children who had the remotest possible chance of a share in the prize took care to have them christened Baskette or Sternhold. There were Sternhold Baskette Browns, Baskette Johnsons, Baskette Stirmingham Slicks, English Baskette Williamsons, and every possible combination of Baskette.

Those who, either by the male or female side, really could show some species of proof that they were descended from the seventeen squatters who were transhipped to the States now numbered no less than one hundred and forty-three individuals—men, women, and children. To distinguish themselves from other claimants, they called themselves "The True Swampers."

But in addition to these, there was a host of other Baskettes, who in one way or another foisted in their names. There were Baskets, Bascots, Buscots, Biscuits, Buschcotts, Bosquettes—every conceivable variation of spelling from every State and territory, who declared that they were related to the parent stem of Will Baskette, the squatter, who was shot by old Sibbold. These might be called for distinction the pseudo-Baskettes.

Then among the True Swampers there was an inner circle, who professed to have prominent "rights" on account of their progenitors having been more nearly related to the original Will Baskette. They argued that the others were not true Baskettes, and had only adopted that name from the chief, while they were real blood Baskettes.

In addition, there was another host of people who made a virtue of proclaiming that they were not named Baskette. They did not profess to be named Baskette—they did not take a name which was not theirs! They were Washingtons, Curries, Bolters, Gregorys, Jamesons, and so on. But they had claims because their father's wives were of the Baskette blood.

Finally, there was another sub-division who loudly maintained that half of the original cotters who landed in New York were not Baskettes, but Gibbs, Webbes, Colborns, and so on, and that they were the descendants of these people. And there were some who went the length of declaring that they were descended from two alleged illegitimate sons of old Romy Baskette!

The Baskette Battalion was therefore made up of—1st. The Pure

Blood Baskettes; 2nd. The True Swampers; 3rd. Demi-Baskettes, who had that name added to another; 4th. Nominal Baskettes, whose names had an accidental resemblance; 5th. The Feminine Baskettes, descended from women of Baskette strain; 6th. Independent Squatters, not Baskettes, but companions; 7th. Illegitimate Baskettes!

Then there were the Sibbolds—such a catalogue! These had been slower to wake up to their "rights" than the Baskettes, but when they did discover them they came in crowds. First, there were the descendants, in a straight line, of the eight sons of James Sibbold, shipped (six with families) to New York. They had multiplied exceedingly, and there was no end to them. The simply Sibbolds, as we may call them, numbered no less than two hundred and eighteen, all told—men, women, and children. Every one of these had some register, some old book—many of these books were worm-eaten copies of Tom Paine's "Rights of Man"—some piece of paper or other to prove that they had the blood of James Sibbold in their veins.

Then there were all the ramifications, pretty much like the Baskette branches; innumerable cadets distantly related, innumerable people whose wife's uncle's mother or cousin's name was Sibbold; and all the various Sibbolde, Sibboldes, Sibald, Sigbeld, Sybels, Sibils, Sibelus, Sibilsons, ad libitum. Illegitimate Sibbolds were as plentiful as blackberries, and all ready to argue the merits of the case with revolver and bowie. If the Baskettes made up a battalion, the Sibbolds formed an army!

Between these two great divisions there was the bitterest enmity. The Baskettes derided the claims of the Sibbolds; the Sibbolds derided those of the Baskettes. The Sibbolds told the Baskettes that they were an ill-conditioned lot; if they had been respectable people, and really his relations, old Sternhold would never have shipped them to America out of his sight. The Baskettes retorted that the Sibbolds were ashamed to stay in England, for they were the sons of a murderer; they were the descendants of a dastardly coward, who shot a man through a window. The Sibbolds snarled, and pointed out that the great chief of the Baskettes was nothing but a thief, caught in the act and deservedly punished; a lot of semi-gipsies, rogues, and vagabonds. Their very name showed that they were but basket-makers; they were not even pure gipsy blood—miserable squatters on another man's property.

Blows were not unfrequently exchanged in the saloons and drinking-stores over these quarrels. The result was the formation of two distinct societies, each determined to prosecute its own claim and to oust the other at all hazards. The Baskette battalion relied upon the admitted non-payment of rent by their forefathers to upset all subsequent agreements, and they agreed also that this agreement which their forefathers had signed was not binding on the remote descendants. The document was obtained by trickery, and the land was not put to the use the vendors had understood it was to be put, as the representatives now alleged, to simple agricultural purposes. Further, each of those who signed the document only gave up his cottage and the small plot of garden round it; they did not sell the waste land between the islands.

The Sibbolds principal argument was that their forefathers could not sign away an entailed estate without previously cutting off the entail, and it was acknowledged that this had not been done. But, said the Baskettes, there was a question if the land ever was entailed; let the Sibbolds produce the deed, and if it was not entailed, where was their claim?

Each of these divisions formed itself into a society, with a regular committee and place of meeting, a minute-book to record accumulated evidence, legal gentlemen to advise, corresponding secretaries, and Heaven knows what. They actually issued gazettes—printed sheets of intelligence. There was the Baskette Gazette and the Sibbold Gazette, which papers carefully recorded all deaths, marriages, and new claims. There was a complete organisation, and a—fine thing it was for the lawyers and some few sharp young men.

Of late these societies had received more or less cordial overtures from the eight building societies at Stirmingham who held the leases. The first four societies encouraged the Baskette battalion, the second held out hopes to the Sibbolds. The cunning building societies, without committing themselves, desired nothing better than protracted litigation between these claimants and the heir, in the certainty that meantime they should reap the benefit.

Among the American corps of claimants there were men of all classes—from common labourers, saloon-keepers, etc, up to judges, editors, financiers, merchants; and many of them were clever, far-seeing persons, who, without putting any weight upon the somewhat strained "rights" they professed to believe in, still thought that there was "something in it, you know," and money might be got by persistent agitation, if it was only hush-money.

Throughout many turbulent States there was at one time quite a feeling aroused against England (which added its venom to the unfortunate Alabama business), as having unjustly kept what was due to American citizens. These societies had their regular agents in Stirmingham and London, whose duty it was to report every change that took place, every variation of the case, and to accumulate evidence and transmit it. These bulletins were received by the "caucuses," and sometimes printed in the Gazettes.

Besides these regular organisations, who had money at disposal and were really formidable, there were several free lances careering over the country, representing themselves as the sons of the elder brother of Romy Baskette, the brother who had disappeared with the gipsies. These were downright impostors, and yet got a living out of the

60

case. Several lecturers also promenaded the States, who made a good thing of it by giving a popular version of the story, illustrated by a diorama of incidents in the lives of the principal actors, from the shooting of Will Baskette to the appearance of Lucia Marese as Lady Godiva. It was singular that no one presented himself as a descendant of Arthur Sibbold; he seemed to have been quite forgotten. So much for America.

From Australia there came, time after time, the most startling reports, as is usual when any cause célèbre is proceeding in the Old World. Now, it was a miner at the diggings who had made extraordinary disclosures; now, some shepherd on a sheep-run, after a fit of illness, found his memory returned, and recollected where important deeds were deposited.

Nothing, however, came of it. The principal seats of disturbance were America and England; for England produced a crop of what we may call Provisional, or Partial Claimants. Here and there, scattered all over the country—from Kent to Cornwall, from Hampshire to Northumberland—were people of the name of Baskette, which is a very ancient English cognomen, and to be found in every collection of surnames.

Most of these were of little or no consequence, but one or two held good positions as gentlemen or merchants. None of these latter made the shadow of a pretence to the estate, but they were fond of speculating as to their possible remote connection with the now famous Baskette stock; and some said that if anything did turn up, if any practical results followed the American attempt, it would be as well to be prepared to take a share in the spoil.

There were also at least three impostors—utter scoundrels, who obtained a profusion of drink and some sustenance from credulous fools in tap-rooms by pretending that they were descendants of the elder brother of Romy Baskette. They had not the shadow of a proof, and ought to have been treated to a dose of "cell."

A gipsy tribe, a travelling clan which went about the country with shooting galleries, merry-go-rounds, peep-shows, and so on, were in the habit of proclaiming that they were the very identical tribe from whom offshoots settled in the historical swamp at Wolf's Glow, in order to attract custom.

Certain persons in and around Stirmingham, whose fathers or ancestors had sold lands to Sternhold Baskette—lands now worth ten, and in some cases a thousand, times the price he had given for them— had a fallacious idea that if the title of the heir was upset, they would have a chance of regaining possession, or at least of an additional payment for the property.

They formed themselves into a loosely-compacted society to protect their interest. It was remarkable that in England, as in America,

61

no one set up a claim to be the descendant of Arthur Sibbold. The real danger was from America, the land of organisation.

But in England there was a class of persons who, without possessing any personal interest in the matter, made it their especial business to collect all the "ana" that could be discovered, and gained a livelihood out of their study of the case. More than one private inquiry office in London received large fees from New York clients to make special investigations. The credulity of mankind is exhibited in a striking manner in the support given to these offices. How should they be supposed to be so devotedly attached to the cause of one client? What is to prevent them having fifty, all with the same end, and from selling the information gained from one to the other?

There were men who made it a speciality of their trade to collect all books, pamphlets, pictures, lectures, genealogies, deeds, documents, letters, papers, souvenirs—anything and everything, from Sternhold Baskette's old hat upwards, that could be twisted into relation with the case.

Those who have never had any leaning towards antiquarian research have no idea of the enormous business done in this way—not only in reference to great cases of this kind, but in reference to matters that would appear to an outsider as absolutely not worth a thought. There is scarcely a scrap of written or printed paper of the last century, or up to within fifty years of the present date, which has not got its value to such a collector, for he knows there will be fools to buy them. Sometimes it happens that an apparently worthless piece of paper or parchment, bought as waste, turns out, under his sharp eye, to be a really awkward thing for some owner of property unless he purchases it.

There were lawyers in a peculiar way of business who did not disdain this species of work, and presently they may cross our path. Such men were in constant communication with people on the other side of the Atlantic, where there is, year by year, an increasing desire manifested to trace out genealogies.

The year in which, in the ordinary course of events, the building societies and the Corporation must relinquish their expired leases was now fast approaching. Some such person as has been described was seized with a brilliant idea, and made haste to advertise it. Why should not all the claimants to the estate meet on the disputed spot at this critical moment? Why should there not be a regular family council, the largest and most important that had ever taken place? The idea was a good one, and spread like wildfire. The newspapers took it up; the American societies thought highly of it. Nothing like a grand demonstration.

The upshot was that Stirmingham began to look forward to the assembling of these would-be monarchs of the city, which was finally, after much discussion, fixed for the next New Year's Day.

This New Year's Day was fast approaching, while Marese and Theodore planned.

Chapter Thirteen

The grand family council was to be held at Stirmingham on the coming New Year's Day. How difficult it is to trace the genesis of an idea! It does not seem to have any regular growth—to begin with a seed and cast out roots, a stem, branches, leaves; it shoots now one way, now this, like those curious creatures revealed by the microscope, or like the germs of fungi. Upon the original thought odd branches are engrafted, accidental circumstances suggest new developments, till at last the full completed idea bears no sort of resemblance to what might have been expected from the embryo.

How the idea was first started neither Marese nor Theodore could tell, nor how it was communicated from one to the other. There is a method of communication which is not dependent upon direct speech; there is a way of talking at a subject without mentioning it. When two clever men's minds are full of one absorbing topic it does not require formal sentences to convey their conceptions. They did not seem even to actually talk of it, and yet it grew and grew, till it overshadowed them like a vast gloomy mountain.

It would not be just to so much as hint at a latent insanity in these men's minds, for it would partly absolve them from responsibility, and would dispose their judges to regard their crimes leniently. Certainly no one, if asked to do so, could have pointed out two keener men of the world than these. Yet, somehow, despite one's reluctance to afford them the shadow of an excuse, there does creep in the conviction that such a ghastly conception could only be formed in a brain lacking the moral organs, if such an expression may be used, in a brain unbalanced with natural human sympathy.

Marese's father, old Sternhold, had certainly been mad at one period of his career. His mother, Lucia, had exhibited a vanity so overweening, and a temper so intense, that at times it resembled lunacy. It may have been that, along with the mental powers of calculation and invention which distinguished old Romy and Sternhold, Marese had also inherited the mental weakness of Sternhold and Lucia.

Theodore had shown a taste for extraordinary studies usually avoided by healthy-minded men. His father, Aurelian, had passed the whole of his time with insane patients, and it is said that too much contact with mad people reacts upon the sane. He had early initiated his son into the mysteries of that sad science of the mind which deals with its deficiencies. The son's youth had been passed in constant intercourse with those harmless and, so to say, reasonable lunatics who are to be met with in the homes and at the dinner-tables of medical men, and whose partial sanity and occasional singular flashes of unnatural intelligence are perhaps more calculated to affect the minds of others than the vagaries of the downright mad.

In one short sentence, this terrible crime, which was looming over Marese and Theodore, was nothing less than the deliberate intention to destroy the whole of the claimants to the estate at once. How it originated it is difficult to imagine, but it did. It might perhaps be partly traced to the injunction in Aurelian's papers to take the weapons out of the hands of the companies; or partly to the oft-expressed wish of Marese's, after the Roman emperor, that all the claimants had but one neck, so that he might cut it. The said emperor has much to answer for.

The announced gathering of the claimants at Stirmingham certainly seemed to bring them all within the reach of the fowler's net, if he could but cast it aright. Marese and Theodore had half-formed ideas of blowing the whole company into the air as they sat at council in the Sternhold Hall on New Year's Day, something after the fashion of Guy Fawkes, but with a deadlier compound than he had at his disposal—nitro-glycerine or dynamite; especially the first might be trusted to do the work much more effectually than gunpowder, which was also more difficult to conceal on account of its bulk.

It will barely be believed that these two men, in the height of the nineteenth century, calmly examined the vault under that famous hall, in order to see if it was fitted for the purpose. This hall or assembly-room had been finished about the time that the agitation commenced over the heir to the estate, just before Sternhold had married, when the Corporation heaped flattery upon him. It had been named after him.

It was a fine room, not too large, and yet of sufficient size to seat an audience. The object was to afford a concert-room for dramatic and theatrical performances, and also for balls. As the site was valuable, and every particle of space had to be utilised in the centre of this mighty city, it had been built over vaults, which were intended for bonded warehouses; but partly on account of the high rent asked, and partly because of the dampness of the cellars—the site was the very centre of the old Swamp—had never been occupied. The access was bad, and there was no place for a display or advertisement, which was another reason why the cellars had not let. There was a certain amount of propriety in holding what was to be called "The Grand Centennial Family Council" in this hall, built upon the centre of the ancient Swamp, and named after the founder of the city.

Marese and Theodore, in disguise, examined the vaults, under the pretence of being agents for London merchants desirous of opening business in Stirmingham. There was hardly any necessity for this precaution, for it was so many years since they had openly resided in the place that few would have recognised them.

To their great surprise, these vaults, whose gloomy darkness they explored by the light of lanterns, extended in one vast cavern, under the whole of the hall. Instead of a series of cellars, there was one huge cavern. This was occasioned by the flooring not being supported upon brick arches, as would have been architecturally preferable, but upon timber posts, or pillars. The place had, in fact, been put up hastily, and the vaults were never completed. The timber pillars were placed in regular order, and it had been intended to build brick partitions; but as no one seemed to care to occupy the cellars, this had never been done. The floor was extremely damp, and the whole appearance of the place repulsive. Snails, toads, and slimy reptiles crawled about, and this under the very stage above, upon which music, song, and dance were wont to enliven the gay hearts of the audiences.

One great obstacle to the idea of blowing up the place was the height of these timber posts, which was full eighteen feet, so that the roof of the vault was high over head, and any explosives, to produce the full effect, would have to be piled up on casks or stands. Then the hall was larger than they had supposed, and it was apparent that the coming council would occupy but a portion of it, and perhaps change that portion now and then, so that it would be uncertain where to place the nitro-glycerine.

The idea, looked at from a distance and in the abstract, seemed feasible enough; but when they came to face the physical difficulties, it was found to be hard of realisation. There was the danger of getting the explosives into the place, the danger of detection, and, finally, the chance of an accident hoisting the engineer with his own petard, especially at that time of the year when nitro-glycerine was notoriously dangerous on account of the crystals which cold formed upon its surface, and the least jar or shake was sufficient to cause an explosion. Obviously, the plan was a cumbrous one, and without hesitation it was abandoned.

But the main idea, that of getting rid of the claimants at one blow, was not abandoned; it grew and grew, and occupied their minds day and night. At last the thought of transferring the Guy Fawkes expedient from the land to the ocean, which, once the deed was successfully accomplished, would tell no tale, occurred to them.

The claimants must come over on shipboard, if only they could be got into one or even two ships; and if these vessels sank upon the voyage suddenly without a warning! This was certainly much safer for the conspirators, as no trace would be left, and it was surer of success, because in the hall some of the victims might escape—at sea they could scarcely do so. They ran over in their minds the various methods of scuttling ships which have been invented from time to time.

There was the good old simple plan of boring holes in the bottom with augurs. There was the devilish coal-shell. A box painted to resemble coal, but really containing powder, was thrown among the coal, and when placed in the furnace blew up the boiler, and destroyed the ship. There was the ship-rat—a contrivance by which the very motion of the vessel caused an augur in a box to bore its way through, and so cause a leak. Some benevolent socialists, anxious for the welfare of man, had also promulgated a notion of exploding nitro-glycerine by clockwork, arranged to go so long, and set to act just as the vessel was farthest from land.

But all these seemed to Marese and Theodore clumsy, risky, and, what was worse, uncertain of operation. It was reserved for Marese to suggest the deadliest of all destructive engines, and he arrived at its conception in this way. He had, as it were, a double mind. He was liable to flashes of inspiration—such as it was—to sudden ideas which shot through him without endeavour. He had also the power of concentrating his thoughts, and bringing the regular forms of logic to his assistance. But this latter method he could only practise with the aid of pen and ink; and it was his constant habit, whenever contemplating an important step, such as a coup upon the Exchange, to write out his plans in a regular sequence, just as he wished them to take place.

This written guide he corrected and enlarged until it seemed beyond any further improvement; and then shutting his eyes to all consequences, resolutely avoiding those secret promptings which suggest that something has been left undone, he was accustomed to rush at the matter in hand, and dispose of it with bold, unhesitating strokes. This method certainly had its advantages, but it had also the disadvantage that if by any accident his notes fell into other hands, he was lost.

Nevertheless, after thinking and thinking in vain over this great problem, and failing of any very brilliant flash of intelligence, Marese at last resorted to his favourite system, and sought the solution by the aid of pen and ink. First he wrote at the top of his rough draft—

"What is it that I desire? Define it. Definition: to destroy the claimants. Who are the claimants? A body of men. How is a body of men to be destroyed? In the same way as a single person. How is man destroyed? By the knife, by bullets, by explosives, by garotting, by fire, by water, by poison, narcotics."

Such were his rough premises. Then he laid the pen down and thought. Why not set the vessels these men were coming over in on fire? That at first seemed to him a most feasible plan, far superior to the uncertain action of explosives. It required some arrangement,

66

which he felt confident the scientific knowledge of Theodore could easily supply, to cause the flames to break out at the proper moment.

He began to grow enraptured with it. It seemed so easy and sure. Then, picturing in his mind the vessel sinking, the thought occurred to him that if the risk was to be run, something might as well be got out of it. Why not put a cargo on board insured far beyond its value, and so kill two birds with one stone?

At one blow to destroy his enemies and fill his own pockets was superb triumph! He called Theodore and explained the idea to him. Theodore was struck with it—especially with the notion of making a profit out of the risk. He was, however, considerably opposed to the insurance dodge, on the ground that it had been tried so often, and people had got so keen that it was ten to one if some suspicion did not arise, especially when it was seen what an object it would be to Marese to secure the destruction of the passengers. Some other plan must be adopted. Suppose, for instance, they took Marese's yacht and followed the vessel, and after its partial destruction, if they could secure only partial destruction, put in a claim for salvage. To do this they must encounter serious difficulties, but it would be far less risky.

Marese wished to know what substances they could employ to produce a fire which could not be extinguished without some special chemical composition. Theodore produced a series of manuscript volumes containing the notes which he had accumulated during his long and curious studies. He turned them over one by one, extracting such information as appeared applicable to their purpose, while Marese, waiting for his friend's reply, amused himself by reading pieces here and there. It was while thus employed that the devilish means by which their end could be obtained occurred to him.

Chapter Fourteen

He happened to light on a volume of notes made upon the remarkable properties of gases. They began with a description of those curious caves and even meadows abroad wherein no animal can live, and the place is strewn with the bones of birds and beasts who have incautiously entered the infected circle. This effect was proved to proceed from a vapour which rose up from the earth, and was no sooner breathed than it produced asphyxiation. Animals who inhaled it fell as if shot, so sudden was the action.

Gases as deleterious were often generated in wells, caves, and confined places, such as the huge tuns or casks used by brewers to keep their beer in, and which had often proved fatal to the men who attempted to scour them out.

Theodore believed that the cold shiver which some persons affected to feel upon entering a churchyard and passing over the graves of the dead, was caused by the presence of a gas in small quantities, evolved from the decaying remains beneath the feet. Then there were gases which upon inhalation caused a profound slumber; others which had precisely an opposite result, and made the patient lively and brisk; and others which rendered the person who took them perfectly insensible to surgical operations.

Marese, a man who had never paid the least regard to science, was deeply struck with these facts, with which the veriest tyro in chemistry is well acquainted. But he did what no tyro or even advanced student would perhaps have done—he applied his discovery—for so it was to him—to his own circumstances.

There are, says Bacon, three modes of reading—one to pass away an idle hour, one to acquire a knowledge of a subject, and the third and the most advantageous method is always to keep your own ends in view, and to apply everything to your object.

In these gases Marese found his desideratum. His engine of destruction burst upon his mind, as it were, complete in a moment. Some such poisonous gas should be shipped on board these vessels, closely confined in a box or other receptacle, and at the proper moment liberated, to spread throughout the steamer a subtle vapour which no man could see coming, and against which strength, skill, and discipline would be perfectly powerless.

Theodore, looking up, saw a change upon Marese's countenance, and immediately knew that something had occurred to him. The heir was pale as death; his own conception, so ghastly and treacherous, filled him with a nameless horror at the same moment that he never hesitated in his purpose.

After a while he took up a pen and added to his already written premises the conclusion—his idea in a few brief sentences—and handed it to Theodore. He left it to Theodore to select the gas, and to arrange the mechanical details. He had sown the seed, the other must patiently tend it. And the other did patiently tend it; and this is what it grew to.

The name of the gas which Theodore at last, after much thought, fixed upon shall not be here disclosed; for although it is well-known to chemists, and any one who can read could easily find it, there is no knowing what imitations might not spring up if they were aware of the means being so ready at hand.

Though suicide is such a simple and obvious expedient in difficulties, yet there are scores who do not commit it because they never think of it. If some kind friend suggested the pistol or the knife they would at once employ it.

Gas had one property which rendered it peculiarly fitted for the purpose in view. Being elastic, it could be compressed to a great extent, and thus an immense volume might be contained in a small compass. Therefore the case or receptacle to hold the vapour poison need not be of large dimensions; and this was a matter of some importance.

The gas chosen was not in any way explosive; on the contrary, it had the property of extinguishing any light which was placed in it—there was thus no danger of any accidental circumstance causing an explosion at an awkward moment. It was absolutely safe—the operator ran no risk, provided always that he did not inhale the vapour.

Theodore sketched out a case about three feet square, which was to be formed of an outer box of deal, and an inner skin of thin iron. Into this case, which would be tolerably strong, he proposed to pump a vast volume of gas, taking care that the pressure should not exceed the power of the box to withstand. The aperture through which it had been pumped was then to be hermetically sealed with molten lead.

The greatest difficulty was to provide for the escape of the devilish vapour at the proper moment; and this caused the projectors much reflection. Clockwork was objectionable; it was liable to injury from jars and shakes. Cases of this character, which looked strong and substantial, and would be placed in the hold, would be certain to receive the roughest of usage.

At one time he conceived the idea of relying upon the cupidity of the seamen. It was suspected that many of the accidents which had taken place at sea, and caused the destruction of hundreds by fire, had arisen through dishonest seamen or employés on board going at night with a candle into the compartment where valuable goods were stowed, and dropping sparks.

Why not utilise this propensity? Mark the case "watches," "jewellery," or "bullion," cause it to be surrounded with a certain amount of mystery and precaution enough to engender suspicion; and leave the rest to the chisel and drill of the would-be thief.

But this, though clever, was too uncertain. Another idea which occurred to him was to have a wooden case only, but a strong one, and to confine in a small hole prepared for the purpose one of the boring insects, which in a certain time would be sure to eat its way through and leave an aperture.

This, too, was more ingenious than practicable. He was delayed for a time. Accident solved the difficulty. Passing through the streets, he was stopped by a crowd which had collected around a quack doctor.

"See," cried the vendor of patent vegetable pills, "here is the horrid stuff the allopathists, the doctors and physicians sell to you at high prices. Here is a common drug used by them in this phial. I will pour some of the liquid upon the hard stone pavement—just see how it acts upon the granite, and then guess how your wretched stomachs must be abused."

He poured it on the stone—the crowd pressed forward, and saw it

69

eat a hole. "Aquafortis," thought Theodore, and the idea was his—aquafortis was the agent he wanted.

He passed on, and left the crowd thoroughly convinced of the tricks played by the medical faculty, and purchasing largely of the vegetable pills. Theodore had found a substance which would eat through his iron and wood cases, and leave an aperture—a substance, too, whose action was equal, and could be regulated to a sufficiently accurate extent.

Upon reflection, however, and after making several experiments, he did not employ ordinary aquafortis, but another acid equally powerful, and which was still more regular in its action. He tried the experiment time after time, till at last he obtained the proper strength, and fixed the requisite amount of acid to eat through a given thickness of iron and wood in a certain time. He repeated the experiment till he was absolutely certain of the result.

The plan had now grown delightfully clear and well-defined—the infernal machine became of the simplest construction. All that had to be done was to place the acid in the case confined in a small and very thin copper vessel (lined with an enamel to resist it), which was to be screwed to one side of the case, then pump the gas in, hermetically seal it, heave the whole thing on board the steamer, and leave it to work its way. Delightfully simple!

He called Marese to look over his drawings, and to witness his experiments with the acid. Marese was enchanted; his confidence in Theodore's scientific resources was confirmed. There was, however, one question he asked—Was the gas so strong and so poisonous that the small quantity confined in a case three feet square would destroy a whole ship's company? Would not the gas escape, rise up, and dissipate itself through the port-holes, up the hatchways, and be further weakened by the breezes that blew and caused draught in various places between decks? These ocean steamers were very roomy.

Theodore was delighted to have an opportunity of explaining the properties and nature of the vapour to his friend. The peculiarity of this gas was that, although an invisible fluid, it was extremely heavy—it was heavier far than atmospheric air. He easily proved that a gas might be heavier than air by a well-known experiment with a vapour (not the one to be used in this case) which he poured out of a glass phial over a candle. The invisible gas descended and extinguished the candle; There was not the slightest chance of the poison-vapour escaping quickly through ports or up hatchways. It would, as it were, cling to the vessel. The pressure inside the case would cause it to issue rapidly from the aperture eaten out by the acid. It would then diffuse itself laterally, and gradually penetrate into every crevice and corner of the ship. The effect would be that one by one every person on board would inhale it, and in an instant, let the quantity breathed be never so small, down he would drop, or grow rigid as he sat—unconscious was the word Theodore used

70

as an euphemism for death. He did not mention another effect it would have, lest the horror of it should cause even Marese to falter.

Theodore traced out the probable course of events on board the fated vessel. First, the persons working or living in the cabins and places nearest the case would feel the effect and succumb. Then there would be alarm and excitement—others would rush to the spot, and they would immediately fall, just as the birds and beast did who entered those fatal caves abroad. One man on board, perhaps, might detect the cause—the surgeon, or any doctor who chanced to be a passenger—and might cry out to man the boats and escape; but who, in the hurry and excitement, would heed him?—he would not have time to escape himself, much less to explain the danger to others. It was doubtful whether even so much as a signal of distress would be hoisted. The crew, the officers, the passengers would be so completely puzzled, so utterly at their wit's end, that no course would suggest itself to them before it was too late.

In this respect the gas had an immense advantage over any apparatus which would set the ship on fire. Let the fire be never so rapid, one boat at least might get away, and on that boat the very person whom it was most desirable should seek the floor of the ocean. Moreover, fire could be seen from a vast distance, and might attract attention from other vessels, who by day would observe the smoke, and by night the glare of the flames.

But in this case probably not so much as a flag would be hoisted. One by one the seamen and passengers, the captain and officers, would succumb to the invisible vapour, first becoming weak and helpless, and next "unconscious." The steersman would fall at the wheel. The engineer would drop at his engine; the stoker as he shovelled up the coal; the passenger would lie in his berth. And the steamer, so long as the fuel in the furnace lasted, would pursue her way unguided over the waves; finally, after a few hours, to float a derelict at the mercy of the wind.

There was a completeness, a finish, an elaboration of detail about this scheme which fascinated the conspirators. It was so novel, daring, and yet safe, it enchanted them. When at last the great horror was discovered, what risk would there be? Nothing on board would excite suspicion. The gas had actually no smell; besides, long before anything was discovered, it would have dissipated itself.

Even if the whole of the cargo was examined, the case itself would offer, no handle to an inquirer. The powerful acid would have eaten its way out, and nothing would be left but a small empty case with a hole in it. Nothing need show who consigned the case. Better still: Marese's yacht would follow the doomed steamer, keeping close on pretence of the safety of having company in a voyage across the Atlantic.

They would easily know when the desired result was obtained by the view of the steamer rolling helplessly in the trough of the waves. By the time that was the case some hours would have elapsed after the catastrophe, and various pretences could be arranged to avoid immediately proceeding on board—especially as from a distance nothing would look the matter—and by then the poisonous vapour would have dissipated itself, or so mixed with the air as to have lost its fatal power. They would then take charge of the vessel and bring it into port, and claim the salvage.

If they contrived to select a vessel which carried a valuable cargo, that salvage money would be something extremely large in amount, added to the value of the steamer itself. They might manoeuvre to get such a cargo stored. This would be far superior to the clumsy dodge of sinking the ship and claiming the insurance money.

As to getting the case on board, it was as easy as could be. Having proceeded to New York in Marese's yacht, taking with them the necessary apparatus for producing the gas (which was very simple), and pumping it into the case, they could ascertain the hour of the steamer's departure, fill the case, regulate the acid for say four, or perhaps three days, and send it on board only a little while before she started. They would then, on board the yacht, proceed to sea on a cruise and keep the steamer in sight.

Delightfully simple! Perfectly complete and scientific in every detail!

Marese once again asked if the gas was really so powerful? Theodore referred to his note-books, and showed him an extract from a newspaper not of so very remote a date, wherein it was stated that at a conference of the various leading European Powers it had been resolved not to employ certain implements in warfare, such as explosive shells or bullets under a certain size, and poisonous gases or vapours which could be thrown into a fortress or town in shells. Marese was convinced, and regarded the engine as perfect.

Thus did two men deliberately plan out the destruction of several hundreds of their fellow-beings without one single thought or reflection upon the misery and suffering they would cause, or upon the intrinsic villainy of the act.

Well was it suggested by a French thinker that certain natures are incapable of feeling, incapable of remorse so long as they remain "faithful to the logic of their type"—i.e. faithful to their own selfish interests and passions.

Chapter Fifteen

With his own hands Theodore constructed the infernal machine and prepared the materials for generating the deadly vapour at the shortest notice. This, the first part of the scheme, having been settled, there remained two great difficulties to overcome. The first was to get the claimants on board one vessel—travelling in a body; and the second was to secure their passage by a steamer carrying a valuable cargo, so as to increase the gain of salvage money to the utmost.

It was not easy to manage the first matter; the latter Marese thought he saw his way through. It happened just then that the payment of the war indemnity to Germany caused a great drain of gold from this country; the value of the precious metals consequently rose, and the imports increased to meet the demand. Gold and silver came in large quantities from New York, both in coin and bullion—especially silver.

Marese intended to take advantage of this fact. By means of certain Stock Exchange operations, with which he was perfectly familiar, having employed them previously on several occasions, he arranged that a very large amount of bullion should be transmitted to London from New York by the splendid steamer Lucca, due to start on December 3rd.

It must be understood that this bullion was not to be despatched to Marese, and that he did not appear in the transaction as having any direct connection with it. He had, in fact, arranged to lose a small sum of money, in order to render the importation of bullion particularly profitable in the week ending December 17th—profitable not to him, but to those speculators who deal in precious metal just as others do in corn or calico. Marese omitted no precaution, spared no pains, and used the whole of his natural and acquired cunning to render this operation a certainty.

The next thing was to tempt the claimants to travel by the steamer Lucca. After considerable hesitation, Marese at last determined to open negotiations with the leading men amongst them. He did not do this in his own person, but through his solicitors. It was represented to the managers of the Baskette and Sibbold Lodges that really their claims and the interests of the heir—i.e. Marese—were not so divergent as had been supposed. The heir was quite as much excluded from the enjoyment of the property as they were, and finding the building societies determined, by every means in their power, to put off the day when they must yield up possession, he wished to make common cause against these companies.

Nor was this statement altogether fictitious. The idea of strengthening the hands of the claimants, and making common cause with them, had often occurred to Marese, for the sole purpose of taking the weapons of the companies out of their hands, as Aurelian had advised.

No sooner was this overture on the part of the heir received in America than both Lodges at once responded, and without a moment's hesitation fell into the snare laid for them. To us, who are acquainted with the infamous designs of Marese, such conduct seems almost senile; but it must be remembered that these men on the other side of the Atlantic had not the slightest suspicion of the deadly engine which had been preparing.

To some extent the sudden overture of the heir caused a cessation of hostilities between the two Lodges, and when Marese's second offer arrived they held a species of jubilee. This offer was nothing less than to convey the whole of the claimants at his own expense, and added that he had already notified to the owners of the Lucca that he might require the entire passage accommodation, or nearly, of that vessel. To the Americans this came as an immense boon. There were many of them comparatively poor men, to whom the cost of the voyage was a serious matter, and who had already begun to hesitate at the prospect before them.

The diabolical foresight of Marese and Theodore had guessed as much. They said to each other, "Half the claimants will not come—only those who are tolerably well off. Then what will be the use of our scheme? We shall destroy only a few, and from the remaining individuals a new crop will spring up to vex us. We must get them all—all!"

This offer was accepted with a fanfaronnade of gratitude. It had one inestimable advantage—it secured the passage of the claimants by the vessel Marese had chosen. The enthusiasm on the other side of the Atlantic was raised to its highest pitch when the heir announced his intention of coming to New York in his yacht, to see that the arrangements, for his friends were properly carried out.

Preparations were at once made to give him an ovation. The authorities of New York city gave orders to do him honour. The papers published biographies of "this distinguished man, upon whom the eyes of all the world were fixed," and who had lately "covered himself with glory by displaying a grand generosity towards the offshoots of the parent stem."

It often happens that in America the descendants of particular families are gathered in and around certain districts, where they form the main part of the population. This was the case with the Baskettes and Sibbolds. The Baskettes chiefly inhabited Caben, a small township west of Philadelphia, and the Sibbolds were mostly to be found at Tandanap, near the shores of Lake Michigan. Numbers of both tribes of course were scattered over the whole country, but these were the strongholds. To suit both parties, and to tend to remove the jealousies which had so long raged, it was arranged that all should meet at Imola, a place about midway and within a hundred and twenty miles of New York, about a week previous to the embarkation.

At Imola (named after a Continental town) there resided perhaps the wealthiest member of the Baskette and Sibbold tribes, for he could claim relationship with both—he offered hospitality to them all; and in return it was agreed that this Reginald Bunker Sibbold Baskette, Esq, should be instituted the leader or president of the expedition. After the mobilisation of the forces at Imola, the army was to move on New York on the 2nd December, and embark the same evening on board the Lucca steamship.

The whole scheme was now complete, and extremely promising it looked; everything had turned out well. Marese had ascertained by secret inquiries that the bullion had been ordered, and that the owners of the Lucca had contracted, under a heavy bond, to deliver it at a certain date. The Lodges had, for a time at least, fused their differences. The engine of destruction was finished, together with a duplicate in case of accident. How extremely simple it looked! Nothing in the world but a strong deal box, apparently nailed together in the usual manner, about a yard square, or a little less. Just such a box as a seaman or passenger, if it chanced to lie about, would choose to sit down on and smoke a pipe. The rough deal planks of which it was made were not even planed smooth—simply a strong packing-case. The conspirators congratulated themselves upon the approaching execution of their schemes, and the success which seemed certain to attend them.

But now Theodore discovered a serious oversight. Reading through Aurelian's papers a second time, he came upon that passage which detailed all that could be learnt of the descendants of Arthur Sibbold. This Arthur, Aurelian wrote, or his descendants, was the most dangerous of all. He was the man who ought to have succeeded to the farm which James Sibbold took possession of. James, or James's sons, had not the slightest right to dispose of the farm to Sternhold Baskette; they were selling what did not belong to them. Arthur was of course dead, but Arthur's heirs still lived; and then followed the address and further particulars.

These heirs were at present quiet; but if they discovered the register of Arthur's marriage, Aurelian could not see what was to prevent them from putting in a claim far superior either to Marese's or to that of any other person. Even if they could not get possession, the Courts would certainly order an immense sum to be paid to them, as compensation; and Aurelian thought himself that nothing in the world could prevent them taking the property which stood on the site of the farm, if not the Swamp. The property on the site of the farm, he thought, must go.

"Now," said Theodore, "what is the use of destroying the American claimants en masse if this even greater danger is to be

75

allowed to remain close at home, within easy reach of the estate, ready at any moment to burst upon us and render nugatory all our risk and labour?"

Marese was thunderstruck. For a time it seemed that their enemies were hydra-headed—no sooner was one head cut off than three sprouted up in the place. But the man was not one to be daunted. This also must be done, he said. They had not much time now to lose. It was already the middle of September, and a fortnight must be reckoned for the passage of the yacht to New York. They spent anxious days and nights considering a variety of plans. There is not time to unravel the strange mazes of the mind and trace the genesis of the idea which at last suggested itself to Theodore. It was only one degree less ingenious, and if anything still more horrible, than the infernal machine of Marese.

Theodore still continued the asylum at Stirmingham. It was an important source of income, in fact. In that asylum there were confined lunatics of all degrees of insanity, most of them having wealthy friends, and some the representatives of large properties. Among these was one more remarkable than the rest. He was the representative of a long line of lunatics, or semi-lunatics. Popular tradition accused a progenitor living two centuries before of a crime too dark to be mentioned, and believed that the lunacy of his descendants was a special punishment from heaven. This particular individual had seemed tolerably sane till he was permitted to marry—a cruel thing. He then rapidly developed his inherited tendencies, living as a married man, left more free from restraint by friends and others.

Though the owner of broad acres and lovely woodlands, he delighted in the society of tinkers, and was himself a clever hand at mending pots and kettles. He had such a fancy for tinkering that he actually promenaded the country for miles in company with gipsies, calling at the farmhouses—on his own tenants—asking for things to mend.

He was also absurdly fond of dogs, and filled the house with them—especially the large mastiff breed, of which he was particularly enraptured, till no one could approach it, and his poor wife was frightened out of her senses. Tinkering, fondling these dogs, and playing the tin whistle occupied his time. His money he scattered far and wide among the gipsies, pedlars, and tinkers, and gave enormous sums for the pure-bred mastiffs.

The countenance of the man expressed the most intense melancholy—that hopeless incurable vacancy of look which is seen on the features of some monkeys while in captivity. His face, and the shape of his head, in fact, much resembled a monkey's; and the ears protruding from the side of the skull, very large and ill-formed, completed the resemblance. He had a favourite resort in one of the woods surrounding the family mansion. Through this wood there ran a stream, and a tree had fallen across it, making a natural bridge.

On this tree, over the stream, he would perch himself astride, his feet nearly in the water, and play for hours upon the tin whistle, while his troop of dogs disported in the woods around. He had a wonderful instinct of music, and really played in a marvellous manner upon this simple instrument, exhibiting skill even in the choice of the whistle—for it is difficult to find one that has a mellow tone.

The spectacle of this being, sitting on the tree trunk in the gloom of the woods, his long legs dangling down to the water, with his melancholy baboon face, performing extraordinary fantasias upon a tin whistle, could hardly be matched.

But he was as cunning as he was mad. Probably from his companions, the gipsies, he had learnt that his ancestors had all been confined in the madhouse. He had sufficient sense to foresee that the moment a son was born to his wife he would himself be confined. But, with the inherent insanity of his nature, he thought that by killing the wife or the son he should escape this danger.

So soon as ever the wretched wife's confinement approached he slew her—and slew her in true fantastic fashion. With his tinker's hammer he drove a nail into her head as she slept. He fled from the place, but was captured; and that was the last time Odo Lechester used his tinker's hammer for some time to come. The dreadful deed, the sight of blood, had developed in him the homicidal tendency—he tried hard to stab his captors. In Aurelian's asylum at Stirmingham he desperately wounded a warder.

This was the being Theodore selected for his purpose. The man had made many violent attempts to escape—he was like a wild beast in a cage, pacing to and fro.

Theodore went down to Stirmingham to his private residence, which adjoined the asylum, to prepare his tool for the deed. It was easy for him, as a physician and the owner of the establishment, to have full and private access to Odo Lechester. He had a fortnight for his task. In that time he succeeded in impressing upon Odo's mind that the persons whose name and address he gave him were those who were responsible for his confinement.

It was not his (Theodore's) fault that he was confined—it was the fault of these persons, and upon them the punishment should fall. The man imbibed the idea thoroughly: he brooded over revenge if ever he should get free. His one-sided mind became absorbed in two great overmastering passions—to revenge his captivity, and to recover his favourite dogs.

Theodore assured him that if ever these persons were out of the way he would be at once reinstalled in his position, and might wander at his sweet will, tinkering and playing his whistle.

Theodore's plan was to let this irresponsible murderer out at large upon the world. The obnoxious persons would be removed, and no one could be punished. He arranged for the escape of Odo Lechester at about the date he and Marese would start for New York.

Their plans were now complete. Theodore, in order to obtain the lunatic's goodwill, had restored to him his whistle; and he roamed to and fro in the court of the asylum, examining the high walls, stone by stone, for a crevice of escape, while his rapid fingers manipulated interminable airs of the merriest kind.

When the engineer approached the ancient Swamp with his level and theodolite, and was followed by an army of workmen in short corduroys and slops, who cleared away the rushes and bull-polls, swept off the willow-beds and watercress, drove the waterfowl away and plucked up the reeds and sedges, then the water-rat knew that his time was come. The teeth that had nibbled away at the willow-tree root till it fell and blocked up the stream, would nibble no more. The nimble feet and black eyes would be seen no more biding among the flags, or plunging out of sight into the water as a footstep was heard.

The lake which the water-rat had made, with its islands and its cotters, was in its way useful, and not altogether despicable. The poor basket-makers, humble as they were, made good and useful baskets, mended pots and pans, split good clothes-pegs, and injured no man till Sibbold fired that fatal shot.

From that hour a curse seemed to hang over the place. A vast city, full of seething human life, had taken the place of the swamp and the bullrushes; the hearths of the poor cotters were gone, and huge hotels, club-houses, theatres, were there instead. Progress and development—yes; but with development came crime.

Under that overgrown city there extended a system of tunnels, sewers—some large enough to drive a horse and cart down them, others hardly large enough to admit the band. But they extended everywhere. Under the busy street, under the quiet office where the only sound was the scratching of the pen, or the buzz of a fly "in th' pane;" under the gay theatre and the gossiping club-house there was not a spot that was not undermined.

And in these subterranean catacombs there dwelt a race nearly as numerous as the human hive above, who worked and gnawed in the dark; they were the domains of the successors of the little furred creatures which nibbled down the ancient willow tree. The grey sewer-rat worked and multiplied exceedingly beneath this mighty city. The grey rat was worse than the water-rat.

He had his human prototypes. What were Marese and Theodore but sewer-rats working in secret, in the dark underground, out of sight, whose presence could hardly be detected by a faint occasional scratching or rustle?

Beside these there were a numerous company of lesser men and masculine brutes, and female fiends, burrowing, fighting in the dark places of this mighty city, whose presence was made known at times by faint sounds of shrieking or devilish glee which rose up, as it were, from the bowels of the earth. The reign of the harmless water-rat was over. The rule of the sewer-rat was now in full force.

End of Volume One

VOLUME TWO

Chapter One

Book Two

Persons

Forty-three miles as the crow flies, south of Stirmingham, there stands upon the lonely Downs a solitary, lichen-grown post, originally intended to direct wayfarers upon those trackless wastes.

In winter, when the herbage, always short, was shortest, and when the ground was softened by rain, there might be detected the ruts left by waggon wheels crossing each other in various directions; but road, or path properly so-called, there was none, and a stranger might as well have been placed on the desert of the Sahara. For time, and the rain blown with tremendous force across these open Downs by the wind, had all but obliterated the painted letters upon the cross-arms, and none but those acquainted with the country could have understood the fragmentary inscriptions.

Some mischievous ploughboys or shepherd lads, tired of arranging flints in fanciful rows, or cutting their names upon the turf, had improved the shining hour by climbing up this post, pulling out the arms, and inserting them in the opposite mortices, thereby making the poor post an unwitting liar. This same section of the population had also energetically pelted all the milestones for far around with flints, till the graven letters upon them were beaten out. Such wooden wit was their only resource in a place where Punch never penetrated; for this lonesome spot was appropriately named World's End, or, it was locally pronounced, Wurdel's End.

The undulating downs surrounded it upon every side, dotted here and there at long distances with farmsteads and a few cottages, and now and then a small village or hamlet of ten or a dozen houses grouped together in a "combe," or narrow valley, where there happened to be a spring of water and a "bourne" or stream. Yet World's End was not altogether to be despised. In this out-of-the-way place there was perhaps the finest natural racecourse in England, to which the uneven uphill course at Epsom, made famous by the Derby, was but an exercise ground.

A level stretch of sweet, elastic turf, half a mile wide, ran in a line something like half a horse-shoe, under the steep Downs, for a distance of two miles, unimpeded by hedge, ditch, or enclosed field, and obstructed only in a few spots by thick bushes of furze and a few scattered hawthorn trees.

A spectator standing upon the Downs had the whole of this Plain, as it was called, at once under his eye; could see a horse start and watch it gallop to the goal. From an ancient earthwork camp or "castle," this Down was known as Berbury Hill, and the level plain was often called Berbury racecourse.

For from time immemorial rustic sports, and local races between the horses of the neighbouring farmers, had taken place twice a year under the Berbury Hill. The sports were held in the early spring; the races proper, according to custom, came off in October. They were of the most primitive character, as may be judged from the following poster, which the kindness of a printer and bookbinder at Barnham—the nearest town—enables us to present to the reader. He had preserved a copy of it, having returned the original to the committee, who sat at the Shepherd's Bush Inn upon the Downs:—

"Take Notiss. The Public is hereby Invite to the Grand open and Hurdle Rases and Steple-Chaces at Wurdel's End which is to come off on Wensday after old Michelmuss Day. All particlars of the Stewards which is Martin Brown, William Smith, Philip Lewis, Ted Pontin. Illegul Beting is stoped."

This copy had in the corner, "Please print two Score and send by Carrier," and the unfortunate printer, ashamed to issue such a circular, sent it back with an amended form for approval; but the carrier forgot the letter, and it was not delivered till a week after the event—not that much was lost by the failure to give this species of publicity to the races. The day was well-known to all those who were likely to attend. The half-dozen gipsies, with the cocoanut sticks and gingerbread stall, duly arrived, and took up their quarters in a fir copse where the ground was dry, and the tree-trunks sheltered them somewhat from the breeze which always blows over the Downs.

Most of the spectators were hill men. There still lingers the old feud between the hill and vale—not so fierce, toned down to an occasional growl—but Nature herself seems to have provided a never-ceasing ground of quarrel. These two races, the hill and the vale men, must always put up opposing prayers to heaven. The vale prays for fine and dry weather; the hill prays for wet. How then can they possibly agree? Not more than three knots of men and half a dozen wenches came up from the vale, and these gave pretty good evidence that they had called en route at the Shepherd's Bush, for they were singing in chorus the lament of the young woman who went to the trysting place to meet her faithless swain:—

But what was there to make her sad?

The gate was there, but not the lad;
Which made poor Mary to sigh and to say
Young William shan't be mine!

The committee were in a moveable shepherd's hut on wheels, where also was the weighing-room and the weights, some of which were stone "quarters."

Just where the judges post was erected the course was roped for a hundred yards to ensure the horses arriving at the right place, but otherwise it was open. By the side of these ropes the traps and four-wheelers and ramshackle gigs of the farmers were drawn up, with their wives and daughters, who had come to see the fun.

Among these there was one pony-carriage drawn by two handsome ponies, with a peacock's feather behind their ears and silver bells on the harness, which, simple enough in itself, had a stylish look beside these battered and worn-out vehicles. It belonged to Jason Waldron, who was generally credited with "Esquire" after his name, and the lady who sat alone in it was his daughter Violet. Mr. Waldron was not there.

Violet was attended by a young man, plainly dressed, very pale, whose slight frame gave him an effeminate appearance in contrast with the burly forms, and weather-beaten faces of those acquaintances who from time to time nodded and spoke as they passed. The pony-carriage was drawn up under an ancient hawthorn tree, whose gnarled and twisted trunk, slow in growth, may have witnessed the formation of the entrenchment on the hill by the Britons themselves. The first frosts of autumn had blackened the leaves, and the mingling of the grey of the trunk and its lichen with the dark colour of the leaves and the red peggles or berries, under a warm, glowing, mellow sunshine, caused the tree to assume a peculiar bronze-like tint.

It may be that the sun in all his broad domains did not shine that day upon a more lovely being than Violet Waldron. Aymer Malet, the young man at her side—whose Norman name ill-assorted with his coarse garments, too plainly speaking of poverty—would have sworn that her equal did not walk the earth, and he would have had good warrant for his belief.

Poor Aymer was out of place in that rude throng, and tormented himself with fears lest he should appear despicable in her eyes, as so inferior to those stalwart men in size and strength. He should have known better; but he was young and had lived so long with those who despised him that a habit of self-depreciation had insensibly grown upon him. It is needless to go back into his pedigree. He was well descended, but an orphan and friendless, except for the single uncle who had given a roof and a bed to lie on to his sister's child.

Martin Brown was a well-meaning man, honest and sturdy, but totally incapable of comprehending that all men are not absorbed in sheep and turnips. He was moderately well off, but, like all true farmers, frugal to the extreme. Never a penny did Aymer get from him. Martin would have said: "Thee doesn't work; thee doesn't even mind a few ewes. If thee'll go bird-keeping I'll pay thee."

Aymer wished for work, but not work of that class. He remembered one golden year spent in London with a friend of his dead father (who had lost his all by horse-racing), where he was permitted to read at will in a magnificent library, and was supplied with money to visit those art-galleries and collections in which his heart delighted. The friend died; the widow had no interest in him, and Aymer returned to the turnips, and sheep. But even in that brief period the impulse had been given; the seed had been sown and had fallen in fertile ground, which gave increase a hundredfold.

The boy—he was but twenty then—was a born genius. He could not help it; it would force him on. What he wanted was books. He could get no money to purchase them; circulating libraries had not yet established agencies upon the open Downs. By a strange contradiction he became a poacher, and the cleverest hand at setting a wire for miles. Tenants were not allowed to shoot in that district, but they might course hares as much as they pleased.

Aymer wired the ground game, sold them to the carriers who went by, and through the carriers got books slowly and one by one from the county town. In this way he bought many of Bohn's fine series—the finest and most useful, perhaps, ever issued—he read Plato and Aristotle, Livy, Xenophon—the poets, the philosophers, the dramatists of ancient Rome and Greece; and although it was not in their original tongue, the vivid imagination of the man carried him back to their day, and enabled him to realise those stirring scenes, to feel their passions, and comprehend their arguments. He bought also most of the English poets, a few historians, and a large number of scientific works, for he was devoured with an eager curiosity to understand the stars that shone so brilliantly upon those hills—the phenomena of Nature with which he was brought in daily contact. When he had mastered a book, his friends the carriers, who called at the Shepherd's Bush, took it back to the county town and resold it for half-price, and these small sums went towards fresh purchases.

It may have been that these very untoward circumstances which would, to all appearance, have checked the growth of his mind, actually tended to assist it. He saw—he felt Nature. The wind, that whistled through the grass and sighed in the tops of the dark fir trees, spoke to him in a mystic language. The great sun, in unclouded splendour slowly passing over the wide, endless hills, told him a part of the secret. His books were not read, in the common sense of the term: they were thought through. Not a sentence but was thought over, examined, and its full meaning grasped and firmly imprinted on the memory.

Poor Aymer! How desperately he longed to escape! How the soft summer breeze seemed to woo him onwards he knew not whither! How the sun seemed to beckon, till he fancied he could hear the echo of the surge as it roared on the far-distant beach!

He did escape once—only for a little while, to be forced ignominiously back again, amid the jeers of his acquaintances. This happened before he knew Violet. By dint of catching hares and rabbits, and by selling off an accumulation of books, and by disposing of his gold watch—his only property—he managed to get some twenty pounds, and with that sum went straight to Florence.

It was in spring, just before the warm summer comes, and he revelled in the beauty of Italian skies and landscapes as he travelled. But his destination was the Palazzo, which contains the statue of ideal woman, known as the Venus de Medici. He stood before the living marble, rapt in thought, and then suddenly burst into tears.

This was perhaps childish. He had his faults; he was extremely proud and oversensitive. The sudden transition from the harsh and rude life at World's End, among the weather-beaten and rough-speaking rustics, to this new world of inexpressible beauty, overcame him. Hastily he brushed those tears away, and recovered himself; but not so quickly as to escape the observation of two sad grey eyes. Inadvertently, as he stood before the statue, he had interfered with the line of sight of a lady who was engaged in sketching. She had paused, and noticing his rapt attention, made no sign that he had interrupted her work. Thus she witnessed his weakness; and being a person of a thoughtful, perhaps too thoughtful, turn, she wondered at and pondered over it.

Day by day Aymer, while his funds lasted and he could stay in Florence, came and stood before the statue, lingering for hours in its close vicinity; so that the artist, as she sketched, had the fullest opportunity of noting the strong contrast between his delicate, intellectual features and slight, tall frame, and the coarse dress he wore. Growing interested, she instructed her attendants to make inquiries, and they easily elicited the name of the stranger, and the place from which he had come.

By a curious coincidence, it so happened that the lady-artist herself was the owner of a family mansion, and moderately large estate but a few miles from Aymer's home. He was, in fact, perfectly familiar with her name, which was a household word at World's End, where distinguished names were few; but moving in his low sphere he had never seen her face.

Lady Lechester—Agnes Lechester to her friends—was "lord of herself, that heritage of woe," and being of an artistic turn of mind, had spent much of her time upon the Continent; another reason being certain unhappy matters connected with the history of the family mansion. She was much struck with the singularity of a mere lad of low and poor estate thus coming to Florence, obviously from pure love of the beautiful. Nothing approaching to affection sprang up in her mind; it must be distinctly understood that her interest was of a different character entirely. But from that moment Aymer unconsciously became the subject of a certain amount of surveillance. He deemed himself despised and unnoticed by all; but there was one who had not forgotten him.

Those happy days in lovely Florence passed like a dream. Even by living on a few fruits and a little bread alone, the scanty stock of money he had carried with him could not be made to last for ever. Barely a month of pure, unalloyed pleasure—pure in every sense of the term—and poor Aymer, who knew not how to get employment in a foreign city, was obliged to return, and Agnes Lechester saw him no more standing in rapt admiration before the famous statue.

Aymer reached Dover with five shillings in his pocket, and walked the whole of the distance, one hundred and fifty miles, to World's End, often sleeping out at night under a rick. Slight as he was in frame, he possessed considerable power of enduring fatigue, and had a way of lounging idly along the road, abstracted in thought, and so walking mile after mile, till he woke up at his destination.

They laughed him to scorn at World's End. The poor fellow wandered about in the daytime on the Downs, hiding in the fir copses, lying on the ancient earthwork entrenchment, and dreaming of his fair Florence, so many hundreds of miles away. He grew dejected and hopeless till he saw Violet. Then in time, the very destiny he deemed so harsh in confining him to that rude spot seemed even superior to the glorious possibilities he had hoped for. For Violet took the place of the marble goddess; yet there never was a beauty less like the Venus de Medici. Lovely as are the ideals men have created for themselves, it sometimes happens that Nature presents us with a rare gem, surpassing those cold conceptions of the mind as far as the sun is above the earth.

Chapter Two

Violet returned from a long visit to friends near London just about the time that Aymer reached home, weary and footsore, from Dover. Although The Place, as Jason Waldron's house was called, was but two miles from World's End, Aymer had never seen her. She was but rarely at home, for Waldron had given her the best education money could buy, and this necessitated much absence from her native hills. But, education and visits over, Violet, with a happy heart, returned to the dear old home at last.

It was on one lovely afternoon in May that Aymer saw her for the first time. He was lying upon the ground hidden in the brake which grew round the hedge of a fir copse on the Downs. Through this copse there ran a narrow green lane or track. He was reading his favourite little book of poetry—one that he always carried in his pocket—the tiny edition of Shakespeare's Poems and Sonnets, published by William James Brown, thirty years since, and now out of print.

Somehow the spirit of those sonnets and that peculiar poetry had penetrated into his mind. The little book was annotated on its narrow margin with notes in his own handwriting, and he knew the greater part of it by heart. He had just read the sonnet beginning—

My mistress' eyes are nothing like the sun;
Coral is far more red than her lips' red.

* * * * *

And yet, by heaven, I think my love as rare
As she belied with false compare,
when the sound of horse's hoofs made him look up.

A lady, riding on a black horse, had entered the green lane, and was passing slowly at a walk. It was Violet. Waldron. All that English beauty which seemed to pervade the poetry of wonderful Will, to Aymer's fancy appeared to be hers. She passed him, and was gone, but her presence was left behind.

Aymer could not have analysed her then—if asked, he could have barely recounted the colour of her hair. Yet she dwelt with him—hovered about him; he fed upon the remembrance of her until he had seen her again. By slow degrees he grew to understand the reason of her surpassing loveliness—to note the separate features, to examine the colours and the lines that composed this enchanting picture. A new life dawned upon him—a new worship, so to say.

It happened that Martin Brown had some business to transact with Jason Waldron. Waldron bore the reputation of being a "scholard;" he was known to be comparatively wealthy; he did not mix with the society of World's End; and he was held in some sort of awe by the rude and uneducated residents in the locality.

Much as he despised that useless Aymer Malet, Martin in his secret heart felt that he was better fitted to meet and talk with Mr. Waldron than himself. Aymer was, therefore, accredited to The Place. He went with no little trepidation, knowing that it was Violet's home, and sharing to some extent the local hesitation to meet Waldron, who, being an invalid, he had never seen. Mr. Waldron received him with a cordial courtesy, which quickly put him at his ease. When the grey-haired, handsome old man, sitting in his Bath-chair in the shadow of a sycamore tree, extended his hand and said: "I had some slight knowledge of your father, Mr. Malet—he came of a good family," poor Aymer forgot his coarse dress, and exhibited the bearing of a born gentleman. He could not help admiring the garden in which he found his host. This evidently genuine admiration pleased Waldron extremely, for the garden had been the solace of his retired manhood, and of his helpless age. He began to talk about it directly.

"It is the trees," he said; "it is the trees that make it look well. Trees are really far more beautiful than flowers. I planted most of them; you have heard the Eastern saying, Mr. Malet—that those who plant trees live long. That yew-hedge?—no; I did not plant that. Such hedges are rare now—that hedge has been growing fully a hundred years—the stems, if you will look, are of immense size. To my mind, the old English yew is a greater favourite than the many foreign evergreens now introduced. The filbert walk?—yes; I planted that. Come and see me in a few months' time, and you shall crack as many as you choose. The old house picturesque?—it is: I wish I had a sketch of it. You draw?—a little; now try. Take out your pocket-book—ah! I see you have a regular artist's sketchbook."

To tell the honest truth, Aymer was not a little pleased to have the opportunity of exhibiting his skill before some one who could appreciate it. He was a natural draughtsman. I do not think he ever, even in later and more fortunate days, attempted colours; but with pencil and crayon, or pen and ink, he was inimitable. Once at work with his pencil, Aymer grew absorbed and forgot everything—even the presence of the invalid, who watched him with interest. The gables and the roof, the curious mullioned windows, the chimney-stacks, the coat of arms and fantastic gargoyles, then the trees and arbours grew upon the paper.

"Ah! that's my window," said a low voice.

His pencil slipped and made a thick stroke—he looked round, it was Violet.

For the first time he looked into her eyes and met her face to face. He could not draw. His hand would not keep steady; he blamed it to the heat of the summer sun. Violet declared it was her fault.

Mr. Waldron seized the incomplete sketch, and insisted upon Mr. Malet (the title, humble as it was, was pleasant to Aymer's ears) returning to finish it next day.

In his confusion Aymer somehow got away, and then remembered that the sketchbook he had left behind was full of drawings, and amongst them there were two that brought a flush to his brow as he thought of them. One was Violet on horseback; the other a profile of her face. He wished to return and claim his book, and yet he hesitated. A sweet uncertainty as to what she would think mastered

87

him. He dared not venture back. The next day passed, and the next—still he did not go—a week, a fortnight.

He could not summon up courage. Then came a note for "A. Malet, Esq"—that "Esq" subjected him to bitter ridicule from rude old Martin—from Mr. Waldron, inquiring if he had been ill, and begging him to visit at The Place, according to promise.

There was no escape. He went; and from that hour the intimacy increased and ripened till not a day passed without some part of it being spent with the Waldrons. Violet had seen her portrait in the sketchbook, but she said not a word. She made Aymer draw everything that took her fancy. Once he was bold enough to ask to sketch her hand. She blushed, and became all dignity; Aymer cowered. He was not bold enough. How could he be? With barely a shilling in his pocket, rough corduroy trousers, an old battered hat, a black coat almost green from long exposure to sun and rain;—after years of ridicule and jeering how could he face her?

His heart was full, but his lips dared not speak. His timidity and over-sensitiveness made him blind to signs and tokens that would have been instantly apparent to others of harder mould. He never saw the overtures that the growing love in Violet's breast compelled her to offer. He tormented himself day and night with thinking how to compass and obtain her love, when it was his already.

The one great difficulty was his poverty. Think how he would, he could discover no method by which it could be remedied. He had no means of obtaining employment, and employment would imply absence from her. How could he make her love him? He turned to his faithful friend and adviser, dear old Will. The tiny volume of poems was carefully scanned, and he lit upon those verses commencing—

> When as thine eye hath chose the dame
> And stall'd the deer that thou shouldst strike.

He asked himself if he had done as the lover was advised—

> And when thou com'st thy tale to tell
> Smooth not thy tongue with filed talk.

Certainly he had not attempted to beguile her with insinuating flattery—

> But plainly say thou lov'st her well,
> And set her person forth to sale.

This he had not done. How dare he say he loved her well? He had not the courage to praise her person.

And to her will frame all thy ways.

This he was willing and ready enough to do. He believed he had done so already; but read on—

Spare not to spend, and chiefly there
Where thy desert may merit praise
By ringing in thy lady's ear.

Here he was at a standstill. He could not spend; he could not even dress as a gentleman. He could not make her rich and beautiful presents.

The strongest castle, tower, and town
The golden bullet beats it down.

He had no golden bullets—to him the castle was therefore impregnable.

Serve always with assured trust,
And in thy suit be humble, true—

Advice such as this last he could and did follow conscientiously.

Have you not heard it said full oft,
A woman's nay doth stand for nought?—

Encouraging to those who could press the question, but he had not even courage to get the first nay. It was the "golden bullet"—the lack of the power to spend—the miserable poverty which pressed upon him with a leaden weight. He did his best to follow infallible Will's advice. He snared twenty hares and sold them; he had still a small gold pencil-case left—it had belonged to his mother. He sold that also.

On foot he walked forty miles to Reading, and spent the whole proceeds in the purchase of a pair of fine jet bracelets, which his instinct told him would look well upon Violet's white wrist. When he had got them, came the difficulty—how could he give them to her? At last he employed a shepherd lad to leave a parcel for Miss Waldron.

He kept away several days, but love was more powerful than shame. He went.

With Violet he strolled up the long shady filbert walk, with the clusters, now ripe, hanging overhead. His heart beat fast, but he said nothing. On her part she was silent. Suddenly she lifted up her arm and reached after a cluster of the nuts high up. Her sleeve fell down; the beautiful arm was bare to the elbow, and there was the bracelet!

Her eyes met his; a lovely colour suffused her cheek. An

89

uncontrollable impulse seized him. He caught her hand and kissed it. Why linger? No one can tell how these things come about. Their lips met, and it is enough.

That was the happiest autumn Aymer ever knew. Even now he looks back at its sweetness with a species of regret. The sunshine was warmer, the blue of the sky richer, the yellow mist that hung over the landscape softer, the bee went by with a joyous hum, the crimson-and-gold of the dying leaves was more brilliant than ever it had been before or since. Love lent his palette to Nature, and the world was aglow with colour. How delicious it is to see everything through the medium, and in the company of a noble girl just ripening into womanhood! I remember one such summer—

> But age with his stealing steps
> Has clawed me in his clutch.

She was very beautiful; it is hard to describe her. It was not perhaps so much the features, the hue of the hair, the colour of the eye, the complexion, or even the shape, as the life, the vitality, the wonderful freshness which seemed to throw a sudden light over her, as when the sunshine falls upon a bed of flowers:—

> Idalian Aphrodite, beautiful,
> Fresh as the foam, new-bathed in Paphian wells,
> With rosy, slender fingers backward drew
> From her warm brows and bosom, her deep hair
> Ambrosial, golden round her lucid throat
> And shoulder: from the violets her light foot
> Shone rosy-white, and o'er her rounded form
> Between the shadows of the vine-bunches
> Floated the glowing sunlights as she moved.

The modern taste for catalogues compels me to name the colour of her eye and hair. Her eye was full, large, and lustrous; that deep black so rarely seen—an eye that gave quick expression to the emotions of the heart—that flashed with laughter, or melted with tenderness. Her hair was not quite golden; it was properly brown, but so near the true golden that a little sunlight lit it up with a glossy radiance impossible to express in words. The complexion was that lovely mingling of red and white, which the prince in the fairy tale prayed his lady-love might have, when he saw the crimson blood of a raven he had slain, staining the translucent marble slab upon which it had fallen. The nose was nearly straight; the lips full and scarlet. She was tall, but not too tall. It is difficult for a woman to have a good carriage unless she be of moderate height. Enough of the catalogue system.

They visited all the places in the neighbourhood where Aymer's pencil could find a subject. Now it was a grand old beech tree; now only a grey stone, set up centuries and centuries since as a "stone of memorial" by races long reduced to ashes; now The Towers, the home of Lady Lechester. With them always went Dando, Waldron's favourite dog, a huge mastiff, who gambolled about in unwieldly antics at Violet's feet.

Aymer listened to her as she played. He sat by the invalid under the shadow of the sycamore tree near the open window, where he could see her sitting at the piano, pouring forth the music of Mendelssohn in that peculiar monotonous cadence which marks the master's works and fills the mind with a pleasant melancholy. Now and then her head turned, a glance met his, and then the long eyelashes drooped again. Presently out she would come with a rush, making old Dando (short for Dandolo) bound and bark with delight as he raced her round the green, tearing her flowing dress with his teeth, and whisking away when she tried to catch him.

The grace of her motions, the suppleness of her lithe form, filled Aymer's heart with a fierce desire to clasp her waist and devour her lips, while the invalid laughed aloud at the heavy bounds of his dog. The old man saw clearly what was going forward, yet he did not put forth his hand to stay it. They were a happy trio that summer and autumn at World's End.

Chapter Three

The summer passed away, as all things do, the winter, and the spring blossomed afresh, and still the course of true love ran smooth with Aymer and Violet.

The winter had been only one degree less pleasant than the summer. Violet had a beautiful voice; Aymer's was not nearly so fine: still, it was fairly good, and scarcely an evening passed without duets and solos on the pianoforte, while old Waldron, animated for the time beyond his wont, accompanied them upon the violin. He had an instrument which, next to his daughter and his dog Dando, he valued above all things. It was by Guarnerius, and he handled it with more care than a mother does her infant, expatiating upon the quality of the wood, the sycamore and pine, the beauty of the varnish, the peculiar, inimitable curl of the scroll, which had genius in its very twist.

Aymer was a ready listener. In the first place, he had grown to look upon Waldron in the light that he would have regarded an affectionate and beneficent father. Then he was, above all things,

91

anxious to please Violet, and he knew that she adored the Silver Fleece, as she called him, in laughing allusion to his odd Christian name, Jason, and to his grey hairs. And, lastly, he really did feel a curiosity and a desire to learn.

Sometimes Aymer gave Violet lessons in drawing, and she repaid him with lessons in French and music, being proficient in both.

After a while Waldron discovered that this boy, without means or friends, had made himself acquainted with the classics, and had even journeyed as a pilgrim to the shrines of ancient art at Florence.

At this he was highly pleased. He at once set to work to ground Aymer in the original languages in which Plato and Livy wrote. He taught him to appreciate the delicate allusions, and exquisite turn of diction, of Horace. He corrected the crude ideas which the self-instructed student had formed, and opened to him the wide field of modern criticism. The effect upon Aymer's mind was most beneficial, and the old man, while teaching the youth, felt his heart, already predisposed, yearning towards him more and more.

To Violet this was especially a happy omen, for she, above all things, loved her only parent, and had not ceased to fear lest her affection for Aymer should be met by his disapproval. As time went on, the ties of intimacy still further strengthened.

Waldron was now often seen in deep thought, and left the young people more to themselves. He busied himself with pen and ink, with calculations and figures, to the subject-matter of which he did not ask their attention.

Even yet Aymer had not thought of marriage; even yet he had not overcome his constitutional sensitiveness so much as to contemplate such a possibility. It was enough to dwell in the sunshine of her presence. Thoroughly happy in her love, he never thought of to-morrow. Perhaps it is a matter to be regretted that we cannot always remain in this state—ever enjoying the ideal without approaching nearer to the realisation, for the realisation, let it be never so glorious, is of the earth, earthy.

It is quite true that women like courage, and that boldness often goes a long way; but it is questionable whether with high-bred natures a subdued, quiet, and delicate manner does not go still further. Aymer was incapable of self-laudation, of that detestable conceit which some think it proper to show when they have made what they are pleased to call "a conquest." Pity the poor castles that have stooped to them!

His happiness had but one alloy—the perpetual remembrance of his own unworthiness, the immeasurable difference in his worldly position, which made it a presumption in him even to frequent her presence, much less to bask in her love. There were plenty who did not fail to remind him of this discrepancy in their mutual positions, for his intimacy at The Place could not, of course, pass unnoticed.

Martin Brown said nothing whatever. If there was any alteration in his manner as the truth dawned on him, it was in favour of Aymer. With such men everything is judged by results. While Aymer went about sketching alone, he despised him and his pencil; the moment the very same talent obtained him the notice of those in a superior station, then Aymer was do longer such a fool. Martin said nothing. He refrained from his former jeers, and abstained from telling Aymer to go and mind the sheep.

It was also to his advantage that Aymer should get rich acquaintances, and so possibly obtain a livelihood, and relieve him of an expense, which, however small, was always a bitter subject with him.

But there were others—farmers' sons—in the district who did not spare Aymer. They despised him; they could not understand him; and they hated him for his luck in carrying off the squire's daughter. They credited him with the most mercenary motives, and called him a beggarly upstart. If Aymer chanced to pass near them he was saluted with ironical bows and cheers, and hats were obsequiously doffed to "My Lord Muck," or "My Lord Would-Be."

He made no reply, but the insult went home. He knew that there was a great deal of ground for this treatment. He knew that his conduct must appear in such a light to others; and yet how welcome they always made him at The Place. He questioned himself if he was doing right; sometimes his pride said "Go; carve yourself a fortune, and then return for her;" but love, strong love always conquered and drove him forward. He deemed that, with the exception of Violet and Waldron, all the world looked upon him with contempt. He was wrong.

In the spring, Violet began to ride again over the Downs. This habit for a moment again lowered Aymer in his own estimation, for he had no horse to accompany her. What was his delight and astonishment when one day Violet took him to the stables and asked him how he liked the new grey horse. It was a handsome animal— Aymer admired it, as in duty bound, and as, indeed, he could not help, yet with a heart full of mortification, when Violet whispered that papa had bought it for him to ride with her. She flung her arms, in her own impulsive way, round his neck, kissed him, and rushed away to don her riding-habit before he could recover from his astonishment.

It was true. In an hour's time they were galloping over the soft springy turf of the Downs, trying the paces of the grey, who proved faster than the black. The rides were repeated day by day; and it often happened that, while thus enjoying themselves, they passed one or more of those very persons who had so often insulted Aymer.

Instead of sitting firmer and with pride in his saddle, Aymer felt that he all the more deserved their censure, and looked the other way as he went by.

He did not know that there was one eye at least that watched him with pleasure, and with something like a quiet envy. It was the same grey eye that had observed, him in the Palazzo at Florence.

Agnes Lechester had returned to England to spend some time at the old Towers, and had not failed to make inquiries for the young pilgrim who, in coarse garb, she had seen at the shrine of art. She heard of the intimacy with Waldron, whom she had once or twice spoken to; and as the lovers rode slowly beneath her grand and comfortless home, she sat at her window, and paused in her art-work, and looked down upon them and sighed. She could not but envy them their joy and youth, their path strewn with roses and lighted by love. She had no need to envy Violet's beauty, for, although no longer young, Agnes Lechester was a fine woman. It was the life, the full glowing life, she deemed so desirable. And she rejoiced that the poor pilgrim had found so fair a lady-love. So that there was one eye at least which, unknown to Aymer, watched him with a quiet pleasure and approval. Had he known it, it would have encouraged him greatly. By precipitating matters it might have prevented—but let us proceed.

Jason Waldron knew that his daughter loved, and was beloved. He was no ordinary man. His life had been spent far from those money-making centres where, in time, the best of natures loses its original bias, and sees nothing but gold. Age, he believed, had given him some power of penetration; and in Aymer he thought he had found one in a thousand—one with whom his darling daughter's future would be safe. "He will not follow the universal idol," thought the old man. "He will be content with art and literature, with nature and with Violet. I can see nothing in store for them but the happiest of lives." He waited long, expecting Aymer to approach the subject in some distant manner. At last he comprehended his reluctance. "He is poor and proud—he is afraid, and no wonder," he thought. "He shall not suffer for that."

The benevolent old man, anxious only to complete the happiness of those he loved, resolved to be the first, and to hold out a welcoming hand. One day he called for Aymer to his study, and motioning him to a seat, averted his face, not to confuse him, and said that he had long seen the mutual affection between Violet and him. He understood why Aymer had refrained from taking him into his confidence—he could appreciate the difficulties of his position. Without any hesitation, he approved of Violet's choice. His own years had now begun to weigh upon him, and he grew daily more anxious that Violet should be settled. He proposed, therefore, that if Aymer would not mind the arrangement, they should be united as speedily as possible, and that after a short trip they should return and live with him at The Place. He could not spare Violet entirely—he must hear the sound of her voice, and see the light of her eyes, while yet the power to do so remained with him. He was not really rich. In that poor district, indeed, he appeared so, but it was only by comparison. Were he to be placed in some great city, side by side with the men whose trade was gold, his

94

little all would sink into the utmost insignificance. Beside rude rustics, who lived from hand to mouth, content if they paid the rent, and perhaps put by a hundred guineas in the county bant, he was well off; but not when weighed against the world.

He had but the house he dwelt in, a few acres of surrounding pasture, and three thousand pounds placed out on loan. This money brought in a good interest, but he had lately thought of calling it in for greater safety, as he felt himself to be getting old in every sense of the term.

It was obvious, therefore, that on the score of expense alone it would be difficult for him to give a dower to Violet sufficient to support a second home. If they could be happy with him, why he should be content.

He turned and held out his hand to Aymer. Aymer took it, but could say nothing. He was literally overwhelmed. To him, after so long a solitude, after so much contempt, this marvellous good fortune was overpowering. Jason pretended not to notice his confusion.

"We understand one another," he said. "It is agreed, is it not?"

Despite all his attempts, Aymer could but incline his head.

"It is a lovely day—take Violet for a ride to Berbury camp."

How Aymer managed to convey what had passed to Violet he never knew, but that was the longest ride they ever had together, and it was dark before The Place was reached.

Aymer did not go home after quitting Violet. He walked away upon the Downs until safe from observation, then threw himself upon the sward, and poured out his heart in thanksgiving. When he had grown a little calmer he leant against a beech-trunk and gazed at the stars. In that short hour upon the solitary Downs he lived a whole lifetime of happiness. There are some of us who can remember such hours—they occur but once to any human being.

To do the rough residents of the district justice, so soon as it was understood to be settled that they were to be married, then the tone of the place changed, and they no longer insulted and annoyed him. Some wished him joy and happiness: not without a tinge of envy at his good fortune, expressed in the rude language of the hills, "I wish I had thee luck, lad."

It was generally agreed that when the marriage took place there should be an arch erected and decorated with flowers, for the bride and bridegroom to pass under; that the path through the churchyard should be strewn with roses, that volleys of firearms should be discharged, and the day kept as a holiday. This was settled at the Shepherd's Bush over foaming jugs of ale.

"Arter all," said an old fellow, "he bean't such a bad sort o' chap. A' mind a' tuk a main bit o' trouble loike to pull a ewe o' mine out of a ditch where hur laid on hur back."

"Ay, ay!" said another; "and a' drawed my little Kittie on the

95

kitchen wall wi' a bit o' charcoal as natural as ever hur walked—zo let's gie 'un a rouser, chaps, and no mistake!"

This was how it happened that at World's End Races that fateful year, early in October, a delicate-looking young man, commonly dressed, stood beside the pretty pony-carriage under the hawthorn tree. The marriage was fixed for that day week.

Chapter Four

The marriage would have taken place earlier but for two circumstances: first, the difficulty of obtaining the wedding outfit for Violet in that out-of-the-way place; and secondly, because Jason insisted upon some important alterations being made in the old house, in order to render it more comfortable for his children.

There is no event in life which causes so much discussion, such pleasant anticipation, as the marriage-day; and at The Place there was not a single thing left unmentioned; every detail of the ceremony was talked over, and it was a standing joke of Jason's to tell Violet to study her prayer-book, a remark that never failed to make the blood mount to her forehead.

She grew somewhat pensive as the final moment approached—with all her youth and spirits, with all the happy omens that accompanied the course of her love, she could not view this, the most important step she would ever take, always with thoughtless levity. She became silent and thoughtful, gave up riding, and devoted herself almost exclusively to attending upon Jason, till Aymer—silly fellow!—grew jealous, and declared it was unkind of her to look forward to the wedding-day as if it was a sentence of imprisonment.

Mr. Waldron had lived so retired that there was some little difficulty in fixing upon a representative to give Violet away, for as an invalid he could not himself go to the church; and this was the only thing he was heard to regret—that he should not see Violet married. However, he consoled himself with the thought that he should see her immediately afterwards, as the church was hardly half a mile distant, down in a narrow combe or valley. After some reflection, Mr. Waldron decided upon asking his solicitor, Mr. Merton, of Barnham, to act as his representative and give the bride away.

Merton, who was an old bachelor, was really delighted at the idea, but with true professional mendacity made an immense virtue of the sacrifice of time it entailed. He really was so busy with a great law case just coming on that really—but then his old friend Waldron, and lovely Miss Violet—duty pulled him one way and inclination another, and beauty, as was proper, triumphed.

Violet had few acquaintances, and it was more difficult still to find her a bridesmaid—not that there were not plenty ready to fill that onerous post—but she disliked the idea of a stranger. Mr. Merton, the solicitor, solved the difficulty by suggesting a niece of his, a merry girl whom Violet had met once or twice.

Aymer could not do less than ask old Martin Brown to stand as his best man, never dreaming that he would accept the task. But what was his surprise when Martin declared that he should enjoy the fun, and would rather miss Barnham fair than not be there. He came out tolerably handsome for him; he offered Aymer a five-pound note to purchase a suitable dress! This note Aymer very respectfully declined to take, and the farmer, half repenting of his generosity, did not press him too hard. Yet he could not help expressing his wonder as to how Aymer meant to appear at church. "Thee bisn't a-goin' to marry th' squire's darter in thee ould hat?"

Aymer smiled and said nothing. Fortune had aided him in this way too. After endless disappointments and "returned with thanks," he had suddenly received a cheque for a sketch of his which had been accepted by an illustrated paper. Immediately afterwards came another cheque for a short story accepted by a magazine. This success, small as it was, elated him, if anything, more than the approaching marriage-day. He had tried, and tried, and tried, and failed again and again, till he despaired and ceased to make the attempt, till the necessity of obtaining some clothes drove him to the last desperate venture. He was elated beyond measure. A successful author, a successful artist, and just about to marry the most beautiful woman in the world!

He resolved to tell Violet nothing about it, but to show her the sketch and the story as they were upon their trip. Thus it was that he was independent of Martin's grudging generosity. Fortune did not stop even here. As if determined to shower delight upon him—to make up at one blow for the cruel isolation, the miserable restraint he had undergone—she never seemed to tire of opening up fresh vistas of pleasure. Both Violet and Aymer would have been satisfied, and more than satisfied, with a simple visit to the seaside; but Jason was not so easily pleased. His daughter was his life—nothing was too good for her—and, besides, such an event happened but once in a lifetime, and it was fit and proper that it be accompanied with memorable circumstances. He announced his intention of sending his children to Florence.

To Florence, the beautiful city, which dwelt for ever in Aymer's dreams—the city he had described time after time to Violet, till the girl thought it the finest upon earth. He was to revisit Florence, and to revisit it with Violet! His heart was full—it would have been impossible to add another blessing.

Violet raced about the house and the garden, teasing Dando to distraction—all her pensiveness dispelled, murmuring "Florence" at every turn. What further joy could there be in store?—it was impossible. It is almost safe to say that these two were the happiest in England. Well they might be. They had all upon their side—i.e., youth.

Violet was to be married upon her twenty-first birthday; Aymer was twenty-three only. Money—not riches—but sufficient for an easy life. Italy in view—the land of the artist and the poet! It was like a fairy dream!

The days flew by. The dresses came—oh, what eager discussions and conferences there were over the dresses! All the farmers' daughters and wives in the neighbourhood to whom Violet was even distantly known, claimed the privilege to see the trousseau. In London it would have been overlooked—there all things are upon a grand scale.

At World's End the ladies were never tired of descanting upon the glories of the silk and satin, the lace and tulle. How can a wretched, unsympathising man describe the sensation produced by Violet's wedding outfit?

The dear girl was in ecstasies. Waldron had gone to the utmost limit of his purse—his friend Merton even frowned a little—but he argued it was only for once—just this once—he must be permitted a little extravagance on Violet's marriage-day.

Aymer was again plagued with his old tormentors—they did not sneer or jeer at him, but he had to run the gauntlet of rude jokes and rustic wit. He forgave them, and asked as many as he could to the breakfast.

The breakfast was to be laid out in that very apartment the window of which opened upon the garden near the sycamore tree, where he had sat so many times listening to Violet playing upon the pianoforte. There was of course a cake, and there was to be what had never before been seen or tasted at World's End from time immemorial—i.e., several dozens of champagne.

If the wedding outfit caused a sensation among the ladies, this champagne was all the talk among the men. They thought of nothing else—it was the subject of endless allusions and unabating anticipation. Here and there was one who could say he had tasted the wine—when after a good hunting spin Lord So-and-So had asked the sportsmen to refresh themselves at his mansion. But the majority had not the faintest notion of what it was like, and formed the most fantastic expectations. There were a few who doubted whether there would be any champagne, and treated it as a myth, till the servants at The Place, proud of their importance, admitted some favoured individuals who were regaled in secret with—the taste?—no, but the view only of certain tall bottles dressed in rosy tissue paper, upon the removal of which stood out the far-famed silver-foil, and doubt was no more. World's End was full of its first champagne treat.

98

Old Martin Brown swelled up into a person of enormous importance, as being the nearest relative of the bridegroom; he was looked upon as an oracle, and his remarks listened to with intense interest at the nightly tobacco parliament at the Shepherd's Bush.

The carriers took fabulous reports of what was to happen at World's End all over the district, and scores of honest people made up their minds to trudge to Bury Wick Church.

Aymer was no longer knocked up at five in the morning, as was the custom, to breakfast at six. He was undisturbed. No more jeers and contempt—he was treated with deference. "My nevvy" was a success; Martin spoke of his "nevvy" as if the connection did him honour.

I hope among the readers of this history there will be many ladies who can remember their feelings on the approach of the marriage-day. Let them kindly recall those moments of wild excitement, of trepidation lest some accident should happen, of a half-hesitation, of a desire to plunge at once and get it over—and approximately they will understand Violet's heart.

Even yet Fortune had not exhausted her favours. On the morning of World's End Races, just one short week before the day, there came a letter in an unknown handwriting, addressed to Aymer Malet, Esq, enclosing five ten-pound notes from an anonymous donor, who wished him every felicity, and advised him to persevere in his art studies.

This extraordinary gift, so totally unexpected, filled Aymer with astonishment. It seemed as if it had dropped from the skies, for he had not the remotest suspicion that Lady Lechester was watching him with interest.

At last the day came. Violet was awake at the earliest dawn, and saw the sun rise, clear and cloudless, from the window. It was one of those days which sometimes occur in autumn, with all the beauty and warmth of summer, without its burning heat, and made still more delicious by the sensation of idle drowsiness—a day for lotos eating. The beech trees already showed an orange tint in places; the maples were turning scarlet; the oaks had a trace of buff. The rooks lazily cawed as they flew off with the acorns, the hills were half hidden with a yellowy vapour, and a few distant fleecy clouds, far up, floated in the azure. A dream-like, luxurious day, such as happens but once a year!

Violet was up with the sun—how could she rest? Miss Merton was with her, chatting gaily. Oh, the mysteries of the toilet! my feeble pen must leave that topic to imagination. All I can say is, that it seemed as if it never would be completed, notwithstanding the reiterated warnings of Jason that the time was going fast.

There came one more pleasant surprise.

A strange man on horseback was seen riding up to The Place. This was so rare an event that Violet's heart beat fast, fearing lest even at the eleventh hour something should happen to cause delay. She waited; her hands trembled. Even the delicious toilet had to be suspended.

Footsteps came up the staircase, and then the maidservant, bearing in her hand a small parcel, advanced to Miss Waldron. With trembling fingers she cut the string—it was a delicate casket of mother-of-pearl. The key was in it; she opened the lid, and an involuntary exclamation of surprise and admiration burst from her lips.

There lay the loveliest necklace of pearls that ever the sun had shone upon. Rich, costly pearls—pearls that were exactly fitted above all jewels for her—pearls that she had always wished for—pearls! They were round her neck in a moment.

Miss Merton was in raptures; the maidservant lost her wits, and ran downstairs calling every one to go up and see Miss Vi'let "in them shiners!"

For a while, in the surprise and wonder, the donor had been forgotten. Under the necklace was a delicate pink note, offering Lady Lechester's sincere desire that Miss Waldron would long wear her little present, and wishing her every good thing. When the wedding trip was over, would Mrs. Aymer Malet let her know that she might call?

Violet was not perfect any more than other girls; she had naturally a vein of pride; she did feel no little elation at this auspicious mark of attention and regard from a person in Lady Lechester's position. The rank of the donor added to the value of the gift.

Mr. Waldron was much affected by this token of esteem. He could not express his pleasure to the giver, because her messenger had galloped off the moment he had delivered the parcel. The importance of the bride, great enough before, immediately rose ninety per cent, in the eyes of Miss Merton, and a hundred and fifty per cent, in the eyes of the lower classes.

Mr. Waldron, examining the pearls with the eye of a connoisseur, valued them at the very lowest at two hundred guineas. The involuntary tears of the poor pilgrim at the shrine of art had indeed solidified into gems!

The news flew over the adjacent village of Bury Wick; the servants at The Place spread it abroad, and in ten minutes it was known far and wide. The excitement was intense. Champagne was grand enough—but pearls! World's End went wild! Champagne and pearls in one day! The whole place turned out to give the bride a triumphant reception.

Aymer was forgotten in the excitement over Violet: forgotten, but not by the bride. All she wished was to be able to show him her present—but etiquette forbade his being sent for on that particular morning; he must meet her at the church.

At the church—goodness! these pearls had delayed the toilet, and ten o'clock had struck. At eleven—ah! at eleven!

Mr. Merton had not arrived yet. He had arranged to bring his carriage; at The Place they had nothing grander than the pony-carriage. Mr. Merton, anxious to do the thing well, as he expressed it, had sent word that he should bring his carriage and pair of greys, to take the bride to the church.

From the earliest dawn the bells at Bury Church had been going from time to time; and every now and then there was a scattered fire of musketry, like skirmishing; it was the young farmers and their friends arriving with their guns, and saluting.

But at a quarter-past ten there was a commotion. The bells burst out merrier than ever; there was volley after volley of musketry, and cheering which penetrated even to the chamber of the bride, where she sat before the mirror with the pearls round her neck. It was Merton driving up in style, with his greys decorated with wedding favours.

Bang! clang! shout, and hurrah! The hand from Barnham struck up. "See the Conquering Hero comes!" There never was such a glorious day before or since at World's End.

"Ncvvy," said old Martin, already a little warm, and slapping Aymer on the back, "nevvy, my buoy! Thee bist th' luckiest dog in Inglandt—champagne and purls—Ha! ha! ha!"

Chapter Five

There was an attempt at order, but it was an utter failure. The men came crowding after Merton's carriage shouting and firing guns, the horses snorted, and when Violet glanced from the window, the excitement of the scene made her hesitate and draw back.

Merton—a regular lady's bachelor, so to say—was equal to the occasion; it was not the first at which he had assisted. He at once became the soul of the ceremonies. He congratulated Waldron, hastened everybody, went into the apartment where the breakfast was laid out, and with his own hands re-arranged it to his satisfaction, shouting out all the time to the bride to make haste.

She came at last. How few brides look well in their wedding-dresses. Even girls who are undeniably handsome fail to stand the trying ordeal; but Violet was so happy, so radiant, she could not help but appear to the best advantage.

Poor old Jason's lip quivered as he gazed at his girl's face—for the last time as his—his lip quivered, and the words of his blessing would not come; his throat swelled, and a tear gathered in his eye. She bent and kissed him, turned and crossed the threshold.

Waldron wheeled himself to the large open window, and watched her walk to the carriage along the carpet, put down that her feet might not touch the ground.

Who shall presume to analyse the feelings of that proud and happy old man? The carriage moved, the crowd shouted, the guns fired; he wheeled his chair a little round, and his head leant forward. Was he thinking of a day twenty-two years ago, when he—not a young man, but still full of hope—led another fair bride to the altar; a bride who had long since left him?

It was an ovation—a triumph all the way along that short half-mile to the church: particularly as they entered the village. The greys pranced slowly, lifting their hoofs well up, champing the bit, proud of their burden. The bride and Miss Merton sat on one seat, Mr. Merton on the other. All the men and boys and children, all the shepherds and ploughboys for miles and miles, who had gathered together, set up a shout. The bells rang merrily, the guns popped and banged, handkerchiefs were waved. Across the village street, but a few yards from the churchyard lych-gate, they had erected an arch—as had been determined on at the Shepherd's Bush—an arch that would have done credit to more pretentious places, with the motto, "Joy be with you."

The bride dismounted at the lych-gate, which was itself covered with flowers, and set her foot upon the scarlet cloth which the good old vicar had himself provided, and which was laid down right to the porch.

The churchyard was full of children, chiefly girls, all carrying roses and flowers to strew the path of the happy couple when they emerged united. In the porch the ringers stood, four on each side, with their hands upon the ropes ready to clash forth the news that the deed was done. The old old clerk was there, in his black suit, which had done duty on so many occasions.

She entered the little church—small, but extremely ancient. She passed the antique font, her light footstep pressed upon the recumbent brazen image of a knight of other days. The venerable vicar advanced to meet her, the sunshine falling on his grey head. But where was Aymer? Surely all must be well: but she could not see him—not for the moment. True-hearted, loving Violet had looked for Aymer with his old battered hat, in the corduroy trousers and the green coat she had known him in so long.

For the moment she barely recognised the handsome, gentlemanly man before her. It was Aymer—oh yes, it was Aymer—and how noble he looked now that he was dressed as became him. Her heart gave another bound of joy—involuntarily she stepped forward; what could be wanting to complete her happiness that day? Certainly it would have been hard to have named one single thing as lacking—not one. The pews were full of women of all classes—they had been mostly reserved for them—the men finding standing room as best they could; and a buzz of admiration went round the church as Violet came into full view. Her dress was good—it was nothing to belles who flourish in Belgravia; but at World's End—goodness, it was Paris itself.

That costume formed the one great topic of conversation for years afterwards. I know nothing of these things; but Miss Merton told me a few days ago that the bride wore a wreath of white rosebuds and myrtle upon her lovely head, and a veil of real Brussels lace. Her earrings were of rubies and diamonds—a present that morning from gallant Mr. Merton. She had a plain locket (with a portrait of Waldron), and wore the splendid necklace of pearls, the gift of Lady Lechester.

Her dress was white satin, trimmed with Brussels lace, and her feet were shod in satin boots. Of course the "rosy, slender fingers" were cased in the traditional white kid, and around her wrist was a bracelet of solid dull gold—the bridegroom's present, only delivered just as she stepped into the carriage. She carried a bouquet of stephanotis, orange, and myrtle.

It is very likely I have misunderstood Miss Merton's lively description, but I think that the above was something like it. Miss Merton herself wore a white silk trimmed with turquoise, blue, a gold locket with monogram in turquoise and pearls, and earrings to match— a gift from Mr. Waldron—and a bouquet, I think, chiefly of white roses and jessamine.

It was a lovely sight. The sunshine fell upon the bride as she advanced up the aisle—fell upon her through the antique panes which softened and mellowed the light. Never did a fairer bride mount the chancel steps.

Aymer waited for her. Till now Violet had been comparatively calm; but now, face to face with the clergyman robed in white, near to the altar and its holy associations, as the first tones of his sonorous voice fell upon her ear, what wonder that her knees trembled and the blood forsook her cheek. Aymer surreptitiously, and before he had a right in etiquette to do so, touched her hand gently—it strengthened and revived her; she blushed slightly, and the vicar's voice, as he gazed upon her beauty, involuntarily softened and fell. While his lips uttered the oft-repeated words, so known by heart that the book in his hand was unneeded, his soul offered up a prayer that this fair creature—yes, just this one—should be spared those pains and miseries which were ordained upon the human race.

The flag upon the church tower waved in the gentle breeze; the children were marshalled beside the path in two long rows, with their hands full of flowers; the women in the cottages were hunting up the old slippers and shoes; the men looked to the caps upon the nipples of their guns; the handsome greys snorted at the gate; and the grand old sun, above all, bathed the village in a flood of light. I cannot linger over it longer.

The solemn adjuration was put, the question asked, and Aymer in an audible voice replied, "I will." The still more solemn adjuration to the woman was repeated—it is but a few words, but it conveys a world of meaning, it sums up a lifetime—and Violet's answer was upon her lips, when, before she could form the words, the chancel side-door burst open, and there—

There before her very eyes, before the bride to whom that day was consecrated, who for that one day was by all law human and divine to be kept from all miserable things, there stood an awe-struck, gasping man, whose white shirt-front was one broad sheet of crimson blood.

It is difficult to gather together, from the confused narratives of those who were present, what really happened in consecutive order, but this is nearly it. Not only was his shirt-front blood, but his grey hair and partially bald head were spotted that awful red, and his trembling hands dripped—the blood literally dripped from them on to the stone pavement. For one awful moment there was a pause—utter silence. The man staggered forward and said in broken tones, but audible over the whole church—

"Miss Violet; your father is dead!" And the bride dropped like a stone before Aymer at her side, or Merton just behind, could grasp her arm. She was down upon the cold stone floor, her wedding-dress all crumpled up, her wreath fallen off, the light of life and love gone from her eyes, the happy glow from her cheek. Even in that moment the clergyman's heart smote him. His impious prayer! That this one because of her beauty should be spared—and struck down before his very eyes in the midst of her joy and triumph. All that they could see in the body of the church was a shapeless heap of satin where but a moment before had stood the most envied of them all.

Aymer knelt and lifted her head; it lay helpless upon his hands. As he did so the wedding-ring, which he had ready, slipped unnoticed from his grasp and was lost. When it was missed, days afterwards, and a search was instituted, it could not be found, and this the superstitious treasured up as a remarkable fact.

Merton raised her up; her frame was limp and helpless in their arms. They carried her to the vestry and brought water. Miss Merton, trembling as she was, did not faint; but, good, brave girl, did her best.

In the excitement over the bride, even the man who had brought this awful news was for the moment forgotten. When they looked for him he was leaning against the altar-rails, as if about to fall, and some of the blood was spotted on the sacred altar-cloth. The men rushed at him; the women, afraid, held back and watched what new harm must come. They deemed that it was some horrible creature; they could not believe that it was only the old gardener at The Place—Waldron's oldest servant.

Only the gardener. He was as helpless as themselves. He had over-exerted himself running to the church with his dreadful tidings, and being subject to heart disease, he could barely stand, and only gasp out that "Master was killed, and quite dead!"

The men, finding nothing could be got from him, ran out, and

104

made direct for The Place. Some leapt on their horses, but those on foot crossing the meadow, as the gardener had done, got there first. All the men made for The Place—all the women stayed to see what would become of the bride.

It was a dead faint, but it was not long before she came to, and immediately insisted upon being taken home. They would have detained her in the vestry till at least confirmation of the dreadful intelligence had arrived. But no, she begged and prayed them to take her; and fearing lest uncertainty should do more harm than certainty, they half-led, half-carried her from the church.

There was not a dry eye among the sympathising women who had remained—not one among those rude, half-educated people whose heart was not bursting with sorrow for the poor shrinking form that was borne through their midst.

But a few short moments since, and how proud and happy had she been advancing up the aisle! The children were gone from the churchyard; their flowers cast away, not in the pathway of the bride, but on the graves. In their haste, they had trod upon the scarlet cloth laid down, and discoloured and stained it. The ringers had deserted the bell-ropes, the village street was empty and silent—only the unconscious flag waved upon the tower, and the arch stood for them to pass beneath, with its motto—now a bitter mockery—"Joy be with you!"

The carriage rolled along the road, and as they approached The Place, Merton began to recover his professional calm; and the return of his mind to a more normal state was marked by doubt—Was it true?

But no sooner had they entered the garden than he saw it was. The faces of the knots of men, their low, hushed voices, all told but one tale—death had been there!

They tried to get Violet to go upstairs to her own room, but she would not. "I must see him!" was her cry. "I must see him!"

She pushed through them. All gave way before her. Not there, surely? Yes, there—in the very room where the wedding-breakfast was laid out, where the cake stood upon the table, and the champagne-bottles at the side; there, in the place of joy, was the dead—dead in his armchair, close to the window, with a ghastly wound upon the once-peaceful brow!

She threw up her hands—she uttered a great cry. Those that heard it say it rings even now in their ears. She threw herself upon him. The crimson blood dyed her veil, as it hung loose and torn, and tinged the innocent pearls around her neck with its terrible hue. She fainted the second time, and would have fallen, but Aymer caught her; and they bore her upstairs, unconscious even of her misery.

The Place was silent. The guns were not fired, the bells were stilled. Men moved with careful footsteps, women hushed their voices, and in the stillness they heard the church clock slowly striking the hour of noon. At that moment she should have been returning, radiant and blissful in triumph, to meet the welcome from her father's lips.

There was one that could not understand it—one dumb beast that could not be driven away. It was Dando, the mastiff dog. Strangely enough, he avoided the chamber of the dead, and crouched at the door of Violet's room.

When Merton saw it he said, "Let the dog go in; maybe, he will relieve her a little."

But Violet, lying on a couch, conscious now and tearless, despairing in the darkened room, motioned him away. "Take him away," she said. "If he had been faithful, he would have watched and guarded."

It was a natural thought, but it was not just. Poor Dando, like the rest, had gone to the church with the crowd; and just at the moment when he was most wanted, then he was absent from his duty.

The great sun still bathed the village in a flood of light, the fleecy clouds sailed slowly in the azure, the yellow mist hung over the distant hills, and the leaves now and again rustled to the ground. But the chamber that should have resounded with laughter and joy was darkened. One more human leaf had fallen from the earthly tree of life. Once more those that were left behind were worse off than those that were taken. In the words of the dear old ballad—

My summer's day, in lusty May,
Is darked afore the noon.

Chapter Six

Great horror fell upon the whole neighbourhood of World's End. Not the oldest man or woman could remember such a deed in their midst. Hitherto the spectre of Murder had avoided those grand old hills. There was no memory of such a thing. The nearest approach to it, which the gossips at the Shepherd's Bush could recall to mind, had happened long before the days of the oldest of them all.

There was one, and one only, who declared that in his youth his father left him in charge of the hayfield one beautiful summer's day, to go and see a man hung on the gallows. It was the custom then to erect the gallows at, or very near, the spot where the crime was supposed to have been committed; often at the cross roads.

His father told him—and having heard the tale so often it was

106

still fresh in his memory—that the gallows in this case was built in a narrow lane, close to a gateway, through which the murderer had fired the fatal shot at his victim. The spot was known to that day as Deadman's Gate.

There was an immense crowd collected to witness the execution, and the sun shone brilliantly on the ghastly machine. The murderer, as seems to have been the fashion in those times, at the foot of the gallows declared his innocence; and there were not wanting people who, in despite of the evidence, believed him.

Just after the horrible ceremony was finished, and the lifeless body swung to and fro, there burst a thunderstorm upon the crowd, which scattered in all directions.

Two men took refuge under a tall tree. One said, "This is dangerous," and went out into the field; before the other could follow he was struck dead by the lightning, so that there were now two corpses.

This man chanced to be one of the principal witnesses against the murderer, and superstition firmly believed that the thunderstorm marked the Divine wrath at the execution of an innocent man.

"The moment before," said the narrator, "the sky was perfectly clear; the storm came without the slightest warning." The fact being that the crowd were so intent upon the spectacle before them that they had not noticed the gathering clouds.

"Ay," concluded the narrator, who evidently shared in the superstition, "it be an awful thing to bear witness about blood. There be them about here as I wouldn't stand in their shoes!"

A dead silence followed. Men understood what he meant. Already public suspicion had fallen upon the gardener.

And Violet? Violet was calm and tearless, but heart-broken. She would not see Aymer till the third day—it was the morning of the inquest, though she did not know it. She saw him in her own room, still darkened. A thrush was singing loud and clear in the tree below the window. The sun still shone as it had done upon the bridal day, but the room was dark.

Miss Merton, despite her horror, had remained by her friend. She left the apartment as Aymer entered, Violet could not speak to him. Her head drooped on his shoulder, and convulsive sobs shook her form.

It is better to leave them together. The soiled wedding-dress, the beautiful pearl necklace tinged with the horrible hue of blood, had been carefully put out of sight. People were searching for the wedding-ring in the chancel at the church, but could not find it.

The inquest was held at the Shepherd's Bush. As had been the case at another inquest a century before, held at a place then almost as retired—at Wolf's Glow—so here the jury was formed of the farmers of the district.

Bury Wick village was so small it had no inn, which was accounted for by the fact that no through road ran by it. The village inn was half a mile from the houses, alone by itself, on the edge of the highway. The Shepherd's Bush was small, merely a cottage made into a tavern, and the largest room barely held the jury.

It is not material to us to go into every detail; the main features of that painful inquiry will be sufficient.

The jury having been sworn, proceeded in solemn procession to The Place. They entered noiselessly, not to disturb "Miss Vi'let," for whom the sympathy was heartfelt. They viewed the body of the good old man, cut down at the very hour when the crowning desire of his heart was in the act of realisation.

Such juries usually hurry through their task, shrinking from the view of the dead which the law compels upon them—a miserable duty, and often quite useless. But in this case they lingered in the room.

Saying little or nothing, they collected in groups of two or three around the coffin, wistfully gazing upon the features of the dead. For the features were placid, notwithstanding the terrible wound upon the top of the head. The peace of his life clung to him even in a violent death.

There was not one man there who could remember a single word or deed by which the dead had injured any human being. Quiet, retired, benevolent, largely subscribing in an unostentatious manner to the village charities, ready always with a helping hand to the poor—surely he ought to have been secure? What motive could there be?

They returned to the Shepherd's Bush. The Coroner asked for the evidence of the person who had last seen the deceased alive. It was at once apparent that numbers had seen him.

Mr. Merton, who attended, self-employed, to watch the case for Violet, and from attachment to his deceased friend—was selected as a representative of the many. He deposed that he had last seen the deceased alive at quarter to eleven on the marriage-day, at the moment that the bride took leave of her father, and received his blessing. This simple statement produced a profound impression. The deceased, who little thought that that parting would last for ever, was then sitting as usual in his armchair, which he could wheel about as he chose, close to the open window—almost in the window—and as witness escorted the bride to her carriage, he looked back and saw the deceased had partly turned round, so that the back of his head was towards the window. He had then his velvet skullcap off, and witness believed that he was engaged in silent prayer. This statement also naturally produced a profound effect. The deceased's head was partially bald, and the little hair he had was grey. The day was very warm and sultry.

Mr. Merton paused, and the next witness was the first person who had seen the deceased after the fatal attack. This was the gardener. He appeared in court, visibly shaking, bearing the marks of recent excitement upon his countenance. He was an aged man, clad in corduroys and grey, much-worn coat—not the suit he had worn on the wedding-day. His name was Edward Jenkins. His wife pressed hard to be admitted to the court, but was forbidden, and remained without, wringing her hands and sobbing. This witness was much confused, and his answers were difficult to get—not from reluctance to speak, but from excitement and fear. He produced an unfavourable impression upon the Coroner, which the medical man in court observing, remarked that he had recently attended the witness for heart disease at the request of the deceased, who took a great interest in his old servant. Even this, however, did not altogether succeed—there was an evident feeling against the man.

His evidence, when reduced to writing, was singularly simple, vague, and unsatisfactory. Why had he not gone to the church to see the wedding, as it appeared every single person had done, not even excepting the dog Dando? He had much desired to see the marriage of his young mistress; but being the only man-servant, it was his duty to see to the wines and to the table; and at the time when the carriage started he was in the garden cutting fresh flowers, for the purpose of strewing the lady's footpath when she returned and descended from the carriage, and also to decorate the breakfast table. How long was it after the carriage started that anything happened? It seemed barely a minute. He was in a remote part of the garden, hastily working, when— almost immediately after the carriage started—he happened to look up, and saw a stranger on the green in front of the house.

"Stay," said the Coroner. "Describe that person."

This he could not do. The glimpse he had caught was obtained through the boughs and branches of several trees and shrubs. He could not say whether the stranger was tall or short, dark or light, or what dress he wore; but he had a vague idea that he had a dirty, grey coat on.

This was an unfortunate remark, for the witness at that moment wore such a coat.

He could not say whether he had a hat or a cap on, nor what colour trousers he wore. The stranger appeared to cross the green diagonally towards the house.

"What did witness do?"

For a moment he did nothing—it did not strike him as anything extraordinary. That morning there had been scores of people about the house, and numbers of strangers whom he did not know. They were attracted by the talk about the wedding, and he thought no harm. He went on with his work as hastily as he could, for he still hoped to have finished in time to make a short cut across the fields, and see a part of the marriage ceremony.

He became so excited with the wish to see the ceremony that he left part of his work undone. As he went he had to pass the open window of the dining-room, where "master" was sitting. He was running, and actually passed the window without noticing anything; but before he had got to the front door he heard a groan. He ran back, and found his master prone on the floor of the apartment, in a pool of blood. He had evidently fallen out of his armchair forwards—started up and fallen. Witness, excessively frightened, lifted him up, and placed him in the chair, and it was in so doing that his shirt-front became saturated with the sanguinary stream, which also dyed his hands. He had on a shirt-front and a black suit, in order to wait at table at the wedding-breakfast. "Master" never spoke or groaned again. So soon as he was placed in the armchair his head dropped on one side as if quite dead, and witness then ran as fast as he could to the church, and crossed the fields by a short cut which brought him to the chancel-door.

The stranger, who had crossed, the narrow "green" or lawn before the house, had entirely disappeared, and he saw nothing of him in the house. In his haste and confusion, he did not see with what the deed had been committed.

This was the substance of his evidence. Cross-examine him as they might, neither the Coroner nor the jury, nor Mr. Merton, could get any further light. The witness was evidently much perturbed. There were those who thought his manner that of a guilty man—or, at least, of a man who knew more than he chose to tell. On the other hand, it might be the manner of an aged and weakly man, greatly upset in mind and body by the frightful discovery he had made. All the jury knew the relations between the witness and the deceased. Jenkins had lived in the service of the Waldrons all his life, as had his father before him, and the deceased had always exhibited the greatest interest in his welfare. He had good wages, an easy occupation, and was well cared for in every way. The most suspicious could conceive of no ground of quarrel or ill-will.

The Coroner directed the witness to remain in attendance, and the first person who had seen the deceased after the alarm was given was called.

This was Phillip Lewis, a farmer's son (one of the stewards at World's End Races), who being swift of foot had outstripped the others in the run from the church to The Place.

Phillip Lewis found the deceased in his armchair, with his head drooping on one side—just as the gardener Jenkins described; only this witness at once caught sight of the weapon with which the fatal blow was given. It was lying on the ground, just outside the open window, stained with blood, and was now produced by the constable who had taken charge of it. It was a small bill-hook, not so large as would be used in cutting hedges, but much the same shape.

The edge of a bill-hook, as every one knows, curves inward like a sickle, and at the end the blade forms a sharp point, or spike. It is, therefore, a fearful instrument with which to deliver a blow upon a bare head.

Phillip Lewis said that the gardener Jenkins recognised this hook as his—the one he usually employed to lop the yew trees, and other favourite trees of the deceased, and for general work in the shrubberies.

This piece of evidence made the jury look very sternly upon Jenkins. He was asked if it was his, and at once admitted it. Where had he left it last? He would not be quite sure, but he believed in the tool-house, which was close to the gate in the garden wall, which led out into the fields. He had used it that morning.

There was a distinct movement among the jury. They evidently began to suspect Jenkins.

The medical man, Dr Parker, was the last witness. He had examined the wound the deceased had received. There was first an incised wound, three inches long, on the top of the skull, extending along the very crown of the head. This wound was not deep, and, though serious, might not have proved mortal. At the end of this wound there was a small space not cut at all, but an inch farther, just at the top of the forehead, was a deep wound, which had penetrated to the brain, and must have caused almost instantaneous death.

These peculiar wounds were precisely such as would have been made if a person had approached the deceased from behind, and struck him on the bare head with the bill-hook produced. He did not think that there was more than one blow. He thought that the deceased when he received the blow must have started up mechanically, and, losing power, fell forward on to the floor. He did not think that the deceased had suffered much pain. There would not be time. The point or spike-like end of the hook had stuck deep into the brain. He had examined the hook, and found clotted gore and a few grey hairs upon the blade.

This concluded the evidence, and the court was cleared—after the Coroner had whispered a few words to the police, several members of which force were present.

The Coroner then summed up the evidence, and in a few brief but terribly powerful sentences pointed out that suspicion could only attach to one man. This man was left alone. He had every opportunity. The tale of the alleged stranger on the lawn bore every mark of being apocryphal. It was obviously a clumsy invention. The witness, who at first could not give any idea whatever as to how the stranger was dressed, had, when pressed, in a manner identified himself as the stranger, by describing him as wearing a grey coat.

In conclusion, he would add that the country had been scoured by the police in the three days that had elapsed, and they had failed to find any trace of the supposed stranger. He then left the jury to deliberate, and going out into the air, met Mr. Merton, who was more firmly convinced than the Coroner as to the guilt of Jenkins.

"There was no motive," he admitted, as they talked it over, walking slowly down the road; "but crimes were not always committed from apparent motives. On the contrary, out of ten such crimes seven

111

would, if investigated, seem to be committed from very inadequate motives. How could they tell that Waldron had not called to the gardener after the carriage had left, and that then a quarrel took place?" He was determined to see that justice was done to his dead friend.

But while the Coroner and Merton thus strolled along together a new complexion had been put upon affairs. The wretched wife of Jenkins, who had heard the muttered communications of the police, and saw that they kept a close look-out upon her husband, had listened as near the door as she could get, and so heard the summing-up of the Coroner. Distracted and out of her mind with terror, a resource occurred to her that would never have been thought of by one less excited. She rushed from the place like mad. "Poor old Sally has lost her head," said the hangers about. She ran across the fields, scrambled through the hedges, reached The Place, tore upstairs, and threw herself upon Violet, beseeching her for the love of God to save her poor husband.

Till that moment Violet had not the least idea that Jenkins, who had carried her in his arms many a time when she was a child, and was more like an old friend than a servant, was under any suspicion. She rose up at once and went downstairs, the first time since the wedding-day. Aymer and Miss Merton tried to stay her.

"Hush!" she said; "it is my duty."

She was obliged to pass the fatal window; she burst into tears, but hurried on. Aymer went with her, and assisted her along the very same route that Sally had come—over ditches and through the gaps in the hedges. Violet reached the Shepherd's Bush bareheaded, panting. Involuntarily, the crowd hanging about, one and all, boors that they were, took off their hats. She knocked at the door where the jury sat astounded, they admitted her. Strung up to the highest pitch she burst upon them, cowed them, overcame them.

"He is innocent!" she cried, in the full tones of her beautiful voice. "He is innocent; let him go free! He served the dead for fifty years; they never quarrelled; they were, like old friends, not master and man. I am the daughter of the dead. I tell you with my whole heart and soul that that man must be innocent; if you injure him, it is you who are murderers!"

She turned and left the room; many started forward to help her, but she clung to Aymer's arm and he got her home as quickly as he might.

It was a noble thing. It was a truly great spectacle to see that young girl standing there and defending the poor fellow upon whom cruel suspicion had fallen, notwithstanding her own irreparable loss. Its effect upon the jury was immediate and irremovable. They were silent for a time. Then one after another found twenty loopholes of doubt where before they had been so positive. After all, why should not the gardener's story be true? It was a simple, artless tale; not one that would be concocted.

One juryman, who had served on the jury at the Quarter Sessions, remembered a great counsel in some important case laying it down as an axiom, that if a man made up a story to defend himself it was always too complete, too full of detail. Said the juryman: "If Jenkins had made up his story, he would have told us what the stranger wore, what colour hat, what sort of trousers, and every particular. There was a total absence of motive. Jenkins was a quiet, inoffensive man, whom they had all known for years and years. Very likely, indeed, for strangers to come to The Place on that day, the fame of which had been talked of everywhere. Perhaps the fellow wished to steal the plate on the breakfast table, and was surprised to find the invalid there. Hearing the gardener coming, he would make off at once, which accounted for the fact that not a single thing was stolen. Why should they condemn one of their own parish on such trivial evidence?" This was the right key, the local one.

When the Coroner was at last called in, he was astounded at the verdict delivered to him by the foreman—"Wilful murder against a person, or persons, unknown." He argued with them, but in vain; the twelve had made up their minds and were firm as a rock. He had to submit with a bad grace!

Poor Sally had a moment of joy, and clasped her husband's neck, but it was of brief duration. A minute afterwards the police sergeant present tapped Jenkins on the shoulder, and took him in custody on a charge of murder.

This is the peculiarity of the law in such cases. A suspected person has to run the gauntlet of two bodies—first, the coroner's jury; next, the magistrates. Many a wretch who has escaped the one has been trapped by the other to his doom.

The handcuffs were slipped on the gardener's wrists and he was led away unresistingly, followed by his weeping wife and a crowd of the villagers.

As the jury emerged from the Shepherd's Bush, which was not till afternoon—for they had stayed to spend their ninepenny fees—there struck on their ears a mournful sound. It was the tolling of the village bell. The medical man had recommended immediate interment. Only three days before those bells had merrily rung for the daughter's bridal; now they tolled for the father's burial. They hastened to the church and watched the solemn ceremony. The low broken voice of the vicar failed at the words, as they stood by the open vault—"He cometh up, and is cut down, like a flower; he fleeth as it were a shadow... In the midst of life we are in death;" and the rest of the service was nearly inaudible.

Chapter Seven

Every one knows what a dull monotony of sorrow succeeds to a great loss. Perhaps it was fortunate for Violet that her mind was in some small measure withdrawn from too consuming grief by the unfortunate position of the poor old gardener. Over the very grave of the dead, as it were, she quarrelled—the word is hardly too strong—with Merton.

Mr. Merton was bitter against Jenkins. His professional mind, always ready to put the worst aspect upon anything, quick to suspect and slow to relinquish an idea, was convinced of the gardener's guilt. In his zeal for the memory of his poor friend, he forgot that he might be injuring an innocent man. He even went so far as to speak strongly to Violet about her visit to the jury. Surely she should have been the last to protect the murderer. He said something like this in the heat of his temper, and regretted it afterwards. It was cruel, unjust, and inconsiderate. Violet simply left the room and refused to see him.

Merton left the house in a rage, and resolved to spare nothing to convict the miserable gardener. Now this quarrel produced certain events—it set on foot another chain of circumstances. Violet was now alone at The Place. Miss Merton could not stay longer. Before she went she asked if she should send back the dog Dando, which Merton had taken to Barnham. Violet, still bitter, in an unreasoning way, against the dog, said no.

"Then," said Miss Merton, "may I take him with me to Torquay?"

She had taken a fancy to the dog. Violet was quite willing—anything so that he did not return to vex her with memories of the dead. Miss Merton took him home, sorry for her friend, and yet glad to quit that dismal house and neighbourhood.

Next day there came a note from Mr. Merton, in which the writer, in a formal way, expressed regret if he had uttered anything which had annoyed her, and asked her to accompany Miss Merton to Torquay for change of scene. Violet thanked him, but refused.

Aymer saw her every day. She did not give way to tears and fits of excited sorrow, but a dull weakness seemed to have taken possession of her. All the old spirit and joy had left her. She wandered about listlessly, stunned, in fact. All the interest she took was in poor Jenkins' fate. Aymer, at her wish, went to Barnham, and engaged a lawyer to defend him. This soon reached Merton's ears, and annoyed him exceedingly; though, to do him justice, he was at that very hour striving to put Violet's affairs into order.

Those affairs were—unknown to her—in a most critical state. The deceased, as he had told Aymer, had three thousand pounds out at interest, as he believed, upon good security, but which he thought of calling in. This money had been advanced to a Mr. Joseph Herring, a large farmer at Belthrop, some ten miles from World's End.

114

Mr. Herring was a successful man and a good man; at all events he had no worse failing than an inordinate love of foxhunting. He had a large family, six sons and eight daughters, but there always seemed to be plenty for them. They lived and dressed well, rode out to the Meet, and one by one, as the sons grew older, they were placed in farms. Foxhunting men, with the reputation of some means, can always find favour in the eyes of landlords. If any one had been asked to point out a fortunate family in that county, he would at once have placed his finger upon the name of Herring.

The original home farm, where dwelt old Herring and his wife, four of the daughters, and one son, who really managed it, was of good size, fertile, and easily rented. The eldest son, Albert Herring, who was married and had children, occupied a fine farm at no great distance; and the two other sons had a smaller farm between them, and with them lived the other four sisters. Of course it was understood that these farms had been stocked partly with borrowed money; but that was a common thing, and there was every indication that all the family were prospering.

It was to this Joseph Herring that Mr. Waldron had advanced three thousand pounds, taking ample security, as was believed, upon stock, and upon a small estate which belonged to Herring's wife. Merton recommended this Herring as a client of his, and conducted the operation. Waldron had given Merton notice that he wished to withdraw the money; but Merton, not thinking there was any hurry, had not mentioned it to Joseph, when there came this awful catastrophe at World's End and drove the matter entirely out of his head. But his attention was drawn back to it in an equally sudden manner. Old Joseph Herring, the foxhunter, while out with the hounds, put his horse at a double mound where there appeared to be a gap. This gap had been caused by cutting down an elm tree, and he imagined that the trunk had been removed.

The morning had been cold, and although the ground was not hard there had been what is called a "duck's frost" in places. The horse's hoofs slipped upon the level butt of the tree, which had been sawn off; the animal fell heavily, and upon his side.

In all probability, even then he would not have been much injured—for falls in the hunting-field are as common as blackberries—had it not been for the trunk of the elm tree. His back, in some way, came against and across the trunk with the weight of the horse upon him, and the spine was broken. He was carried home upon a hurdle, still living, and quite conscious.

A more terrible spectacle could not be conceived than this strong burly man lying upon his bed, conscious, and speaking at times faintly, without a visible wound, and yet with the certainty of death.

His sons and daughters gathered round him; all were at hand except the eldest, Albert, and he was sent for. Joseph, who had seen too

115

many accidents not to know he was doomed, even if it had not been visible upon the faces of his wife and children, betrayed the greatest uneasiness. He kept asking for "Albert" and for "Merton." Messenger after messenger was despatched after both, and still they did not come.

Merton, when the messenger reached him, was in the Petty Sessional Court at Barnham, watching the preliminary proceedings against poor Jenkins, which happened to take place that day. He was much excited.

The lawyer whom Aymer had engaged to defend Jenkins was a professional rival—a keen and clever man, and he had so worked up the case, and suggested so many doubts and probabilities that the Bench of magistrates hesitated to commit him.

It was in the thick of the fight that the messenger from the death-bed arrived. Will it be believed, so great was the professional rivalry between these men, and so determined was Merton to succeed in committing poor Jenkins, that he paused, he hesitated, finally he waited till the case was finished.

"After all," he said to himself, "very likely the accident to Joseph is much exaggerated—people always lose their heads at such times. At all events his neck's not broken, and he's alive; the messenger doesn't know exactly where he's hurt. There's no particular hurry."

But it so happened that there was a particular cause for hurry. While Merton persuaded himself that he was looking after the cause of his murdered friend and revenging him, that friend's dearest one—his Violet—was fast losing her patrimony. Even when the second messenger came with more exact intelligence, Merton thought— "Sometimes men lie for days with broken backs, and what does he want me for? His will is made; I've got it in my office, and a very just will it is. All his affairs are arranged, I believe. It's all fuss and fidget."

However, he ordered his carriage to wait at the door of the Court, and half an hour afterwards the Bench reappeared.

The Chairman said that although there was very little evidence against the prisoner Jenkins, although his character had been proved excellent, and although his solicitor had most ably conducted the defence, yet the Bench felt that the crime was one too serious for them to think of dismissing a suspected person. The prisoner would be committed for trial at the Assizes, which fortunately for him came on that day fortnight.

A smile of triumph lit up Merton's face as he gathered up his papers. The rival solicitor smiled too, and assured Aymer who was present to tell Violet what happened, that the grand jury would be certain to throw out the bill. There was not a tittle of evidence against the prisoner.

With this assurance Aymer mounted and rode back to Violet. At the same time Merton, telling his coachman not to distress the horses,

116

drove leisurely towards the death-bed, where he had been so anxiously expected for hours.

The scene at that death-bed was extremely dreadful. The poor dying man gradually became more and more restless and excited; nor could all the efforts of Dr Parker, the persuasions of the clergyman, nor the tears of his wife and children, keep him calm.

The thought of death—the idea of preparing for the hereafter never seemed to occur to him. His one wish was to see "Albert" and "Merton;" till feverish and his eye glittering with excitement, all that he could ejaculate was those two names.

He remained for four hours quite conscious, and able to converse; then suddenly there was a change, and he lost the power of answering questions, though still faintly repeating those names. The scene was very shocking.

"Why doesn't Albert come?" said poor Mrs Herring. "He might have been here two hours ago. If Merton would not, Albert, my son, might have come."

What do you suppose Albert was doing at that moment? It is incredible, but it is true. He was in the field superintending the placing of two new steam ploughing engines and their tackle, watching the trial of the new engines, as they tore up the soil with the deep plough. They had arrived that morning, just purchased; and had it not been for their coming, he would have been in the hunting-field with his father when the accident happened.

He could not, or would not, leave his engines. He busied about with them—now riding himself upon the plough, now watching the drivers of the engines, now causing experiments to be made with the scarifier. He paid little attention to the first messenger. "Tell them I'll be there," he said. Another and another messenger, still Albert remained with his plough.

"He asks for me, does he?" he said. "I'll be there directly." Still he made no haste. After quitting the engines he went out of his path to visit a flock of fat sheep, and putting up a covey of partridges in the stubble, stayed to mark them down.

At the house he calmly refreshed himself with cheese and ale. As he mounted his horse another messenger came, this time with a note from Dr Parker. Albert mounted with much bustle, and made off at a gallop. Two miles on the way he pulled up to a walk, met his shepherd, and had a talk with him about the ewes; then the farrier on his nag, and described to him the lameness of a carthorse. All this time his father lay dying. Strange and unaccountable indifference!

Merton reached Belthrop Farm first, and was too late. Joseph Herring was dead. He had died without even so much as listening to the words of the clergyman—yet he had to all appearance been a good, and even pious man while in health. Why was he so strangely warped upon his death-bed?

"Oh! Albert—Albert, my son, my son! Why did you linger?" cried poor Mrs Herring as he entered.

"Father?" said Albert, questioningly.

She shook her head.

"Ah!" said the son; and it sounded like a sigh of relief.

Let the grief for the dead be never so great, there quickly follows the commonplace realities of money and affairs to be settled.

The dead man's will was read by Merton. It was a fair and just will. Next came the investigation into his effects, and then came the revelation. Joseph Herring left no effects. This discovery fell upon his wife, three of the sons, and all the daughters, like a thunderbolt. They had always believed they should be left tolerably provided for. But when all the debts were paid there would not be a ten-pound note.

They began to murmur, and to question, as well they might. What had become of the three thousand pounds Herring had had of Waldron? They did not know that their father had borrowed so much as that; they knew there was a loan from Waldron, but never suspected the amount.

Merton, hard as it was, felt that he must draw that money in; and who was to pay it? Why, there were no effects whatever. To pay the other debts would take all the money that could be got, and part of the stock must be sold even then.

But this three thousand pounds. To make that good all the stock, the corn, the implements—everything would have to be sold; including Mrs Herring's little estate, and the small sums that had been advanced to the two sons who lived on one farm must be withdrawn. It was complete ruin—ruin without reserve.

They were literally stunned, and knew not which way to turn. They could not understand, neither could Merton, what had become of the three thousand pounds; there was not a scrap of paper to show. Joseph had never been a good accountant—few farmers are; but one would have thought that he would have preserved some record of such a sum. But no—not a scrap.

Then, as said before, these children began to murmur, as well they might. Then they began to understand, or guess dimly at the extraordinary excitement of the dying man. It was this that weighed upon his mind, and caused him to continually call for his eldest son and for Merton, in order that he might make some provision.

There grew up a certain feeling against Albert. Why had he not come at once—if he had done so, perhaps this might have been averted. A vague distrust and suspicion of him arose. It was intensified by the knowledge that he alone was safe. He had had a longer start and a better farm; he had the reputation of having even saved a little money. No injury could befall him. Yet they had not got the slightest evidence against him in any way; but a coolness—a decided coolness arose between the brothers and sisters, and Albert, which Albert, on his part, made no effort to remove. Ill-natured people said he was only too glad to quarrel with them, so as to have a pretext for refusing them assistance.

It happened, however, that one day a strange gentleman called upon Robert and John, the two brothers, who worked one farm together. He was an agent of an agricultural implement manufactory in a distant county, and his object was to induce them to purchase implements of him—especially steam traction engines. The poor brothers smiled in a melancholy way at the very idea. They buy engines—they should soon scarcely be able to buy bread! The agent expressed his surprise.

"But your brother seems a wealthy man," he said. "He paid for his engines in cash."

"In cash!" they cried. "He told us that he paid one-fifth only, and the rest remained in bills."

The agent saw he had got on delicate ground; but they pressed him, and he could not very well escape. It then came out that Albert had paid sixteen hundred pounds in hard cash for the engines, by which, as the factory had been pressed for money, he got them at little more than two-thirds of the value, which was considered to be two thousand three hundred pounds.

The brothers were simply astounded. They went home and talked it over with the fourth son, who managed the Belthrop Farm. They could not understand how Albert came to have so much ready cash. At last the conclusion forced itself upon them—the three thousand pounds borrowed from Waldron must have been lent by their father to Albert. They remembered that something had been said of an opening Albert had heard of, to add another farm to his already large tenancy.

This was the secret—poor old Joseph, a bad accountant, had given the money to Albert, and, never thinking of dying, had postponed drawing up the proper deeds. Without a moment's delay they proceeded in a body to Albert's residence. He received them in an off-hand manner—utterly denied that he had had the money, challenged them to find the proof, and finally threatened if they set such a tale about the county to prosecute them for slander. This was too much.

It is wretched to chronicle these things; but they must be written. High words were followed by blows; there was a fight between the eldest and the next in succession, and both being strong men, they were much knocked about. The other brothers, maddened with their loss, actually cheered on their representative, and stripped to take his place as soon as he should be fatigued. But at that moment poor old Mrs Joseph Herring, who had feared this, arrived, driving up in a pony-carriage, and sprang between the combatants. She received a severe blow, but she separated them, and they parted with menacing gestures.

Once back at Belthrop, a kind of family council was held. Merton was sent for, but nothing could be done. There was not a scrap of proof

119

that Albert had had the money. Mrs Joseph, went to him, reasoned with him, entreated him. He turned a deaf ear to her remonstrances, and cursed her to her face. The miserable woman returned to her despairing younger children, and never recovered the terrible blow which the selfish, and inhuman conduct of her eldest son had inflicted upon her. Ruin stared them in the face. Waldron's loan was due, and everything was already advertised for sale.

Chapter Eight

How suddenly the leaves go in the autumn! They linger on the trees till we almost cheat ourselves into the belief that we shall escape the inevitable winter; that for once the inexorable march of events will be stayed, till some morning we wake up and look forth, and lo! a wind has arisen, and the leaves are gone.

Absorbed in the one miserable topic—the one thought of Waldron's terrible fate—Violet and Aymer spent several weeks almost unconsciously. When at last they, as it were, woke up and looked forth, the actual tangible leaves upon the trees had disappeared, and, like them, the green leaves of their lives had been shaken down and had perished.

Even yet they had one consolation—they had themselves. The catastrophe that had happened at the very eleventh hour, at the moment when their affection and their hope was about to be realised, after all had only drawn them closer together. She was more dependent upon him than ever. There was no kind Jason to fly to now; the resources he could command were gone for ever. Had Aymer been as selfish as he was unselfish, that very fact would not have been without its pleasure. She could come to him only now in trouble, and she did come to him.

It may be that all that happy summer which they had spent together, strolling about, sketching under the beech and fir; all that happy winter, with its music and song; all the merry spring, with its rides, had not called forth such deep and abiding love between these two as was brought into existence by these weeks of sorrow, the first frosts of their year. They were constantly together; they were both orphans now; they had nothing but themselves. It was natural that they should grow all in all to each other.

There was one subject that was never alluded to between them, and that was the interrupted marriage. It was too painful for Violet, too delicate a subject for Aymer to mention. It was in both their minds, yet

120

neither spoke of it. They were, and they were not, married. In a sense—in the sense of the publication of the banns; in the sense of the public procession to the church, the sanction of friends, the presence of the people—in this sense they were married. But the words "I will" had never left Violet's lips, however willing they were to utter the phrase; and, above all, the ring had never been placed upon her finger. Nor could that ring be found. They were half married.

It was a strange and exceptional case, perhaps unequalled. Morally, Violet felt that she was his legally, Aymer feared that she was not his. He feared it, because he knew that it would be impossible to persuade Violet to undergo the ceremony a second time, till the memory of that dreadful day had softened and somewhat faded. It might be months, perhaps years. The disappointment to him was almost more than he could bear. To be so near, to have the prize within his reach, and then to be dashed aside with the merciless hand of fate.

It would not be well that the ancient belief in destiny should again bear sway in our time; it is contrary to the thought of the period, and yet hourly, daily, weekly, all our lives, we seem to move, and live, and have our being amidst circumstances that march on and on, and are utterly beyond our power to control or guide. "Circumstances beyond my power to control" is a household phrase—we hear it at the hearth, on the mart, in the council-chamber. And what are circumstances? Why are these apparently trivial things out of our power? Why do they perpetually evolve other circumstances, till a chain forms itself—a net, a web—as visible, and as tangible, as if it had been actually woven by the three sisters of antique mythology.

The unseen, awful, inscrutable necessity which, heedless alike of gods and men, marches with irresistible tread through the wonderful dramas of Sophocles, seems to have survived the twilight of the gods, survived the age of miracles and supernatural events. Of all that the ancients venerated and feared, necessity alone remains a factor in modern life. What can our brightest flashes of intelligence, our inventions, our steam engine and telegraph, effect when confronted with those "circumstances over which we have no control?" It is our nineteenth-century euphemism for the Fate of the ancient world.

It is not well that we should scrutinise too closely the state of poor Aymer's mind. His joy and elation before that terrible day were too great not for the fall to be felt severely. The iron of it entered into his soul. For one moment he almost hoped against hope.

The clergyman who had officiated at the interrupted bridal came daily to see Violet, and his true piety, his quiet parental manner, soothed and comforted her. He whispered to Aymer that it would be well if the marriage ceremony were completed in private, as could be done by special licence.

Aymer naturally grasped at the idea. He had still twenty pounds left of the gift which had been sent to him anonymously. He was eager to spend it upon the special licence, but he confessed that he dared not mention it to Violet.

The vicar undertook that task, but failed completely. Violet begged him to spare her—to desist; she could not—not yet.

After that day she was more and more tender and affectionate to Aymer, as if to make up to him for his loss. She said that he must take heart—they had no need to be unhappy. In a little while, but not yet—not yet, while that fearful vision was still floating before her eyes. But Aymer must be happy. They had sufficient. He had left them all he had. That was another reason why they should wait, in affection for his memory. They could see each other daily—their future would be together. And Aymer, miserable as he was, was forced to be content.

Merton had not been to The Place. Not one word had he said about the difficulty in Herring's affairs, and the loss of the three thousand pounds. Violet was utterly ignorant that her fortune was gone. She spoke very bitterly of Merton. "If he had loved poor papa," she said, "he would never have persecuted his faithful servant," for nothing could shake her belief in Jenkins' innocence, and she did all she could to comfort the poor gardener's desolate wife.

Merton, on his part, did not care to approach her after the share he had had in the commitment of Jenkins, and because he hesitated, he dreaded to face her, and to tell her that her fortune, entrusted to his hands, was gone. He blamed himself greatly, and yet he would not own it. He ought to have hastened to Herring's death-bed. Had that dying man but left one written word, to say that Albert had had the money, all would have been well.

In the fierce attempt to revenge his old friend, he had irreparably injured that friend's daughter, and he dreaded the inevitable disclosure. He put it off till the last, hoping against hope, and doing all that his lawyer's ingenuity could suggest to recover some part of the amount. In endeavouring to succeed in this, he pressed hard—very hard—upon the Herring family. He pushed them sorely, and spared not. He was bitterly exasperated against them. Unjustly, he openly accused them of a plot to rob his client and dishonour him.

He abused the dead man as one who had repented too late upon his death-bed. He would take everything—down to the smallest article. Neither the persuasions of the sons, the tears of the daughters, nor the silent despair of the widow could move him. Of all this Violet knew nothing.

It happened that one evening not long after the lamp had been lit at The Place, that there was heard a slight tapping or knocking at the front door. Now, this door was close to the window where the terrible deed had been committed. By this door the bride had stepped forth in all her gay attire; by this door the corpse of her father had been carried forth. Villagers, and all isolated people, are superstitious; the beliefs of those days, when all people were more isolated than they are now, linger amongst them. By common consent, this door was avoided by day and night. A dread destiny seemed to hang over those who passed beneath its portal. It had been kept locked since the funeral—no one had used it.

Violet and Aymer, sitting in the breakfast-parlour—which was the most comfortable room in the house—were reading, and looked up mutually at the sound of those unwonted knocks. They listened. There was a pause; and then the taps were repeated. They were so gentle, so muffled, that they doubted the evidence of their ears—and yet surely it was a knocking.

The servants in the kitchen heard the taps, and they cowered over the fire and looked fearfully at each other.

One thing was certain—no person who knew The Place, no one from the village, would come to that door. If it was any mortal man or woman, it must be a stranger; and the last time a stranger had crossed the "green," all knew what had happened. If it was not a stranger, then it must be the spirit of poor "master." They were determined not to hear.

The taps were repeated. Violet and Aymer looked at each other.

Something very like a moan penetrated into the apartment. Aymer immediately rose and went to the front door. He asked if any one was without; there was no answer. He opened the door; the bitter wind, bearing with it flakes of snow, drove into his face. For a moment, in the darkness, he could distinguish nothing; the next, brave as he was, he recoiled; for there lay what looked like a body at his feet. Overcoming his dread he stooped and touched—a woman's dress. He lifted her up—the form was heavy and inanimate in his hands.

"Violet, dear!" he said, "it is a woman—she has fainted; may I bring her in?"

Violet's sympathies were at once on the alert. The woman was carried in and laid upon the rug before the fire, the servant came crowding in to render assistance brandy was brought, and the stranger opened her eyes and moaned faintly. Then they saw that, although stained with travel and damp from exposure to the drifting snow her dress was that of a lady.

Under the influence of the warm fire and the brandy she soon recovered sufficiently to sit up. She was not handsome nor young her best features were a broad, intellectual looking forehead, and fine dark eyes. So soon as ever she was strong enough to speak she turned to Violet, and begged to be alone with her for a little while.

Aymer, with all a lover's suspicions, demurred, but Violet insisted, and he had to be content with remaining within easy call.

He had no sooner left the room than the lady, for such she appeared to be, fell upon her knees at Violet's feet, and begged her for the sake of her father's memory to show mercy.

"Oh! spare us," cried the unhappy creature, bursting into tears, and wringing her hands, "spare us—we are penniless. Indeed we did not do it purposely. We never knew—I am Esther Herring!"

It was long before Violet could gather her meaning from these incoherent sentences. At last, under her kind words and gentle questions, Esther became calmer and explained the miserable state of affairs. Violet sighed deeply. In one moment her hopes were dashed to the ground: her money was gone; how could she and Aymer—

But she bore up bravely, and listened patiently to Esther's story. How the widow's heart was breaking, how the sons were despairing, and the daughters looking forward to begging their bread. How the sale approached—only five days more; and that thinking, and thinking day and night over the misery of it, Esther had at last fled to Violet for mercy—to Violet, who was ignorant of the whole matter. Fled on foot— for all their horses were seized—on that wild winter afternoon, facing the bitter wind, the snow, and the steep hills for ten long miles to World's End. Fled to fling herself at Violet's feet, and beg for mercy upon the widow and the fatherless children. The fatigue and her excitement had proved too much, and she had fainted at the very door. Esther dwelt much upon Mr. Merton's cruelty, for his insults had cut her to the quick.

Violet became very pale. She went to the door and called softly, "Aymer." He came, and Esther attempted to dry her tears. Violet told him all, and took his hand.

"This cannot be," she said; "this surely must not be. I will do—we will do—as of a surety my father would have done. The innocent shall not suffer for the guilty. We, Aymer and I, will give up our claim. Tell them at your home to be comforted and to fear not."

Esther saw that her mission was accomplished, and the reaction set in. She became ill and feverish. Violet had her taken upstairs and waited upon her. Aymer was left alone. He walked to the window, opened the shutters, and looked forth. The scud flew over the sky, and the wan moon was now hidden, and now shone forth with a pale feeble light. The heart within him was very bitter. He did not repent the renunciation which he had confirmed; he felt that it was right and just. But it was a terrible blow. It cut away the very ground from beneath his feet.

The poor fellow—he was poor Aymer again now—looked forward to the future. What could he do? The talents he possessed were useless, or nearly useless, in a pecuniary sense. Unable to earn sufficient to support himself, how could he marry Violet? The thought was maddening. To continue in the old, old life at Wick Farm without a prospect was impossible. To wander a beggar from door to door would be preferable. When he found that Violet could not leave Esther, he walked home to Wick Farm; over the wild and open Downs, and his heart went up in a great and bitter cry.

The blow that had struck down poor Waldron had struck him

down also. It is ever thus with evil. The circle widens, and no man knows where it will end. Yet he did not falter.

Next day Violet wrote a curt letter to Mr. Merton, requesting him to forbear proceedings, and upbraiding him for his cruelty. She desired that he would relinquish the charge of her affairs.

Merton, had he so chosen, might have made a difficulty about this—under the will of Waldron—but he did not. He was, to say truth, glad of a pretext to wash his hands of a matter in which he had figured so ill.

Violet sent for the same solicitor who had defended Jenkins, Mr. Broughton, and desired him to see that proceedings were stayed. The Herrings were saved. Esther was sent home in the pony-carriage with the good tidings. Other debts, unsuspected before, ate up most of the effects of Joseph Herring. The widow's little property had to be sold to meet them. With the trifle that was left they removed to the farm where the two brothers worked together, and by dint of careful management escaped starvation. Neither were they unhappy, for misfortune and a common injury bound them closer together—all but the widow, who never overcame the duplicity of her eldest son.

Their conduct towards Violet appears extremely selfish, but it must be remembered that Waldron had borne the reputation of being a rich man. They never dreamt that they had taken Violet's all. But so it was. The dear, dear ponies had to be sold, the servants dismissed; Violet could not keep the house on, and in that isolated position it was difficult to let it, even at a nominal rent.

Her friends in London made no sign. She had been a favoured guest while Waldron lived and was reputed wealthy. Now they had lost sight of her.

To Aymer all this was as gall and wormwood. It was a comment upon his own weakness, and impotency to aid the only one he loved. He wrote, he sketched; but now with the strange inconsistency of fortune these works were returned, as "not up to the standard required." Perhaps his misfortunes affected his skilfulness. He knew not which way to turn. At home—if Wick Farm could be called home—the old state of things began to gradually return. The old covert sneers and hints at his uselessness crept again into the daily conversation. Martin, like Hercules—

Rude, unrefined in speech.
Judging all wisdom by its last results,

looked upon him as a failure, and treated him accordingly. To do the young men justice, those who had formerly taunted him now never lost an opportunity of expressing their regret. Poor Aymer felt this worse than their sneers and gibes. He had the fault of pride, and yet he

125

depreciated himself habitually. He was punished severely for his brief period of elation. What hurt him most was his helplessness to aid Violet. And Violet, noble girl! was calm, resigned, fearless in her trust—strong in her love of Aymer.

But the inevitable approached—"the circumstances over which we have no control." The day was coming when she must go, and go—whither?

Chapter Nine

Down to one firm faith in this day of scepticism and cynicism. It may be a despicable weakness—that cannot be helped—but nothing will ever overthrow it. My faith is firm in the good which is possible in woman.

There is much vice, much evil, much folly; but, after all, these faults are chiefly caused by weakness, therefore they are more or less excusable. It is difficult for women to do good—so many and so complex are the restraints which surround them as in a net—yet they do it. Were I in sorrow, in trouble, or in fear, to them I should go, as hundreds—ay, countless numbers—have previously gone, certain of assistance if assistance were possible, and of compassion and sympathy, even if my crimes were too evil to speak of.

There was heard one afternoon at The Place the roll of carriage-wheels—a sound that had not been heard since the fatal bridal day. It was a damp, cold day, and Violet had been unable to go out. A fog hung over the fields, creeping slowly along the fallows, clinging in shapeless clouds upon the hill tops. There was no rain, but the bare hedges were dripping large drops of water condensed from the mist, and the dead leaves upon the ground were soddened with damp. On such days as these, when she could not walk out and dispel her gloom by exercise, Violet naturally felt the loss of poor Jason the more.

Aymer could not be always with her. Although their intercourse was little, if at all, fettered by the etiquette which would have barred it in more civilised neighbourhoods, yet he could not be always at The Place, and of late he had been working hard at sketches and literary matters, which occupied time and kept him from her side.

She was very lonely, longing for the evening, when he would be certain to come. The roll of these carriage-wheels was therefore an event. Looking from the window upstairs—that very window whence, in all the splendour of her beauty and her wedding-dress, she had timidly glanced forth to watch the approach of the greys—she saw a stylish brougham rapidly nearing the house, and as it came nearer recognised the horses, and knew it was Lady Lechester's.

Agnes, not waiting for the footman to announce her visit, sprang out, and walked at once to the front door. Once more there came a tapping at that dread portal.

Conquering her fluttering heart, Violet, in a maze of bewilderment, opened it herself. Agnes held out her hand, and kissed her twice upon the cheek and forehead.

"Forgive me!" she said. "Forgive me for coming so soon after—. But I wanted to see you; I had much to say to you."

Violet began to thank her in a confused way for the pearl necklace. Agnes stopped her; it was not that—it was about Violet herself that she had come to talk. Even in her surprise and confusion, Violet could not help thinking that Agnes was very beautiful. It was a species of beauty that was precisely the opposite of Violet's. Both gained by the contrast of the other's style.

Agnes Lechester was at least thirty—she might have been a year or two older—and there hovered over her countenance an indefinable air of melancholy, as if the memory of a past sorrow was for ever before her mind. There was not a wrinkle, not a groove upon her pale brow, but the impress of pain was none the less unmistakable upon her features. Her hair was very dark, as near as possible to the raven's hue, so often spoken of, so rarely seen. Her eyes were large and grey, deep-set under delicate eyebrows, well-marked, and slightly arching. Her forehead high and intellectual. The features, the nose and mouth, were small and well-made, the ears especially delicate. High blood and long descent spoke out clearly in her every aspect, down even to the quiet subdued manner—the exquisite tact, and consideration for others, which distinguished her in conversation and in daily life.

She was about the same height as Violet, but appeared taller, being more slightly made. She wore a simple black-silk, extremely plain, and one mourning-ring—no other jewellery.

Violet, whose position was not a little embarrassing, found herself in a few moments entirely at her ease, and conversing as with an old friend. Agnes did not in a direct manner recall the terrible past, but she had a way of asking what may be called sympathising questions, which quickly drew forth Violet's confidence.

For the first time she found a sister to whom she could express her feelings unrestrainedly; and even that brief hour of companionship did her much good. Not till all trace of distant formality had been removed, not till there had been a certain degree of familiarity established between them, did Agnes allude to the real object of her visit. She had come to ask Violet as a favour—so she put it—to spend a little time with her. The Towers were so very, very lonely—she said this in a tone that was evidently sincere—she had so few visitors, practically none, and she should be so glad if Violet would come. Violet saw in an instant that it was really out of kindness to her that the invitation was given; she wished to accept it, and yet hesitated. Agnes pressed her. Then she remembered Aymer—what would he say? If she went, he would be alone—he would not see her, and she would not see him. Thinking of him, a slight blush rose to her cheek. Perhaps Agnes guessed what was passing in her mind, for she said—

"Mr. Malet will, of course, come and see us—often. You must ask his permission, you know. I will come again to-morrow and fetch you in the brougham."

So it was practically settled, and Agnes, after a warm farewell, departed. Violet waited for Aymer, almost fearing he would upbraid her; but then the separation would only be for a little time. A little time!

When Agnes Lechester came to ask her to The Towers, she came with a full knowledge of Violet's position—of her monetary loss, and of the noble self-sacrifice she had made.

It chanced—"circumstances over which we have no control" again—that Mr. Broughton, to whom Violet had transferred her affairs, had succeeded to the business of an uncle, an elder Mr. Broughton, who was almost the hereditary solicitor of the Lechester family. The position was one of great emolument, and gave some social precedence; hence, perhaps, part of the jealousy exhibited towards him by Mr. Merton—an older man, and not so fortunate. From him Agnes learnt the whole of the details. The frightful catastrophe—the mystery of the murder of poor Waldron—had greatly impressed her, and the sad circumstances of the interrupted bridal trebled the interest she had taken in Violet and Aymer. She had instructed Broughton to inform her of everything, and especially of how matters stood with Violet now her father was no more. As he had now the charge of Violet's affairs, it was easy for him to do this; and being a comparatively young man, and with a heart not yet quite dead to feeling, he was himself much interested in the woman who could so willingly give up the last fragment of her fortune.

Agnes Lechester was deeply impressed by Violet's generosity and abrogation of self—she felt the warmest sympathy and desire to assist her—she really was anxious to make her acquaintance, and the result was her visit to The Place. Ostensibly the invitation was for a little time only; but Agnes knew that the house, which alone was left to Violet, could not support her, and intended to prolong the invitation indefinitely. She really was lonely, and really did look forward to a companion in whom she could trust.

Aymer was overjoyed when he heard what had happened, and insisted upon Violet accepting the invitation. Violet's isolation, and the daily increasing awkwardness of her position, troubled him greatly. He knew not what to do for her. Here was a resource—a haven of safety for a while at least. Never mind about himself—doubtless he could see her sometimes; so long as she was safe and comfortable he should be happy, much happier even than in their present unrestricted intercourse—though this was said with a sigh.

He lingered long with her that evening, longer than he had ever done before; it was the last, perhaps, they should ever spend together in that house, which was still very dear to them, notwithstanding the tragedy it had witnessed. The time came at last when they must separate. It was the saddest walk that night that he had ever had across the Downs. They were enveloped in a thick mist—only instinct and long use kept him in the path—an impenetrable gloom hung over him. Even the fir trees were silent; there was no breeze to stir them, to produce that low sighing sound that seems to mean so much to those who will pause and listen.

The morrow was brighter; there was a little sunshine, clouded and feeble, but still there was a little. It would be difficult to explain the process by which it came about. There are means of communication between persons without direct words. Thus it happened that almost by a species of volition, Agnes Lechester, Violet, and Aymer, before the hour to depart arrived, walked slowly and mournfully to the old, old church, across the meadows by the well-worn path, which the morning's frost had left hard and dry. Since that terrible day Violet had never been—she could not. But now, somehow, with this newly-found companion, strengthened by two loving hearts, one on either side, it seemed to her as if a holy peace might perhaps descend upon her if she could visit her father's tomb.

With her face hidden by a thick veil, the tears standing in her eyes, the poor girl walked between them. Few words passed—silence was more natural and fitting than speech. They met two or three persons, all of whom knew Violet and Aymer; but these paid the homage to sorrow which the rudest tender, and went by silently, raising their hats. No one interrupted them; no one stared with vulgar curiosity. These three were alone—alone with the memory of the dead. And strangely enough, all three were orphans. It was Agnes Lechester who reminded them of that fact as they stood before the tomb; it was, she said in a low voice, another bond of union between them.

The inscription had not yet been put up; the slab was plain. Their visit was very short; it was more than Violet could bear. The tomb was just without the church. Agnes motioned to Aymer to leave them; he walked away a few paces. Together the two women entered the church; they were alone in the sacred edifice. With slow steps poor Violet, leaning on Agnes's arm and sobbing bitterly, walked up that very aisle, over that very figure of the ancient knight in brass, past the antique font—the very aisle where she had gone in all her wedding splendour amid the admiration of the gathered crowd. And now she came again— came with a stranger—in silence and sorrow, to kneel on the steps that led up to the chancel to pray as best her throbbing heart would permit. Was that prayer more for the living, or the dead?

Violet had been reared a Protestant in the Articles of the Church of England, yet I question whether in that supreme moment her soul was not fuller of prayer for him who had gone before, than for herself and those who still lingered on earth. Those among us who can remember bitter hours of agony, say truly for whom have they prayed? Let us not penetrate further into the sanctuary of sorrow.

The carriage rolled away, and Aymer was alone. He watched it go down into the valley out of sight. He turned and ascended the Downs, not daring to look back upon the old, old house. At the summit he could command an extended view. Far away the white road ran up over a hill, and he could see a black dot crawling slowly up it. He knew it was the carriage; he watched it reach the top and disappear over the brow—then she was gone.

For the first time since love had arisen in his heart he was separated from her. It was true that it was not total separation. They were bound together by ties which nothing could sever, and yet—the happy past was gone, to return no more. He was at liberty to see her at The Towers; Agnes Lechester had done her best to impress upon him that he could come whenever he chose, and would be always welcome. But Aymer had the vaguest ideas of what life with the upper ranks was like; he had a vague shrinking from entering this house; he felt that he should be restrained and at a loss. There could never be that free intercourse between him and Violet that had existed. He felt in his heart that she would never more return to The Place. The house was to be closed that evening; would it ever be opened again?

He crushed back his despair as best he could, and went home to his cold, lonely room at the Wick Farm. Martin grudged him a fire even. Aymer crushed back his heart, and tried to work. It was very difficult. When the hand and the body are numbed with physical cold, when the heart is chilled with grief, it is hard indeed to call the fancy into play and to amuse others. Was it not Goldsmith who wrote the "Vicar of Wakefield" to pay the expenses of his parent's funeral?

Perhaps no greater proof of his wonderful genius could be given than is presented by that oft-repeated and simple anecdote. Only a transcendant genius could have forced itself out under such miserable circumstances. Aymer certainly had talent, perhaps even genius, but he had not yet found his opportunity—he was not quite certain wherein his ability really lay. All his efforts were tentative. They failed one and all—failed just at the moment when what he most wanted was a little encouragement. He did not spare himself; he worked the whole day, saving only an hour put aside to walk upon the Downs for health's sake.

He had still fifteen pounds remaining of the munificent, and anonymous present he had received. This he husbanded with the utmost care; it was his capital, his all. With it he formed schemes of reaching London, and finding employment. He only waited till a work upon which he was now engaged was finished before he started. Now

Violet was gone, there was no inducement to remain at World's End; far better to go out and face hard facts, and conquer them.

But as the days went by, and the work was half finished, a deadly despair seemed to seize him. Of what use was it? Every slow post that reached that almost forgotten spot returned to him work rejected and despised. His sketches, he was told, "wanted spirit;" his literary labours "wanted finish, and bore marks of haste."

If these were useless, of what good was it to complete this book he was writing? It would only end in another disappointment. He ceased to open his letters; he flung them on one side. For a day or two he did nothing—he wandered about on the open Downs, seeking consolation from Nature, and finding none. At last, accusing himself of a lack of energy and fortitude, he set to work again. So it was not till two days after date that he read the following letter, which had been cast upon one side with the rest:—

"2, Market Cross, Barnham.

"Dear Sir,—I am requested by Mr. Broughton to ask you to call upon him at your earliest convenience. He has some employment to offer you.

"With esteem, etc, etc."

He went. Broughton received him kindly, and explained that he wanted a clerk, not so much for technical work as for correspondence, and to give general assistance. Aymer being a novice and completely ignorant of such duties, could not of course expect much salary. However, he would have thirty-five shillings per week. This offer was made partly through Lady Lechester's influence, partly out of the interest he himself took in Aymer. But a true lawyer, he could not help doing even good as cheaply as possible. Aymer thanked him, and accepted the post.

Chapter Ten

Aymer would in times gone by have regarded the employment he had now obtained as a great step in advance, and have rejoiced accordingly. But he had been too near the prize for it to give him even so much as hope for the future. He wished to be grateful for what he had got; he tried to look upon it as a wonderful thing, but it was impossible. The contrast between the actual, and what had been within his very grasp was too intense.

It was an easy place. Beyond a little correspondence to write for Mr. Broughton, and sometimes a little copying, he had practically nothing to do. His hours were short for the business—only from ten till four; he had plenty of time at his own disposal.

The fact was that his salary came, not directly, but indirectly from Lady Lechester, and he was favoured accordingly. If he had known this he would have been still more dissatisfied.

The office in which he was placed was a kind of library or retiring apartment, opening by double doors into Mr. Broughton's private room; and he was often called upon to bear witness to certain transactions of a strictly private nature, and in which the solicitor told him he relied upon his honour as a gentleman, to preserve secrecy.

Broughton really meant him well, and did his best now and then to start him on in the acquisition of a knowledge of the law. Books were put into his hands, and he was told what parts of them to study, and had to prepare extracts from them occasionally. Aymer did his best, conscientiously, but he hated it—he hated it most thoroughly. It was not altogether that the reading in these books was dry and uninteresting to the last degree. Flat, tame, spiritless, meaningless,—a mere collection of decisions, interpretations, precedents—such they appeared at first. Aymer had talent and insight sufficient to speedily observe that this forbidding aspect was not the true one.

All these precedents, rules, decisions—these ten thousand subtle distinctions—were much like the laws or rules of a game at chess. They decided in what way a pawn should be moved or a bishop replaced. The science of law seemed to him like a momentous game at chess, only the pieces were living human creatures.

These subtle distinctions and technical divisions, formalities though they appeared, had a meaning, and a deep one. Following his employer, Mr. Broughton, into the petty law courts at Barnham, he saw how the right and the wrong, the sorrow or the joy of human beings depended almost upon the quibble of a word, the incident of a slip of the pen. It was a game—a game requiring long study, an iron memory, quick observation, and quicker decision; and he hated it—hated it because the right appeared to be of no consequence. Truth, and what he had always thought was meant by justice, were left entirely out of sight.

It was not the man who had the right upon his side who won. If that was the case, what use would there be for lawyers? Too often it was the man who had the law upon his side, and the law only. He actually heard magistrates, and even judges, expressing their regret that the law compelled them to give decisions contrary to the true justice of the cause before them.

By degrees he became aware of the extraordinary fact, that with all the cumbrous system of law phrases—a system that requires a special dictionary—there was not even a word to express what he understood as justice; not even a word to express it!

Justice meant a decision according to the law, and not according to the right or wrong of the particular case proceeding; equity meant a decision based upon a complex, antiquated, unreasonable jumble of obsolete customs. The sense of the word "equity"—as it is used in the sublime prophecy, "With equity shall he judge the world"—was entirely lost.

In the brief time that he had sat beside Mr. Broughton in these Courts, Aymer conceived an intense loathing for the whole system. After all, what was the law, upon which so much was based, which over-rode equity, justice, truth, and even conscience? What was this great fetish to which every one bowed the knee—from the distinguished and learned judge downwards, the judge who, in point of fact, admitted and regretted that he decided against his conscience? It was principally precedent. Because a man had once been hung for a murder committed in a certain manner, men must always be hung for murder. Because a judge had once given a verdict which, under the circumstances, was as near the right as he dared to go (and our judges do this), then every one who came after must be dealt with by this immovable standard.

The very passage of time itself—the changes introduced into society, custom, and modes of thought in the course of the years—was in itself a strong and all-sufficient argument against this fetish precedent.

That was not all. Aymer in his position—to a certain extent confidential—had a glimpse behind the scenes. Quick of observation and comprehension, he saw that even this game of argument, and precedent, and quibble was not conducted honestly. He had heard and read so much of the freedom, the liberty of England, the safety of the subject, the equal justice meted out to all, that he was literally confounded when the bare facts stared him in the face.

There was jobbery, corruption under the whole of it; there was class prejudice operating in the minds of those on the judgment-seat; there were a thousand-and-one small, invisible strings, which palled this way and that behind the scenes. It was, after all, a species of Punch and Judy show, moved by wires, and learnt by rote by the exhibitor.

It sickened and wearied him. Sitting on those hard benches, he longed for liberty—longed to escape from the depressing influence of the atmosphere of chicanery in which he was plunged. The very sight of those hideous faces which are sure to congregate in the criminal justice-room, seemed to weaken the fresh young spirit within him.

Yet, as said before, Mr. Broughton used him kindly. He found Aymer lodgings cheap and fairly comfortable. Aymer had often desired to escape from his solitary room at Wick Farm; but even that cold, lonely apartment was better than this. These four walls had no association—they were walls only—partly concealed with a few common prints. One of these, over the mantelpiece, looked down upon him as he sat by his fire in the evening. He saw it night after night, till at last that engraving seemed to almost live, and he watched to see when the labour of the prisoner should be completed. For it was the picture of the prisoner sitting in his cell upon a stone bench, painfully chiselling out upon the stone wall—just where a single beam of sunlight fell—the figure of Christ upon the Cross, with the rude tool of a common iron nail.

He grew to understand the feelings and the thought, to sympathise in the work of the prisoner in his dungeon. The solitary ray of sunshine that fell upon his life was the love of Violet. He was himself confined, imprisoned by the iron bars and the strong walls of poverty, and the tools he had at hand for his labour of love were scanty and rude. How could he in that contracted sphere, without travel, without change of scene and conversation with other men, ever hope to find materials for works with which to please the world, and obtain for himself fame and position? He understood now the deep meaning of the words put in Ulysses' mouth—"I am a part of all that I have met." They applied with tenfold force to the artistic, and to the literary career. It was only by extended experience, by contact with the wide, wide world, that he could hope to comprehend what it wanted. Yet it sometimes happened that even the prisoner in his cell, by sheer self-concentration, and with the aid of the rude tools and material within his reach, produced a work which could not be surpassed. The poor prisoner of the picture reminded him constantly of this. He tried. He thought and thought, till at last, in the quiet and solitude of his lonely room, an idea did occur to him—not a very great or remarkable idea either, but still one which, he felt, if properly carried out, might produce substantial results.

Evening after evening, upon leaving the office, he laboured at his new conception, illustrating his book with his own pencil, spending hour after hour upon it far into the night. So absorbed was he upon it, that he almost neglected Violet's letters—almost, he could not quite—but his notes were so short and so unlike his usual style, that she, with her knowledge of his character, saw at once what he was doing, and kept begging him not to overwork himself.

"Circumstances over which we have no control." There are other circumstances still more powerful—i.e., those circumstances which we never even think of controlling, which happen so quietly and whose true significance is so little apparent at the time, that we pass them by without a thought.

It happened that Mr. Broughton was engaged in a cause which necessitated extracts to be made from a file of old newspapers. Being overworked himself, and his staff also in full employment, he asked Aymer to do this, and to do it especially well and carefully. Aymer began the work, and at first found it dry enough, but as he got deeper into it, the strange contrast presented by this contemporary chronicle with the present day gradually forced itself upon him, and he ceased to cast aside the papers so soon as the particular extract required was made.

Presently the idea occurred to him of writing an article for the London papers, founded upon the curiosities of these old sheets of news. With this view, after he had finished the work he was set to do, he got into the habit of carrying two or three of the papers home, and re-reading and studying them, and making notes by his own fireside. The file was really interesting. It began in the year 1710. The Barnham Chronicle was one of those extremely old papers published in county towns, which live on from year to year without an effort, because they meet with no opposition. The circle of its readers, in all probability, at that date—more than a century and a half after its establishment—was scarcely larger than in the first year of publication. It had been taken and read by whole generations. The son found it taken by his father, and when he succeeded to the farm, to the mill, or to the shop, continued the old subscription.

Looked at in the light of the present day, when intelligence is flashed from end to end of the kingdom in a few hours, the Barnham Chronicle was all but ridiculous. Its news was a week old or more, stale and unprofitable. It did not even advance so far as to have a London letter; but perhaps that was no great loss to its readers.

Yet the Barnham Chronicle was a "property" in more than one sense; it paid, as well it might, at fourpence per copy, and with the monopoly of auctioneer's and lawyer's advertisements in that district. And it could boast of a more than patriarchal age.

Reading slowly, paragraph by paragraph, through this enormous file, his note-book at his side, Aymer came upon one advertisement, simply worded, and with no meretricious advantage given to it by large type or other printer's resource, yet which he read with a special interest. It contained the name of Waldron, of The Place, Bury Wick; and that name was sufficient to attract him. It ran thus:—

"Notice of Change of Name.—I, Arthur Sibbold, tea-dealer, of the City of London, in the county of Middlesex, do hereby give notice, that it is my intention to apply for permission to add to my present baptismal names the name of Waldron, upon the occasion of my approaching marriage with Miss Annica Waldron, of The Place, Bury Wick, co. B—, etc, etc. And that I shall be henceforward known, called, and designated by the name of Arthur Sibbold Waldron in all deeds, writings, etc, etc."

To us who are acquainted with the history of the city of Stirmingham, this entry has a wide significance; to Aymer it had none beyond the mere fact of the mention of Waldron. He copied it into his

135

note-book with a mental resolve to show it to Violet, and thought no more of it. An event that happened about this time made him forget all about what appeared to him a trivial matter. This was the trial of Jenkins, the gardener, for the murder of Jason Waldron. Mr. Broughton, who was engaged for the defence, to instruct counsel, naturally made much use of Aymer's local knowledge and perfect acquaintance with the details of that terrible day, and was thereby furnished with fresh and overwhelming arguments.

Aymer worked with a will, for he knew that Violet was much concerned and extremely anxious as to the result, and he watched the proceedings on the fateful day with intense interest. It is needless to recapitulate the details of the case, which have been already given. The result was an acquittal. The Judge summed up in favour of the prisoner, observing that it was monstrous if a man must be condemned to the last penalty of the law, because it so chanced that a tool belonging to him had been snatched up as the readiest instrument for a murderous attack. To his experience the murder did not appear at all in the light of an ordinary crime. In the first place, there was an apparent absence of motive. So far as was known, Waldron had no enemies and no quarrel with any man. Evidently it was not committed with the intention of theft, as not a single article had been missed. It appeared to him like the unaccountable impulse of an unreasoning being; in plain words, like the act of a lunatic with homicidal tendencies. The jury unanimously acquitted the prisoner, and Aymer hastened to send the news to Violet. He could not post with it himself, as Mr. Broughton had other cases to attend to.

Poor Jenkins was free—and lost. The shock had stunned him, and he was too old and too much weakened by disease to ever recover from it. He could not face his native village, the place where his family, though humble, had for generations borne a good character. He had an almost childish dread of meeting any one from Bury Wick or World's End, and even avoided Aymer, who sought him in the crowd.

How truly was it said that "service is no inheritance!" After two generations of faithful service, these poor people were practically exiled from home and friends, and this without fault of their own. Violet would have gladly done what she could for the aged couple. They might have, at all events, lived at The Place and taken care of the old house, but she and Aymer lost sight of them entirely.

All that was known was that a few weeks after the acquittal, a waggon came and fetched away their goods from the cottage, and Jenkins was heard of no more—for the time. He had, in fact, found work, and buried himself, as he hoped, for ever out of sight. There was a certain natural pride in him, and it had been cruelly trampled upon. Suffer what he might, he would not ask for aid—not even from Violet. And he did suffer—he and his poor shattered wife. With not exactly a bad character, but the stigma of "murder" clinging to him, he wandered about seeking work, and nearly starved.

Even in Bury Wick, where he was so well-known, had he returned, he would have found a certain amount of reluctance to receive him into the old grooves. In distant villages where the dreadful tale of blood had penetrated, and where the people had had little or no opportunity of hearing the facts, there was still a strong prejudice against him; and it must be owned that from an outsider's point of view, it did look suspicious that he should have been alone near the house when the deed was committed. So it was that he found it hard to get employment, especially now the winter was come, and labour less in demand.

At length, worn-out and exhausted with hunger and wandering, he accepted the wages of a boy from Albert Herring, and a waggon was sent to fetch his goods.

Albert Herring had the reputation of being a hard master, and it was well deserved. Hard work, long hours, small pay, and that given grudgingly, and withheld on trivial pretences—these were the practices which gained for him the hatred of the labouring population. Yet with singular inconsistency they were always willing to work for him. This is a phenomenon commonly to be observed—the worst of masters can always command plenty of men.

With Jenkins it was a matter of necessity. If he could not get work he must starve or go into the union—dreaded almost as much as the prison. Albert kept him several days after his application—he would see about it—he was in no hurry. He laid much stress upon the gardener's age, though the other assured him that willingness would compensate for that Jenkins had been a gardener, not a labourer. It was doubtful if he would understand his duties if he was put on to cut a hedge.

"Oh, yes!" said the old man, eagerly; "I can use an axe or a bill-hook."

"Ay, ay," said Albert, brutally. "Thee can use a bill-hook, so I've heard say."

Jenkins bowed his head, and his lip quivered.

The upshot was that he was put on at nine shillings per week—one shilling to be deducted for rent of a small cottage.

Chapter Eleven

This trial of poor Jenkins took up Aymer's time, so that he had no leisure for his new book, which had to be laid aside; and when he was in hopes of returning to it, another incident again interrupted him. The work he had to do was very little after all; it was not the amount, but the character of it, that he disliked.

Yet, notwithstanding his hatred of the law, he could not help imbibing some small smattering which afterwards proved extremely serviceable. The change from World's End was also beneficial in another manner—it opened his eyes to much that he had never suspected. If anything, his inclination hitherto would have been to have taken most people pretty much at their word. This may sound childish to the young men of the period, who—in the habit of frequenting billiard saloons, horse-races, card parties, hotels, and all places where people congregate—naturally pick up a good deal of knowledge of the world sufficient to astonish their parents, at all events.

Aymer certainly was not a model young man. Without a doubt, if he had been placed where such amusements were easily accessible, he would have done much as others of his age did; but it so happened that living at World's End, entirely out of society, he had no such opportunities. After a month or so at Broughton's office his eyes began to open, and he saw that things are very different under the surface to what they appear outwardly. He became less ready to accept what people said, or did in the sense they wished others to see them, and commenced a habit of deducting a large percentage from the price they put upon themselves.

He had been three times to see Violet—staying only a few hours—and was agreeably surprised with the pleasant reception he received from Lady Lechester, who took an opportunity of informing him privately that she wished Violet to continue with her. Violet was well, but dull. She was no sentimental heroine to pine away at separation from Aymer; but it was only natural that she should miss the old associations. Particularly she begged Aymer not to overwork himself at night with his private labour.

Lady Lechester seconded this, saying that she had known a gentleman who, much of the same disposition as Aymer, had lost his wits through incessant application. He was a relation of hers, and was now confined in an asylum at Stirmingham. To save speculation, it will be as well to at once mention that this person was not Odo Lechester.

Aymer's reply was that he feared he should never complete his book, for something always seemed to happen to delay it, and now he should soon have to accompany Mr. Broughton to Stirmingham.

It was in this way. Mr. Broughton, before removing to Barnham, where he inherited the practice and most of the fortune of a deceased uncle, had lived in Stirmingham, working as the junior partner in a firm there. He was no longer a partner, but still continued on friendly relations with the firm; and having much confidence in his ability, they frequently sent for him in difficult cases.

138

Now this firm—Messrs Shaw, Shaw, and Simson—had one very good client, who had been to them almost equal to an estate, bringing in a yearly income, and paying cash without dispute. This client, or rather these clients, was one of those very building societies which had leased old Sternhold Baskette's incomplete houses for a term of years.

House property is, as every one knows, fruitful in causes of litigation—repairs, defaulting tenants, disputes, and what not; and, in addition, there is the task of collecting the rents, and a vast variety of smaller pickings. All these Shaw, Shaw, and Simson had enjoyed for fully half a century, till they had come to look upon them as their legitimate right, and as certain to descend into the hands of their successors. But as time went on, they began to get anxious, and to perceive that there was a great deal of truth in the ancient maxim, "This too shall pass away," for the term of the lease, long as it was, rapidly approached expiration.

Obviously, it was their interest to delay the delivering up of the property to the heir, John Marese Baskette, as long as possible; and they felt the stake to be so great, that they did not spare their own money in the effort to oust him from his just claim.

Messrs Shaw, Shaw, and Simson were all three old and experienced men—safe men, in every sense; but they hesitated to trust entirely to their own ingenuity in this complicated business. They had, in fact, entrusted it to Mr. Broughton, who was not only more energetic, but was full of resources which would never have occurred to such steady persons as the three partners.

So it happened that, as the fall of the year advanced, Broughton had his hands full of the building societies' business, and had engaged to proceed to Stirmingham as their legal representative, at the great family council of the claimants in the Sternhold Hall, which was to open in three or four days.

Another circumstance that brought Aymer into still closer contact with the great case, was the fact that this firm of Shaw, Shaw, and Simson had an American client, who was himself one of the claimants. His name was another variation upon the old stem.

Anthony Baskelette was tolerably well to do. He had a great business, and had large transactions with manufacturers in Stirmingham. These necessitated an agent there, and Shaw, Shaw, and Simson had for years looked after his affairs. He was one of the Original Swampers. He really could prove his direct descent from one of old Will Baskette's cousins, and held ample documentary evidence; and being moderately wealthy, thought he would have a trial at the monster estate at Stirmingham. He instructed Shaw, Shaw, and Simson to get up his claim in a legal form, and announced his intention of accompanying the body of the claimants to England in the steamer Lucca, which had been so generously chartered by Marese.

139

All the correspondence from him to Shaw and Company was sent on to Barnham; and in this way Aymer, who had much to do with Broughton's correspondence, began to have some idea of the magnitude of the interests at stake. Though constitutionally averse to the law, and hating its formalities, he could not help feeling some considerable excitement about this tremendous case, and perhaps showed more genuine alacrity in executing Broughton's instructions relating to it, than he had with other matters.

At all events, Broughton told him that he should want him to act as his clerk, or notary, during his approaching visit to Stirmingham. The lawyer had begun to feel a certain amount of trust and confidence in Aymer, who never failed to fulfil his orders, though obviously against the grain, and especially as Aymer's demeanour was quiet and gentlemanly. If he did venture to throw out a suggestion, it was in the most respectful and diffident manner.

In this way it happened that Aymer became well up in the latter part of the history of Stirmingham, especially in that section of the case which concerned the Baskettes, and in time it grew to be almost the leading thought in his mind. His letters to Violet were full of it. The history was so romantic—so extraordinary, and yet so true—that it took strong hold upon his imagination.

He looked forward with pleasure to his approaching visit to Stirmingham. Like all men with any pretence to brains, though he delighted in Nature and loved the country, there was a strong, almost irresistible, desire within him to mingle in the vast crowds of cities, to feel that indefinable "life" which animates the mass. A great city to such a man as Aymer was like a wonderful book—an Arabian Night's tale, an endless romance which would afford inexhaustible pleasure in the study of its characteristics.

Though it would involve at least a month's absence from Violet, he looked forward to the visit with impatience—not without a secret hope that he might in some unexpected manner find a chance of rising in the scale, and getting a little nearer to the object of his life.

He had a number of commissions to execute for Lady Lechester—particularly one. This was to search the old bookstalls and the curiosity shops, in out-of-the-way corners, for antique Bibles. Agnes had a weakness, if it may be so-called, for collecting old editions of the Bible, and possessed a large and extremely interesting library filled with them. One or two particularly rare copies had hitherto escaped her search, and if there was such a thing to be found in Stirmingham she felt sure that Aymer would be precisely the man to find it.

He had also a commission to purchase for her a few pictures, with which to decorate the walls of a new wing she was adding to The Towers. She had a curious dislike to the old family mansion, and yet wished to live in the neighbourhood from a sense of duty. She held it as a doctrine that the owners of large estates should pass a part of their time, at all events, at home—there were so many ways in which they could do good, not only by charity, but by encouraging local industries.

The new wing was being built to enable her to reside at home, and yet gratify the innate dislike to The Towers which she cherished. Aymer's artistic taste was so marked that she felt confident he would select her suitable pictures. There were plenty of old paintings in the galleries of The Towers which could have been spared for the new wing, but she preferred to be surrounded with fresh objects, even down to the very footstool.

The day for the assembling of the great family council came nearer and nearer, and the letters from Anthony Baskelette more frequent. The daily papers, which Aymer saw now and read with the closest attention, began to devote a space to notes upon the preparations, and some sent specials to Stirmingham in advance, who described the city in a series of sketches, which excited Aymer's curiosity to the highest pitch.

News came at last that the claimants were assembling at Imola; then the date of the sailing of the Lucca came and passed. They knew that she must sail upon that day, because her owners were under contract to deliver the bullion entrusted to them on a fixed date in London, where its approaching arrival had already had an appreciable effect upon the money-market. Seven hundred thousand pounds in coin, in gold bars and Mexican dollars, is a sum which cannot be transferred from one country to another at once, without causing some fluctuations upon the Exchange. The owners of the Lucca were under a bond by which they forfeited a heavy sum if the vessel did not start to time. Therefore there was no doubt that the Lucca had sailed, though no announcement had reached London of the event, for it happened that the Atlantic cables were out of order, and there were not then such a number of cables as at present. Still, no one doubted for an instant that she was upon the seas; and one well-known illustrated paper announced that a special artist of theirs was on board, who, the moment he landed, would present the public with sketches of the incidents of the voyage, portraits of the claimants, and other subjects of interest. It was also generally understood that the heir, in his yacht, had started from New York to accompany the steamer.

What was Aymer's surprise and regret, upon opening the paper on the second morning after, to see the following telegram, one of the cables having got into partial working order again:—

"New York, Tuesday Night.
"The Lucca sailed on Friday at noon, but without the claimants. She brings the specie announced."

Then there was an editorial note to the effect that several other words of the telegram could not be read, on account of the unsatisfactory state of the wires. The evening papers had further particulars:—

"The Lucca, and the yacht of John Marese Baskette, Esq, have passed Sandy Hook. All well. A snow-storm blocked the line from Imola to New York, and the claimants could not arrive in time. They follow per Saskatchewan."

Next day additional particulars came to hand. It appeared that the heir, Marese, had on the Wednesday gone to Imola, and received an ovation from the assembled claimants. He was to accompany them to New York on the Friday, and to follow the Lucca in his yacht. On Thursday night there came a heavy fall of snow—and a strong wind, which caused immense drifts. Notwithstanding these the special train, with Marese and one hundred and fifty claimants, started from Imola with a pilot-engine in front, the station-masters along the line having telegraphed that they would clear it in time. They did partially succeed in the attempt; but the storm came on again, the wires were blown down; and telegraphic communication for a part of the way interrupted.

In the thick snow the special crept along, with the pilot in front; but, despite of all their caution, the pilot-engine ran into a drift and stuck fast. The special came up, but there was no collision. To proceed was, however, impossible; every moment made it more so, and they began to fear lest the return to Imola should be also blocked up.

After much consultation it was decided to run back to Imola, and proceed by a more circuitous route. There was just a chance that, if this other route was clear of snow, they might get to New York in time. They put on steam and pushed as fast as possible, and the consequence was a narrow escape from a serious disaster. The wind, since they had passed, had blown down a large pine tree, which fell across the line. The engine of the special struck this tree, but being provided with cow-guards, was not thrown off the line. Some of the machinery was, however, damaged, and the special came to a standstill. After a long delay, consequent on the interruption of telegraphic communication, a second train was sent up, and the passengers re-embarked in it, and at last got back to Imola. It was now, however, too late to reach New York in time, especially as the longer route was equally encumbered with drifts of snow. The result was that the Lucca was obliged to start without them.

Chapter Twelve

The Saskatchewan was to start on the next Friday. The claimants had arrived at New York on the Sunday, after much trouble and a long journey, having to make an immense détour. The council could not now hold its first meeting on New Year's Day, but was expected to assemble on the 6th January (Twelfth Day).

For two days they were without intelligence at Barnham and Stirmingham, the cables being wrong again, but on the third Aymer was sent for to the private residence of Mr. Broughton at seven in the morning. The London dailies had not yet arrived, but he had received a private telegram from Shaw, Shaw, and Simson, with the most extraordinary news. The yacht of Mr. Marese Baskette had brought the steamship Lucca back to port a derelict, having found her helpless on the high seas, with every passenger and every one of the crew dead.

Presently the papers came and contained the same announcement, though they one and all expressed a strong doubt as to the accuracy of the news. By-and-by down came a second edition of the Telegraph, repeating the former telegram, with additional particulars. By night it was known as a fact over the length and breadth of the world, that the Lucca had been found lying like a log upon the waste of waters with a crew of corpses—a veritable ship of the Dead. The ghastly news was only too true. Excitement rose to the highest pitch; edition after edition of the papers sold out; men congregated in groups, discussing this new horror which had saddened civilisation. All were completely in the dark as to how it had happened, and in the eagerness for further insight the brief telegram announcing that the claimants had started on board the Saskatchewan was overlooked. There were plenty, however, who pointed out to each other the fortunate escape the claimants had had. If the snow had not fallen on that particular night; if the wires had not been broken by the falling posts; if the pine tree had fallen on one side instead of crossing the line, they would in all human probability have one and all shared the fate of those on board the Lucca.

Only one circumstance caused any abatement of the intense alarm which this fearful occurrence created. It was this: The greater portion of the space allotted for passenger accommodation on the Lucca had been taken by Marese for the claimants, and as it was not certain up to the last moment whether they would come or not, the ship started with less than a third of her full complement of passengers. There was not, therefore, such a death-roll as might have been; but, even as it was, it was extended enough.

No one could understand how it had happened; not the slightest explanation was given, and the public mind was exercised in speculating upon the cause of the disaster. The passage from America to England had long lost the character of a voyage. The height to which perfection had been carried in the great steamship lines, was such that it had become a mere ocean promenade. No one thought of danger; the perils of the deep had been so thoroughly overcome. In the midst of this security came a shattering blow, which dispelled the confidence slowly built up by such an expenditure of skill and money as had perhaps never been equalled in the history of the world. The mystery seemed impenetrable. If the vessel had disappeared like the City of Boston; if it had sunk, there would have been several explanations possible. But to be brought back into port perfect, uninjured, and yet a derelict, with a dead crew—it was inexplicable.

The Saskatchewan arrived on the 2nd January, and with her came the claimants—all but Marese—and these immediately proceeded to Stirmingham. It was hoped that she would have brought fuller particulars as to the fate of the Lucca; but having started on the very day that the Lucca returned to port, nothing more was known on board than the simple fact.

On the 4th, however, another steamer came into Liverpool, bringing the New York papers up to date, and the contents of these were at once published in London.

By the steamer came a letter from Anthony Baskelette. He had left the Saskatchewan on hearing of the Lucca's return, in great anxiety about some consignment he had made by her to his agent in Stirmingham. He had met the heir, and had been invited to accompany him to England on board his yacht, which would not reach Liverpool till the 9th. He was full of the Lucca catastrophe, and his long letter contained more particulars than four papers.

Aymer read it with the deepest interest. It ran:—

"You will of course attend the council on the 6th, both in the interest of the building society and of myself. I am delayed by the necessity of seeing after the consignment I had made on board the unfortunate Lucca, which consignment is too valuable to be left to agents. I am in the greatest anxiety, because it is uncertain yet in what light the rescue of the Lucca will be regarded.

"There can be no doubt that if the owner of the yacht—Mr. Marese Baskette—likes, he can put in a heavy claim for salvage. The question is—whether in his position as the ostensible heir, and as a gentleman, he will insist upon his right, or, at all events, moderate his demands?

"I have met and conversed with him, and I gather from him that personally he is averse to making any claim at all. He considers that his yacht simply performed a duly, and a duly that was imperative upon her captain. To take money from those unfortunate persons who had consigned goods, or bullion in the Lucca he thought would be contrary to every sentiment of honour and humanity.

"But, unfortunately, he is not altogether a free agent. It appears that at the time when the salvage of the Lucca was effected, there was on board the yacht a certain Mr. Theodore Marese—a cousin of Mr. Baskette's, who is only in moderate circumstances, and naturally looks upon the event as a windfall which may never occur again—as I hope and pray it never will.

"Mr. Theodore Marese, it seems, performed some personal service in rescuing the Lucca, and was considered to have run considerable risk to his life.

"A certain sum will have no doubt to be paid to Mr. Theodore, and I cannot blame him if he insists upon his right. He was practically the master of the yacht at the time, and it seems was on his way—with Mr. Baskette's permission—to London, to attend to some very urgent business there, which the catastrophe of the Lucca has delayed and greatly injured, causing him pecuniary loss.

"Then there is the captain of the yacht, and the crew. It is a fine vessel—some 300 tons or more, I should think—a screw steamer, and very fast. She carries a rather numerous crew, and all these are ravenous for plunder, and it is hard to see how these claims are to be avoided. Still further, it seems that Mr. Baskette himself is not altogether a free agent. He freely admitted to me that he was not without his debts—as is probable enough to a man of fashion, with a certain position to maintain.

"These creditors may take advantage of the Lucca business to push him, and say that he must take the salvage in order to meet their demands. Of this he is greatly afraid.

"Baskette is a most pleasant man, easy to converse with, very open and straightforward—quite a different person to what I should have expected. He has been particularly agreeable to me, promising his best efforts to curtail my loss, and has given me a cabin in his now famous yacht, the Gloire de Dijon.

"I cannot drive the subject of the salvage from my mind. The saloons, bars, hotels—everywhere people talk of nothing else. It has quite eclipsed the tragedy, as well it might, from the magnitude of the sums involved.

"First of all, there is the vessel herself—found upon the high seas, a derelict, without a hand at the wheel or at the engines. She is a splendid steamer, fully 3000 tons, and estimated at half a million of dollars, or, say, 100,000 pounds. The cargo she carried was immensely valuable—the bullion you know about: it was 718,000 pounds in exact figures—but the cargo must be worth at least another 75,000 pounds.

"Then there is a very large amount of personal property, for half the claimants who were to go by her had forwarded their luggage previously; and there are the effects of the poor creatures who died. But these last, Mr. Baskette declares, shall under no circumstances be touched. Happen what may, they are to be returned to the owners of their heirs undiminished.

145

"Putting it all at the lowest estimate, the value of the vessel, the bullion, and cargo cannot be less than 893,000 pounds; and the salvage will equal a gigantic fortune.

"So far I have dealt only with the salvage question. I will now proceed to give you a more detailed account than you will be able to get from the papers, of the terrible fate which overtook the Lucca. These I have learnt from Mr. Baskette and from Mr. Theodore Marese, who was on the yacht.

"The reporters are, of course, incessant in their inquiries, but there is much that has escaped them, as a certain amount of reticence must of necessity be observed. These gentlemen have, however, made no reserve to me—I must beg of you not to publish this letter, or any part of it, lest there should appear to be a breach of confidence.

"It appears that the Lucca started at noon on the Friday, as per bond, with a full complement of crew, but a short list of passengers. About two hours after she had left, the Gloire de Dijon put out to sea. Mr. Baskette was at that time still at Imola, unable to get to New York. He and his cousin, Mr. T. Marese, were to have gone together in the yacht to London, where Mr. Theodore's business was very pressing.

"When Mr. Baskette found himself unable to reach New York, he telegraphed to Mr. Theodore telling him to take the yacht and go on to London as had been previously arranged, thereby showing the same character of consideration for others which he has since exhibited to me.

"Mr. Theodore put to sea in the Gloire de Dijon, and says that next morning they overtook the Lucca, or nearly so, the yacht being extremely swift. It occurred to him that, after all, as the Atlantic is still the Atlantic, notwithstanding steam, and there are such things as breaking machinery, it would be well to keep in company with a powerful vessel like the Lucca as far as the coast of Ireland.

"They did so, and even once spoke the steamship, which replied, 'All well.' All that day the two ships were not half a mile apart, and the night being moonlit, the Gloire de Dijon followed close in the other's wake till about four in the morning, when, as often happens at thick fog came on. Afraid of collision, the captain of the yacht now slackened speed to about six knots, and kept a course a little to the starboard of the steamer ahead.

"The fog continued very thick till past noon, and then suddenly lifted, and they saw seven or eight sail in sight, one of which was the Lucca on their port bow, and about four miles off. She was running, as usual, at a good pace, and the sea being quiet, was making all thirteen knots. The Gloire de Dijon increased speed, and drew up to within a mile and a half by three in the afternoon. The Lucca then bore due east, and they were in her wake. The wind was west, with a little southerly, and just ahead of the Lucca was a large square-rigged ship, with all sail set, but making very little way on account of the trifling breeze.

"An extraordinary thing now happened. The Lucca was observed by the captain of the yacht to be making straight for the sailing ship ahead, and had now got so close that a collision appeared inevitable. He called to Mr. Theodore, who came up from below. The Lucca ran dead at the sailing ship, though she was making thirteen knots to the other's four, and the slightest turn of her wheel would have carried her free. On account of the direction of the wind, the ship was sailing almost right before it, and the steamer appeared to be aiming at her stern.

"On the yacht they could see the crew of the sailing ship making frantic signs over the quarter to the steamer, but not the slightest notice was taken. The captain of the sailing ship had relied upon the steamer giving way, as is usual, and had allowed her to come so close that, it seems, he lost his head. Seeing this, the mate sang out to put the helm a-starboard, and run straight before the wind. This was done, and only just in time, for the steamer actually grazed her quarter, and carried away their boom. Knowing that the captain of the Lucca was an old sailor, and a steady, experienced man, they were astonished at this behaviour, especially as, without staying to inquire what damage had been done, she kept on her course at still greater speed.

"The captain of the yacht now put on speed, being desirous of speaking the steamer; but after an hour or two it was evident that the Lucca was drawing ahead, and had increased her lead by at least a mile. They could not understand this, as the yacht was notoriously faster, and it became evident that the engineer of the Lucca must have got his safety-valve screwed-down.

"Night, as every one knows, falls rapidly at this time of the year, and the darkness was increased by the fog, which now came on again. During the evening all their conversation was upon the Lucca. Surely she would not keep up her speed in such a fog as this? The yacht had slackened, and was doing, as before, about six knots.

"The night wore on, till about two o'clock, when the wind freshened, and blew half a gale. At four the fog cleared, and the watch reported that the Lucca was on their starboard quarter, a mile astern, with her engines stopped. Mr. Theodore was called, and came on deck. There lay the steamer in the trough of the sea, rolling, heaving—so much so that they wondered her sticks did not go. No smoke issued from her funnel, and the steam-pipe gave no sign. The usual flag was flying, but no signal was shown in answer to the Gloire de Dijon's inquiry. There was no sail on her.

"It was at once evident that something was wrong, and Mr. Theodore ordered the yacht to be put about. They tried the signals, but, as I said, no notice was taken. On approaching the Lucca, which had to be done with some caution, as she slewed about in a helpless manner, and was drifting before the sea, an extraordinary spectacle presented itself. As she rolled, her deck came partly into view, and they saw, with what feelings may be imagined, several men lying on the deck, and thrown now this way, now that, as the rollers went under her, evidently either dead or unconscious.

"Filled with alarm and excitement, they attempted to board the vessel, but found it impossible. The waves made all but a clean breach over her. She staggered like a drunken man, and swung now this way, now that. Some of the standing rigging had given way, and they could hear the masts creak. They were afraid to get under her lee in case they should fall.

"At length the captain of the yacht thought of a plan. He got a hawser ready with a loop, and watching his opportunity, ran the yacht close to her bow, and with his own hand, at great risk, hurled the rope, and by good luck the loop caught in the fluke of one of her anchors. They paid the hawser out over the yacht's stern, and gradually got her in tow. It strained fearfully; but as soon as they had got the Lucca before the wind, they had her right enough, though there was even then some danger of being pooped. The sea was high, but not so high that the jolly-boat could live, and they manned her and boarded the Lucca.

"The sailors were eager enough to get on board, but so soon as they were on deck the superstition of the sea seemed to seize them, and not one would venture from the gangway; for towards the stern there lay the bodies that they had seen, still and motionless, and evidently dead.

"A terrible mystery hung over the ship—terrible, indeed!"

Chapter Thirteen

"Not one of the seamen could be got to go below, or to approach the corpses on the deck; and even the mate, who did touch these last, had a reluctance to descend. It was, however, necessary to get another hawser attached to the Lucca, and this occupied some little time; and by then the men became more accustomed to the ship, and at last, led by the mate, they went down.

"At the foot of the staircase a terrible sight met their gaze. A heap of people—seamen, passengers, all classes—lay huddled up together—dead. They were piled one over the other in ghastly profusion, having been probably flung about by the rolling of the ship when she got broadside on. So great was the heap that they could not advance without either stepping upon the bodies, or removing them; and in this emergency they signalled to the yacht, which sent another boat, and in it came Mr. Theodore.

148

"He at once gave orders to make a passage and to explore the steamer thoroughly, which was done, and done speedily, for the sailors, having now conquered their superstitious fears, worked with a will. From that heap thirty-five bodies were carried up on deck, and laid upon one side in an awful row. They exhibited no traces of violence whatever. Their faces were quite calm; though one or two had the eyeballs staring from the head, as if they had struggled to escape suffocation.

"A search through the steamer revealed a cargo of the dead. Passengers lay at the doors of their berths, some half-dressed; and five or six were discovered in their berths, having evidently died while asleep. The engineer lay on the floor of the engine-room with three assistants—stiff, and with features grimly distorted. They had apparently suffered more than the rest.

"The crew were found in various places. The captain lay near the engine-room, as if he had been on his way to consult with the engineer when death overtook him. Bodies were found all over the ship, and exclamations constantly arose as the men discovered fresh corpses. The air between decks was close and confined, and there was a fetid odour which they supposed to arise from the bodies, and which forced them sometimes to run on deck to breathe. This odour caused many of the sailors to vomit, and one or two were really ill for a time.

"It appeared that the whole ship's crew and all the passengers had perished; but one of the sailors searching about found a man in the wheelhouse on deck, who on being lifted up showed some slight trace of life. The sailors crowded round, and the excitement was intense. Mr. Theodore, who is a physician by profession, lent the aid of his skill, and after a while the man began to come round, though unable to speak.

"The captain of the yacht had now come on board, and a consultation was held, at which it was decided to run back to New York. But as the wind was strong and the sea high, and the hawsers strained a good deal, it was arranged to put a part of the crew of the yacht on board the Lucca, to get up steam in her boilers, and shape a course for the States. To this the crew of the yacht strongly objected—they came aft in a body and respectfully begged not to be asked to stay on board the Lucca. They dreaded a similar fate to that which befel the crew and passengers of that unfortunate steamer.

"The end of it was that Mr. Theodore ordered the hawsers to be kept attached, and the yacht was to partly tow the steamer and she was to partly steam ahead herself—the steam was to be got up, and the engines driven at half speed. This would ease the hawsers and the yacht, and at the same time the crew on board the Lucca would be in communication with the yacht, and able to convey their wishes at once.

"All agreed to this. Steam was easily got up, and the Lucca's boilers and her engines were soon working, for the machinery was found to be in perfect order. By the time that this arrangement was

149

perfected, and the ships were, got well under weigh, the short day was nearly over, and with the night came anew the superstitions of the sailors. They murmured, and demurred to working a ship with a whole cargo of dead bodies. They would not move even across the deck alone, and as to going below it required them at once to face the mystery.

"After an hour or so a clamour arose to pitch the dead overboard. What on earth was the use of keeping them? An abominable stench came up from between decks, and many of them could barely stand it. Mr. Theodore and the captain begged them to be calm, but it was in vain. They rose en masse, and in a short space of time every one of these dead bodies had been heaved overboard.

"The gale had moderated, and the splash of each corpse as it fell into the water could be distinctly heard on board the yacht ahead. Such conduct cannot be too much deplored, and there was a talk of prosecuting the men for mutiny; but, on the other hand, there appears to be some excuse in the extraordinary and unprecedented horrors of the situation.

"Mr. Theodore remained on board the Lucca, doing all that science and patience could do for the sole survivor, who proved to be the third officer. Towards sunrise he rallied considerably, but Mr. Theodore never had any hopes, and advised the captain to take a note of his depositions, which was done.

"His name, he said, was William Burrows, of Maine. He could only speak a few sentences at a time, and that very faintly, but the substance of it was that all went well with the Lucca up till early that morning, when first the fog came on. Very soon after the mist settled down, and speed was reduced, there was a commotion below, and a report spread through the ship that three men were dying. In ten minutes half a dozen more were taken in this manner. They complained merely of inability to breathe, and of a deadly weakness, and prayed to be taken on deck. This was done; but then ten or twelve more were affected, and those who went below to assist them up on deck fell victims at once to the same strange disorder. Every one throughout the ship complained of a faint, sickly odour, and no sooner was this inhaled than a deadly lethargy seized upon them, and increased till they fell down and died. He happened to be on deck in the wheelhouse at the time, and saw half a dozen sailors and three of the passengers brought up, but remembered no more, for the sickly smell invaded the deck. He heard a singing in his ears, and the blood seemed to press heavily, as if driven upwards against the roof of his skull. He remembered no more for some hours. Then he, as it were, awoke, and got up on his legs, but again felt the same lethargy, and fell. When the disorder first attacked the ship's company, the captain talked of stopping the steamer and signalling for assistance; but it appeared to be useless, for the fog was so thick that any flag, or rocket, or light would have been unnoticed at half a cable's distance. Preparations were made to fire a gun, and the steam blast was ordered, but the engineer was dead, and no one would go below. The captain then descended to go to the engine-room, and was seen no more. Meantime the steamer continued her way. When he got on his legs in the wheelhouse, it was just after the bow of the Lucca had carried away the boom of an unknown sailing ship, and he could feel that she was then going at a tremendous speed. The fog had cleared, and if he had had strength enough he could have made signals, but the deadly sleep came over him again, and he was unconscious till picked up by the crew of the Gloire de Dijon.

"This was all he could tell, and it threw no light upon the cause of the disaster. After he had signed this in a shaky hand—I have seen the original document—he sank rapidly, and, despite of every remedy and stimulant, died before noon. His body was the only one brought into port, and it was interred yesterday in the presence of a vast assembly. A post-mortem examination failed to detect the slightest trace of poison or indication of disease; and all those who assisted in removing the dead bodies on board the Lucca, declare that they presented no known symptoms of any epidemic—for the prevailing belief in New York at first was that some epidemic had broken out—a kind of plague, which destroyed its victims almost as soon as attacked. But for this there seems no foundation whatever. None of the sailors of the yacht caught the epidemic. One or two were unwell for a day or so, but are now well and hearty.

"I think Mr. Theodore's suggestion the best that has been made—and it gradually gains ground with educated men, though the mass cling to the fanciful notion of foul play in some unheard-of way—Mr. Theodore thinks that it was caused by the generation of coal-damp, or some similar and fatal gas, in the coal-bunkers of the Lucca; and everything seems to favour this supposition. It is well-known that in cold weather—especially in cold weather accompanied by fog—coal-damp in mines is especially active and fatal. Most of the great explosions which have destroyed hundreds at once have occurred in such a state of the atmosphere.

"Now the fog which came on that fatal morning was peculiarly thick and heavy, and it so happens that the coal in the Lucca's bunkers came from a colliery where, only a fortnight ago, there was an explosion. The vapour, or gas, or whatever it was that was thus generated, was not the true coal-damp, or it would have been ignited by the furnaces of the boilers, or at the cook's fires; but in all probability it was something very near akin to it. All the symptoms described by poor Burrows, are those of blood-poisoning combined with suffocation, and such would be the effects of a gas or vapour arising from coal. Fatal effects arising from damp coal in close bunkers are on record; but this is the worst ever heard of.

"It would seem that after the engineer and the crew fell into their

151

fatal slumbers, the steam in the boilers must have reached almost a bursting pressure—the boilers being untended—and the engineer, in falling, had opened the valve to the full, which accounts for the extraordinary speed of the Lucca when pursued by the yacht. Being a very long vessel and sharp in the bows, and going at a very high speed, she would naturally keep nearly a direct course, as there was little wind or sea to interfere with her rudder. So soon as the fires burned out the engines stopped, and the sea rising, she became entirely at the mercy of the waves.

"When Burrows fell a victim he saw nine or ten men on deck lying prone in a fatal sleep—when the Gloire de Dijon sent a boat's crew on board there were but three bodies on deck; the rest had rolled, or been washed, overboard.

"These are the principal particulars of this unprecedented catastrophe. This is a long letter, but I am sure that you will be eager for news upon the subject, and, to tell the truth, I cannot get it out of my mind, and it relieves me to write it down.

"What a narrow escape we have all had. And especially me, for I came on to New York from Imola before the rest started, and got clear through without any snow. When it was found that they could not reach New York in time, I was in doubt whether to go by the Lucca, or remain and accompany the main body in the Saskatchewan. Accident decided. I met an old friend whom I had not seen for years, and resolved to take advantage of the delay, and spend a day or two with him. So I escaped.

"But had it not been for the snow-storm, which caused so much cursing at the time, we should one and all have perished miserably. The impression made upon us was so deep that just before the Saskatchewan started the whole body of the claimants attended a special service at a church here, when thanksgivings were offered for the escape they had had, and prayers offered up for future safety.

"I look forward with much pleasure to my voyage in the Gloire de Dijon yacht, at Mr. Baskette's invitation. A finer, more gentlemanly man does not exist; and I am greatly impressed with the learning of Mr. Theodore."

Aymer was much struck with the contents of this letter of Anthony Baskelette's. The whole tragedy seemed to pass before his mind; his vivid imagination called up a picture of the Lucca, steaming as fast as bursting pressure could drive her with a crew of corpses across the winter sea. He made an extract from it, and sent it to Violet. Next day they were en route for Stirmingham.

At the same moment the designer of this horrible event was steaming across the Atlantic in his splendid yacht, gulling weak-minded, simple Baskelette with highest notions of honour, and what not. When Marese found that the snow had blocked the line and prevented access to New York, his rage and disappointment knew no bounds; but he was sufficiently master of himself to think and decide upon the course to be pursued.

Although that part of the diabolical scheme which aimed at the wholesale destruction of the claimants had failed, all the other sections of it were in train to succeed. The bullion was shipped, the cargo a rich one, the steamer herself valuable—no better prize could ever fall to him. Therefore he telegraphed to Theodore in cypher to proceed as had been arranged.

The infernal machine, concealed in the simple aspect of an ordinary strong deal-box, was sent on board the Lucca, and everything happened just as Theodore had foreseen. If the conspirators were somewhat disturbed in their calculations by the snow-storm, on the other hand their designs were assisted by the heavy fog which had occurred at sea. Undoubtedly this fog rendered the poisonous gas escaping from the case still more effective, as it would prevent it dispersing so rapidly, and at the same time it hid any signals the Lucca might have made.

Nothing more fortunate for the conspirators than this fog could have happened, for its service did not end here—it furnished a plausible explanation of what would have otherwise been inexplicable.

Theodore easily contrived the removal of the fatal case, now empty, on board the Gloire de Dijon after the Lucca had returned to port. The case had been consigned to Liverpool, which was the port the Lucca was bound for, and the excuse for sending it by the Lucca was all cut and dried—i.e., that the Gloire de Dijon was for London.

Nothing was more natural than that, after this narrow escape, it should be wished to transfer the case to the Gloire de Dijon. This was done; and while at sea Theodore quietly removed his machine and pitched it into the water at night, and it sank in the abyss, being lined with iron inside.

The question of salvage bid fair to occupy the Courts in New York for some considerable time, and to be a boon to the lawyers; but the two conspirators were far too keen to let their prize slip from them in that way. They managed to have the matter referred to arbitration, and the final result was that 400,000 pounds was awarded. This amount they at once transferred to London, and with it plunged at once into fresh schemes.

Chapter Fourteen

The great city whose ownership was at stake, knew that the eagles were gathered to the living carcase, and yet did not feel their presence. What are one hundred and fifty people in a population of half a million? They are lost, unless they march in order and attract attention by blocking up the streets. Disband a regiment of the Line in Saint Paul's Churchyard at London, and in ten minutes it would disappear, and no one would notice any unusual prevalence of red coats on the pavements.

The newspaper people were woefully disappointed, for the Press were not admitted. They revenged themselves with caricature portraits of the claimants, and grotesque sketches of their manners and conduct. Although the Press were excluded; there were several present who could write shorthand, and amongst these was a clerk from the office of Shaw, Shaw, and Simson, whose notes I have had the opportunity of consulting.

The Sternhold Hall, in which the council was held, was built, as has been stated, upon a spot once the very centre of the Swamp, now surrounded with noble streets of mansions and club-houses, theatres, picture-galleries—the social centre of Stirmingham. The front—you can buy a photograph of it for a shilling—is of the Ionic order of architecture—that is, the modern mock Ionic—i.e., the basement is supported by columns of that order, and above these the façade consists of windows in the Gothic style, which are, after all, dumb windows only. The guide-books call it magnificent; it is really simply incongruous.

The whole of the first two days was spent by the one hundred and fifty claimants in wrangling as to who should take the chair, how the business should be conducted, who should be admitted and who should not. All the minor differences suppressed while on the voyage broke out afresh, the moment the eagles had scented the carcase. Two days' glimpse at the wealth of Stirmingham, was sufficient to upset all the artificial calm and friendship, which had been introduced by the generous offers of Marese Baskette. One gentleman proposed that a certain section of claimants should be wholly excluded from the hall. This caused a hubbub, and if the incident had happened in the States revolvers might have been used. The Original Swampers declared that they would not sit under a chairman drawn from any other body but themselves. The outer circle of Baskettes considered that the conceit of the Swampers was something unbearable, and declined to support them in any way. The Illegitimate Swampers alone supported the Originals, in the hope of getting up by clinging to their coat-tails. The Primitive Sibbolds were quite as determined to sit under no president

154

but their own, and, the ranks of the other Sibbolds were split up into twenty parties. The clamour of tongues, the excitement, the hubbub was astounding.

Aymer, as clerk to Mr. Broughton, had a first-rate view of the whole, for Shaw, Shaw, and Simson had provided for the comfort of their representative by purchasing for the time the right to use the stage entrance of the room. Their offices were for the nonce established in the green-room. Their clients mounted upon the platform or stage, and passed behind the curtain to private consultation. This astute management upset the other seven companies, whose representatives had to locate themselves as best they might in the midst of a stormy sea of contending people. From the rear of the stage, just where the stage-manager was accustomed to look out upon the audience and watch the effect upon them of the play, Aymer had a good view of the crowd below, and beheld men in every shade of cloth, with rolls of paper, yellow deeds, or old books and quill pens in their hands, gesticulating and chattering like the starlings at World's End.

For two whole days the storm continued, till at last Mr. Broughton suggested that the debate should be conducted in sections; each party to have its own president, secretary, committee, and reporter of progress; each to sit apart from the others by means of screens, and that there should be a central committee-room, to receive the reports and tabulate them in order. This scheme was adopted, and something like order began to prevail. Anthony Baskelette, Esq, who had now arrived per the Gloire de Dijon, was pretty unanimously voted to the presidentship of the central committee, or section, the members of which were composed of representatives from every party. Screens were provided at no little expense, and the great hall was portioned out into thirty or forty pens, not unlike the high pews used of old in village churches.

Aymer was intensely interested and amused, as he stood at his peep-hole on the stage, from which he could see into every one of these pens, or pews, and watch the eagerness of the disputes going on between the actors in each.

The first great object the sections had in view was to reduce their claims to something like shape and order; for this purpose each section was numbered from 1 to 37, and was to deliver to the central section, Number 38, a report or summary of the general principles and facts upon which the members of the section based their claim. This summary of claim, as it was called, was to be short, succinct, and clear; and to be supported by minute extracts of evidence, by the vouchers of the separate individuals, so to say, showing that the summary was correct.

These extracts of evidence attached to the summary were really not extracts, but full copies, and had to contain the dates, names, method of identification, and references to church registers, tombstones, family Bibles, and so forth.

Aymer was astounded at the magnitude of these volumes of evidence—for such, in fact, they were. He had an opportunity of just glancing at them, as they were laid upon the table of the central section one after another. The summaries were reasonable and tolerably well expressed. The minutes of evidence were something overwhelming. A section would send up in the course of a day—first, its summary and a pile of folios—seventy or eighty large lawyer's folios of evidence to be attached to it. On the morrow it would beg for permission to add to its evidence, and towards the afternoon up would come another huge bundle of closely-written manuscript.

This would go on for several days, till the central committee at last issued an order to receive no more evidence from section Number—.

Then section Number — would hold an indignation meeting and protest, till the central committee was obliged to receive additional bundles of so-called evidence. Half of this evidence was nothing better than personal recollection.

The method pursued in the sections was delightfully simple and gratifying to every member's vanity. He was supplied with pen and ink, and told to put down all he could recollect about his family. The result was that in each section there were five or six people—and in some more—all busily at work, writing autobiographies; and as everybody considered himself of quite as much consequence as his neighbour, the bulk of these autobiographies can easily be imagined.

If any one had taken the trouble to wade through these personal histories, he would have been highly gratified with the fertility of the United States in breeding truly benevolent, upright, and distinguished men!

Out of all that one hundred and fifty there was not one who did not merit the gratitude of his township at least, and some were fully worthy of the President's chair at the White House. Their labours for the good of others were most carefully recorded—the subscriptions they had made to local charities far away on the other side of the Atlantic, to schoolhouses, and chapels, town-halls, and what not.

"There," ran many a proud record,—"you will see my initials upon the corner-stone—'J.I.B.,' for 'Jonathan Ithuriel Baskette,' and the date (186-), which is in itself good evidence towards my case."

All this mass of rubbish had to be sifted by the central committee, to be docketed, indexed, arranged, and a general analysis made of it.

They worked for a while without a murmur, and suddenly collapsed. It was impossible to meet the flood of writing. Fancy one hundred and fifty people writing their autobiographies all at once, and each determined to do himself justice! Such a spectacle was never witnessed since the world began, and was worthy of the nineteenth century. The central committee flung up their hands in despair. A resource was presently found in the printing-press.

When once the idea was started, the cry spread to all corners of the hall, and rose in a volume of sound to be echoed from the roof. The Press! The Spirit evoked by Faust which he could not control, nor any who have followed him.

It was unanimously decided that everything should be printed—sectional summaries, minutes of evidence, central committees analysis, solicitors arguments, references and all. There was rejoicing in the printing offices at Stirmingham that day. Now the Stirmingham Daily Post reaped the reward of its long attack upon the family of the heir, upon Sternhold Baskette, and Marese, his son. The contract was offered to the Daily Post, the Daily Post accepted it, and set to work, but soon found it necessary to obtain the aid of other local printers.

Now a new source of delay and worry arose. The moment everybody knew they were going into print—why is it print sounds so much better than manuscript?—each and all wanted to revise and add to their histories. First, all the sections had to receive back their summaries and minutes of evidence, to be re-written, corrected, revised, and above all extended. The scribbling of pens recommenced with redoubled vigour, and now the printer's devils appeared upon the scene. The cost of printing the enormous mass of verbiage must have been something immense, but it was cheerfully submitted to—because each man looked forward to the pleasure of seeing himself in print.

Acres upon acres of proofs went in and out of the Sternhold Hall, and meantime Aymer grew impatient and weary of it. His time was much more occupied than at Barnham. He had to conduct all Broughton's correspondence, and when that was finished lend a hand in arranging the minutes of evidence for the committee, who had applied for assistance to the solicitors. He had only reckoned on a month at Stirmingham at the outside. Already a fortnight had elapsed, and there seemed no sign of the end.

His letters to Violet became tinged with a species of dull despair. All this scribbling was to him the very acme of misery, the very winter of discontent—meaningless, insufferable. There was no progress in it for him: he could not find a minute's spare time now to proceed with his private work. Not a step was gained nearer Violet.

When at last the scribbling was over; when the proofs had been read and re-read and corrected till the compositors went mad; then the speechifying had to begin. This to Aymer was even more wearisome than the other. For Mr. Broughton having discovered his literary talent, employed him to listen to the debate and write a daily précis of its progress, which it would be less trouble to him to read than the copious and interminable notes of the shorthand writer.

157

This order compelled Aymer to pay close attention to every speech from first to last; and as they one and all followed the American plan of writing out their speeches and reading them, most were of inordinate length. To suit the speakers a new arrangement of the hall had to be made. The screens were now removed, and the sections placed in a kind of semi-circle, with the central section in front. Those who desired to speak gave in their names, and were called upon by the president in regular rotation.

The first subject discussed was the method to be pursued. Some recommended that the whole body of claimants should combine and present their claims en masse. Others thought that this plan might sacrifice those who had good claims to those who had bad ones. Many were for forming a committee, chosen from the various sections, to remain in England and instruct the solicitors; others were for forming at once a committee of solicitors.

After four or five days of fierce discussion the subject was still unsettled, and a new one occupied its place. This was—how should the plunder be divided? Such a topic seemed to outsiders very much like reckoning the chickens before they were hatched. But not so to these enthusiastic gentlemen. They were certain of wresting the properly from the hands of the "Britishers," who had so long kept them out of their rights—the Stars and Stripes would yet float over the city of Stirmingham, and the President of the United States should be invited to a grand dinner in that very hall!

The division of the property caused more dissension than everything else taken together. One section—that of the Original Swampers—declared that it would have, nothing should prevent its having, the whole of the streets, etc, built on the site of the Swamp. The Sibbolds cared not a rap for the Swamp; they would have all the property which had grown upon the site of old Sibbold's farm at Wolfs Glow. The Illegitimates claimed pieces here and there, corresponding to the islands of the Swamp. Some one proposed that the meeting should be provided with maps of Stirmingham, and the idea was unanimously adopted.

Then came the day of the surveyors. One vast map was ordered—it had to be made in sections—and was estimated to cover, when extended, a mile in length by three hundred yards in breadth; and then it did not satisfy some of the claimants. Then followed a terrible wrangle over the maps. Everybody wanted to mark his possession upon it with red ink, and these red ink lines invariably interfered with one another. One gentleman proposed, with true American ingenuity, to have the map traced in squares—like the outlying territories and backwoods of America—and to assign to each section a square! But this was too equal a mode to satisfy the more grasping.

Finally, it was resolved that all the minutes of evidence should be gone through by the central committee, and that they should sketch out those portions of the city to which each section was entitled. This took some time. At the end of that time the great Sternhold Hall presented an extraordinary spectacle. The walls of the hall, from the ceiling to the floor, and all round, and the very ceiling itself, were papered with these sections of the map, each strongly marked with lines in red ink. Near the stage there was a vast library of books, reaching half-way to the ceiling; this was composed of the summaries, minutes of evidence, etc.

All round the room wandered the claimants in knots of two or three, examining their claims as marked upon the sections of the map. Many had opera-glasses to distinguish the claims which were "skyed;" some affected to lie down on their backs and examine the ceiling with telescopes; scores had their volume of evidence in their hands, and were trying to discover upon what principle the central committee had apportioned out the city.

Of course there was a general outcry of dissatisfaction—one section had too much, another too little, and some sections, it was contended, had no right to any. The meeting then resolved that each section should visit the spaces marked out for its claim, and should report to the central committee upon its value. Away went the sections, and there might have been seen five or six gentlemen in one street, and ten or twelve round the corner, with maps and pencils, talking eagerly, and curiously scanning the shops and houses—poking their noses into back courts and alleys—measuring the frontage of club-houses and theatres. The result was an uproar, for each section declared that the other had had a more valuable portion of the city given to it; and one utterly rejected its section, for it had got the Wolf's Glow district—the lowest den in Stirmingham!

After a long discussion, it was at last arranged that each section should retain, pro tem, its claim as marked out, and that token the property was realised, any excess of one section over the other should be equally divided. These people actually contemplated the possibility of putting the city up to auction! To such lengths will the desire of wealth drive the astutest of men, blinding their eyes to their own absurdity.

After these preliminary points were settled, the meeting at last resolved itself into a committee of the whole house, and proceeded to business. The first business was to verify the evidence. This necessitated visits to the churches, and public record office to make extracts, etc, and two days were set apart for that purpose. It was a rich harvest for the parish clerks of Stirmingham, and especially for the fortunate clerk at Wolf's Glow. After this the meeting, beginning to be alarmed at the enormous expense it had incurred, resolved on action, and with that object it decided to hold a secret session, and to exclude all persons not strictly claimants.

This relieved Aymer from his wearisome task of chronicling the proceedings; but he could not leave or get a day to visit Violet. As he left the hall he stopped a moment to look at the stock-in-trade of an itinerant bookseller, who had established his track in front of the building since the family congress began. His stock was principally genealogical, antiquarian, and topographical—mostly old rubbish, that no one would imagine to be worth a sixpence, and yet which, among a certain class, commands a good sale.

The title of a more modern-looking volume caught Aymer's eye. It was "A Fortune for a Shilling," and consisted of a list of unclaimed estates, next of kin, persons advertised for, etc. He weighed it in his hand—it tempted him; yet he despised himself for his weakness. But Violet? He should serve her best by saving his shilling. He put it down, and went his way.

Chapter Fifteen

Their mouths watered for the great city, yet it seemed no nearer to them than when three thousand miles away on the other side of the Atlantic. They talked loudly of their rights, but there was the little difficulty of possession, which is sometimes a trifle more than nine points of the law. I have conversed with unreasonable members of a certain Church, which claims to be universal, who considered that half England—half the vast domains owned by lords and ladies, by the two hundred and fifty proprietors of Great Britain—was really the property of the Church, if she had her rights.

There are those who consider that Algeria ought to belong to the Arabs, that Africa belongs to the blacks, and India to the Hindoos. Sat there comes this awkward item of possession. You have to buy the man in possession out, or else pitch him out; and the difficulty in this case was that there were so many in possession. Eight companies and a Corporation are not easily ejected.

The fact was, the grand family council was a farce, and fell through. Even as a demonstration it completely failed. The members of it might just as well have stayed at home, and sent a monster petition to the House of Lords, several hundred yards long (as per the usual custom now-a-days), and their progress would have been about as great.

The Stirmingham Daily News, which had published the life of Sternhold Baskette, and defended his legitimate line, poured bitter satire upon it, and held the whole business up to ridicule—as well it might. The News was now Conservative. The intense self-conceit of the Yankees—to imagine that they were going to quietly take possession of a great English city, and hoist the Stars and Stripes on Saint George's Cathedral at Stirmingham!

The American gentlemen fumed and fussed, and uttered threats of making the Stirmingham claim a feature in the next Presidential election—it should "leave the low sphere of personal contention, and enter the arena of political discussion;" so they said. It should be a new Alabama case; and if they could not have Stirmingham, they would have—the Dollars!

Meantime the dollars disappeared rather rapidly, and, after a month or six weeks of these endless wranglings in the Sternhold Hall, there began to be symptoms of an early break-up. First, three or four, then ten, then a dozen, crept off, and quietly sailed for New York, lighter in pocket, and looking rather foolish. The body, however, of the claimants could not break up in that ignominious manner. It was necessary for them to do something to mark the fact that they had been there, at all events.

The final result was that they appointed a committee of solicitors—one for each section that chose to be represented. Twenty-two sections did choose, and twenty-two solicitors formed the English committee who were to promote the claims of one hundred and fifty able-bodied Baskettes and Sibboldians, who represented about three times that number of women and children. Then they held a banquet in the Sternhold Hall, and invited the Mayor of Stirmingham, who, however, was very busy that evening, and "deeply regretted" his inability to be present. The council then broke up, and departed for New York.

Aymer was indeed glad; now he should be able to see Violet again, and resume his book so long laid aside. But no; there came a new surprise. A certain recalcitrant borough in the West returned unexpectedly a member of the wrong colour to Parliament, and the House was dissolved, and writs were issued for a general election. Three days afterwards an address appeared in the Stirmingham Daily News, announcing Marese Baskette as a candidate for that place in the Conservative interest. The heir had resolved to enter the House if possible, and his proclamation fell on Stirmingham, not like a thunderbolt, but like the very apple of discord dropped from heaven.

First, it upset poor Aymer's little plans and hopes. The companies were desperately alarmed, and not without reason; for if Marese got into Parliament he would, no doubt, very quickly become in himself a power, and would be supported by his party in his claim upon the building societies. It would be to the interest of his party that he should obtain his property—it would be so much substantial gain to them. Practically, Marese Baskette would have the important borough of Stirmingham in his pocket; therefore the party would be sure to do all they could to get his claim fully admitted. Imagine that party in power; fancy the chief at the head of Government!

161

Every one knows that justice and equity are immaculate in England, and that no strain is ever put upon them for political purposes, or to gratify political supporters. The fact is so well understood, so patent, that it is unnecessary to adduce any proof of it. But there is, nevertheless, a certain indefinite feeling that the complexion of the political party in power extends very widely, and penetrates into quarters supposed to be remote from its centre. Whichever happens to be uppermost—but let us not even think such treasonable things.

At all events the companies had a real dread—a heartfelt fear—lest Marese Baskette should get into Parliament, and so obtain political support to his claim. They had foreseen something of the kind; they had dreaded its happening any time ever since he came of age; but they had reckoned that his known poverty would keep him out, especially as there was a very popular landlord in the county, Sir Jasper Norton, who, with another prominent supporter of the Liberal Government, had hitherto proved invincible. It had hung over their heads for years; now it had fallen, and fallen, of all other times, just at the very moment when their leases were on the point of expiring. A more unfortunate moment for them could not have been chosen. With one consent they resolved to fight him tooth and nail. This was fatal to poor Aymer's hopes. For the company (Number 6) which employed Shaw, Shaw, and Simson could not possibly spare Mr. Broughton's energetic spirit; he must help them fight the coming man. Broughton, seeing good fees and some sport, resolved, to stay, and with him poor Aymer had to remain.

The whole city was in a ferment. Marese Baskette's name was upon every lip, and as the murmur swelled into a roar it grew into something very like a cheer for the heir. That cheer penetrated the thick walls of many a fashionable villa and mansion, and was listened to with ill-concealed anxiety. Many a portly gentleman, dressed in the tailor's best, with broad shirt-front, gold studs, and heavy ring, rubicund with good living, as he stood upon his hearth-rug, with his back to the fire, in the midst of his family circle, surrounded with luxury, grew thoughtful and absent as that dull distant roar reached his ears. Banker and speculator, city man, merchant, ironworker, coalowner, millowner, heard and trembled. For the first time they began to comprehend the meaning of the word Mob.

That word is well understood in America; twice it has been thoroughly spelt and learnt by heart in France. Will it ever be learnt in England? Outside those thick walls and strong shutters in the dingy street or dimly-lit suburban road, where the bitter winter wind drove the cold rain and sleet along, there roamed abroad a mighty monster roused from his den. They heard and trembled. Before that monster the safeguards of civilisation are as cobwebs. He may be scotched with Horse Guards and Snider rifles, beaten back into his caverns; but of what avail is that after the mischief is done? In sober earnest, the middle classes began to fear for the safety of Stirmingham. You see, the grey sewer-rats had undermined it from end to end!

It happened that the ironmasters and the coalowners, and some of the millowners, had held out long and successfully against a mighty strike: a strike that extended almost to a million of hearths and homes. They had won in the struggle, but the mind of the monster was bitter against them. They were Liberal—nearly all. Let them and their candidates keep a good look-out!

It happened also that the winter was hard and cold, work scarce, provisions dear; everything was wrong. It is at such times that, in exact opposition to all rules, the grey rat flourishes!

Finally, it happened that the party who had so strangely abdicated power just at the time when they seemed so firmly fixed, had committed a singularly, an exceptionally, unpopular act. They had robbed the poor man of his beer! They had curtailed his hours for drinking it, and to all appearance in an arbitrary way. Rumour said that they contemplated an alliance with the Cold Water Pump—that horror of horrors, the Temperance party. They had robbed the poor man of his beer! And the grey rat showed his teeth.

Marese Baskette issued his pronunciamento, and at once opened the campaign. Everybody read it, from the club-house to the grimy bar of the lowest public-house. The club-house smiled, and said, "Clever;" the pot-house cheered, and cried, "He's our man." He was their man. Even yet, at this distance of time, there lingered in the minds of the populace a distinct recollection of the great saturnalia which had been held in the days of old Sternhold Baskette, when their candidate was born.

History magnifies itself as time rolls on; the memory of that brief hour of unlimited riot had grown till it remained the one green spot in the life of the Stirmingham populace. This was the very man—this was the very infant whose advent, almost a generation ago, had been celebrated with rejoicings such as no king or queen in these degenerate days ever offered to the people.

When old Sternhold Baskette in the joy of his heart poured out wine in gallons, spirits in casks, and beer in rivers, he baptised his son Marese, the Child of the People. And it bore fruit at this great distance of time.

John Marese Baskette was, as we know, a clever man; he had a still more subtle man at his elbow. Between them they composed his address and his first oration. Be sure they did not forget the memory so dear to the people. Not one single thing was omitted which could tend to identify Marese Baskette with the populace. The combination of capital against them, the hard winter and price of provisions, all were skilfully turned to advantage; and, above all, the beer. When the publicans had read his address they one and all said, "He's our man."

163

Licensed victuallers, beer-house keepers, "off the premises" men, gin-palace, eating-house, restaurant, hotel—all joined hands and marched in chorus, praising the man who promised to turn on the beer.

> For he's a jolly good fellow,
> And so say all of us!

But Marese Baskette did not wholly rely upon the poorer classes: he gained the goodwill, or at least the neutrality, of two-thirds of the middle classes, by openly declaring that when he came into his property, as he grandly designated half the city, he should devote one-third of it to the relief of local taxation, to form a kind of common fund for sewers, gas, water, poor-rates, paving, etc. He went further—this he did not promulgate openly, but he caused it to be spread industriously abroad from house to house—and said that, when he inherited his rights, the house rents should be reduced from their present exorbitant figure.

Now it was notorious that the companies only waited to see whether they could tide over the year of expiration of their leases before they raised the rents. The arrow therefore went home. Baskette had hit the nail upon the head. The other party began to threaten petitions for bribery—contending that these promises were nothing short of it.

The Daily Post published a leader on "Glaring Corruption and Wholesale Venality." Baskette and Theodore smiled. What would be the use of unseating him if, as they clearly saw, the opposite party was gone to utter destruction?

Baskette met with a triumphant reception at his first meeting. Whenever he appeared in the streets he was cheered to the echo.

The building societies and the Corporation were desperately alarmed. Though so bitterly opposed to each other at ordinary times, a common fear gave them unity. They held a secret meeting—at least they thought it was secret, but such things are impossible in our time. The pen is everywhere—its sharp point penetrates through the thickest wall. They united, formed themselves into an association, voted funds—secret also—hired speakers and hired roughs.

It all leaked out. The Stirmingham Daily News—Baskette's paper—came out with a report and a leader, and held up the poor heir to the commiseration of the people. See what a combination against him!—anything to keep him out of his rights. Hired speakers to talk him down—hired roughs to knock him on the head. Vested interests arrayed against him—poor heir! How deeply to be pitied! How greatly to be sympathised with! The paper used stronger language than this, and hinted at "gangs of foul conspirators," but that was not gentlemanly.

The exposure was worth a thousand votes to Baskette. But

though exposed, the Corporation and the companies never ceased their efforts. Between them they comprised almost all of the rich employers of labour. They had one terrible engine—a fearful instrument of oppression and torture—invented in our modern days, in order that we may not get free and "become as gods." They put on the screw.

There is not a working man in England, from the hedger and ditcher, and the wretch who breaks the flints by the roadside, up to the best paid clerk or manager of a bank—not one single man who receives wages from another—who does not know the meaning of that word.

Let no one imagine that the "screw" is confined in its operation to the needy artisan or the labourer. It extends into all ranks of society, poisons every family circle, tortures every tenant and householder—all who in any way depend for comfort, luxury, or peace upon another person. There is but one rank who are free—the few who, whether for wages or as tenants, never have to look to others.

Society is divided into two sections—the first, infinitely numerous, and the second, infinitely few—i.e., the Screwed-down, and the Screw-drivers. Now, the Corporation and the companies were the screw-drivers, and they twisted the horrible engine up tight.

Perhaps they gave it one turn too many; at all events the mob set up a yell. They formed processions and marched about the streets with bundles of screws, strung like bunches of keys, at the end of poles. Squibs flew in all directions—too personal to be quoted here. Somebody wrote a parody on "John Brown's Knapsack"—representing old Sternhold Baskette as John Brown, and his soul as marching on. This, set to music, resounded in every corner.

It is sad, but it is true. Everything might still have gone off pretty quiet, had it not been for religion, or rather pseudo-religion. There were in the city vast numbers of workmen of the lowest class from Ireland, and when the watchwords "Orangemen" and "Papists" are mentioned, every one will understand. Fights occurred hourly—a grand battle-royal was imminent. The grey rats did all they could to foster the animosity, and got up sham quarrels to set fire to the excited passions of the mob. Their game was riot, in order that they might plunder. While the fools were fighting and the wise men trying to put them down, the grey rats meant to make off with all they could get.

Aymer, having by this time made for himself some little reputation for intelligence and quick observation, was sent out by the committee, of which Broughton was chairman, to watch the temper of the people; to penetrate into all the corners and out-of-the-way places; to hang on the skirts of the crowd and pick up their hopes and wishes, and to make reports from time to time as anything struck him. He was even to bring in the lampoons and squibs that were circulated, and, if possible, to spy out the secret doings of the other party—a commission which gave him liberty to roam. He wished to be gone, but this was better than the close office-work. He should see something of life; he should see man face to face. (In gilded salons and well-bred society it is only the profile one sees—the full face is averted.) He put on his roughest suit, took his note-book, and strolled out into the city.

The first thing he had to report was that an insinuation which had been spread abroad against Baskette was actually working in his favour. It had been thrown out that he was upon too familiar terms with a certain lady, singer and actress, the fame of whose wonderful beauty was sullied with suspicions of her frailty. With a certain section of the people, who prided themselves upon being "English to the backbone," this was resented as unfair. With a far larger portion it was at once believed, and, amid sly nods and winks, taken as another proof that Baskette was one of themselves.

Aymer wandered about the city; he saw its horrors, its crime. At such a period the sin, the wickedness and misery which commonly lurks in corners, came out and flaunted in the daylight. A great horror fell upon him—a horror of the drunkenness, the cursing, the immorality, the fierce brutishness. He shuddered. Not that he was himself pure, but he was sensitive and quick to understand, to see beneath the surface. He was of an age when the mind deals with broad generalities. If this was the state of one city only—then, poor England!

His imagination pictured a time when this monster might be uppermost. One night he ascended the tower of a great brewery and looked down upon the city, all flaring with gas. Up from the depth came the shouting, the hum of thousands, the tramp of the multitudes. He looked afar. The horizon was bright with blazing fires—the sky red with a crimson and yellow glow. Not a star, was visible, a dense cloud of smoke hid everything. The iron furnaces shot forth their glowing flames, the engines puffed and snorted. He thought of Violet and trembled: when the monster was let loose, what then?

He descended and wandered away he knew not exactly whither, but he found himself towards midnight mixed in a crowd around the police station. Jammed in amid, the throng he was shoved against the wall, but fortunately a lamp-post preserved him from the crush. However, he could not move. The gas-light fell upon the wall and lit up the proclamations of "V.R."—the advertisements of missing and lost, the descriptions of persons who were wanted, etc.

One sheet, half-defaced with the wind and rain and mud splashed against it, caught his eye—

"Escaped," so ran the fragment, "from... mingham Asylum, a lunatic of homicidal tendencies... Stabbed a warder... killed his wife by driving a nail into her head... Is at large. His description—Long grey hair, restless eye, peculiar ears, walks with a shambling gait, and has a melancholy expression of countenance. Plays fantastic airs upon a tin whistle, and is particularly fond of tinkering."

A new bill, "Two Hundred Pounds Reward," for the apprehension of a defaulting bank manager, blotted out the rest.

166

But Aymer had read enough. A sickening sensation seized him—this horrible being loose upon society, tinkering, playing upon a tin whistle, and driving nails into women's heads! In his ears sounded the din of tremendous shouts, "Baskette for ever!" and he saw a carriage go by from which the horses had been taken, and in which a man was standing upright, with his hat off, bowing. It was Marese Baskette returning from an evening meeting, and dragged in his carriage by the mob to his hotel.

Aymer caught a glance of his dark eye flashing with triumph, and it left an unpleasant impression upon him. But the shouts rose up to the thick cloud of smoke overhead—"Baskette for ever! Baskette for ever!"

"Oh! my love," wrote Aymer to Violet, "this is, indeed, an awful place. I begin to live in dread of my fellow-creatures. Not for worlds—no, not for worlds, would I be the owner of this city (as so many are striving to be), lest I should be held, partly at least, responsible hereafter for its miseries, its crimes, its drunkenness, its nameless, indefinable horrors."

These words, read by what afterwards happened, are remarkable. Aymer's last vision of Stirmingham was the same man drawn again in his carriage amid tenfold louder shouts than before, "Baskette for ever!" He headed the poll by over 1000 votes.

The grey rats were triumphant.

End of Volume Two

VOLUME THREE

Chapter One

Book Three

Results

After a life in which each day was spent in happy anticipation of the pleasures of the next, the calm, quiet existence at The Towers would have been dull and cheerless to Violet. But following so soon upon the death of Waldron, under such awful circumstances, the life with Lady Lechester seemed to her, for a while at least, like that in a haven of refuge where the storm without could not reach. And had Aymer been there, or near at hand, she would in a quiet way have been happy.

For Lady Lechester was singularly kind. She made no show of sympathy, she did not ask, as some pretentiously hospitable people do every morning, if she were comfortable and had all she wished. But Agnes possessed a rare and delicate tact, the power of perceiving what others felt, of anticipating their smallest fancies.

She accommodated herself and her habits to Violet, and there grew up between them a firm friendship, and more than that—a companionship. Agnes kept no secret from Violet. Violet had none to hide from her.

There was one topic only which Violet never of her own volition approached, but she was perfectly aware that something of the kind was going on. In an indefinable manner she had learnt that Agnes had a suitor. It came to her knowledge that he was extremely wealthy, but low born in comparison with her long descent. How Agnes looked upon him it was hard to say. She was fully five-and-thirty, and that is an age at which women begin to feel that now, if ever, is the time when they must choose a companion.

On the other hand it is an age when the glamour of early hope and youthful fancy, are hardly likely to gild the first figure that approaches with a beauty not really its own. It is an age when the mind can choose calmly and deliberately, in the true sense of the word. Violet had never seen this man, or heard his name, but she knew that there was correspondence between them, for she had seen the letters with a foreign postmark. She gathered that he was in America. After which Agnes whispered that he would shortly be home, and would visit her.

"He is very handsome," she said, for the first time speaking directly upon the subject. "He is a man who could not be passed in a crowd, even were it not for exceptional circumstances surrounding him. And yet. I do not know—I do not know."

Then she was silent again for several days, but presently approached the inevitable topic again.

Would it be possible for a woman to really banish that topic from her mind? Agnes could the more easily confide in Violet, because she was fully aware of her love for Aymer. It is easier to speak to those who have had similar experiences, than to those who are as yet ignorant.

"He is in England, now," said Agnes, one day. "He is not far distant. Why should I conceal it any longer? Your friend Mr. Malet meets him daily, I daresay; he is a candidate for Stirmingham. It is Mr. Marese Baskette."

"I must congratulate you," said Violet. "He is the richest man in the world, is he not?"

"He will be if he succeeds in obtaining his rights. To tell you the truth, I think the great battle he is fighting with these companies and claimants, gives me more interest in him than—than—well, I don't know. You will see him soon. He will come directly the election is over. Now you know why I took so much interest in your letters from Mr. Malet, describing the course of the family council. But I think he is wrong, dear, in the last that you showed me. I think I should like to be the owner of that great city—it is true there would be responsibilities, but then there would be opportunities, he forgets that. Think what one could do—the misery to be alleviated, the crime to be hunted out, the great work that would be possible."

Her eyes flashed, her form dilated. It was easy to see that to the ambition innate in her nature, the idea of having an immense city to reign over, as it were, like the princesses of old, was almost irresistible. A true, good woman she was, but it would have been impossible for her not to have been ambitions.

"With his talent," she said—becoming freer upon the subject the longer she dwelt upon it—"with his talent, for he is undoubtedly a clever man, with the love the populace there have for him, with my long descent—perhaps the longest in the county—which enables me to claim kindred with powerful families, with a seat in Parliament, there seems no reasonable limit to what we might not do. That is the way to put it. You shall see his letters."

Violet read them. Marese Baskette was gifted with the power of detecting the points which pleased those he conversed or corresponded with, and upon these he dwelt and dilated. It was this that made his speeches so successful in Stirmingham. As he spoke he noted those passages and allusions which awoke the enthusiasm of the audience. Next time he omitted those sentiments which had failed to attract attention, and confined himself to those which were applauded. In half

169

a dozen trials he produced a speech, every word of which was cheered to the echo.

So, in his intercourse with Agnes Lechester, the same faculty of perceiving what pleased, led him to disregard the ordinary method of lovers; he avoided all mention, or almost avoided, expressions of affection, or of love, and harped upon the string which he had found vibrated most willingly in her breast. The theme was ample and he did not hesitate to work upon it. He compared his position and that of Agnes when united, and when his rights were conceded, to that of the royal reigning dukes of Italy a hundred years ago—dukes whose territory in area was not large, but whose power within that area was absolute.

The city of Stirmingham was in effect a grander possession than Parma or Milan; far more valuable estimated in coin, far more influential estimated by the extent of its commerce. Without a doubt, when once he had obtained possession, the Government would soon recognise his claims and confer upon him a coronet, unless indeed Agnes preferred a career of perhaps greater power in the House of Commons. He candidly admitted his ignoble descent.

"My ancestor," he wrote, "was a poor basket-maker; there is no attempt on my part to conceal the fact. I am perfectly well aware that upon the score of blood I am far, far, your inferior, and unable to offer a single claim to equality. The Lechesters, I know, were powerful auxiliaries of William, the Conqueror of England. The name is preserved in the Roll of Battle Abbey; it occupies an important place in the 'early chronicles.' Heralds have blazoned its arms, genealogists recorded its descent, poets have sung its fame. Yet remember, even in this view of the matter, that the great William himself, the feudal lord of the Lechesters, was descended upon the mother's side from a tanner. I cannot compare my father, grand old Sternhold, with William the Conqueror; and yet, in this age when wealth is what provinces and conquered countries used to be, perhaps there may be some faint resemblance."

Then he went on:—"I will not disguise from you the fact that in your long descent, and in your connections with the highest families in the land—not even excepting ancient royalty—I place much of my hope for recovering my legitimate possessions and for fighting my myriad enemies. To me the alliance is simply invaluable. To yourself I would fain hope it would not be without its charms. I do not approach you with a boy's silly affection expressed in rhyme and love-sick glances. I do not follow your footsteps from place to place. It is long since I have had even ten minutes conversation with you. I have treated you as I should an equal (not in position, for there you are superior), but as my equal in mind and ability; not as your sex is commonly treated. I have not wooed you as a woman. I have asked you to be my partner, something more than my partner in the kingdom—for so in fact it is—which is mine by right."

This tone was exactly fitted to the mind of the person he addressed. Delicate and full of benevolence, kind, thoughtful, anxious always for others good, there was still at the root of Agnes Lechester's mind a strong vaulting ambition. An ambition which some said had warped her mind with overweening pride, which had cut her off from the natural sphere in which she should have moved, leaving her with little or no society, and which, if rumour spoke correctly, had in earlier days forced her to stifle the heart that beat responsive to another's love.

To Violet, this calm, reasoning courtship, full of coronets and crowns, thinking of nothing but power, was inexplicable. Her heart wrapped up in Aymer, she could not understand this species of barter—of long descent and good family against wealth and property. It seemed unnatural—almost a kind of sacrilege. She fancied that Agnes was not without twinges of conscience, not without hesitation, and naturally put down her apparent vacillation to feelings, similar to those which would have animated herself under the same circumstances.

This is not the place to argue upon marriage; but in passing it does appear that both sides are right and both wrong. It does not of necessity follow that marriage must be for love only; but on the other hand it does not follow that marriage should be for convenience always, and never for affection. In the present instance, to all appearance the parties were exactly fitted to each other. It was notorious that although Lady Lechester had a sufficient income for all her purposes, and even a superfluity, that the revenue from her large estates was greatly reduced by encumbrances upon it. There were surmises that this comparatively inadequate income was one reason why Agnes saw so little society; she was too proud to mingle in a circle for which her purse was unfitted.

Marese, the moment he had an opportunity, did not lose this chance either. In a letter, which Violet was permitted to read, he gradually and by degrees approached the subject of the mortgages and other encumbrances upon the Lechester estates. Instead of being an obstacle, this very fact, he argued, was one reason why their union was singularly appropriate. At the same moment that her family and connections gave him a position for which otherwise he might have striven in vain, his wealth (Marese always kept up the belief in others that he was, even at present, extremely wealthy) would free those ancient estates, and restore them to their pristine splendour.

Then came a brief telegram, announcing that he had won the representation of Stirmingham by a majority of 1000 votes. Agnes was visibly elated. She moved with a prouder step—there was a slight flush upon her usually pale cheek. It was a proof of his genius—of that godlike genius which commands men. He possessed the same qualities which in the ages past had made the Lechesters members of the ruling race.

Violet saw that the balance bowed in his favour. If he were to come now—and he did come.

171

Scarcely three days after the election, Marese drove up to The Towers, and was received with a stately courtesy—a proud indifference which bewildered Violet. She knew, or thought she knew, that Agnes's heart was beating with excitement—yet how calm, how distant and formal she appeared.

Violet looked with interest upon Marese, having heard so much of him from Aymer and Agnes.

On his part, meeting her attentive gaze and hearing her name, Marese slightly started, recovered himself, and bowed profoundly. His attention was wholly bestowed upon Lechester; the conversation between them seemed to Violet constrained and cold to the last degree. She could not help acknowledging that Marese was a handsome man— far handsomer in features and figure than was Aymer. But how different! In her heart of hearts she pitied poor Agnes if such was her choice.

They betrayed no desire whatever to be alone; on the contrary, Agnes particularly desired Violet to remain in the apartment with them. Their talk was of distant things, till it travelled round to the scene of Marese's candidature, and finally fixed itself upon the great case. Marese was extremely sanguine in his language, and indeed he was so in reality. He had gained two important steps he said. In the first place he had partly paid off the claims of the companies for expenses incurred during their tenure of the leases, on the pretence of improving the estate. These expenses reached a preposterous figure; he had succeeded in getting them taxed and considerably reduced, and he had also succeeded in obtaining an order from the Court of Chancery that the payment of these claims should be made by instalments. He casually mentioned that the first instalment of 100,000 pounds had been paid yesterday. The second step was his admittance to Parliament, which, properly worked, would enable him to obtain the support of the party now in power.

Still further, the great family council had blown over without result. The mountain had been in labour, and a mouse had sprung forth. That spectre which had hovered over the city of Stirmingham so long—the spectre of the American claims—had at last put in its appearance, and was found to be hollow and unsubstantial. He did not think there was anything more to be dreaded from that spectral host. The building societies even, despaired of being able to prolong the contest by supporting the American claims. They could no longer refuse to give up possession on the ground that they did not know who was the true heir. It could not be denied who was the heir.

Marese stayed but one afternoon. He was too wise to make himself common. Before he went he formally asked for a private interview. What passed Violet easily gathered from what Agnes said to her afterwards.

"Mr. Broughton will be here in a day or two," she said; "tell Mr.

Malet to come with him. The mortgages I have told you of are to be paid off; Broughton will manage it."

From which it was evident that a definite understanding had been come to with Marese. Agnes was silent and thoughtful all the evening. Towards the hour when they usually retired, she called Violet to the window, and put her arm round her neck.

"Suppose," she said, "all the meadows and hills you see out there were yours, and had been your ancestors for so many centuries—remember, too, that we may die however well we feel—should you like to think that the estate would then fall into the helpless hands of one of two lunatics?"

It was clear that the natural hope of children to inherit had influenced her. Violet had heard something of the lunacy inherent in certain branches of the Lechester family:

Chapter Two

The manner in which Marese Baskette became acquainted with Lady Lechester affords another instance of those "circumstances over which we have no control," which have already been so strongly illustrated in this history. In the course of his purchases of land and property, old Sternhold Baskette was so shrewd and far-seeing, and so difficult to impose upon, that only once did he make any considerable mistake.

It happened that among other land which he bought at no great distance from Stirmingham, there was a small plot of not much more than two acres, which was included in a large area, and not specified particularly in the agreement. This plot had been in the hands of tenants who had lived so long upon it that they believed they had acquired a prescriptive right. They sold their right to a person whom we may call A, and A sold it in common with other property to Sternhold Baskette. The thing was done, no questions asked, and apparently no one thought anything more about it. But what piece of land is there so small that it can escape the eagle eye of an English lawyer? And especially when that lawyer is a new broom, and a rising man determined to make his mark.

So it happened that Mr. Broughton, Lady Lechester's new solicitor (and successor to his uncle's practice), in going over the map of the estate, and comparing it with older maps, found out that there was a certain two-acre piece missing; and being anxious to recommend himself to so good a client as Lady Agnes, lost no time in tracing out the clue to it.

He had not much difficulty in discovering the facts of the case, but it was very soon apparent to his legal knowledge that although the documentary claim of Lady Agnes, and her moral right, were indisputable, yet the whole value of the little property would probably be swallowed up in costs, if an attempt was made to recover it. He represented the fact to her, but Lady Agnes at once instructed him to proceed.

The same over-mastering pride which was the one fault of her character, lent an almost sacred value to every piece of land, however small, which had once formed part of the estate of her ancestors. Not one rood of ground would she have parted with, not one perch should remain in the hands of strangers whilst she had the means of disputing possession. Yet this was the very woman who, with open-handed generosity, was ever ready to succour or assist the poor, and would not hesitate to spend large sums of money to give another person a pleasure.

Mr. Broughton went to law and quickly found it a tough job, for this was one of those small properties which old Sternhold had been able to keep in his own hands, and his son Marese was not disposed to part with it, especially as with lapse of time—although situated far from the city proper—it had increased in value some twenty-five per cent.

Broughton advised Lady Agnes not to go to the inevitable expense of protracted litigation; but she was firm, and the battle began in the Courts, when suddenly, as the forces advanced to the fight, the enemy gave in and surrendered without firing a shot.

It was a piece of Theodore's work. That subtle brain of his had perceived a means by which Marese might, if he played his cards rightly, obtain the value of this little plot of land ten times over. Why not marry this Lady Lechester? She would give him exactly what he wanted—a position and connections among the nobility which all the wealth of old Sternhold could not buy.

"Who is Lady Lechester?" asked Marese.

Theodore told him. He knew, because in the asylum at Stirmingham there were two lunatics of that family, the most profitable of the patients the asylum contained.

"If any accident should happen to either of those patients," said Theodore, "Lady Lechester's property would be doubled; if an accident happen to both of them, it would be trebled. Accidents sometimes happen in the best regulated asylums. The easiest way to get rid of a lunatic who exhibits homicidal tendencies is—to let him escape. He kills two or three, and then—he cuts his own throat. With a lunatic who has not got homicidal tendencies, and whose madness is, between ourselves, a matter of opinion—with such persons there are other methods; but no matter, get Lady Lechester first." And Marese, seeing that his (Theodore's) words were good, did as he was advised.

One day there called at The Towers a gentleman, who was received by Lady Agnes in the most distant manner, for she recognised his name as that of her opponent. Marese met her with a species of mingled deference and pride, exactly suited to the person he addressed. He begged pardon for his intrusion; he felt that an apology was due to Lady Lechester which written words could not convey. His lawyers had involved him in a mistaken and ungentlemanly contest. When he had learnt that his antagonist was a lady, and a lady of distinguished position, he had looked into the matter personally, and at once saw that whatever claim the chicanery of the law gave him, was far overbalanced by the moral and social right of Lady Lechester. He had at once stayed proceedings, had ordered his solicitors to immediately restore possession to Lady Lechester, and had come in person to offer his sincere apology for the trouble he had inadvertently caused.

Be sure that Marese's personal appearance had something to do with his success. At all events Lady Agnes was deeply impressed with his conduct, which she easily ascribed to a nobility of mind; and not to be outdone, while she freely accepted the land, she insisted upon disbursing a sum sufficient to cover the money that had been spent on it.

From that hour Marese was a favoured visitor at The Towers. He came but rarely, but when he came his presence lingered after him. His name, as the heir of Stirmingham, was constantly before her in the papers and on everyone's lips. Add to this his own deep artifice, and it is not to be wondered at that he made progress.

At last it came to pass that Broughton was engaged in arranging the clearing off of certain heavy incumbrances upon the Lechester estate, with money which Marese had received for salvage of the Lucca. Such an arrangement could only mean marriage.

Not long after Marese's visit to The Towers, Aymer arrived with Broughton, bringing with him a collection of pictures, old Bibles, and some few bronzes for Lady Lechester, and a heart full of affection for Violet. He was invited to stay several days, and did so, and for that brief time the joys they had shared at The Place seemed to return. The weather of early spring was too chilly for much out-of-door exercise; but they had all the vast structure of The Towers to wander over—galleries and corridors, vast rooms where they were unlikely to be interrupted, for now the new wing had been built, very few of the servants ever entered the old rooms, and Lady Agnes never. Aymer had come with his mind full of a thousand things he had to say—of love, of hope, of projects that he had formed, and yet when they were together, and the silent rooms invited him to speak, he found himself instead listening to Violet's low voice as she told him all about her life at The Towers, and her feelings for him. It was natural that, the first pleasures of their meeting over, Violet should speak of Lady Agnes, and Aymer of the heir, with whose fortunes he had of late seemed to be mixed up. Violet was full of a subject which she had long wanted to confide to Aymer, and yet hardly liked to write. It was about some singularities of Lady Agnes.

She was very kind, very affectionate and considerate, and yet, Violet said, it seemed to those who lived with her constantly that she had something for ever preying upon her mind. She was subject to fits of silence and abstraction, which would seize her at unaccountable times, and she would then rise and withdraw, and shut herself up in her own room for hours; and once for as long an two days she remained thus secluded.

At such times she generally used a small room in the new wing, the key of which never left her hands, and which no one entered but herself. Another singular habit which she had was going out at night, or after dusk, into the most unfrequented portion of the park. She would seem to be seized with a sudden desire to escape all notice and observation, would put on her hat, wrap herself in a plain shawl, and let the weather be what it might, go forth alone. The servants were so well acquainted with this habit that they never offered to accompany her—indeed, it was part of the household etiquette to affect not to notice her at these times. Her absence rarely exceeded an hour, but knowing that poachers were often abroad, Violet owned that these nocturnal rambles filled her with alarm while they lasted. Another peculiar thing was that Lady Agnes seemed at times as if she believed there was a third person in the room, invisible to others. Once, Violet going into her apartment, surprised her talking in an excited tone, and found to her astonishment that there was no one near her. She was about to retire, when she was transfixed with astonishment to see that Agnes held a naked sword in her hand, which she would point at some invisible object, and then speak softly in a tongue that Violet did not understand, but believed to be Latin. Violet saw that she was not perceived. Agnes' eyes were wide open, but fixed and staring, as if she saw and yet did not see. Afraid, and yet unwilling to call assistance, Violet remained in the ante-chamber, and presently there was a profound silence. She cautiously went in and found the sword returned to its position over the mantelpiece, and Lady Agnes fast asleep in her armchair.

What ought she to do? Ought the family physician, Dr Parker, to be made acquainted with these facts, or was it best to pass them unnoticed? Violet was half afraid to say so, but at these times an ill-defined dread would arise lest Agnes' mind was partly affected. Insanity was well known to run in the Lechester family. Violet's gentle and affectionate mind was filled with fear lest her benefactress should suffer some injury. What had she better do?

It was a difficult question, and Aymer could not answer it. To him, Lady Lechester appeared to be of perfectly sound mind; he could hardly believe the strange things Violet had told him. At all events it would be best not to take any action at present; better wait and watch if these symptoms developed themselves. Violet should keep as close a watch upon Lady Agnes as was compatible with not arousing her suspicions, and yet—

The selfishness of the true lover came to the surface. He did not like to leave his love in a house where the mistress was certainly given to odd habits, and might possibly be really insane—not even though that mistress had shown the most disinterested and affectionate interest in her. But what could he do? His time was up, he must return to Broughton and recommence the old dreary round of labour, to recommence the book he was writing in his solitary apartments. The poor fellow was very miserable at parting, though Agnes asked him to come when he chose.

Violet was less moved than her lover. The truth was she had an unlimited confidence in Aymer's genius, and believed it would triumph over every obstacle.

It was very strange, but these symptoms she had described to Aymer, seemed to increase and strengthen directly afterwards. Lady Lechester seemed to desire more and more to be alone: she wandered more frequently out into the park, not only by night but in the open daylight; and Violet watching her, and yet ashamed to watch, learnt which way her steps tended, and was always prepared, if any alarm was given, to start at once for the spot.

That spot was about half-a-mile, perhaps a little more, from The Towers, and just within the park walls. It was concealed from The Towers by the intervening trees which dotted the park, but there was no wood or copse to pass through in reaching it.

Wherever a rapid river eats its way through a hilly country, and where streams dash down from the hills to join it, there singular tunnels, or whatever the proper name may be, are often found. The Ise (obviously a corruption of Ouse) was a narrow, clear stream, extremely rapid, and confined between high banks, which made it, for two-thirds of its career, practically inaccessible.

At this particular place, in days gone by, it appeared as if a stream, perhaps flowing from some long extinct glacier, had cut its way down to the river by boring a narrow, circular tunnel through the bank of the river. This tunnel was narrow at the top, not larger than would admit the body of a man, but widened as it descended, till where it reached the river there was a considerable cave, and any one kneeling on the sward above could look down upon the water of the river in the dim light, and hear its gurgling, murmuring sound rise up, greatly increased in volume by the acoustic properties of the tunnel, which somewhat resembled the famed Ear of Dionysius, though of course irregular in shape. When the river was swollen with rain or snow, the water came halfway up the tunnel, and the gurgling noise then rose into a hissing, bubbling sound, like that from a huge cauldron of boiling water. Hence, perhaps, its popular name of "Pot." Such "Pots" are to be found, more or less varied in construction, in many parts of England, and generally associated with some local tradition of supernatural beings, or of ancient heroes.

This particular funnel was known as Kickwell Pot—an apparently unmeaning name. The antiquaries, however, would have it that Kickwell was a degenerate form of Cwichhelm, the name of a famous chieftain in the days when the Saxons and Britons fought for the fairest isle of the sea. Probably, they added, Cwichhelm, in one of his numerous battles, was defeated, and perhaps forced to take refuge in this very cave, which was accessible in a canoe or small boat from below, and may have been larger and more capable of habitation then than in our time. At all events, Kickwell Pot had a bad name in the neighbourhood, and there were traditions that more than one man had lost his life, by attempting to descend its precipitous sides in search of treasure temptingly displayed by a dwarf. This may or may not have been founded upon some old worship of a water-spirit or cave-god. The effect was that the common people shunned the spot.

It was a wild place. The beech trees and the great hawthorns, which half-filled that side of the park, completely hid all view of the mansion, and on the right and left were steep downs, so thinly clad with vegetation that the chalk was bare in places. In front swirled along the dark river, whose bank rose twenty feet almost sheer cliff, and opposite was a plantation of fir. On the left hand, facing the fir plantation, was the low stone wall of the park which ended here. Near the mouth of "The Pot," round which some one had built up a loosely-compacted wall of a few stones without mortar, to keep sheep from falling in, was the trunk of a decayed oak tree, once vast in size and reaching to a noble height, now a mere stump, but still retaining a certain weird grandeur. Its hollow trunk formed a natural hut, facing "The Pot" and the dark fir plantation.

This was a singular spot for the mistress of that fair estate to frequent almost at all hours of the day and night. No wonder that Violet, having ascertained its character, grew more and more alarmed, and kept a closer watch.

Chapter Three

When even the most strictly logical mind looks round and investigates the phenomena attending its own existence, perhaps the first fact to attract attention by its strongly marked prominence, is the remarkable loneliness of man. He stands alone. He may have brethren, but they are far below, and like Joseph's seen in the dream, must bow the knee to his state. There extends, as it were, behind him a vast army of bird, beast, reptile, fish, and insect, thronging the broad earth in countless myriads, whose ancestry goes back into periods of time which cannot be expressed by notation. And every one of these, from the tiniest insect to the majestic elephant, is man's intellectual inferior; so that he stands alone on a pedestal on the apex of a huge pyramid of animal life. He looks back—there are millions of inferior creatures. He looks forward—where is his superior? His mind easily grasps the idea of a superior, but where is it? He cannot see, feel, touch, or in any way indisputably prove the existence of a superior being, or race of beings. Yet the mind within is so wonderful and so complex, that it will not accept the conclusion that he really stands alone; that he is the completion and the keystone of creation. A little thought convinces him of his own shortcomings, tells him how far he is from perfection, and the analogy of all things teaches him almost instinctively to look above into the Unknown for a superior being, or a race of beings. It is contrary to all reason and logic, to all analogy and all imagination, that there should be so many myriads behind, and nothing in front. There must be beings in front of him in the scale of existence, just as he is in front of the beings in his rear. Where are they?

The answer to that question has peopled the whole universe with invisible beings. The solid earth beneath our feet has, according to one form of mythology, its gnomes and dwarfs, low of stature, grimy of aspect, but mighty in strength; or it has its Pluto and its Proserpine, its Titans struggling under Etna. The air and the sky above us teem with such shapes; they follow us night and day as our good and evil genii, or they engage in mighty battles—Armageddons of the angels in the empyrean, echoes of whose thundering charges reach our ears on earth.

Such a belief has existed from the earliest days; it has spread over the whole world, it dwells in our midst at this very hour; for what is the so-called spiritualism but a new development of the oldest of all creeds? Even the very atheists, or those who deny the existence of a Supreme Deity—all-creating, all-sustaining—even these admit that there is no logical argument conclusively proving that there are not races of beings superior to our imperfect bodies. Modern science goes a step farther, and all but positively asserts that there are such creatures. It has long speculated as to the possibility of life in some shape or another in the stars and suns of the firmament. One grey-headed veteran, foremost in the ranks of the hardest of all science (anatomy), gravely, and step by step, argues out and demonstrates the fact, that all known living beings are developed, as it were, from one archetypal skeleton. And he concludes with the remarkable statement that, according to all laws of geometry (another hard science), this archetypal skeleton is not exhausted yet; it is still capable of further modification, of fresh development—nay, even that the strange beings with wings and wheels seen by Ezekiel in his vision, are possibilities of the same skeleton. The belief in itself is therefore not a matter for ridicule, however much we may deplore some of the forms which it has taken.

Violet, watch how she might, never learnt the whole secret of Agnes Lechester's apparent vagaries. The genesis of an idea in the mind is difficult to trace; but substantially the circumstances were these.

Fifteen years since, Lady Agnes Lechester was seen and loved by a certain Walter de Warren, a cornet in a dragoon regiment: a lad of good family but miserably poor. Agnes returned his affection: her heart responded to his love, but her pride forbade a marriage. He was not only poor, but had no kind of distinction: nothing whatever to mark him out from the common herd of men except a handsome face and figure. Even then the innate pride of the Lechesters was stirring in Agnes's inner mind, and love as she might, nothing would induce her to listen to him.

This disposition on her part was encouraged by the trustees of the estate, or rather guardians, who, under pretence of keeping up the dignity of the family, represented to her that such a union would be disgraceful. Let the young man win his spurs, and then his poverty would be no obstacle in their sight. They had an object in view in retarding the marriage of their ward. It was true that no salary or commission was allowed for the management of the estate; but all wise men know that there are ways and means of making a profit in an indirect manner. Evil report said that more than one of the mortgages which encumbered the property had been incurred, not from necessity, or from the consequences of extravagance, but simply in order that these parties might receive a handsome gratuity for the permission given to put out large sums at a safe interest.

De Warren was deeply affected when Agnes calmly told him her view of the matter, admitted without reserve that she liked him—loved she could not say, though that was the truth—but added that marriage or further intercourse was impossible, so long as he remained unknown and unheard of among men.

He kissed her hand, and swore to win distinction or to perish. He at once exchanged or volunteered—I forget which, but I think the latter—into a detachment going to China.

When once Agnes had received a letter, which had travelled with its message of love and admiration over those thousands and thousands of miles of ocean, then she realised how she had cut herself off from her own darling; and her heart, before so cold and hard, softened, and was full of miserable forebodings. She lost much of her youthful beauty—the incessant anxiety that gnawed at her heart deprived her cheeks of their bloom, and her form of its graceful lines. She grew pale, even haggard, and people whispered that the heiress was fast going into a decline. Hours and hours she spent alone in the room of the old mansion where the parting had taken place. Sitting there in the Blue Room, as it was called, her mind filled with pictures of war and its dangers, her soul ever strung up to the highest pitch of anxious waiting, what wonder was it that Agnes began to see visions and to dream dreams—visions that she never mentioned, dreams that she never told. It would be easy to argue that what happened was a mere coincidence; that her fears had excited her mind; and that if the actual event had not lent a factitious importance to the affair, it would have passed as a mental delusion.

Certain it was that in May, about ten months after De Warren's departure, Agnes grew suddenly cheerful—the very opposite to what she had been. She sang and played, and danced about the old house. She said that something had told her that De Warren was coming home. No letter had reached her to that effect; the war was still going on, and yet she was perfectly certain that for some reason or other the cornet was returning—and, what was better, was returning covered with honours. Those in the house looked upon this sudden change of spirits and manner as a certain sign that something would happen to the heiress, and her faithful old nurse (dead before Violet's advent) kept a close watch upon her.

One day, a curious thing happened. In the midst of lunch, Lady Agnes sprang up from table with a joyful but hysterical laugh, and declared that Walter was coming on horseback, and she must go and meet him. Quick as thought she had her hat on, and rushed out of the house, the nurse following at a little distance, anxious to see what would happen.

Lady Agnes walked swiftly across the park to a little wicket-gate in the wall, where Warren used to meet her. Then she stopped and looked along the path, while the nurse hid behind the trunk of a beech tree at a short distance. In a few minutes Agnes cried out, "I hear him—I hear him; it is his footstep." Then a minute afterwards she flung out her arms as if embracing some one, and cried, and seemed to kiss the air, uttering warm words of affection. The nurse saw nothing—only a light puff of wind stirred the leaves and caused a rustling.

Agnes in a few moments turned to the right, and began to walk, or rather glide, as it seemed to the excited fancy of the nurse, at a swift pace, all the while talking as if to some person who accompanied her, and every now and then pausing to throw her arms round his neck, and uttering an hysterical sob. She made straight for "The Pot," and went quickly round the oak stump. The nurse followed rapidly, and as she peeped round the oak there was Lady Agnes facing her on the other side of "The Pot," with both arms extended and her face white as death. "Walter," she said, distinctly; "Walter, what does that red spot on your forehead mean? Are you angry?" Then she fell prone on the grass in a dead faint, and the nurse had immense trouble to get her home again.

Just a month afterwards came the news that Walter was dead, having been shot in the forehead with a ball from a matchlock while leading on his men. He had won much praise by his desperate courage, and the last despatch recommended him for promotion, and for the Cross for saving life under heavy fire.

Now, looked at dispassionately by others, the whole incident resolves itself into a case of excitement and over-anxiety acting upon a naturally sensitive organisation. But it was easy to see how to Lady Agnes the affair wore a very different light. To her the imaginary shape, invisible to others, which had met her at the little wicket-gate, was real—the spirit of her lover, which had come from the wilds of China, over thousands of miles, to acquaint her in dumb show of the destruction of its body.

From that moment she became a devout believer in the power of the dead to revisit their friends. She was not alarmed. On the contrary, the thought soothed her. She expected and waited for Walter's second approach, and spoke lovingly when he came again. For he, or the unsubstantial vision in his form, did come again and again, and always in one of two places—in the Blue Room, or beside "The Pot." That strange freak of Nature had been the favourite resort of the lovers in the bygone time. Agnes counted the time for the approach of the spirit; those who waited upon her could tell when she believed the time for the appearance was near, by the peculiar light in her eyes, and the glow upon her cheek. At such times the superstitious servants hastened to get out of the room. After a while Agnes became conscious that these things were noticed and commented upon, and it became her practice, when she felt the time coming, to retire to her own room and lock herself in.

Reflecting upon these periodical visits of what she really believed was the spirit of her dead lover, Agnes naturally went on to consider the whole question of the existence of supernatural beings. She purchased works upon demonology and witchcraft, and being an accomplished scholar did not confine her studies to her own language, but read deeply in Agrippa, and the necromancers of the Middle Ages. There were those who said that while upon the Continent she plunged into these forbidden mysteries, and found in the recesses of foreign capitals, men with whom there still lingered the knowledge how to control the spirits of the air. In part this was true; whether self-deceived or not, it was certain that Agnes really believed there were genii with whom she could converse almost at pleasure. How was it then that, always anxious for Warren's presence, she yet disliked The Towers?

Soon after she began to study these magical books, and to attempt to penetrate the veil which covers the ethereal world from the eyes of poor humanity, it appeared to her that whenever Walter came, his face wore a sad aspect, almost of upbraiding. And beside him there rose up a Darkness: something without form and void, and yet which was there—something which chilled her blood. After a while it began to take the shape of a thin column of darkness; even in the broad sunlight there was this spot where no light would penetrate. It came too without Walter; it rose up in the middle of the room where she sat—a dark presence, a shadow which haunted her everywhere.

I cannot explain this; I can only record that it was the case. It was this that made Agnes dislike The Towers, and live in the new wing. Yet even there she did not escape. The shadow took a shape.

There is a sentence in a certain grand old book, which prays that we may be delivered from the pestilence which walketh in darkness. The thought of that is awful enough. But there is something more awful still. Ancient books, which mention such things in a far-off manner, as if one were speaking under the breath, refer in a dim way to the noonday phantom—the phantom which meets the huntsman at midday in the green and shady wood; which stops the maiden at the fountain with her pitcher, in the glare of the sunbeams; which addresses the shepherd suddenly upon the hillside as he watches his sheep under the blue vault of the sky. To the darkness and the night, the spirits seem to have a natural claim—it is their realm; the boldest of us have sometimes felt an unaccountable creeping in the thick darkness. But at noonday, when one would naturally feel safe, by one's side in the daylight, this is a thousand times worse. The noonday phantom came to Agnes. The dark shadow, the thin column of darkness like smoke, took to itself a shape.

Chapter Four

Ever since the world began it has been the belief of mankind that desolate places are the special haunt of supernatural beings. To this day the merchants who travel upon camels across the deserts of the East, are firmly persuaded that they can hear strange voices calling them from among the sandhills, and that at dusk wild figures may be seen gliding over the ruins of long-lost cities. It is useless to demonstrate that the curious noises of the desert, are caused by the tension which the dead silence causes upon the nerves of the ear, or by the shifting of the sand, and the currents of air which the heated surface of the sand makes whirl about. The belief is so natural that it cannot be entirely eradicated. In the olden times in our own fair England, and not so very long ago either, there was not a wild and unfrequented place which had not got its spirit. The woods had their elves and wild huntsmen, the meadows their fairies, the fountains their nymphs, the rocks and caves their dwarfs, and the air at night was crowded with witches travelling to and fro.

Let any one who possesses a vivid imagination and a highly-wrought nervous system, even now, in this nineteenth century, with all the advantages of learning and science, go and sit among the rocks, or in the depths of the wood and think of immortality, and all that that word really means, and by-and-by a mysterious awe will creep into the mind, and it will half believe in the possibility of seeing or meeting something—something—it knows not exactly what.

Agnes Lechester went into the desolate places fully expecting to meet her lover, and she met—

A more desolate place than the Kickwell Pot could not easily be found in highly-cultivated England, so near to an inhabited mansion. Even in winter, when the leaves were off the trees, there was not a place where a view could be got of it from the mansion, and when there the visitor was, to all intents and purposes, isolated from the world. In summer it was still more hidden, for the thick leaves above, and the tall brake fern growing luxuriantly beneath, obstructed the view, and it was impossible to see for more than a dozen yards. There was but one spot from whence it was possible to overlook "The Pot," and that was from the summit of the Down on the right. But this Down was totally deserted. The very sheep kept aloof from it. Its steep sides were almost inaccessible even to their nimble feet, and the soil was so thin—that no herbage grew to reward the bold climber. Shepherds kept their flocks away from that neighbourhood, for if a sheep lost its footing and stumbled, there was no escape. The body must roll and rebound till it reached the swift river below, which running between steep banks was not easy to get at, and death by drowning was certain. In the course of time many had been lost in this way, and now care was taken that the flocks should not travel in that direction. Animal life almost entirely avoided the bare chalk cliffs. Sometimes a hawk would linger on the edge, as it were, poising himself on his wings but a few feet above the ridge, as if glorying in defiance of the depth below. Sometimes a solitary crow would alight upon the hill, to devour the spoil it had carried off, in peace and undisturbed. In the fir plantation on the other side of the river a few pigeons built, and now and then a loud jay chattered, and a squirrel peeped out from the topmost branches among the cones. The woodpecker might be heard now and then tapping in the great beech trees, and a brown rabbit would start out from among the fern. But so far as man was concerned the spot was totally desolate: no path passed near, the common people avoided it. It was a desolate place.

In summer time a place to meditate in. To sit upon the sward, leaning back against the vast trunk of the dead oak tree, listening to the gentle murmur of the river, as it rose up out of the mouth of "The Pot" close to the feet. In winter a weird and sinister spot, when the trees were bare and dark, the fir trees gloomy and black, when the snow lodged in great drifts upon the Downs, and the murmur of the river rose to a dull, sullen roar, resounding up the strange, natural funnel. When the grey clouds hung over the sky, and the mist clung to the hill, and the occasional gusts of bitter wind rustled the dead beech leaves— then indeed it was a desolate place. It was here that the darkness, the thin column of smoke-like darkness, began to grow into form and shape; and as it took to itself a figure, so the vision of poor Walter faded away, and lost its distinctness of outline.

Agnes saw before her a something that was half-human and half-divine; and yet which a species of instinct told her was not wholly good, perhaps only apparently good. The face was human and yet not human—so much grander, nobler, full of passions, stronger, more irresistible than ever yet played upon the features of a man. The brow spoke of power illimitable, of foresight infinite, of design, and deep, fathomless thought. The chin and mouth spoke of iron will, of strength to rive the solid rock and overthrow a tower, of a purpose relentlessly pursued. The eyes were unbearable, searching, burning like a flame of fire. The form uncertain, ill-defined, yet full of a flowing grace and majestic grandeur. It was winged. There was a general resemblance between this being and those strange creatures—half man, half deity— which are depicted upon the slabs from the palace at Nineveh; only that those pictures are flat and tame, spiritless, mere outline representations. This was full of an intense vitality—a magnetic vigour.

It did not speak; yet she understood its thoughts and its wishes. They filled her with a swelling hope, and yet with unutterable dread:— to place herself willingly, unhesitatingly, without a grain of distrust, within those arms; to be folded to its breast; to feel the wings spread out, and to rush with breathless haste into space, seeking the home of the immortals, the bride of a spirit. The pride of her mind found an unspeakable joy in the belief that such a fate was possible for her—nay, was ever waiting for her—it was but for her to step forward, and in a moment—

The illimitable ambition of her soul urged her on. She never doubted the possibility—"And the sons of God saw that the daughters of men were fair"—what happened then could happen now. Yet something held her back, and that something was Walter—the faint indistinct vision of Walter. He seemed to shake his head mournfully, to beckon with his hand, to grow paler and unhappy, as her frame of mind disposed her more and more to join the ineffable being which stood

185

before her. The warfare, as it were; the struggle between the two grew insupportable; she was torn with conflicting thoughts, doubts, and fears. This was one reason why she so earnestly desired companionship; and in the presence of Violet she found temporary relief.

The offer of Marese Baskette introduced a new element of trouble and confusion in her mind. She had, as it were, a double existence; she lived two lives. One, visible to others with men and woman, mortal like herself; the other, unseen, was spent with the spirit of the dead, and with a spirit which had never known mortality. Yet it was not two minds, but one mind; for all through this dual nature there ran the same master chord. As in the physical life, so in the mental. In the physical life, the proud position Marese offered her attracted her irresistibly; so, in the mental life, the figure of Walter grew fainter and fainter, and that of the Genius, offering supremacy and superiority, became more distinct, larger, and more powerful. The struggle now lay between Marese and the Genius—the vision of the dead Walter faded entirely away. Which should she choose—an earthly kingdom, or little less, with opportunities such as had never before fallen to the lot of a mortal; or should she soar up into the empyrean on the breast of that wonderful and glorious being who grew brighter, more lovely, the longer she gazed upon him?

It was the spirit she went to meet by day and night at the side of "The Pot."

It was the belief among the ancients that persons afflicted with certain diseases, or of unsound mind, were possessed by spirits; and still further, they seem to have quite understood that the possessed person had, as it were, two evils at once. The disease was not the spirit, nor the spirit the disease. These were distinct. Those who could exorcise the spirit had also to cure the disease, though the one generally followed the other.

It is hard to understand the intense reality of the vision seen by Agnes, except upon some similar theory. That the inherent insanity of the Lechester family had developed itself in her mind, unsuspected by others, there can be no doubt; but even to the persons who are subject to illusions of the mind, the reality of their visions is seldom, if ever, so absolutely believed in as these were by Lady Agnes. There is just the possibility, even atheists will not deny the possibility—but it is better not to argue the matter. It is sad, indeed, to record the affliction which had fallen upon this most estimable and generous woman, if we regard it as insanity only; if we go a step further, and admit the possibility alluded to, it is sadder still.

At home, in the new wing, the darkness rarely came now, though there was the sense of a presence. It was by the side of "The Pot" that the figure showed itself fully. It rose up from the strange funnel, as if a mist hardened and solidified into shape. It stood before her silent, yet speaking unutterable things.

186

In the cold winter, when the sky was grey with cloud, the firs black and gloomy, and the drifted snow lay in heaps upon the Downs, there mingled with the sullen roar of the river resounding up "The Pot," a voice from this mysterious being, which in the savage, fierce desolation of that place spoke of a pride, of an ambition, which rose above even utter failure and degradation. Of a strength of mind which gloried even in its fall; which defied the very heavens in its grandeur; which could not be subdued—immortal in its pride.

As the spring stole on and the soft rain fell, as the buds sprang forth and the thrush sang with joy, the figure grew brighter; an intense vitality seemed to pass from it to her—a glow of life which said, "Come with me; we will wander amid forests such as earth even in its youth never saw, by the shore of lakes such as mortal eye never gazed upon; we will revel in an immortal youth—in a sunshine inconceivable in beauty."

It was but a step to those arms; she longed, yet she did not take it. At night, when the sky glittered with stars and a solitary planet beamed in the west, the eyes of the shape grew into blazing coals, and her soul was aware that it was thinking of unutterable mysteries, of knowledge locked up for ages and ages, in the infinite space beyond those points of light. Oh, to penetrate into that silent chamber, to walk with reverent footsteps in that library of the universe, to read the wondrous truths written there—to read which was, in itself, life eternal! This, in brief, the spirit spoke to her.

It will now be understood why the strange behaviour of Lady Agnes seemed to grow stranger after the last visit of Marese Baskette and her practical acceptance of his offer. The moment she had in a manner given her hand to him, the claims of the other and supernatural life appeared to be infinitely superior—as is the common case when one has decided, the other course always seems preferable. Yet she could not easily withdraw from her word, nor indeed did she altogether wish to do so; and this indecision drove her into a restless frame of mind. Her visits to "The Pot" became more and more frequent—some times she would go there four times in the course of the day, and once again in the evening. She shut herself in her private room—the one room Violet was never asked to enter—for hours almost every day. There was a restless gleam in her eyes, usually so mild and pleasant.

One evening, after a more than ordinarily restless day had been spent, Agnes suddenly rose up, and retired to her private room. This was usually her custom before going out alone into the park, but on this occasion, Violet watching her, saw to her intense surprise that, instead of leaving the house, she unlocked a door which led into the old mansion, and entered the long deserted apartments of The Towers proper. Such a step would have been under any ordinary circumstances nothing to take notice of, but Violet had gradually worked herself up into a state of alarm, and this unusual proceeding created more

187

surmises in her mind even than the lonely walks in the darkness. She slipped out of the house thinking to watch Agnes' progress through The Towers by the light she carried, which would show which rooms she went into. It fell out exactly as she had supposed—she saw the light of the little lamp flit about from window to window and along the corridors, now disappearing from sight entirely, and now suddenly flickering out again, till at last it stopped in what Violet well knew was the Blue Room. This room was so called from the colour employed in decorating the walls. They were painted instead of being papered, much in the same style as the houses at Pompeii, only in larger panels, and the ground colour was blue. From the lawn in front of the house Violet could just see Agnes seated at a table in this room, and before her was a small desk—a desk she had often noticed in that room, thinking how incongruous a plain gentleman's writing-desk, with brass handles, looked amidst the elegant furniture and decorations.

Out of this desk Agnes was taking what, at that distance, Violet could only conjecture were letters, and burning them one by one in the flame of the lamp.

Presently she paused, and Violet saw her kiss something which looked like a curl of chestnut hair. Then not fancying her self-imposed task of watching her benefactress, and convinced that there was no danger, Violet stole away.

Agnes was, in fact, destroying her memorials of Walter De Warren, which she had kept in his own desk in the room in which she had last seen him alive. She had determined to cast aside all remembrance of him; his memory should not embarrass her in the course she would pursue. Freed from the slightest control by him, she thought that she would be the better able to choose between the earthly and the immortal destinies offered to her. Yet she still lingered, still hesitated. She could not say to Marese "I will," nor could she say "I will not." She permitted his money to be used in freeing her estate of encumbrance, and this gave him a moral claim upon her hand. After that was done, it seemed to her that the spirit who visited her at "The Pot" visibly frowned, and the great eyes were full of reproach.

What was this feeble earthly glory to that which was offered to her in the sky? She had chosen wrongly, contrary to the spirit of the proud and ambitious Lechesters; she was acting in opposition to the traditions of her race. Marese, after all, was a low-born upstart. The ancestry of the spirit had no beginning and no end. Again she hesitated.

About this time there came a letter from Miss Merton, dated Torquay, written in a formal but polite manner, begging to be informed what she had better do with the dog Dando. She did not wish to get rid of him—she had become quite attached to the dog and he to her—but she was not the actual owner, and she did not like the responsibility of having so valuable an animal with her.

It seemed as if the value of the dog was well known, for at least two deliberate attempts had been made to steal it within a few days. And these attempts had not a little alarmed Miss Merton. To find that her steps were watched and followed by a wild-looking tramp, or tinker fellow, bent upon carrying off the dog was, to say the least, extremely unpleasant.

The man—an ill-looking fellow—was always about the house, and would not go away. He played a tin whistle, and whenever the dog heard some peculiar notes, he became greatly excited, and began to dance about in a curious manner. Not only that, but if the tramp varied the tune in some way, then the dog grew frantic to run after him, and twice she had the utmost difficulty to recover him.

What was she to do? She did not like to part with the dog, and yet really it was very awkward.

Violet in reply asked Miss Merton to send her Dando. She had now got over her prejudice against him and felt that her anger had been unjust. She should like to have him back again. As to the tramp, she was not surprised, for she remembered that her poor father had bought the dog, when quite young, from a band of strolling gipsies, and there were certain tunes which had always excited him to dance and frisk about as if he had been trained to do so.

Violet, of course, asked Lady Lechester's permission, whose reply was that she should be glad to have the dog; there was plenty of room for him, and he would be company, and add to the safety of the somewhat lonely Towers. Violet herself thought that it would be a great advantage if Dando should happen to please Agnes' fancy; he might be allowed to accompany her in her lonely dark walks, and would be some protection.

A week afterwards Dando came, and at once recognised Violet. He had grown considerably larger, and was a fine, noble animal.

As Violet had hoped, Agnes took a great fancy to him, and the dog returning it, they became inseparable companions. This relieved Violet of much of her anxiety.

Chapter Five

A fortnight after Dando's establishment at The Towers, Aymer came. He looked ill, pale, and careworn, and at once announced that he had left Mr. Broughton, and was going to London, literally to seek his fortune.

The monotony had at last proved too much for him, and worse than that was the miserable thought that, after all this work and patience, he was no nearer to Violet. Perhaps after ten or fifteen years of unremitting labour, nine-tenths of which time must be spent at a distance from her, he might, if his health lasted and no accident happened, be in receipt of one hundred and fifty pounds per annum; and how much more forward would he be then?

Not all the poverty and restraint of the years upon Wick Farm at World's End, not all the terrible disappointment on the very day when every hope seemed on the point of realisation; nothing could dull his vivid imagination, or make him abate one iota of the future which he had marked out for Violet.

In truth, she wondered why he had never asked her to come to him—to be married and live with him in his humble lodgings at Barnham. She would have been happy and content. But to Aymer the idea was impossible. All the romance of his life was woven around her head; he would not bring her to miserable back rooms, to a confined narrow life in a third-class street. It would have been to admit that his whole being was a failure; that he had formed hopes and dreamed dreams beyond his power ever to grasp, and his spirit was not yet broken to that. No, he would struggle and work, and bear anything for Violet's sake. Anything but this miserable monotony without progress. Had there been progress, however slow, he might have tamed his impatient mind and forced himself to endure it.

Day after day passed, the nights came and went, and each morning found him precisely in the same position as before. His organisation was too sensitive, too highly wrought, eager, nervous, for the dull plodding of daily life. He chafed against it, till dark circles formed themselves under his eyelids—circles which sleep would not remove. These were partly caused by overwork.

Broughton, on returning from Stirmingham, found his affairs at Barnham had got into a fearful state of muddle, and Aymer had to assist him to clear the Augean stable of accumulated correspondence, and satisfy neglected clients. Often, after a long day's work, he had to carry accounts or correspondence home with him and finish it there, and then after that he would open his own plain simple desk—much such a desk as the one that had belonged to poor Cornet De Warren—and resume his interrupted MS.

After a while it became unbearable; the poor fellow grew desperate. He might not have so soon given way, had not a slight attack of illness, not sufficient to confine him in-doors, added to the tension of his nerves. He determined to stay on until his MS was finished—till the last word had been written, and the last sketch elaborated—then he would go to London, no matter what became of him. If all else failed he could, at the last, return to Wick Farm; they would give him a bed and a crust, and he would be no worse off than before.

He toiled at his book at midnight, and long hours afterwards, when the good people of Barnham town were calmly sleeping the sleep of the just, and permitting the talent in their midst to eat its own heart. At last it was finished, and he left.

Mr. Broughton wished him to stay, offered to increase his salary, said that he had become really useful, and even, as a personal favour, begged him to remain. Aymer thanked him sincerely, but was firm—he must go. So far as was possible he explained to Broughton the reason, and the lawyer, hard as he was, had sufficient power of understanding others to perceive the real state of affairs. He warned Aymer that certain disappointment awaited him in London, that no publisher would issue a book by an unknown author unless paid for it. Aymer shook his head sadly—he had known that well enough long ago, but he must go.

Broughton shook hands with him, gave him a five-pound note over and above his salary, and told him if in distress, as he prophesied he would certainly soon be, to write to him, or else return.

Aymer again thanked him, packed his modest little portmanteau, and taking with him his manuscript, went to The Towers to say farewell to Violet.

When Agnes understood the course he had decided on, she said that she thought he had done right. To any other she should have said differently; to any other of a less highly organised mind she should have said, "Why, you cannot find a better opening." But what would have been meat to others was poison to Aymer. Therefore she applauded his resolution, and told him to go forth and conquer, but first to stay a few days with Violet.

This language greatly cheered poor Aymer, and for a few days he was in a species of Paradise.

It was not even yet fully spring—the wind was cold at times, but still they could go out freely; and with Violet at his side, and Dando bounding along in front, it seemed almost like a return to the old joyous times at World's End.

The hours flew by, and when the last day came it seemed as if but a few minutes had elapsed. It happened to be a wet day—the spring showers were falling steadily, and, unable to go out, they rambled into the old mansion, and strolled from room to room.

The groom had been ordered to get the dog-cart out by a certain time to take Aymer seven miles to the nearest railway station. That station was but a small one, and two up-trains only stopped there in the course of the day—if he missed this he would not reach London that night.

Forgetful of time, perhaps half purposely forgetful, Aymer lingered on, and could not tear himself away.

At length the groom, tired of waiting in the rain, and anxious about the time, waived all ceremony, and came to seek his passenger.

Aymer pressed Violet's hand, kissed it, and was gone, not daring to look back.

The wheels grated on the gravel, and Violet remained where he had left her.

Agnes came presently and found her, and started. The farewell had been given in the Blue Room.

"You did not say farewell here?" said Agnes, with emphasis.

Violet admitted it.

"Good Heavens—what an evil omen!" muttered Agnes, and drew her from the spot.

From that very room De Warren had gone, forth to his fate: from that room Aymer had started to win himself a way in the world.

It was late at night when he reached London. Nothing could be done till the morning. As he had no experience of the ways of the metropolis, Aymer naturally paid about half as much again as was necessary, and reckoning up his slender stock of money, foresaw that he could not long remain in town at this rate.

Mr. Broughton had given him a written introduction to a firm of law-publishers and stationers with whom he dealt—not that they would be of any use to him in themselves, but in the idea that they might have connections who could serve him.

Upon these gentlemen he waited in the morning, and was fairly well received. They gave him a note to another firm who were in a more popular line of business. Aymer trudged thither, and found these people very off-handed and very busy. They glanced at his manuscript—not in their line. Had he anything that would be likely to take with boys?—illustrated fiction sold best for boys and girls. Ah, well! they were sorry and very busy. Suppose he tried so-and-so?

This process, or pretty much the same process, was repeated for two or three days, until poor Aymer, naturally enough, lost heart.

As he left one publisher's shop, a clerk, who was writing at his desk near the door, noticed his careworn look, and having once gone through a somewhat similar experience, and seeing "gentleman" marked upon his features, asked him if he would show him the work.

Aymer did so. The clerk, an experienced man, turned over the illustrations carefully, and then appeared to ponder.

"These are good," he said; "they would certainly take if they were published. But so also would a great many other things. The difficulty is to get them published, unless you have a name. Now take my advice—It is useless carrying the MS from door to door. You may tramp over London without success. Your best plan will be to bring it out at your own cost; once out you will get a reputation, and then you can sell your next. I don't want to be personal, but have you any money? I see—you have a little. Well, you need not pay all the cost. Go to so-and-so—offer them, let me see, such-and-such a sum, and not a shilling more, and your business is done."

Aymer, as he walked along busy Fleet Street and up into the Strand, thought over this advice, and it sounded reasonable enough—

too reasonable. For he had so little money. When all he had saved from the gift of fifty pounds, his salary, and Broughton's present, were added together, he had but forty-seven pounds. Out of this he was advised to expend forty pounds in one lump; to him it seemed like risking a fortune. But Violet? His book? He could not help, even after all his disappointments, feeling a certain faith in his book.

Westwards he walked, past the famous bronze lions, and the idea came into his mind—How did the hero of Trafalgar win his fame? Was it not by courage only—simple courage? On, then. He went to the firm mentioned. They haggled for a larger sum; but Aymer was firm, for the simple reason that he had no more to give. Then they wanted a few days to consider.

This he could not refuse; and these days passed slowly, while his stock of money diminished every hour. Finally they agreed to publish the work, but bound him down to such conditions, that it was hard to see how he could recover a tenth part of his investment, much less obtain a profit. He signed the agreement, paid the money, and walked forth.

He went up the steps to the National Gallery, barely knowing what he did. He stood and gazed down upon the great square, with the lions and the fountains, and the busy stream of human life flowing for ever round it. A proud feeling swelled up within. At last his book would be seen and read, his name would be known, and then—Violet!

Days and weeks went by, and yet no proofs came to his humble lodgings, or rather sleeping place, for all day he wandered to and fro in the great city. When he called at the publishers' office they treated him with supercilious indifference, and—"Really did not know that the immediate appearance of the little book was so important." There were other works they had had in hand previously, and which must have priority.

Aymer wandered about, not only into the great thoroughfares and the famous streets of the City and West End, but eastwards down to the docks, filled with curiosity, observing everything, storing his mind with facts and characteristics for future use, and meantime starving—for it was rapidly coming to that; and the descent was facilitated by a misfortune which befell him in Shoreditch, where, as he was standing near a passage or court in a crowd, a thief made off with three pounds out of his remaining five.

It is easy to say—Why did not Aymer get work? But how was he to do so with no money to advertise, no introductions, no kind of security to give, a perfect stranger? He did try. He called upon some firms who advertised in the Telegraph. The very first question was—Where do you come from? The country! That answer was sufficient. They wanted a man up to London work and to the ways of the City. Aymer modestly said he could learn. "Yes," they replied, "and we must pay for your education. Good morning."

193

Economise as much as he would, the two pounds left dwindled and dwindled, till the inevitable end came, and the last half sovereign melted into five shillings, the five shillings into half-a-crown, the half-a-crown into a single solitary shilling. Driven to the last extremity, Aymer hit upon the idea of manual labour. He was not a powerful man, he could not lift a heavy weight, but he could bear a great deal of fatigue. He looked round him, he saw hundreds at work, and yet there did not seem any place where he could go and ask for employment.

By a kind of instinct he wandered down to the river and along the wharves. There he saw men busy unloading the barges and smaller craft. Summoning up courage, he spoke to one of the labourers, who stared, and then burst into a broad grin. Aymer turned away, but was called back. The ganger looked him up and down and offered him half-a-crown a day; the others earned three shillings and sixpence and four shillings, but they were strong, strapping fellows. Aymer accepted it, for indeed he could not help himself and in a few minutes the poet, author, artist, with his coat off, was rolling small casks across the wharf. At first he was awkward, and hurt himself; the rest laughed at him, but good-humouredly. Some offered him beer.

At six o'clock he, with the rest, was called to a small office and received his day's wages—two shillings and sixpence. He made a meal, the first that day, at a cheap eating-house, and then set out to return to his wretched lodgings, tired, worn out, miserable, yet not despairing, for he had found a means which would enable him to live, and to wait— to wait till the book came out.

For a fortnight Aymer worked at the wharf, and had become a favourite with the men. Noting his handiness and activity, and seeing that he was well educated, he was now put into an office of some little trust, to check the goods as they were landed, and received an advance of eighteen-pence, making a daily wage of four shillings. This seemed an immense improvement; but he was obliged to borrow a week's extra salary in advance to buy a new pair of boots, and was therefore very little better off.

Strolling slowly one evening up Cannon Street, Aymer met the great stream of city men and merchants, clerks and agents, which at that time pours out of the warehouses and offices, setting across London Bridge towards the suburbs.

He walked slowly, all but despondently. It was already a week since he had written to Violet—that in itself was a strong proof of his condition of mind. It is very easy for those who have got everything, to pray each Sunday against envy, and to repeat with unction the response after the command not to covet thy neighbour's goods. It is a different matter when one is practically destitute, when the mere value of the chain that hangs so daintily from my lady's neck—ay, the price of the muff that warms her delicate hands—would be as a fortune, and lift the heart up out of the mire.

194

He could not help thinking that if he had but the money, the value, of a single much-despised pony that drew a greengrocer's cart he should be almost a prince.

He passed under Temple Bar, and entered the busy Strand, walking, as it happened—events always happen, and no one can say what that word really means—on the right hand pavement, facing westwards. Painfully and wearily walking, he came to the church where the pavement makes a détour, and hesitated for a moment whether to cross to the other side or go round the church, and decided, as the road was dirty, and his old boots thin and full of holes, to follow the pavement. "Circumstances over which we have no control"—these circumstances generally commence in the smallest, least noticeable trifles. It so happened—there it is again—will anyone explain why it so happened?—that as he reached the entrance to Holywell Street, he glanced up it, and saw for the first time that avenue of old books. The author's instinct made him first pause, and then go up it—he was tired, but he must go and look. Dingy and dirty, but tempting to a man whose library had been obtained by wiring hares. He thought, with a sigh, how many more books he could have bought with his money had he known of the existence of this cheap mart, or had he had any access to it. Here was Bohn's Plato—for which he had paid a hardly got thirty shillings— marked up at fifteen shillings, slightly soiled it was true, but what did that matter? Here was old Herodotus—Bohn's—marked at eighteen- pence, the very book which had cost him three hares, including carriage. The margins were all scribbled over—odd faces and odder animals rudely sketched in pen and ink, evidently some schoolboy's crib. But what did that matter, so long as the text was complete—he cared for nothing but the text. As he lingered and heard the bells chiming seven o'clock, his eye caught sight of a little book called "A Fortune for a Shilling."

It was a catching title; he remembered seeing it lying upon the itinerant bookseller's stall in front of the Sternhold Hall. He looked at it, weighed it in his hand. He smiled sadly at his own folly. He had but fifteen pence in his pocket, and to think of throwing a whole shilling away upon such a lottery! It was absurd—childish; and yet the book fascinated him. The bookseller's assistant came out, ostensibly to dust the books—really to see that none were pocketed. Aymer ran his eye down the pages of the book, feeling all the while as if he were cheating the bookseller of his money. The assistant said, "Only one shilling, sir; a chance for everybody, sir, in that book." Aymer shut his eyes to his own folly, paid the money, and returned into the Strand with threepence left.

Chapter Six

He repented his folly very speedily, for the landlady had advanced him half-a-crown two days before for some necessaries, and now asked him for the money.

Not all the hunger and thirst of downright destitution is so hard to bear to a proud spirit as the insults of a petty creditor. He could not taste his tea; the dry bread—he could not afford butter—stuck in his throat. If he had not spent that shilling, he might have paid a part at least of his debt.

He took up the book—the cause of his depression—and, still ashamed of himself, began to search it for any reference to his own name. In vain; Malet was not mentioned, there were no unclaimed legacies, no bank dividends accumulating, no estates without an owner waiting for him to take possession—it was an absolute blank. The shilling had been utterly wasted.

As he sat thinking over his position, the idea occurred to him to see what mention the book made of the great estate at Stirmingham.

There were pages upon pages devoted to Sibbolds and Baskettes, just as he expected. Aymer ran down the list, recalling, as he went, the scenes he had witnessed in the Sternhold Hall.

At the foot of one page was a short note in small type, and a name which caught his eye—"Bury Wick Church." He read it—it stated that it was uncertain what had become of Arthur Sibbold, the heir by the entail, and that inquiries had failed to elucidate his fate. There was a statement, made on very little authority, that he had been buried in Bury Wick Church, co. B—, but researches there had revealed nothing. Either he had died a pauper, and had been interred without a tombstone, or else he had changed his name. It was this last sentence that in an instant threw a flood of light, as it were, into Aymer's mind—changed his name.

Full of excitement, he rushed to his little portmanteau, tore out his note-book, and quickly found the memorandum made in the office of Mr. Broughton, at Barnham.

There was the explanation of the disappearance of Arthur Sibbold—there was the advertisement in a small local newspaper of his intended marriage and change of name. Doubtless he had afterwards been known as Mr. Waldron—had been buried as Waldron, and his death registered as Waldron. As Waldron of The Place, World's End! Then poor old Jason Waldron, the kindest man that ever lived, was in reality the true heir to the vast estate at Stirmingham.

Jason was dead, but Violet remained. Violet was the heiress. He sat, perfectly overwhelmed with his own discovery, of which he never entertained a moment's doubt. He ransacked his memory of what he had heard at the family council; tried to recall the evidence that had been produced at that memorable fiasco; but found it hard to do so, for at the time his mind was far away with Violet, and he had no personal interest in the proceedings. Had he only known—what an opportunity he would have had—he might have learnt the smallest particulars.

Thinking intently upon it, it seemed to him that the name of Arthur Sibbold was rarely, if ever, mentioned at that conference, it was always James Sibbold; Arthur seemed to have dropped out of the list altogether.

If he could read a copy of the "Life of Sternhold Baskette," perhaps he might be able to get a better understanding of the facts.

He deeply regretted now that he had not purchased a copy, as he might have done so easily at Stirmingham, on the stall of the itinerant bookseller. Then he had a little money; now he had none.

He called his landlady, took up his great coat, and gave it to her—could she sell it? She looked it over, found many faults, but finally went out with it. In half an hour she returned with eighteen shillings.

Aymer had given three pounds for it just before his wedding-day. He paid the old lady her half-crown, and hurried back to Holywell Street. The book he wanted, however, was not so easily to be found. All had heard of it—but no one had it.

In time he was directed to a man who dealt in genealogical works, sold deeds, autographs, and similar trash. Here he found the book, and had a haggle for it, finally securing it for seven shillings and sixpence; the fellow would have been glad of three shillings, for it had been on his shelves for years, but Aymer was burning with impatience. In the preface he found a scanty account of the Sibbolds, not one-fifth as much as he had reckoned upon, for the book was devoted to Sternhold, the representative man of the Baskettes. There was, however, a pretty accurate narrative of the murder of Will Baskette, and from that Aymer incidentally obtained much that he wanted. Reflecting upon the murder, and trying to put himself in Arthur Sibbold's place, Aymer arrived at a nearly perfect conception of the causes which led him to bury himself, as it were, out of sight.

One of two things was clear—either Arthur Sibbold had actually participated in the murder, and was afraid of evidence unexpectedly turning up against him; or else he had been deeply hurt with the suspicion that was cast upon him, and had resolved for ever to abandon the home of his ancestors.

Probably he had travelled as far as possible from the scene of the murder—perhaps to London (this was the case) got employment, and, being successful, finally married into the Waldron family, and changed his name. He would naturally be reticent about his ancestors. The next generation would forget all about it, and the third would never think to inquire.

Had the vast estate been in existence before Arthur Sibbold's death, most probably he would have made himself known; but it was

197

clear that it had not grown to one-fiftieth part of its present magnificence till long after.

The silence of Arthur Sibbold, and Arthur Sibbold's descendant, was thus readily and reasonably accounted for. Reading further, Aymer came to the bargain which Sternhold Baskette had made with the sons of James Sibbold, and of their transhipment to America. Here the legal knowledge that he had picked up in the office of Mr. Broughton enabled him to perceive several points that would not otherwise have occurred to him. That transaction was obviously null and void, if at the time it was concluded either Arthur Sibbold, or Arthur Sibbold's descendants, were living. They were the lawful owners of the old farm at Wolf's Glow, and of the Dismal Swamp, and it was impossible for James Sibbold's children to transfer the estate to another person. All then that it was necessary to prove was that Violet was the direct descendant of Arthur Sibbold, and her claim would be at once irresistible. Then it occurred to him that at the family council he had often heard mention made of a certain deed of entail which was missing, and for which the members of the Sibbold detachment had offered large sums of money.

The long, long hours and days that he had spent in the Sternhold Hall chronicling the proceedings of the council, and which he had at the time so heartily hated soon proved of the utmost value. He could at once understand what was wanted, and perceive the value of the smallest link of evidence. Here was one link obviously wanting—the deed. Without that deed the descent of Violet from Arthur Sibbold was comparatively of small account. It was possible that even then she might be a co-heiress; but without that deed—which specially included female heiresses—she would not be able to claim the entire estate. Yet even then, as the direct descendant of the elder brother, her claim would be extremely valuable, and far more likely to succeed than the very distant chance of the American Sibbolds or Baskettes, all of whom laboured under the disadvantage that their forefathers had sold their birthright for a mess of pottage. Another and far more serious difficulty which occurred to him as he thought over the matter, far into the night, was the absence of proof of Arthur Sibbold's marriage. It was clear from the little book whose notes had opened his eyes, that the register of the church at Bury Wick, World's End, had been searched, and no record found. His memorandum of the advertisement of change of name described Arthur Sibbold as of Middlesex; the marriage therefore might have taken place in London. Probably Sibbold had met the Miss Waldron he had afterwards married in town. Where then was he to find the register of marriage? Middlesex was a wide definition. How many churches were there in Middlesex? What a Herculean labour to search through them all!

He was too much excited to sleep. Despite of all these drawbacks—the disappearance of the deed, and the absence of the

198

marriage certificate—there was no reasonable doubt that Violet was the heiress of the Stirmingham estates. The difficulties that were in the way appeared to him as nothing; he would force his way through them. She should have her rights—and then! He would search every church in London till he did find the register of Arthur Sibbold's marriage. It must be in existence somewhere. If it was in existence he would find it. Towards two o'clock in the morning he fell asleep, and, as a result, did not wake till ten next day. Hurrying to his daily task, he was met with frowns and curses for neglect, and venturing to remonstrate, was discharged upon the spot.

Here seemed an end at once to all his golden dreams. He walked back into the City, and passing along Fleet Street, was stopped for a moment by a crowd of people staring into the window of a print and bookshop, and talking excitedly. A momentary curiosity led him to press through the crowd, till he could obtain a view of the window. There he saw—wonder of wonders—one of his own sketches, an illustration from his book, greatly enlarged, and printed in colours. It was this that had attracted the crowd. The humour and yet the pathos of the picture—the touch of Nature which makes the whole world kin—had gone straight to their hearts. On every side he heard the question, "Whose is it?"—"Who drew it?"—"What's the artist's name?" Then the title of the book was repeated, and "Who's it by?"—"Who wrote it?"— "I'll get a copy! Third Edition already—it must be good."

Gratified, wonder-stricken, proud, and yet bewildered, Aymer at last got into the shop and made inquiries. Then he learnt that the publisher had stolen a march upon him. They had never sent him the proofs; they had in fact thought very little of the book, till one day it happened (it happened again) a famous artist came into the office, and chanced to turn over a leaf of the MS, which was lying where Aymer had left it, on the publisher's wide desk. This man had a world-wide reputation, and feared no competitor; he could therefore do justice to others. He was greatly struck with the sketches.

"This man will make hid fortune," he said. "Why on earth do you let the book lie here mouldering?"

The publisher said nothing, but next day the manuscript was put in hand, hurried out, and well advertised. The first and second edition sold out in a week, and Aymer heard nothing of it till accident led him into the crowd round the shop window in Fleet Street.

It will be pardoned if I say that Aymer was prouder that day than ever he had been in his life. He went straight to the publisher's with a glowing heart. The agreement had been that the publisher should have two editions for his trouble and the use of his name; in the third, the author and artist was to share. In point of fact, the publisher had never dreamt of the book reaching even a second edition.

Aymer was received coldly. He asked for his share. Impossible— the booksellers had not paid yet—the expense had been enormous—

advertising, etc, there would barely be a balance when all was said and done. Aymer lost his temper, as well he might, and was very politely requested to leave the premises. He did so, but hastened at once to his adviser—the clerk who had told him to publish at his own risk. This man, or rather gentleman, said he had expected him for days, and wondered why he had not come.

"Wait till one o'clock," said he, "and I will accompany you."

At one they revisited the offices of the publisher. The upshot was that Aymer was presented with a cheque for fifty pounds, being his own forty pounds, and ten pounds additional.

"Now," said his friend, "you call on my employers—I will mention your name—and offer them a work you have in hand."

Aymer did so, and obtained a commission to write a work for them, to be illustrated by himself, and was presented with a twenty-pound note as earnest-money. Thus in a few hours, from a penniless outcast, he found himself with seventy pounds in his pocket—with a name, and with a prospect of constant and highly remunerative employment. If this continued, and of course it would—not all his disappointments could quench his faith in his destiny—he would marry Violet almost immediately. With this money he could search out, and establish her claim; he would employ her own late employer, Mr. Broughton. He was anxious to write to Violet, but he had not tasted food that day yet. He entered a restaurant and treated himself to a really good dinner, with a little of the generous juice of the grape. Towards five o'clock he sat himself down in his old room to write to Violet, and to Mr. Broughton.

He wrote and wrote and wrote, and still he could not conclude; his heart was full, and he knew that there was a loving pair of eyes which would read every line with delight. First about his book— sending, of course, two copies by the same post—one for Violet, one for Lady Lechester—telling Violet of the excitement it had caused, of the crowd in the street, of the anxiety to learn the author's name, of the first, second, third edition, and the fourth in the press. Was it to be wondered at that he dilated upon this subject?

Then he told her of his troubles, of his work at the wharf, and explained why he had not written, and finally came to the discovery that Violet was the heiress of Stirmingham. He had a difficult task to explain to her how this arose; he had to review the whole history of the case in as short a compass as possible, and to put the links of evidence clearly, so that a non-technical mind could grasp them. He finished with a declaration of his intention to spare neither trouble, time, nor expense to establish Violet's right; he would search every church register in London; she should ride in her carriage yet. If only poor Jason had been alive to rejoice in all this!

This was the same man, remember, who not many weeks before had written to Violet from Stirmingham in the midst of the turmoil of the election, expressing his deep sense of the responsibility that must of necessity fall upon the owner of that marvellous city; he would not be that man for worlds. The self-same man was now intent on nothing less than becoming, through Violet, the very thing he had said he would not be at any price. Still the same omnipotent circumstances over which we have no control, and which can alter cases, and change the whole course of man's nature.

To Broughton he wrote in more businesslike style. He could not help triumphing a little after the other's positive prophecy of his failure; he sent him also a copy of the third edition. But the mass of his letter referred to Violet's claim upon the estate, and went as fully into details as he could possibly do. He referred Mr. Broughton to the number and date of the Barnham newspaper, which contained the advertisement of Arthur Sibbold's change of name. Would Mr. Broughton take up the case?

Who can trace the wonderful processes of the mind, especially when that mind is excited by unusual events, by unusual indulgence, and by a long previous course of hard thinking? That evening Aymer treated himself to the theatre, and saw his beloved Shakespeare performed for the first time. It was Hamlet—the greatest of all tragedies. Who can tell? It may be that the intricate course of crime and bloodshed, he had seen displayed upon the stage, had preternaturally excited him; had caused him to think of such things. Perhaps the wine he had taken—a small quantity indeed, but almost unprecedented for him—had quickened his mental powers. Be it what it might, towards the grey dawn Aymer dreamt a dream—inchoate, wild, frenzied, horrible, impossible to describe. But he awoke with the drops of cold perspiration upon his forehead, with a great horror clinging to him, and he asked himself the question—Who murdered Jason Waldron, true heir to Stirmingham city? His legal knowledge suggested the immediate reply—Those who had an interest and a motive so to do. The man who had an interest was—John Marese Baskette.

There was not a shadow of proof, but Aymer rose that morning weighed down with the firm moral conviction that it was he and no other who had instigated the deed. He recalled to his mind the circumstances of that mysterious crime—a crime which had never been even partially cleared up. He thought of Violet—his Violet—the next heir. Oh, God! if she were taken too. Should he go down to her at once? No; it was the fancy of his distempered mind. He would conquer it. She was perfectly safe at The Towers; and yet Marese came their sometimes. No; where could she be safer than amid that household and troop of servants? But he wrote and hinted his dark suspicions to her; warned her to be on her guard. This, he said, he was determined upon—he would establish her right, and he would punish the murderer of poor Jason. That very day he had commenced his search among the churches.

Chapter Seven

When Aymer's first and longest letter reached The Towers, together with the copy of his book, Violet could hardly contain herself with pleasure. His triumph was her triumph—his fame her fame—and in the excitement of the moment she but barely skimmed the remainder of his letter, and did not realise the fact that she was the heiress to the most valuable property in England. Her faith in Aymer had proved to be well-founded; he had justified her confidence; his genius had conquered every obstacle. As she had read Marese's letters to Agnes, so it was only natural that she should proudly show this letter to her.

Agnes fully sympathised with her, and declared that the sketches (she had already looked cursorily through the copy of his book which Aymer had sent her) were wonderfully good. But it was natural for her to be less excited than Violet, and therefore it was that the second part of the letter made a greater impression upon her. Violet the heiress of the Stirmingham estate? It was impossible—a marvel undreamt of. Marese was the heir—there could not be two—and in Marese she was personally interested. Together they re-read that portion of Aymer's letter, and wondered and wondered still more. His line of argument seemed laid down with remarkable precision, and there was no escape from his conclusions—but were his premises correct; was he not mistaken in the identity?

The whole thing appeared so strange and bizarre, that Agnes said she really thought he must be romancing—drawing on his imagination, as he had in the book she held in her hand.

Violet knew not what to think. She could not doubt Aymer. She warmly defended him, and declared that he was incapable of playing such practical jokes. She had a faint recollection of poor old Jason once telling her that her great-grandfather's name was Sibbold, or something like that—she could not quite be sure of the name. She remembered it, because Jason had instanced it as an example of the long periods of time, that may be bridged by three or four persons' successive memories. He said that his father had conversed with this Sibbold, or Sibald, and he again had met in his youth an old man, who had fought at Culloden in '45. If it had not been for that circumstance, the name would have escaped her altogether.

The more Agnes thought of it, the more she inclined to the view that Aymer, overworked and poorly-fed, had become the subject of an hallucination. It was impossible that Marese could lay open claim to be the heir if this were the case—perfectly impossible. A gentleman of the highest and most sensitive honour like Marese, would at once have renounced all thought of the inheritance; he would have been only eager to make compensation. Why, even Aymer said that the matter had never been mentioned at the family council—surely that was in itself sufficient proof. It was an insult to Marese—to herself—to credit such nonsense. Aymer must be ill—over-excited.

Violet kept silence, with difficulty, from deference to her generous friend; but she read the letter the third time, and it seemed to her that, whether mistaken or not, Aymer had given good grounds for his statement. She was silent, and this irritated Agnes, who had of late been less considerate than was her wont. It seemed as if some inward struggle had warped her nature—as if in vigorously, aggressively defending Marese, she was defending herself.

The incident caused a coolness between them—the first that had sprung up since Violet had been at The Towers. Violet was certainly as free from false pride as Lady Lechester was eaten up with it; but even she could not help dreaming over the fascinating idea that she was the heiress of that vast estate, or at least a part of it. How happy they would be! What books Aymer could write; what countries they could visit together; what pleasures one hundredth part of that wealth would enable them to enjoy! Thinking like this, her mind also became thoroughly saturated with the idea of the Stirmingham estate. Like a vast whirlpool, that estate seemed to have the power of gradually attracting to itself atoms floating at an apparently safe distance, and of engulfing them in the seething waters of contention.

In the morning came Aymer's second letter, imputing the worst of all crimes to Marese Baskette, or to his instigation.

Violet turned pale as she read it. Her lips quivered. All the whole scene passed again before her eyes—the terrible scene in the dining-room, where the wedding breakfast was laid out—the pool of blood upon the carpet—Jason's head lying helplessly against the back of the armchair—the ghastly wound, upon the brow. Poor girl! Swift events and the change of life, and her interest in Agnes, had in a manner chased away the memory of that gloomy hour. Now it came back to her with full force, and she reproached herself with a too ready forgetfulness—reproached herself with neglecting the sacred duty of endeavouring to discover the murderer. To her, the facts given by Aymer—the interest, the motive—seemed irresistible. Not for a moment did she question his conclusion. She thought of Marese as she had seen him for a few hours: she remembered his start as he heard her name—it was the start of conscious guilt, there was no doubt.

A great horror fell upon her—a horror only less great than had fallen that miserable wedding-day. She had been in the presence of her father's murderer—she had eaten at the same table—she had shaken hands with him. Above the loathing and detestation, the hatred and abhorrence, there rose a horror—almost a fear. Next to being in the presence of the corpse, being in the presence of the murderer was most awful. She could not stay at The Towers—she could not remain, when at any hour he might come, with blood upon his conscience if not upon

203

his actual hands—the blood of her beloved and kindly father. A bitter dislike to The Towers fell upon her—a hatred of the place. It seemed as if she had been entrapped into a position, where she was compelled to associate with the one person of all others whom love, duty, religion—all taught her to avoid. She must go—no matter where. She had a little money—the remnant left after all. Jason's debts had been paid—only some fifty pounds, but it was enough. Mr. Merton had sent it to her with a formal note, after the affairs were wound up. At first the idea occurred to her that she would go back and live at The Place which was still hers; but no, that could not be—she could not, could not live there; the spirit of the dead would cry out to her from the very walls. She would go to some small village where living was cheap; where she could take a little cottage; where her fifty pounds, and the few pounds she received for the rent of the meadow at The Place, would keep her—till Aymer succeeded, and could get her a home. She hesitated to write to him—she half decided to keep her new address a secret; for she knew that if he understood her purpose he would deprive himself of necessaries to give her luxuries.

That very day she set to work to pack her trunk, pausing at times to ask herself if she should, or should not, tell Lady Agnes that her lover was a murderer. Well she knew that Agnes would draw herself up in bitter scorn—would not deign even to listen to her—and yet it was wrong to let her go on in the belief that Marese Baskette was the soul of honour. Clearly it was her duty to warn Agnes of the terrible fate which hung over her—to warn her from accepting a hand stained with the blood of an innocent, unoffending man. One course was open to her, and upon that she finally decided—it was to leave a note for Agnes, enclosing Aymer's letter.

It was Agnes' constant practice to go for a drive about three in the afternoon; Violet usually accompanied her. This day she feigned a headache, and as soon as the carriage was out of sight sent for the groom, and asked him to take her to the railway station.

The man at once got the dog-cart ready, and in half an hour, with her trunk behind her, Violet was driving along the road. She would not look back—she would not take a last glance at that horrible place. The groom, in a respectful manner, hoped that Miss Waldron was not going to leave them—she had made herself liked by all the servants at The Towers. She said she must, and offered him a crown from her slender store. The man lifted his hat, but refused to take the money.

This incident touched her deeply—she had forgotten that, in leaving The Towers, she might also leave hearts that loved her. The groom wished to stay and get her ticket, but she dismissed him, anxious that he should not know her destination. Two hours afterwards she alighted at a little station, or "road," as it was called. "Belthrop Road" was two and a half miles from Belthrop village; but she got a boy to carry her trunk, and reached the place on foot just before dusk.

On the outskirts of Belthrop dwelt an old woman who in her youth had lived at World's End, and had carried Violet in her arms many and many a time. She married, and removed to her husband's parish, and was now a widow.

Astonished beyond measure, but also delighted, the honest old lady jumped at Violet's proposal that she should be her lodger. The modest sum per week which Violet offered seemed in that outlying spot a mine of silver. Hannah Bond was only afraid lest her humble cottage should be too small—she had really good furniture for a cottage, having had many presents from the persons she had nursed, and particularly prided herself upon her feather beds. Here Violet found an asylum—quiet and retired, and yet not altogether uncomfortable. Her only fear was lest Aymer should be alarmed, and she tried to devise some means of assuring him of her safety, without letting him know her whereabouts.

Circumstances over which no one as usual had had any control, made that spring a memorable one in the quiet annals of Belthrop. The great agricultural labourers' movement of the Eastern counties had extended even to this village; a branch of the Union had been formed, meetings held, and fiery language indulged in. The delegate despatched to organise the branch, looked about him for a labourer of some little education to officiate as secretary, and to receive the monthly contributions from the members.

Chance again led him to fix upon poor old Edward Jenkins, the gardener, who still worked for Mr Albert Herring, doing a man's labour for a boy's pay. The gardener could write and read and cipher; he was a man of some little intelligence, and, though a new comer, the working men regarded him as a kind of "scholar." He was just the very man, for he was a man with a grievance. He very naturally resented what he considered the harsh treatment he had met with after so many years faithful service, and he equally resented the low pay which circumstances compelled him to put up with. Jenkins became the secretary of the branch, and this did not improve his relations with Albert Herring. Always a harsh and unjust man, his temper of late had been aroused by repeated losses—cattle had died, crops gone wrong; above all, an investment he had made of a thousand pounds of the money that should have been Violet's, in some shares that promised well, had turned out an utter failure. He therefore felt the gradual rise in wages more severely than he would have done, and was particularly sore against the Union. He abused Jenkins right and left, and yet did not discharge him, for Jenkins was a cheap machine. His insults were so coarse and so frequent that the poor old man lost his temper, and so far forgot himself (as indeed he might very easily do) as to hope that the Almighty would punish his tormentor, and burn down, his home over his head.

Early in the spring the labourers struck, and the strike extended to Belthrop. The months passed on, the farmers were in difficulty, and meantime the wretched labourers were half-starved. Albert was furious, for he could not get his wheat sown, and upon that crop he depended to meet his engagements. Yet he was the one of all others, at a meeting which was called, to persuade the farmers to hold out; and above all he abused Jenkins, the secretary; called him a traitor, a firebrand, an incendiary. The meeting broke up without result; and it was on that very evening that Violet arrived. The third evening afterwards she was suddenly called out by gossiping old Hannah Bond, who rushed in, in a state of intense excitement—

"Farmer Herring's ricks be all ablaze!"

Violet was dragged out by the old woman, and beheld a magnificent, and yet a sad sight. Eight and thirty ricks, placed in a double row, were on fire. About half had caught when she came out. As she stood watching, with the glare in the sky reflected upon her face, she saw the flames run along from one to another, till the whole rickyard was one mass of roaring fire. The outbuildings, the stables, and cow-houses, all thatched, caught soon after—finally the dwelling-house.

The farm being situated upon the Downs, the flames and sparks were seen for miles and miles in the darkness of the night, and the glare in the sky still farther. The whole countryside turned out in wonder and alarm; hundreds and hundreds trooped over Down and meadow to the spot. Efforts were made by scores of willing hands to stay the flames—efforts which seemed ridiculously futile before that fearful blast; for with the fire there rose a wind caused by the heated column of air ascending, and the draught was like that of a furnace. Nothing could have saved the place—not all the engines in London, even had there been water; and the soil being chalky, and the situation elevated, there was but one deep well. As it was, no engine reached the spot till long after the fire was practically over—Barnham engine came in the grey of the morning, having been raced over the hills fully fifteen miles. By that time, all that was left of that noble farmhouse and rickyard, was some two-score heaps of smoking ashes, smouldering and emitting intense heat.

Hundreds upon hundreds stood looking on, and among them there moved dark figures:—policemen—who had hastily gathered together.

And where was Albert Herring? Was he ruined? He at that moment recked nothing of the fire. He was stooping—in a lowly cottage at a little distance—over the form of his only son, a boy of ten. The family had easily escaped before the dwelling-house took fire, and were, to all intents and purposes, safe; but this lad slipped off, as a lad would do, to follow his father, and watch the flames. A burning beam from one of the outhouses struck him down. Albert heard a scream; turned, and saw his boy beneath the flaring, glowing timber. He shrieked—literally shrieked—and tore at the beam with his scorched hands till the flesh came off.

At last the on-lookers lifted the beam. The lad was fearfully burnt—one whole shoulder seemed injured—and the doctors gave no hope of his life. (As I cannot return to this matter, it may be as well to state that he did not die—he recovered slowly, but perfectly.) Yet what must the agony of that man's mind have been while the child lay upon the bed in the lowly cottage? Let the fire roar and hiss, let roof-tree fall and ruin come—life, flickering life more precious than the whole world—only save him this one little life.

In the morning Albert turned like a wild beast at bay, shouting and crying for vengeance. "Vengeance is mine, saith the Lord;" but when did man ever hearken to that? He marked out Jenkins, the gardener; he pointed him out to all. That was the man—had they not heard him say he hoped Heaven would burn the farm over his head?

That was true; several had heard it. Jenkins had been the last to leave the premises that night.

The gardener, utterly confounded, could not defend himself. The leader of the Unionists! The police looked grave, and the upshot was he was taken into custody.

Feeling ran high in the neighbourhood, as well it might. There were grievances on both sides, and the great fire had stirred up all uncharitableness. The justices' room was crowded, and a riot was feared. The Union had taken up poor Jenkins' defence, and had sent down a shrewd lawyer who put a bold face on it, but had little hope in his heart. Suspicion was so strong against the prisoner.

His poor old wife was perhaps even more frenzied than she had been at the coroner's inquest. Such a circumstance as Violet's arrival at Belthrop, though trivial in itself, was, of course, known in the village; she once again rushed to Violet for help. Violet, though anxious to keep quiet, could not resist the appeal, she was herself much excited and upset about the matter. She went with the miserable wife to the Court, and being a lady, was accommodated with a good seat. Out of her little stock she would have willingly paid for a lawyer, but that was unnecessary. The counsel retained by the Union was a clever man; but he could make no head against the unfortunate facts, and in his anxiety to save the prisoner he made one great mistake—justifiable perhaps—but a mistake. He asked who would profit by the fire, whose interest was it? Was not hard cash better than ricks, and an uncertain and falling market? In a word, he hinted that Albert himself had fired the ricks.

A roar of denial rose from the farmers present, a deafening cheer from the labourers. It was with difficulty that the crowd was silenced, and when the proceedings were resumed, it was easy to see that the Bench had been annoyed by this remark.

The solicitor on the other side got up, and asked the justices to consider the previous character of this man the prisoner—who had been on his trial for murder—was there a single person who would speak to his good character?

"Yes," said Violet, standing up. Amid intense surprise she was sworn. "My name is Violet Waldron," she said, nerving herself to the effort. "I am the daughter of—of—the person who was—you understand me? I have known this man for years—since I was a child. He and his served us faithfully for two generations. He is incapable of such a crime—I believe him innocent—he is a good man, but most unfortunate."

She could not go further, her courage broke down. They did not cross-examine her.

The prosecution professed great respect for Miss Waldron, whose misfortunes were well known, but of what value was her testimony in this case? She had not even seen Jenkins for a long time; circumstances warped the best of natures.

The end was, that Jenkins was committed for trial at the assizes within two months. Thus did circumstances again involve this victim of fate in an iron net. Here again I must anticipate. Jenkins was sentenced at the assizes to twelve months imprisonment with hard labour. Nevertheless the imputation against Albert Herring was never quite forgotten; to this day the poor believe it, and even the police shake their heads. At all events he profited largely by it. The corn had been kept in the hope that the markets would rise, but they had fallen. The insurance-money saved him from irretrievable ruin.

The prisoner's poor wife was reduced to utter beggary. Violet did her best to keep her, but she could not pay the debts the gardener, with his miserable pay, had of necessity contracted. Ten pounds still remained unpaid. At last the poor woman bethought her of an ancient treasure, an old bible;—would Miss Violet buy it? It really was Violet's—it had been lent by Violet's grandmother to the poor woman, and never returned. Violet at once remembered Lady Lechester's fancy for such books, and recommended her to take it to The Towers. The woman went, and returned with the money.

Now, the immediate effect upon our history of this fire was that Violet Waldron became a prominent name in the local paper published at Barnham, and that local paper had been taken for years regularly at The Towers. And at The Towers at that time Theodore Marese was temporarily staying, under circumstances that will shortly appear.

Chapter Eight

When Lady Lechester returned from her drive and learnt with intense surprise that Violet was gone, her first thought was that she had been hurt by the remarks made upon Aymer's hallucination the previous evening. Agnes reproached herself for her momentary irritation; but when she found a note for her from Violet on her dressing-table, and had read both it and the enclosed letter from Aymer, her anger was thoroughly aroused.

Not unnaturally she took it in the worst sense, and looked upon it as a downright insult. To pretend that a gentlemen of Marese's position and character was not the heir that he affirmed himself to be—that he had wooed her under false pretences—that was bad taste enough, and utterly unjustifiable. Still, it might have passed as the hallucination of an over-tasked mind. But to deliberately accuse the same gentleman of the blackest crime it was possible for human beings to commit, was inexcusable.

All the pride of her nature rose up in almost savage resentment. Her first impulse was to tear up the letters and burn them; but this she refrained from doing, for on second thoughts they might be instrumental in obtaining the punishment of the slanderer. It was all the more bitter, because she felt that she had done her best both for Aymer and Violet, and the latter she had really loved. Certainly Agnes was far too proud and high-minded to regret for one moment a single shilling that she had spent for the benefit of others; but the reflection of Violet's ingratitude did add a sharper sting. Agnes was in truth touched in her tenderest place—her pride:—she engaged, or partially engaged to a pretender, and worse than that, to a murderer—a Lechester, impossible!

Before she had decided what to do, Mr. Broughton arrived from Barnham, bringing with him Aymer's letter to him. He was utterly unprepared for the mood in which he found Agnes, and unwittingly added fuel to the fire by saying that he had searched the file of old newspapers, and found the very advertisement mentioned by Aymer.

Lady Agnes' indignation knew no bounds. She reproached him for even so much as daring to investigate the matter—for deeming it possible that anything of the kind could be. Let him leave the house immediately—she regretted that she had demeaned herself so much as to admit him to see her.

This aroused Mr. Broughton—who was not without his professional pride—and he answered rather smartly, that Lady Lechester seemed to be forgetting the very dignity to which, she laid claim; and added that if he should mention Aymer's discovery to the building society in Stirmingham, who were his clients, they at least

209

would think Miss Waldron's claim one well worth supporting. With this parting shot he bowed and left the room.

No sooner was he gone, than Agnes took up her pen and wrote direct to Marese Baskette, enclosing Aymer's second letter—which accused Marese of being the instigator of the murder—and giving the fullest particulars she could remember of his first—relating to Violet's claim. She did not forget to describe her interview with Mr. Broughton, nor to mention his threat of the building society taking the matter up. She assured him that she looked upon the matter as a hoax and an insult; and only related the story to him in order that he might take the proper proceedings to punish the author of the calumny.

This letter reached Marese at his club in London, and, hardened man that he was, it filled him with well-founded alarm. Till that moment he had believed that no one on earth was aware of the Waldron claims but himself and Theodore, who had learnt it from perusal of his father Aurelian's papers. As for any one suspecting him of complicity in the death of Jason Waldron, he had never dreamt that detection was possible.

If ever a crime was managed skilfully, that had been; and as to the old story that "murder will out," it was of course an exploded superstition. Had it been Aymer alone who was on his track, he would not so much have cared; but Aymer had not kept the secret to himself: he had written to a lawyer, giving his proofs; the lawyer had verified one of them, at least, and Marese well knew what lawyers were. Then there was the threat of the building society, just as he was on the point of making a favourable composition with them, and was actually to receive a surrender of some part of the property in a few weeks' time. He appreciated the full force of Broughton's remark, repeated by Lady Agnes, that the building society, his client, would be sure to support Violet Waldron's claim. Of course they would. A fresh litigation would be set on foot, and possession of the estate indefinitely delayed; if that was delayed, his marriage with Lady Lechester would be also thrown back.

Yet despite all these serious reflections, Marese would have made comparatively light of the matter had it not been for the accusation of crime—for the fact that Aymer had obtained a faint glimpse of the truth. He was not the man to hesitate one moment at crime, or to regret it after it was done; but he dreaded detection, as well he might, for from the height to which he had risen, and was about to rise, his fall would be great indeed. He smiled at Lady Agnes' suggestion that he should prosecute Aymer for libel or slander. Prosecute him in open court, and at once fix ten thousand eyes upon that dark story; perhaps bring a hundred detectives, eager to hunt out the secrets of a rich man, upon his track! That would be folly indeed.

Aymer must be silenced, and Violet removed; but not like that.

The first thing he did was to telegraph for Theodore, who came up by the express from Stirmingham.

They had a long and anxious consultation. Theodore persuaded Marese to go at once to The Towers to see Agnes and deny the imputation—to secure her, in fact. Marese thought that this would hardly do; he knew Agnes better than Theodore. She would think that he had put himself out unnecessarily, that he had taken it too greatly to heart, and would simply ask him why he had not at once instituted legal proceedings against Aymer.

In his secret heart of hearts, Marese did not care to visit that neighbourhood more often than was absolutely necessary. And he really did think that Agnes' transcendent pride would be better suited if he treated the matter in an off-hand way, and dispatched only an agent to represent him—a species of ambassador. Another reason was that Broughton, if he was on the watch, would take Marese's visit to The Towers as a proof that there was something in it, else why should he be so anxious to deny it?

Theodore was willing to go, and he did not long delay his departure. "For all the time that we waste in thinking," said Marese, "this fellow, Malet, is at work. It will take him some time to search all the London churches; but it may so happen that he may hit upon the very entry he wants at the first church chance leads him to."

There was no time to be lost. Very probably Aymer himself, of whose whereabouts in London they were quite ignorant, might go down to The Towers expecting to see his affianced, Violet. Theodore might meet him there, and—

Above all things, Theodore was to so work upon Lady Agnes' mind as to turn this apparent disadvantage to a real good, and use it to precipitate the marriage. Could not she be brought to see that her proudest course would be to marry Marese, in despite of all these foul calumnies, at once, in defiance? It would be difficult for Marese to put this himself, but his agent could do so.

Theodore went to The Towers, and it fell out much as Marese had foreseen. Agnes was gratified. Theodore said that Marese looked upon the whole affair with the deepest contempt, and disdained to proceed. The hallucination of that unfortunate young man, Aymer, would prove in itself sufficient punishment for him. Marese desired no vengeance upon a poverty-stricken youth whose brains were not very clear. Then he delicately hinted at a more immediate marriage, and saw with satisfaction that Agnes did not resent the idea, but seemed to ponder over it.

But where was Violet? She had left The Towers, and no one there knew her place of abode.

This disturbed Theodore. He wished to know what the enemy was doing; if he could foresee their designs, then Marese was safe, because they could be outwitted. It was awkward to have these persons working against them in the dark—i.e., Violet, Aymer, and Broughton.

Violet had left no address. Agnes remembered Aymer's, but Theodore found on secret inquiry that he had moved. He waited at The Towers in the hope that Malet might come. Being a man of versatile talent, and clever in conversation, Lady Agnes was pleased with him, and invited him to stay as long as was convenient.

While Theodore was at The Towers, the great fire happened at Belthrop, and the flames were visible from the upper windows of the mansion, where Lady Agnes, Theodore, and the servants watched them with interest.

Shortly afterwards the Barnham paper was published, with a special account of the preliminary examination of the supposed incendiary, poor Jenkins, before the justices, and Theodore came across the name of Violet Waldron. In this way he learnt that one of the parties, and the most important, was at that moment living in an obscure village, not much more than fifteen miles distant.

He was preparing to pay a visit to Belthrop—ostensibly to see the ruins of the fire—when Aymer Malet arrived at The Towers.

His coming was very natural. He could not understand why he did not hear from Violet. He had written to her fully twenty times, addressing his letters to The Towers, and had received no answer. This greatly alarmed him, and he resolved to go down and see her. All these letters were meantime at the General Post Office in London.

Lady Agnes, determined to cut off every connection with Malet and Violet, had given the servants strict orders not to take in any letters addressed to either of them. Aymer's letters, therefore, went back to the local post office, and from thence to London, and doubtless in due time they would have returned to him.

When he found himself with seventy pounds in his pocket, he had taken a better lodging, having previously written to Violet to apprise her of his removal, but as she never had his letter, her note to him was delivered at the old address, and Aymer's old landlady, irritated at his leaving her, coolly put it on the fire.

Violet had only written once, for she too was astonished, and a little hurt, because Aymer did not write to her, and in addition, she had been much disturbed by the great fire and the trial of poor Jenkins. The upshot was, that Aymer leaving his monotonous labour in the London churches, took train and came down to the nearest station to The Towers.

Never doubting his reception, he drove up to the mansion, and was surprised beyond measure when the servants, respectfully and regretfully, but firmly announced that Lady Lechester would not see him. Where was Miss Waldron? Miss Waldron had left—the newspaper said she was at Belthrop, but that was a day or two ago.

Bewildered, and not a little upset, Aymer mechanically turned on his heel—he had dismissed his fly at the park gates—and set out to walk to Belthrop. He had almost reached that very little wicket-gate where Lady Lechester had met the apparition of Cornet De Warren, when he heard a voice calling his name, and saw a gentleman hastily following him. It was Theodore, who had requested the servants, and enforced his request by a bribe, to at once inform him when Mr. Malet called.

Theodore had a difficult task before him; but he approached it with full confidence in himself. Without a moment's delay he introduced himself as Marese Baskette's cousin, and at once noted the change that passed over Aymer's countenance. Ah!—then Mr. Malet was aware of the previous intimacy that had existed between him and Mr. Baskette? That intimacy was now at an end. He frankly admitted that he had come to The Towers in the interest of Marese; but upon his arrival he had heard, to his intense surprise, of Mr. Malet's discovery of the Waldron claim. To him that claim appeared indisputable: he had written as much to Mr. Baskette, and the consequence was a quarrel. They had parted: and he was now endeavouring to persuade Lady Lechester to break off her association with that man.

He had heard with great interest the career of Mr. Malet—he had seen his book; and while he regretted his misfortunes, he rejoiced that circumstances enabled him to offer Mr. Malet a most lucrative and remunerative post—a post that would at once give him ease and leisure to promote his literary labours; which would supply him with funds to continue his researches into the Waldron claims—and perhaps to bring the guilty to justice; which would even—this in a delicate manner—it would even permit of an immediate union with Miss Waldron.

Further, as this post was in the city of Stirmingham, Mr. Malet would be on the very spot, and within easy reach of London. The only difficulty was that it required Mr. Malet's immediate presence in Stirmingham, as it would be necessary to fill the place at once. Probably from the direction of Mr. Malet's steps he was on his way to visit Belthrop, and to congratulate the truly heroic Miss Waldron upon her gallant attempt to save an innocent man from punishment. At the same time, perhaps, Mr. Malet would really serve Miss Waldron's interest better by at once proceeding to Stirmingham that very afternoon with Theodore.

What was this post? Mr. Malet had been in Stirmingham, and was aware that he (Theodore) had inherited a very large asylum for the insane there. As he was himself averse to the science of the mind, he had rarely resided on his property, but left the chief management to a physician, and the accounts to a secretary. His secretary had left about a month ago, and the affairs were in much confusion. He had great pleasure in offering Mr. Malet the place. The salary was seven hundred and fifty pounds per annum, and residence. This residence was sufficiently large for a married man.

Aymer modestly objected that he was hardly fit for so important a trust.

Theodore said that he had read his book, and a man who was capable of writing like that was capable of anything. Besides, he had heard of his ability while in Mr. Broughton's service.

The end was that Aymer accepted the engagement, as indeed he could hardly refuse it. Still he wished to see Violet. That was certainly unfortunate; but could not Mr. Malet write from the railway station and send it by a messenger. On arrival in Stirmingham, and taking possession of his place of trust, Mr. Malet could at once write to Miss Waldron to come, and there was plenty of room at the asylum, and more than one respectable matron residing there with whom she could remain until the marriage could take place. He was so sorry that Lady Lechester cherished a prejudice against Mr. Malet—that would wear off—he had done his best to remove it. Still, at present, Mr. Malet was not welcome at The Towers. Would he so far stretch politeness as to stroll gently on the road to the station? He (Theodore) would speedily overtake him with a carriage.

An hour and a half afterwards Theodore and Aymer were en route to Stirmingham. Theodore had explained his sudden departure by a telegram. He had received a telegram, it was true, as he constantly did; but it was as usual a Stock Exchange report of no importance.

From the station Aymer sent a short note to Violet at Belthrop, by special messenger, acquainting her with his good fortune.

They reached Stirmingham the same evening, and next day Aymer was formally installed in possession of a bundle of papers, ledgers, and account books, which he was to balance up. He was shown the secretary's residence—a fine house, closely adjoining the asylum—and at night he wrote a glowing letter to Violet, enclosing money to pay her fare first-class, and begging her to come at once.

On the second morning came a note telling him that she should start that very day, and full of joyful anticipations. She would arrive towards night. Aymer dined with Theodore, and took wine with him afterwards. Presently he rose to prepare to go to the railway and meet Violet. He reached his private room with a singular sensation in the head, a swimming in his eyes, and a dryness of the tongue. He plunged his face in cold water to recover himself; but it seemed to increase the disorder. His head seemed to swell to an enormous size, and yet to grow extremely light, till it felt like an inflated balloon, and seemed as if it would lift him to the ceiling. Sitting down to try and steady himself, he fancied that the chair rose in the air, and cried out in alarm. He managed to pull the bell, and then felt as if he was carried away to an immense distance, and could look down upon his body in the room beneath.

A servant answered the bell, who stared at him, smiled, and said—"Ah, your fit's on at last." Aymer's last consciousness was that he was talking very fast, without exactly knowing what he was saying. After that there was a blank.

Meantime Violet was met by Theodore Marese at the railway station; and a message in cipher flew along the wires to a certain club in London. Marese Baskette breathed again, for the cipher read—"They are here." A simple sentence, but enough.

Chapter Nine

A fashionable London newspaper came out one morning with the statement that a marriage had been arranged in high life, and that preparations were already in progress. J. Marese Baskette, Esq, of Stirmingham, and Lady Agnes Lechester were to be shortly united in holy matrimony. This announcement was of the very greatest value to Marese. Not all the wealth, or reputed wealth he possessed—not even the honour of representing so important a city, could obtain for him the position in society which was secured by an alliance with the blue blood of Lechester. His money affairs wore at once a more roseate aspect.

It was well known that Lady Lechester owned large estates, and they were naturally reported to be even larger than they were. It was whispered abroad that, under careful nursing, certain incumbrances had been paid off, and that the rent-roll was now something extremely heavy even for England, the land of long rent-rolls.

People who had previously fought a little shy of the handsome heir, and asked hard terms to discount his paper, now pressed forward, and were anxious to obtrude their services. At the clubs, persons who had affected to ignore the richest man in the world as a matter of principle, on account of his ignoble descent, now began to acknowledge his existence, and to extend the tips of their aristocratic fingers. It was remembered that the doubts and difficulties which had beset his claim to the vast Stirmingham estate like a dark cloud, had of late in great part cleared away. The family council had "burst up," and there were really no competitors in the field. Marese Baskette, Esq, in the course of a year or two, so soon as the law affairs could be settled, would be the richest man in the world.

At the clubs they freely discussed his wealth. When realised it would put the Rothschilds, and Coutts, and Barings, and all the other famous names—the Astors of New York and even the princes of India—into the shade.

Stirmingham, the busiest city in England, surrounded with a triple belt of iron furnaces, undermined with hundreds of miles of coal galleries, was it possible to estimate the value of that wonderful place? Why, the estate in the time of old Sternhold Baskette was roughly put at twenty millions sterling—that was thirty years ago or more—what must it be worth now? There really was no calculating it. Suppose he got but one quarter of what he was entitled to—say property worth only five millions—there was a fine thing. What on earth had the ladies been thinking of all these years that they had not secured so rich a prize?

Lady Lechester was not a little envied. County families and others, from whom she had kept aloof for years, overlooked the disrespect, and called upon her with their congratulations. Invitations poured in upon her; the whole county talked of nothing else but Lady Lechester's wedding; even the great fire was forgotten.

In London circles the name of Agnes Lechester, which from long retirement had almost dropped out of memory, was revived, and the old story of the attachment to the dragoon and his untimely end in the East, was dug up and sent on its way from mansion to mansion. It was nothing but pride that made her refuse poor De Warren who was a handsomer man than Baskette, and came of quite as good a family as her own. However, fortune seemed to favour these creatures—why, she must be five-and-thirty; five-and-thirty, ay, closer on forty; older than Marese—much older.

To Agnes, all the conversation that went on around, and the echo of which reached her, was happiness itself. The intense pride and ambition of her nature, which had partly kept her in retirement, blazed out in all its native vigour. Her step was slow and stately; her manner grew cold and haughty; her conversation distant. When poor old Jenkins's wife came with the ancient Bible, she bought it, indeed, and put it on the library table, but barely looked at it. Six months before she would have criticised it carefully, and entered a descriptive record of it in the catalogue which she kept with her own hand. Now it was disdainfully tossed upon one side.

A point that was sometimes discussed between these formal and distant lovers was the place of their future residence, and as Lady Lechester hated The Towers, and Marese said that the country house near Stirmingham had of late been closely approached by the coal mines, it was finally settled that they should reside in a mansion near Regent's Park, which belonged to Lady Lechester, until Marese could build a suitable place. This he announced his intention of doing upon a magnificent scale.

It was singular that old Sternhold, whose life was spent in adding stone to stone and brick to brick, had never contemplated the idea of building himself a palace.

His son determined to surpass all the mansions of England; and the plans, when once they had been decided upon, were sent down to Lady Lechester for her approval. They were placed upon a table in the reception room, so that every visitor who called could not avoid seeing them; and it became one of the pleasures of Agnes' daily life to point out the beauties of the new mansion, and to show her own sketches for improvements. To such littleness did this once noble and generous nature descend. The Stirmingham estate seemed to be endowed with the power of degrading every character that came into contact with it.

It was understood that Lady Lechester was to lay the first stone of this grand mansion when they returned from the wedding trip. They were to go to Italy, and make excursions in the Mediterranean in Marese's yacht Gloire de Dijon, the name of which he now altered to Agnes.

Marese's life at this time was one long continued triumph. The only danger that had threatened him was crushed; both Aymer and Violet were in safe keeping.

Theodore was still at Stirmingham watching them; perhaps a sterner keeper than Theodore might turn the key upon one or both ere long. He set his teeth firmly with a frown as he thought of that possibility. Marese was not the man to be threatened with impunity. At all events they were quite safe for a good length of time—till long after his marriage. The marriage once over and he feared nothing. No scandal could seriously injure him after that. He should be secured with a triple wall of brass—of wealth, power, position.

The property at Stirmingham was falling into his hands like an over-ripe pear. Let the companies strive how they might, they could no longer discover any pretext to delay its surrender. The American claimants had vanished into the distance—that great dread had departed. He had paid off in hard cash a large share of the claims the building societies made upon him, for expenses they had incurred in improving the property. He had obtained a rule that the remainder of the claims should be discharged by instalments; and as now in a short time he should enjoy almost unlimited credit, there would be no difficulty in raising the necessary sums.

With other societies he had corresponded; with the Corporation he was on the best of terms, having used his influence in Parliament already to pass a private bill of theirs, and they had no legal power to prevent his seizure of his rights. With the rest of his creditors he was not only on good terms—he was pressed to borrow more. Literally he felt himself, as he surveyed his monetary affairs, the richest man in the world.

Another success came to him. He had delivered his maiden speech in the House, and whether it really was clever or appropriate, or whether people were predisposed in his favour, certain it was that it had produced an impression. The papers were full of it; the reviewers considered it an omen of an honourable parliamentary career. It was quoted from one end of the kingdom to the other. His party begun to cast an eye upon him. Here was that rare combination—a rich man with talent. Could they not turn him to account?

Then came the announcement of the engagement with Lechester, and they went a step further, and said something must be done. Something was forthwith done. An office was offered to him—not a high office, nor very remunerative, but still an office; and one only a degree beneath that of a Minister. It was well understood that no man ever filled that post without subsequently becoming a Minister. It was a kind of political cadetship. Marese accepted the office, and wrote to Lady Lechester, who saw in this a new proof of the career in store for her; and he received in reply the warmest note he had hitherto had.

Lastly, he was about to marry into one of the oldest families in England. This marriage was the sure and certain prelude to a coronet; not that he would take it till he had exhausted his powers, and felt it time to retire to the House of Lords. Yet it was this marriage that alone caused any anxiety to Marese. He grew, for him, nervously anxious as the time approached. It certainly was not affection for her personally; it was the extraordinary good fortune which now smiled upon him. Once a gamester—still largely gambling upon the Stock Exchange—he had imbibed a little of the superstition of the race. Hard as he was—cool, self-possessed, and equal to any emergency—there arose in his mind a certain feverish eagerness to get it over; not sufficient to curtail his rest, or cause him to exhibit any outward sign, or even to diminish his glory in his success; but there was just this dash of uncertain bitter in the cup that was rising to his lip. He dared not hurry on the ceremony, knowing Lady Lechester's temperament too well: he must await the arrival of the date that she herself had fixed.

There was some little difficulty at The Towers as to where the marriage should take place. The church at Bury Wick was the natural resort, easiest of access, and nearest; but Agnes, even in her pride and self-will, could not altogether make up her mind to be married in that church. The memory of the wedding-party so strangely and fearfully interrupted there, had not yet died away. It would seem like a bad omen to be married there.

Barnham was so far, and the vicar a Low Churchman, and not to her taste. Marese suggested Stirmingham: but no, that would not do. My lady would be married from her own ancestral Towers; and finally hit upon the plan of resuscitating the ancient family chapel at The Towers, and having the ceremony performed in it. This could be done by a special licence: which, of course, was no obstacle. It was true that she disliked and even hated The Towers; but the pride of family and long descent overcame that feeling. She would be married in the old chapel. Accordingly, workmen were sent for, and the sound of hammer and plane resounded through the place. The chapel, disused ever since the Lechesters left the Church of Rome—about a century ago—was completely renovated, cleaned, painted, gilded, and adorned in every possible manner.

Time flew, and Agnes' pen was busy in marking the list of names of those who were eligible to receive an invitation to the marriage. The dresses were ordered. Agnes was very hard to please—even a simple village maiden likes to exercise her choice for that once in her life. Judge, then, of the difficulty of pleasing the mistress of The Towers, soon to be the richest lady in the world. Nothing was good enough: the orders were countermanded day after day, and nothing but the enormous sums that were to be expended could have reconciled the tradesmen to her incessant caprices.

Yet through all this loud sound of preparation, through all this silk and satin, through everything that could be devised to make the heart content, there penetrated a trouble. Agnes would at times retire to her private room, and remain secluded for hours. After these solitary fits her step was slower, and her countenance pale and melancholy, till she gradually recovered herself. She had broken off her habit of visiting the Kickwell Pot. It had been a great trial to her to do so; but she had at last firmly made up her mind, and had conquered the singular fascination which drew her thither. She had decided upon the earthly career: she would close her eyes to the immortal one. But the memory of the spirit was not so easily effaced: she mused on its shape, its graceful, swaying elegance of motion, the glow in its wonderful eyes, and felt at times the thrill of its electric touch. It required immense strength of mind to resist the temptation to converse once more with her phantom-lover.

Who that had for a moment contemplated the proud and happy position of Lady Lechester, the observed of all observers, would have credited that such a hankering, such an extraordinary belief, still possessed her mind?

Time flew, and there remained but one brief week till the marriage day. Marese was to come to The Towers on the morrow, and stay till the day previous to the ceremony when he was, in obedience to the old etiquette, to sleep at Barnham. For one day only would she be alone at The Towers. Marese came; the hours flew; some little warmth infused itself even into their cold intercourse. Just before dinner he left The Towers for Barnham. After dark, Lady Agnes went out alone, wrapped in her plaid shawl, and made her way to "The Pot."

The morrow was her wedding-day, yet the old fascination had conquered—she could not resist it. Once more, for the last time, she would look upon the face of that glorious being, and beg his forgiveness. It was May now—beautiful May. The beech trees were covered with foliage, the air was soft and warm, and there was a delicate odour at times of the hawthorn blossom borne upon the gentle breeze. Only in places there was a low white mist, a dew hanging like a light cloud a few feet above the earth. A thin column of such a mist hung over the mouth of "The Pot," spectral, ghost-like. There had been heavy rains previously, and the river was swollen and turbid. Its roar came up in a sullen hoarse murmur through the narrow tunnel. Over the steep down or cliff there shone one lucent planet—the evening star.

Agnes stole out from among the fern and beech trees, and stood beside the great decaying oak trunk, leaning lightly against it. Before her but two steps was the mouth of "The Pot," and over it hovered the thin mist.

The old, old fascination fell upon her, the same half unconsciousness of all surrounding things. The star grew dim, the roar of the river receded to an immense distance, and then arose the spirit. What intercourse they had cannot be told: whether she half yielded to the desire to soar above this earthly ball, and stepped forward to his embrace—whether she eagerly implored for pardon for her weakness, dazzled by worldly glory.

The dog Dando had followed her unchidden. He alone of all that had pertained to Aymer and Violet, Agnes had retained. He knew the old path so well. He crouched so still at the foot of the great oak trunk. So quietly, so heedlessly, taking no heed of the figure, the shadow that stole onward in the dark beneath the beech trees—stole forward from trunk to trunk, from bunch of fern to hawthorn bush.

A grey shadow in the form of a man—a crouching, stealthy, gliding approach—yet the dog Dando made no sign. And Agnes stood with arms extended almost over the mouth of "The Pot." And the grey shadow reached the hollow oak trunk.

In the left hand of this shadow was a tin whistle.

Chapter Ten

After a while, Aymer awoke from the stupor into which the drug that had been administered to him had thrown his senses. His awakening was more painful than the first effects of the poison. His head felt as heavy as lead, and there was a dull pain across his brow. A languid helplessness seemed to possess his limbs, he could not walk across the room, and with difficulty stretched out his hand to the bell-rope. Then all the designs upon the wall-papering got mixed up before his eyes in a fantastic dance, which made him giddy, till he was obliged to shut them. His consciousness had as yet barely sufficiently returned for him to notice that he was in a different apartment to any he had hitherto occupied at the asylum. He must have had partial returns to consciousness previously, for he found himself sitting in a large armchair, half clad, and wearing a dressing-gown. A second pull at the bell-rope brought footsteps outside the door, which sounded heavy upon the boards, evidently uncarpeted. Then a key turned in the lock outside, at the sound of that Aymer opened his eyes quickly, and a strong-looking man, whom he had never seen before, peered in.

"Where is Mr. Theodore?" said Aymer. "Is Miss Waldron come? Tell them I am better. Ask her to see me. What has been the matter with me?"

"You've had one of your fits, sir," replied the man, very civilly, but in an indifferent tone.

"My fits! I never have fits. Why do you stand in the doorway? Why was the door locked?"

"All right sir—don't excite yourself. There, you see you can't stand. It's your head, sir, your head."

"Send me a doctor instantly," said Aymer.

"A doctor? He's been to sec you three or four times."

"Three or four times! How long have I been ill, then?"

"Oh, five days, I think. Let's see, you were brought over here on the Tuesday I remember—yes, five days."

"Brought over here? What do you mean? Who the deuce are you?" said Aymer, for the first time growing suspicious, and standing up by dint of effort.

"Do sit still, sir, and keep calm, or you'll have another fit. My name's Davidson; I'm a warder; and I'll take good care of you, sir, if you'll only keep quiet."

The truth flashed into Aymer's mind in an instant.

"Do you mean to say I am in the madhouse?" he asked, quietly.

"Well, no, sir, not quite so bad as that. This is an asylum, sir."

"How did I get here?"

"You were carried over in your fit."

"And where's Miss Waldron? Tell her to come to me at once."

"There's no Miss Waldron, sir; your head is not quite clear yet."

"What! you don't mean to say that you believe me mad?"

"Well, your papers is all right, sir."

Aymer lost his temper, as well he might.

"Mr. Theodore must be mad," he said. "Tell him to come at once; no, I'll go to him."

With an effort he reached the door; but Davidson easily kept him back with one hand, in his weak state.

"Now do keep quiet, sir—do sit down."

"I tell you I'm the secretary," said Aymer, his breath coming fast and thick, for he began to feel that he was trapped.

"Ay, ay, sir; they all say that, or something like it. You see, we likes to get people to come quiet, without any noise. One gent came here thinking it was his family mansion, and he was a duke. If you'll sit down, sir, I'll get you anything you want."

Poor Aymer was obliged to totter to his chair.

221

"And where's Violet—where's Miss Waldron?" he said.

"There isn't no such person, sir. 'Tis your head; you'll be better presently. I'll look in again by-and-by."

The door shut, the lock turned. Aymer knew that he was a prisoner. For a few minutes he really was mad, frenzied with unusual passion and indignation, to be trapped like an animal lured on by provender, and for what purpose? Ah, for what purpose? Violet—it must be Violet—her claim to the Stirmingham estate. He was trapped that he might not follow up the clue. Where was she? Doubtless spirited away somewhere, or perhaps expecting him at Belthrop, thinking he was coming to her. They would be sure to keep them as far apart as possible. Theodore was Marese Baskette's cousin, his friend, his confidant; he saw it all—he had been drugged, stupefied, made to utter every species of nonsense, to appear literally mad. He looked round the room; it was to all appearance an ordinary apartment, except that the door was strong, and without panels to weaken it. He staggered to the window, he put it up; there were no bars, no iron rods to prevent him getting out; but he looked down—a drop of twenty feet—into a narrow, stone-paved courtyard. A bitter thought entered his mind: they would rather like him to commit suicide out of that window. Opposite, about ten feet distant, ran an immensely high stone wall, crenelated on the top, and over that he could catch a glimpse of the blue May sky. He understood now why the corridor was evidently uncarpeted; if by any means he should get out at the door, his steps would sound, and give the alarm at once. He sat down and tried to think; either the excitement, or the natural strength of his constitution was fast overcoming the poison. His head was clearer, and he could see distinctly, but his limbs were still feeble. What could he do?

At this moment the key again turned in the lock, and Davidson entered, bearing a tray with an appetising dinner.

"How do I know these things are not drugged also?" said Aymer.

"Drugged, sir? That's always their delusion. Them's good victuals. I'll taste if you like." And he did so.

While his head was turned, Aymer, weak as he was, made a rush at the door. The warder turned and seized him, and led him back to his chair like a child. Aymer, mad with passion, threatened him, and snatched at a knife upon the table.

"Ay, ay; steady, sir," said the warder, quite coolly; "that's no use, my waistcoat is padded on purpose. I've had him padded ever since Mr Odo made a stab at me. Now, now, sir, do be quiet; you're only a hurting yourself. Eat your dinner and get stronger, and maybe then you can have a wrestle with me."

He glanced with a half smile at Aymer's slight, panting figure, and then at his own sturdy proportions, winked, and withdrew.

As his steps died away in the passage, Aymer started to his feet in intense astonishment. He had heard his own name; he could not believe his senses—was he really mad?

"Aymer Malet, Esq."

The voice was low, but distinct. It might come from the doorway, the window, the wall, the ceiling. He was startled, but replied—

"Yes; I am here."

"Young man," said the voice, very low, but quite audible, "take my advice: control your temper. If you stab a warder they will have a pretext to keep you here all your lifetime."

"Ah," said Aymer; "thank you, I understand. But who are you?— who are you?"

"I am a young old man. Who are you?"

"I am a young man," said Aymer, growing curious, and for the moment forgetting his position. "My name you know—I can't tell how. I come from World's End."

"Ah!" said the voice, sadly; "I had hoped you were sane."

"So I am."

"Why then say you came from the world's end?"

"I did not. I said from World's End; it is a place near Bury Wick."

"You are sane then so far. I know that World's End very well. I only tried you. I overheard your name when you were carried in. Now, answer me. Why are you here?"

"There, that is what I want to know."

"If you do not know, you are not sane. Cannot you see the motive for your confinement?"

"Certainly I can. It is easy to see that."

And Aymer briefly related the circumstances.

"And where is your Violet?"

"Doubtless at Belthrop, or spirited away—perhaps abroad. Far enough from me, at all events."

"Not so: she is in this very place."

"I don't believe it. They would keep her away."

"I am sure of it. What should you do if you got out?"

"I should go straight to Belthrop—or, stay, perhaps I should go to Mr. Broughton. He would protect me."

"Broughton—ah! he is a lawyer. I see you are sane. I must have a look at you. Turn your face towards the picture of the 'Last Supper.'"

Wondering and yet curious, Aymer did as he was bid. On the wall above a side-board was a large copy of Vinci's "Last Supper." In a few seconds the voice came again; and soon he found it came from the picture.

"I see you. I have read you. You have talent, perhaps genius; but your chin is weak. You know not how to fight men. You do not comprehend that men are beasts, and that it is necessary to be always fighting them. Still you are sane, you are young—eat, and get strong— you will do. Your name is familiar to me. Who was your father?"

223

Aymer told him. The voice replied—"I knew him—a clever man, and, excuse me, a fool. How came you to reside at World's End?"

Aymer told him. "But who are you?" he said, eagerly. "Let me see you also."

"Very well. Look at the dog under the table in the picture. Now."

Aymer saw a slender white finger suddenly protruded through the body of the dog.

"But I only see your finger."

"Well, that is me. Don't you know that the hand is the man, and the claw is the beast? You can see by my finger that I have a hand."

It was evident that the stranger was proud of his white hand and slender finger.

"Who on earth are you?" said Aymer, beginning to get excited. "If you do not answer me I will pull the picture down."

"If you do, you will ruin us both."

"Well, tell me who you are."

"I am a prisoner like yourself. My name is, or was, for I am dead now, Fulk Lechester."

"Fulk Lechester—Lady Agnes' cousin! Ah! I have heard of you," said Aymer. "You were very clever, and you went—well, I mean—"

"Ha! ha! ha! I will convince you that I am as sane as yourself— saner; for what a goose you were to be so easily trapped."

"So I certainly was."

"Would you like to get out? Of course. So should I. Let me see. First, I have seen you—your physiognomy is good; next, I have read of your book, for I see the papers; thirdly, I knew your father, at least I knew all about his career; fourthly, you come from World's End, and that is my neighbourhood; fifthly, you are young; sixthly, you are in love, which is a strong stimulus to exertion. Yes, you will do. Now eat your dinner; you must get strong."

"I will not touch it till I see you. I will tear the picture down."

"Oh, rash, headstrong! Lift it up instead."

Aymer tried. "I can't," he said.

"No, because I have fixed it. Now try."

The picture lifted easily, and Aymer was face to face with the stranger. He saw a little man, a head and a half shorter than himself, elegantly made, and dressed in the fashion. His brow was very broad and high, his eyes dark and large, deeply set; his lips perfect. He had a small moustache but no beard or whiskers. His complexion was the worst part of his appearance; it was almost yellow. Fulk smiled, and showed good teeth.

"I am yellow, I know," he said. "So would you be if you had not been out of doors for two years. I look forty, I know; I am really just thirty-three. Nipped in the bud. Ha! ha! However, there is no time to waste—the warder will return. Eat your dinner. Let us shake hands."

Aymer readily extended his hand. Suddenly he said—

"How do I know that this is not a new trap?"

Fulk smiled sadly. "A week ago you believed everybody," he said; "now you run to the other extreme. That is youth. I am young; but I am also old. Trouble makes men old, thought perhaps still older. For seven years I have done nothing but think."

"For seven years!" echoed Aymer, in horror. "Have you been here seven years?"

"Yes; I was then twenty-six, now I am thirty-three. Ah! I blossomed too fast. It is a bad sign, friend Aymer, when life is all roses too early; the frosts are sure to come."

"True," said Aymer, thinking of his wedding-day, so strangely, so dreadfully interrupted.

"I was a Secretary of State at twenty-six. I had everything—money, youth, power, a career, a loving wife. A few hours changed it."

"May I ask, how?"

"Certainly; companions in misfortune have no secrets. My wife was thrown from her horse; her beautiful neck was broken. I had no son. We Lechesters are perhaps a little wild. Odo was certainly wild. Well, grief made me eccentric. I threw up my career. I was young then, like you. I resigned; I went down to Cornwall; I built a hut among the rocks, and said I would live a hermit's life. I did so. I began to feel better. The sea soothed me; I learnt much from Nature. You see, I had lived hitherto all my days with men. If I had stayed there, I should have written something great. But there were men who had their eyes on me. My property is large, you know; trustees or guardians do not get pay direct; but there are indirect profits in managing estates. My wife was dead; her friends did not trouble to protect me. Perhaps I did seem eccentric. Hermits are out of date. For years it has been the custom to put Lechesters in an asylum. I was put here; but not so easily as you. I fought; it was no use. I might as well have been calm."

"And you have been here all these years?"

"All these years, but not without trying to escape. I pretended to be harmlessly mad—quite satisfied with my condition. I was allowed to wander in the grounds. One day I got up a tree, and before they could follow I was on the wall, I dropped over but broke my leg. Well, I recovered, but I still limp a little; after a while, I went into the grounds with a keeper. I tried cunning. I became harmlessly mad again—my fancy was to fly kites. To one kite I attached a long letter with an account of my imprisonment. I let it loose, and it fell in the midst of Stirmingham. But it was no good—it made a stir—people came here, and I answered their questions calmly. No good. They were determined to see that I was mad. If I misspelt a single word in a sentence, it was a proof that a highly-educated mind had partially broken down. Like you, I got violent—I tried to despatch a warder and get out. Ever since then I have been in this room."

"Two years?"

"Two years. Hush—eat your dinner—Davidson comes."

The picture fell into its place, and Aymer tried to eat the dinner, which had grown cold.

Chapter Eleven

After Davidson was gone with the tray, Aymer could hear him opening other doors along the corridor, and waited till all was quiet.

"Fulk!"

"Aymer!"

The picture was lifted, and Fulk's head appeared in the orifice.

"Remember," he said, "your first object is to get strong; unless you get strong, neither of us can escape. Therefore, eat and drink, and above all, sleep. If you fidget yourself, you will waste away. The sooner you get strong, the sooner you will get out and find your Violet. Push your armchair up close under this picture, and speak low, lest a warder should steal along on tiptoe. Take a book in your hand as if reading."

Aymer did as he was told. Fulk's head receded. "It is difficult for me to keep long in that position," he said; "I am not tall enough. But we can talk just as well."

"How came that hole in the wall?" asked Aymer.

"How came your book published?" said Fulk. "By the same process—patience and perseverance. No credit to me though. When a man is confined for two years in one room, he is glad enough of something to do."

"Why did you make such a hole—how did you do it? It was very clever."

"It was very easy. The poker did a part, the steel to sharpen the dinner knife did another part!"

"But were they not afraid to leave such instruments in your room?"

"Not they. Theodore knows very well that I am not mad. He knows that I have too much mind to attempt suicide. As to the warders, they are strong, their clothes are impenetrable to an ordinary stab. Besides, I feign to be harmless, and at last worn out."

"There is no poker in my room," said Aymer, "and they have taken the knives away."

"That is because, as yet, they do not know your temperament. They think they know mine. So far as conveniences, and even luxuries, are concerned, certainly Theodore does not treat me amiss. I have

226

everything I could have if I were free—papers, books—everything but tools or liberty—but I can improvise tools."

"How is it they do not discover this hole in the wall?"

"Simply because on your side it is hidden by the picture, and behind the picture I have preserved the papering. On my side, it is hidden by a mirror; when I open the aperture, I unscrew the mirror."

"But how did you know there was a picture on this side?"

"A person who was confined as you are told me."

"Was he sane then? What became of him?"

"Don't ask me. He was sane. It was a terrible disappointment when he went."

"But did he not return to get you out?"

"You do not comprehend. He lies in the grave. It is my belief—but I should alarm you."

"They killed him?"

"Well, not so violent as that. He died—that is it—before our arrangements were complete."

"Then you have tried to escape with others?"

"Yes, three times, and three times accident has baulked it. For that reason I wish you to get strong speedily, lest you should be removed to another room—"

"Or the grave!"

"Let us talk on other subjects. You do not ask how the hole was made, nor why. I will tell you. In the first place, it was made because I had hopes of escaping through your room, which was then unoccupied, and the door left open. That was vain, for it was afterwards occupied; then the hole was enlarged to let me and one of your predecessors converse, and to let him get into my room, as you will have to do."

"Why?"

"Because your window is a French one; mine has a bar or upright up the centre, which is an essential element of escape."

"Go on—how did you make the hole?"

"With the steel and with the poker—grinding the bricks into dust, and mingling the dust with the ashes of the fire, so that the warder himself carried them away."

"And why not escape this way?"

"Because, in the first place, the door of that room is kept locked; secondly, because it opens also into the same corridor, and at the end of that corridor is the guard-room, where there is always a warder. Your bell rings in that room."

"How did you learn all these things?"

"How did you learn all the little traits of human nature, which the reviewers say you put in your book? By observation, of course. I had to walk along that corridor to reach the grounds, when I was allowed to go out."

"But you could bore a hole into the corridor?"

227

"Yes, and the bits of broken plaster would tell the story—that would be simple. Besides, to what end? Once I thought of boring under the corridor."

"How do that?"

"By lifting up one of the planks of the floor here; there is a space between the flooring and the ceiling, and that corridor has a kind of tunnel along under it. What for? why the hot-water pipes, to warm the cells, are carried along it—the cells of the violent, whose rooms have no fire-grates—that is of no use, for the tunnel at one end comes to the furnaces, where there is usually a man, neither could I get through the heat. At the other there is the thick outer wall of stone, and just beneath is Theodore's own room—his ears are sharp. Useless, my friend. This knowledge of the premises seems to you wonderful, simply because you have been here so short a time. Why, I have never seen the outside of this side of the building, except a partial glimpse when I was brought, gagged and bound, in a closed carriage; yet look at this."

He handed to Aymer a sheet of paper, on which was an elevation plan.

"I can't see how you got at this," said Aymer, beginning to have a high opinion of the other's ability.

"It was difficult; but patience and observation will accomplish all things. I learnt much of the outline by the shadow on the ground. Here is another plan, more minute; this is a ground plan."

Aymer examined it.

"Why, you have got even the locks and bolts of the doors," he said, in admiration.

"Yes, I should have made a splendid burglar—what a career lost!"

"But," said Aymer, "I see here 'water-canal' marked. I have seen that canal; why, it runs just outside the high wall just across the courtyard here."

"Ay, and that is the awkward part of it. First, a narrow courtyard or chasm to bridge; then a high wall to surmount; then a broad and deep canal—especially broad here, for, as you will see on the plan, there is a double width of water for the barges to turn round in. Finally, an unknown maze of streets."

"Not unknown," said Aymer. "I can be of some use there;" and he told Fulk of his residence in Stirmingham during the family council and the election. He had a fair knowledge of the streets.

"That is extremely fortunate," said Fulk. "You must trace out a plan for me, in case we should get separated. So you were at the family council—I read much of it in the papers which they allow me. By-the-by, Marese Baskette is about to marry my cousin. I wonder she has escaped the asylum so long—the common fate of us poor Lechesters. Tell me now about your Violet's claim."

Aymer did so.

Fulk mused a little while.

228

"I begin to see daylight," he said. "I see much that I did not previously comprehend. If we only wait, and keep watching, everything comes plain in time. Waldron—I knew the Waldrons well—very respectable people, and well descended. Waldron is mentioned in Domesday—Waleran Venator—i.e., Walron, the Huntsman. Jason Waldron—I wonder if I had better tell you what I know?—he was murdered, and—but you will not rest nor eat."

"I shall certainly not eat or sleep unless you tell me."

"Very well, but do keep calm; we shall be out all the sooner, unless indeed some unforeseen circumstance stops it, as it has hitherto done. Ay di me!"

"Do you know anything of Jason Waldron's murder?" asked Aymer, impatiently.

"I do; you have yourself told me. I had my suspicions—almost certainty—before, but I could not see the motive; now I see the motive—poor, miserable Odo!"

"Odo! what has Odo, to do with it? Do go on; I am wild."

"Very well. Odo Lechester murdered your friend Jason Waldron!"

"But Odo Lechester is in a lunatic asylum, incurable."

"Odo Lechester was in this very asylum, but he escaped nearly a year ago. He escaped by permission."

"I am in the dark—explain."

"By permission, directed to destroy Jason Waldron. He had homicidal tendencies, you know."

"Homicidal tendencies!—escaped! Stay a minute, let me think. I remember now. Oh! what a fool I have been. Why, I saw the description of him posted up against the police station in Stirmingham, during the election; it was partly destroyed—evidently an old bill. I see—I see. But why should Odo Lechester kill Jason?"

"He was instructed to do so. Your dear friend Theodore, who so kindly offered you a secretaryship at seven hundred and fifty pounds a year, told him to do so."

"Why—how—how could he—"

"Work on Odo's mind? Easily enough. Poor Odo—he is a beast, born in the shape of a man: it is not his fault—he is not responsible. Odo is a tinker and a whistler; he is at home among the gipsies and the woods, playing on his tin whistle, mending pots and kettles. His three great passions are tinkering, dogs, and—liberty. Theodore simply assured him that it was Waldron who was the cause of his confinement. Jason dead, Odo would be for ever free. Shall I add one more word? If Jason's daughter were also dead, Odo would be still safer in his freedom."

"Good God! he may be killing her now. Let me out—help me."

"Silence! Be quiet. She is safe—your cries will ruin all. She is safe in this very building."

229

"Impossible—I can't believe it; it is all a blind. I must go to Belthrop; I must see Broughton. Good God, how weak I am!"

He fell exhausted back into his chair.

"How foolish of you!" said Fulk, gently. "But I can understand it. Now, I will tell you how I learnt all this. It was very simple. When I found that there was no escape through your room, I tried the other wall. I removed the clock from the bracket, and bored a small hole. Frequently I had to stop, because I heard voices. I found the next room to mine was one of Theodore's own private apartments: it is the sitting-room, in fact. Beyond it is his laboratory. I should like to know what is in that laboratory: if we escape, I will know. He and Marese used to meet here and converse. I heard them; I listened. I tell you I heard things that would make your flesh creep. Are you better?"

"Yes; oh, that I was stronger! There is wine on the table. Do you think I might drink it safely?"

"Certainly not; but you had better pretend that you have. Pour some behind the grate; get rid of it somehow, or they will put the poison in your food. Well, I heard things about a certain ship, the Lucca."

"The Lucca—she was found a derelict."

"Yes, I know; I could tell you how she became a derelict. But Odo. Well, I heard them discuss that plan. He was to be instructed, and then allowed to escape. He did escape. I only wish I was strong, and could climb like him. What he did, you know. If he is still at large, I will wager a hundred pounds I find him. I know his old haunts. But I could not understand the object of—of—I see now. Waldron was the descendant of Arthur Sibbold. Are you superstitious? No. Well, I am—a little. In this case, now, does it not seem as if the blood of old Will Baskette, shot at the cider barrel, had revenged itself from generation to generation? Stirmingham was, as it were, founded with blood. Your poor friend Jason was a descendant of the murderer Sibbold, who shot the thief; and here is a Baskette continuing the vendetta."

"For God's sake, tell me how to escape."

"I will. But is it not Fate? Look at the chain of events— 'circumstances' they are called now: the ancients called them Fate, Sophocles called them Necessity. But you are eager about escaping. Hush—they are coming!"

The picture dropped; Aymer looked down at his book. Davidson entered, and asked him how he felt. He replied better, and asked if Miss Waldron was in the asylum?

Davidson smiled. "Still on that, sir? I tell you honestly that no such person is here."

He looked Aymer in the face, and Aymer believed him. Davidson lit the gas, left several newspapers and books, and retired. So soon as his steps had died away, the picture was lifted again.

230

"I told you so," said Aymer; "she is not here. He evidently spoke the truth."

"He did so—so far as he knew. But this is an immense building; and you forget—you were not brought here at first—there is a residence, as they call it, detached. Davidson's duties never take him there, unless specially sent for."

"Well, well; let me escape, that is all."

"You have looked out of window; you have seen the courtyard—the wall. You know that beyond the wall is the canal: all that is plain in your mind?"

"It is. First, we must get across the courtyard, then we must climb the wall, then descend and swim the canal."

"Ah," said Fulk, "I cannot swim."

"I can," said Aymer; "I learnt in the sea." He remembered his few bright months of wandering before he had met Violet.

"I am glad of it, though I had provided for that. The bladders that would have supported you, can carry our dry clothes to change."

"The bladders—have you got some to float you?"

"I have; but, first of all, the courtyard and the wall. We must not descend into the courtyard, because at one end there is a window— Theodore's window—and he is here now; at the other it opens on the grounds, and warders are sometimes about. It is the wall we must attack."

"All we want now is a rope and a grapnel."

"I have a rope and a grapnel. Where? In my bed. What rope? Bell-rope partly, partly bed cording. How did I get it? By being mad. By picking everything to pieces with my fingers, as mad people will. They humoured me, and I secreted half the pieces while they carelessly removed the other. I have a long, strong rope; long enough to go up the wall and down the other side. I have also a grapnel."

"That is fortunate. How did you make a grapnel?"

"I did not make it; the warder brought it to me. You wonder. But you noticed the crenelated wall: that is the secret. My grapnel is simply a very long, strong ruler, such as are used in keeping ledgers, and in some mechanical drawing; I had it ostensibly for drawing. This ruler must be tied across the rope; when the rope is flung over the wall, the ruler will catch across the crenelation. There is the grapnel. The rope at its lower end will be fastened to the upright pillar, or whatever the technical name may be, which divides my window into two. There's the ladder."

"And the swimming bladders?"

"I made them out of an old Macintosh, which I also tore up: I sewed them together. Mad people have whims: one of mine was to mend my own clothes; so I got needles and thread. They are also in my bed. They have simply to be inflated with air; they have cords to fasten to the body."

231

"How clever! I should never have thought of such things. But why did you not escape before I came? You had all the materials required."

"True—all the means; but not the physical strength, nor the physical courage. I could not do it without a companion to assist me. You forget my leg was broken; it is still weak. You forget that I have been confined without exercise for two years—enough to weaken any man; and I was never strong. I used to envy Odo as he climbed trees, like the wild man of the woods he is by nature. Besides, I wanted courage; don't despise me. I have moral courage, but I have no physical courage. I jumped from the wall—yes; but under extreme excitement—this must be done coolly; and I could not climb the rope. You must climb first, and drag me up by sheer force."

"I will do it somehow," said Aymer. "But why not tie loops in the rope for your feet and hands? Is it long enough?"

"Plenty; I never thought of that. Two heads are better than one. I will do that this very night. How long do you think it will take you to recover yourself?"

"I will try it to-morrow," said Aymer.

"No; that is too soon. Say the night after. We must go as early in the evening as is compatible with being unseen, so as to have the whole night to escape in. Now sleep. I shall not say another word."

He withdrew, and Aymer vainly tried to slumber. He could not sleep till morning, and he did not wake till far into the day. His breakfast was waiting for him. As he sat down to it with a better appetite, Fulk spoke to him from the picture.

"You look better," he said; "your long sleep has refreshed you. Shall we try it to-night? I own I am afraid lest some trifle should delay us."

"To-night, certainly," said Aymer. "I feel quite well now. It was simply a heaviness—a drowsiness—a narcotic, perhaps. Let it be to-night. I must go to Violet."

"Ah, Violet!" sighed Fulk. "That was my poor wife's name too. I shall love your Violet. I will help you. I know more of the world than you do."

The day passed slowly. They conversed in low tones nearly all the time. Aymer, led on by Fulk's gentle ways, frankly told him all his struggles, his disappointments, his hopes. Fulk was deeply interested. At last he said—

"At ten we will do it, or perish. I have a mind," he said, "to let you go alone; you are stronger than I am. Very likely my nervousness or weakness will spoil the whole enterprise; but you could do it certainly."

"I will not hear of such a thing," said Aymer; "I will not attempt it without you. Do you think I am a cur?"

The dusk fell gradually—so slowly that it tried Aymer's patience terribly. Davidson lit the gas, and left him the evening paper.

232

"Glad to see you getting better, sir," he said, civilly.

He withdrew, and nothing now remained between them and the task except the twilight. Aymer kept urging to commence. Fulk thought it was not dark enough. At half-past nine a cloud came over the sky.

"Now," said Fulk; "I have got the rope ready. Take the picture down, and scramble through the hole. No; hand me your change of dress first. There is the rope."

Aymer had no difficulty in getting through, and at once picked up the rope. At one end he found a heavy knob of coal fastened.

"That is to throw it up by," said Fulk, "and to make the rope hang down the other side. I hid it for that purpose."

Fulk put the window open, shading the gas by the blind. Aymer coiled up the rope on his left arm to let it run out easily; and was glad now of the physical education he had unwillingly imbibed at old Martin Brown's. Many a time he had cast the cart-line over a tall waggon-load of straw. He looked out, measured the height, and hurled the knob of coal. It flew straight up into the air, carrying with it the destinies of two men, like a shot from a mortar over a ship in distress. A moment of suspense—it cleared the wall, the rope ran out quickly, till but a few feet were left in Aymer's hands. Fulk opened the other half of the window; the rope was passed round the upright and secured. Next the air-belt had to be fastened under Fulk's chest and inflated. Aymer tied his change of clothes and Fulk's in the other air-belt, and adjusted them to his back. These incumbrances gave him some little uneasiness. He pulled at the rope—it was firm; the ruler had caught the crenelations. Then arose the difficulty as to who should go first; Aymer, with a lurking suspicion lest Fulk's heart should fail, compelled him to take the lead. He helped him at the window, and saw a new danger. Their shadows were projected on the wall opposite; if any one looked that way it would be seen in an instant that something was going forward. Below on the right was a bow window, and from this bow window a stream of light fell upon the rope. However it was too late to hesitate.

Folk clung like a cat till he got his foot into the first loop, then he went up fairly well. As soon as he was up, and Aymer could see his form dimly astride of the wall, he followed. Halfway up, as he looked down, he saw a man in the bow window approach and draw down the blind. If he had looked out he must have seen the rope and Aymer, but he did not. When the blinds were down the rope became invisible. With a beating heart Aymer found himself at the top of the wall, astride, facing Fulk, who pressed his hand.

"I feel all right now we have started," he whispered; "I think I shall manage it yet."

There were no loops for the descent. Aymer, after one glance at the city lights before him, slid down first, and let himself into the water gently. He adjusted the load on his back on the float: then shook the line as a signal to Fulk, who came halfway down well, but his nervous excitement overcame him, and he rather fell than slid the remainder, reaching the water with a splash. His head did not go under, but they feared lest any one had heard it. In a few seconds, as all was quiet, Aymer struck out, pushing the float in front and dragging Fulk behind. He had no load to support, but simply to force his way through the water. It was chilly, but not so cold as he had feared. It smelt unpleasant—some chemical works discharged into it. Though a fairly good swimmer, Aymer had a hard struggle to cross the broad canal, and more than once paused to recover his strength. At last they landed on the towing path, and without a moment's delay got over a low wall into some back garden and changed their clothes, wrapping the wet things round a loose brick from the wall and dropping them in the water. They then made haste along the towing path, Aymer leading, and emerged at a bridge into a broad thoroughfare, gaslit but deserted.

"Come on," whispered Aymer. "There is the station; we shall catch the up 10:15 train to London."

"Is that the station?" said Fulk. "Then here we part. Good-by."

"Part? What do you mean?"

"I mean this: that I owe you my liberty—I shall repay you. I shall stay here and watch for your Violet—I am sure she is here."

It was useless arguing with him: Fulk was determined.

"I shall easily hide in this great city," he said. "We shall be on the watch in two places at once—you at Belthrop and World's End, and I here. Make haste. By-the-by, can you lend me a pound or two? I have no money with me."

Aymer insisted upon dividing the sixty-five pounds he had left. Then they shook hands.

"Stay," said Fulk, "our rendezvous?—Where shall we meet again? Quick!—your train."

"At The Place, World's End," said Aymer at a venture, and with one more rapid handshake ran off. He caught his train, and by one in the morning was in London.

Poor Fulk, wandering he hardly knew where on the look out for a quiet inn, came suddenly into a crowded street, and amidst a number of carriages evidently waiting. He looked up—it was some theatre or other. There was a large poster announcing that the famous singer Mademoiselle F—o would perform that evening in the Sternhold Hall, and as he read, he heard a loud encore which reached even to the street.

"I remember her," he thought. "I saw her at Vienna the year before I was captured. They said she was this Marese Baskette's mistress—a splendid creature. I've half a mind—I haven't heard a song for so long—"

He hesitated. Prudence told him to go away; but talk of prudence to a man who has just escaped into liberty! He walked in; the performance was nearly over, but he paid and went into the pit. "After

234

all," he tried to persuade himself, "there's more safety in a crowd. When I go out, I can take a cab and drive to an hotel and say I've lost my train through the theatre; that will account for my having no luggage."

As he struggled in among the crowd, he glanced up at the boxes; his pushing caused a little movement, and people in the boxes looked down. He caught an eye watching him—he turned pale. It was Theodore, who rose at once and left his box. Poor Fulk gasped for breath; he pushed to get out. The audience was annoyed at the movement and disturbance—some gentlemen held him down—the notes of the singer's voice floated over, musically sweet. Poor Fulk!

Chapter Twelve

Science, as illustrated by the printing press, the telegraph, the railway, is a double-edged sword. At the same moment that it puts an enormous power in the hands of the good man, it also offers an equal advantage to the evil disposed.

Theodore Marese was a man of science; and he was a typical man of science—hard, clear, bright, pitiless as the dissecting knife. Unfortunately, he applied his knowledge and his undoubted ability to the worst of uses. One pursuit to which he had devoted special effort, and over which he had spent many thoughtful hours, was the problem how to dispose of a dead human body. There was an old superstitious saying that the earth will not hide blood—it will out. Theodore was of a different opinion. Science had conquered everything: science could conquer this. Yet it certainly was a difficult task. Did you ever contemplate the difficulty? Suppose you slay your enemy—slay him secretly, effectually: now, what next? Try to bury it: the loose earth speaks for itself. Exhalations will rise. Quicklime it, and hasten its decomposition: there will remain, perhaps, only a brass button, or some coin left in the pocket. Throw it into the water: it will rise to the surface. Burn it, and all the city will know from the odour. The more you think over it, the more difficult it will appear. But Theodore had found the solution.

In that laboratory of his which Fulk wished to explore, and which was a harmless-looking room—without so much as a phial or a microscope in view, there was at one corner, not very far from the fireplace, a long upright cupboard, reaching from the floor to the ceiling. Or, rather, the cupboard rose about halfway, and a bookcase reached the remainder. It was a shallow cupboard. There were no locks to the doors. Any one could pull them open, and see a few trifles within—such trifles as might be found in any bachelor's room. The bookcase was also shallow, but there was depth enough back for some rows of books. The books were harmless enough—mostly medical works, just such works as any one can purchase who cares to. Nothing certainly here to excite suspicion. Yet behind that cupboard and bookcase was concealed the most deadly, insidious, awful engine ever constructed by man—an engine about which no secrecy exists either, and which living men have seen in operation; which has been described in the papers; and which the legislature must put down, or strictly regulate.

Upon removing one of the books, Theodore had merely to push aside a small brass plate, which looked like part of a hinge, and there was a keyhole; turn the key, and the whole cupboard swung bodily out into the room. It was, in fact, a blind, placed in front of a narrow inner door, which rose to the ceiling. When the door was open, there stood revealed an iron box, not unlike an extremely long coffin, placed on end. There was a keyhole—two key-holes—to this iron box. Open the first, and there was a large cavity, tall enough for a man to sit on a bar which went across it, without his head touching the iron roof. In this iron roof there was an opening, not unlike a small grating. Put the key in the second keyhole, above the first, and there was the apparatus, greatly improved by Theodore, but in substance the same as used in other places—the apparatus for absorbing the smell of the gases which arise from a human body when consumed by heat. Every one knows that if the smoke of a pipe be passed through water in a peculiar way, it loses its pungency, and you can inhale it with more comfort: this is the hookah. Everybody also knows that manufacturers in great towns are compelled to consume their own smoke, and all have seen a lump of loaf sugar suck up a spoonful of tea. A combination of these principles formed Theodore's deadly engine, which was nothing more or less than a private cremation stove. The ordinary fire in the harmless-looking fireplace produced sufficient heat, when a draught was caused by turning a winch with a multiplying wheel placed at the lower part of the cupboard, just beneath the cavity which was to receive the body. This body, made thoroughly insensible and unconscious by being saturated with chloroform or strong drugs—or, if you like, still more insensible with a trifle of arsenic—had merely to be lifted into its iron coffin, the door closed, the blast applied, and in a couple of hours or so there would remain a little heap of ashes, and a little melted metal, brass buttons, coins, and such like, things easily dropped into a canal, dust easily mixed with the ashes under the grate. Now, where was all that superstitious nonsense about the difficulty of getting rid of a dead body?

Whether Theodore had ever used this awful engine was never known; but it existed, and it may exist at this present hour in other equally unsuspected places. What I say is, that the legislature should take cremation in hand. If any one had been shut up in that iron box alive—only stupefied for a few minutes with a drug, put in asleep; if they had been awakened by the red-hot iron, of what use would their screams have been—deadened by the confinement, deadened by thick walls?

"I am extremely sorry," said Theodore Marese, meeting Violet at the railway station, and handing her to a carriage; "I regret very much that Mr. Malet could not come. He has, in fact, gone upon a special mission. A gentleman in the Isle of Man, who owed us a large sum, died suddenly; his affairs are in confusion, and Mr. Malet was obliged to start this afternoon to see to our debt. I am the bearer of his regrets. At all events, he will not be absent more than a week."

Violet was naturally much disappointed, but after all, it was only a week or ten days, and they treated her with great courtesy at the residence at the asylum. A matron was always ready to afford her companionship; no intrusion was made upon her privacy. Theodore occasionally called upon her in the most respectful way. Books, papers, anything she seemed to wish for came at once. The matron, a lady-like person, took her into the town to do some shopping. Everything but a letter from Aymer. However, that was easily explained—the sea-post was always uncertain. Theodore took her over a great part of the asylum; she was astonished at its size, and the number of its inmates. It saddened her, and she still more longed for Aymer to return.

Why it was that she was not confined like Aymer was never wholly explained, but there is some reason to think that Marese Baskette had a faint idea of marrying her himself. He was, as we have seen, nervous about his marriage with Lady Lechester: lest anything should happen to prevent or delay it. This girl, Violet, he well knew, had a good claim to the estate; suppose he married her? She was a second string to his bow. As to the rumour of his being her father's murderer, he would trust to his own wit and handsome face to overcome that. He never questioned his power to have her if he chose— but Lady Lechester first. Theodore had therefore his instructions to treat her well, and give her seeming liberty, and above all to keep her in good temper. Theodore did as he was bid. This seems the natural solution of the problem. If she had known that Aymer was so near!

It happened at this time that, on the seventh day after Violet's arrival, the famous singer, Mademoiselle F—o, of whom all the world was talking, was to sing for one night only in the Sternhold Hall. Theodore, finding that she was getting restless and thoughtful, seized upon this opportunity to while away her gloom. He proposed that she should accompany him to the theatre or hall, and Violet, who had never heard an opera in her life, was naturally enough delighted to go. They went, and as it chanced it was the very night that Aymer and poor Fulk chose to make their escape. Thus it was that Theodore's eye caught

237

sight of Fulk, the moment the commotion caused by his late entrance attracted his attention. Violet was extremely pleased; the notes of the music and song filled her with an exquisite enjoyment. She was very beautiful, leaning over the front of her box, and scores of glasses were directed at her. Had she known that at that very moment Aymer was risking his life to escape!

The difficulty in this history-writing is to describe two or three events at the same moment. The eye can only read one line at a time, how then are you to bring two scenes at once before it? Some allowance must be made for the infirmities of the pen. There were two scenes proceeding at the moment that Theodore's eye fell upon Fulk—three scenes, if you reckon the opera on the stage. First, poor Fulk shivering with terror, struggling to escape, the crowd round execrating him, his mind in a whirl, reproaching himself with his folly, and the tall figure of Theodore, who had come down from the box, pointing him out to an attendant and pushing forward to seize him. On the stage, La Sonnambula was uttering her sweetest trill; Marese Baskette's mistress in the full height of her glory, with hundreds upon hundreds of the élite of that great city intent upon her every accent—hundreds upon hundreds of well-dressed, fashionable, wealthy ladies and gentlemen, most of whom knew her connection with Marese, the popular M.P., were there. This very knowledge attracted them in shoals. This was scene two.

The third scene was underneath. There in the darkness and gloom of the cellars, amid the slimy pools of water, the hideous fungi, the loathsome toads and creeping things, the grey sewer-rats were at work. You have seen a ship launched—she stands firm as a rock till the last wedge is knocked away, then glides into the water. Something of the same kind was going on here beneath the feet of several hundred human beings. These musty cellars and vaults under the Sternhold Hall, with their awkward approach, had been let at last. A London firm had given a small sum for them, and established a store of whisky casks. A dozen or so of whisky casks had been rolled down, a name put upon the door, and an advertisement in the newspaper. Nobody could do business with this firm, their terms were too high. The whisky casks, in truth, contained pure spring water. It was an excuse, however, for men in rough jackets, who had evidently been at work, to go in and out of these vaults, and to take with them saws and chisels, hammers, and other harmless tools. The firm was, in fact, composed of a dozen or more of the sharpest sewer-rats in Stirmingham. Their little game was so delightfully simple—only a little gnawing to be done! When Theodore and Baskette went down into this place, they found the floor supported by timber pillars. Their idea was to blow it up. The sewer-rats were much cleverer—their idea was to saw through the wooden pillars, and let the roof or floor down, and with it many hundred shrieking, maimed, and mutilated human beings. How simple great

238

ideas appear when once they are described! There is nothing novel in the idea either: the holy Saint Dunstan tried it at Calne, and found it answer admirably.

Some say odd accidents have happened to grand stands at race meetings, through iron bolts being inadvertently removed. When hundreds of well-dressed, fashionable people, ladies and gentlemen, with gold rings and diamonds, earrings and bracelets, watches, money, bank-notes, and similar valuables about them, not to mention rich cloaks and perhaps furs, were shrieking, struggling, groaning, maimed, mutilated, and broken to pieces, with jagged ends and splinters of deal sticking into their bodies, how nice and benevolent it would be to go in among and assist them; to lift up the broken arm, and lighten it of the massive gold bracelet; to pull the horrid splinter out of the leg, and extract the well-filled purse; to alleviate the agony of the bruised shoulder or the broken back, and remove the choice fur or necklace of diamonds! Thoughtful of the sewer-rats to provide this banquet of Christian charity!

The one difficulty had been to get the several hundred people there. They had all in readiness for months, watching. They had it ready while the family council sat, and had deliberated about knocking the last wedge out at that time, but on reflection it was doubtful whether the Americans had much coin about them. Finally, one shrewd sewer-rat hit upon the idea of engaging Mademoiselle F—o to come down and sing. They paid her one hundred pounds in advance, with travelling expenses to come afterwards; and it would have been a good speculation in itself, for they took three hundred and fifty pounds, including the boxes. These boxes were a worry. They could not be let down, they were not built on wooden pillars; however, it was easy to shut one of the folding-doors at the entrance, and let the bolt drop into the stone—easy to raise a cry of "Fire!"—easy to imagine the crush at the door.

Easy also for me to enter into a catalogue of broken limbs, ribs, fractures, contusions, gashes, etc, etc—I shall leave it to the surgical imagination. But when hundreds of people, closely packed, are suddenly precipitated eighteen feet, amid splintering planks and crushing beams, it is probable that the hospitals will be full. This was the third scene preparing underneath.

Just as Fulk felt Theodore close to him—just as F—o uttered her sweetest trill—just as Violet was in the height of her enjoyment—the grey rat gave his last nibble—the last wedge was knocked away; and the floor went down. Poor Violet saw it all. She saw fourteen hundred hands suddenly thrown up into the air; she heard one awful cry, she felt the box tremble and vibrate, and the whole audience sank—sank as into one great pit. She turned deadly pale; she clung with both hands to the balustrade; but she did not faint. It was all too quick.

Fulk was in a stooping position, struggling to escape. That saved him. He fell with his body across a joist, which with a few others had not been sawn—some few had to be left to keep the floor apparently safe. His arms flew out in front, his legs struggling behind; he was poised on the centre of his body. At any other time one might have laughed. In that terrible moment the instinctive love of life endowed him with unusual strength. He knew not how he did it, but he got astride of the joist; he worked himself along it; he reached one of the slender iron columns or shafts which supported the boxes and gallery. He who mistrusted his power to climb a rope, in that hour of horrors went up that shaft with ease, assisted by the scroll-work on it. He got into the very box where Violet sat, with straining eyes gazing into that bottomless pit. Exhausted, he fell on his knees beside her. Exhausted, he heard the cry of "Fire!"—heard the rush to the doors. He remained on his knees, gazing, like her, down into the pit.

The cry that rose up—the shouts, the groans, the shrieks—will ring in Fulk's ears till his death. Violet never heard a sound; her whole faculties were concentrated in her eyes. Heaps of human beings striving, heaving; fragments of dresses, opera cloaks fluttering from joists in mid-air; splinters with pieces of torn coats—Ah! I cannot write it; and she dares not tell me. One dares not dwell on this scene. One more word only. Fulk glanced at the stage: still the lights burnt there; the painted scene was untouched; the singer, F—o, had fled by the stage staircase.

It is odd, but the idea since came to me—she was the cheese; the hall, the trap. The simile will hardly bear close investigation.

It was those few minutes that Fulk and Violet spent in motionless horror that saved them. They thereby escaped the crush at the door; that is to say, they escaped being in it; it was impossible to go out without seeing it. Fulk recovered himself a little: his first instinct was that of a gentleman—the lady beside him. He caught her arm, and dragged her up from her seat; and she came with him unresistingly out of the box into the corridor: he could feel her whole frame tremble. Perhaps, reasoning after the event, they might as well have sat still; but remember the awful cry of fire, the instinctive desire to escape, and that Fulk was still fearful of being re-captured! They reached the staircase—descended it to within a few feet of the passage. There they saw a black mass, writhing, heaving: it was a mass of men and women who had fallen, and been trodden down. It extended along the whole passage to the open air. Then Violet fainted, and hung in his arms inert, helpless. Poor girl! it was enough to unnerve the boldest man. Fulk grasped her round the waist—he was short remember—he struggled with her; got his feet on that awful floor of moving bodies; he stumbled, and staggered towards the air, gasping for breath, dragging, half-trailing her behind him. He cried for help—his arms failed him; his poor, weak leg—the one that had been broken—slipped down into a crevice between two fallen men, and strive how he would he could not get it out. A mist swam before his eyes; but he did not let go—gallant little Fulk!

Strong arms seized him. Cabmen, police, coachmen, grooms—idlers who had rushed to the doors—seized him, and pulled him out, and set him on his legs, and pushed the brandy flask between his teeth. And still Fulk instinctively held tight to his burden.

"Where shall I drive you, sir?" said one cabman.

"To—I don't know. Where is a good hotel?"

"The 'Dragon,' sir."

"Help to lift her in."

Fifteen minutes afterwards they were at the "Dragon." Fortunate, indeed; for all the city—the great city—was pouring in vast crowds to that horrible doorway; and those who were extricated found it difficult to get away.

Fulk and Violet were well cared for at the "Dragon," as, indeed, they would be after so terrible a catastrophe had brought out all the sympathy there was latent in that city. Besides, they were well-dressed, and Fulk was found to have money in his pocket-money, to do them justice, not one farthing of which was touched while he and Violet lay in adjoining rooms helpless—for they were helpless, utterly exhausted for six whole days. When Fulk, conscious that he must be stirring, did pull himself together and got out of bed, and into the sitting apartment, the first thing he saw was a newspaper on the table, the Stirmingham Daily News, which had come out with a deep line of black round every page, and in which was a list of the dead and wounded; the killed were very few in proportion to the injured. Fulk looked for Theodore Marese; he found his name among the dead. Theodore was gone to his account; he had been found on the floor of the vault face downwards, quite dead. There was a deep wound in his forehead, and it was thought that, in falling, his head had struck the iron-bound edge of one of the supposed whisky casks.

Violet, when she heard that Fulk was up, came out of her room and held out her hand. She was still dreadfully pale; but Fulk thought he had never seen a more beautiful face. She thanked him with tears in her eyes; and Fulk in vain tried to make her think that he had done nothing. "I was up yesterday," she said, "but I could not go till you were better. Now, will you please take me back to the asylum?"

"The asylum?" said Fulk, in amazement.

"Yes; Mr. Theodore will be anxious about me. I sent a message yesterday to him, but I have had no reply."

"Theodore Marese is dead," said Fulk, quietly. "I trust you have had nothing to do with him?"

"Dead!" Violet shuddered. "But I must go to the asylum; perhaps Aymer has returned."

"Aymer—what Aymer?"

An explanation followed, which will be readily understood. It was

241

long before Violet could believe him; till at last his reiterated statements, and the little incidents he related, shook her incredulity. Even then she was partially doubtful, till Fulk chanced to look at the paper on the table. There was an advertisement in large type—"Escaped from the Asylum, Fulk Lechester and Aymer Malet." She could no longer doubt.

"How miserably I have been deceived," she said, and burst into tears.

Fulk was greatly shocked.

"You see now that I must hasten away," he said. "Doubtless this great catastrophe has occupied men's minds, and interfered to prevent a strict search; but now I have found you it is a folly to remain here. My rendezvous with Aymer is at The Place, World's End. We will go to World's End at once."

"Aymer will be there?" said Violet, brightening a little.

"Yes, Aymer will be there," said Fulk.

That evening they paid the bill—to the honour of the "Dragon," it was a very small one—and reached the station in a fly. The same train that had taken Aymer to London took them also. They stayed that night at an hotel, and next afternoon travelled down to the little station nearest to World's End. Another fly took them to the outskirts of Bury Wick village; and from thence they walked to The Place. Violet's heart sank; it was dark, not a light in the window, not a sign of life; the doors were fast. They broke a pane of glass, and Fulk opened the window, got in, and unbolted one of the back doors. Fulk had taken the precaution to bring with him a few provisions, and had also bought the local paper—The Barnham Chronicle—and stuffed it in with the ham in the basket, for he was anxious to read about his cousin Lady Agnes' marriage. Violet made a fire, and got some tea: she had provided that. Where was Aymer?

A strange night that at The Place. Fulk felt safer now he was out of the city: but Violet had too vivid a memory of the past. In the very house where so many happy hours had been passed she was alone with a perfect stranger, or one who was a stranger but a little while before. And Aymer?

"Where could Aymer be?" was the question she constantly asked.

Fulk said, "Aymer was doubtless at Belthrop, trying to find her."

"But Hannah Bond knows I started for Stirmingham," objected Violet. "If Aymer should see her, and go back to Stirmingham. I must write to her—or will you?"

"I will go and see her," said Fulk; "certainly I will. But remember that I am in hiding; it must be at night. Wait till to-morrow night. Give Aymer that little time to come, then I will go."

"Hannah must come and live here with me," said Violet, musingly. "I think I shall stay at The Place till—till—where is your newspaper?"

"I—I—burnt it," said Fulk. "I burnt it helping you to light the fire."

It was the truth, yet it was a lie. He had burnt it, that Violet might not see something in it. Aymer was not at Belthrop. Aymer's name was in the paper.

"How shall I amuse you?" said Violet. "This is my home; I must amuse you. I will play to you one of the airs that Aymer likes. Poor Aymer!" she added, half to herself.

The gentle, melancholy music of Mendelssohn filled the room from the long unused piano.

"Poor Aymer!" repeated Fulk to himself. Poor Aymer, indeed!

Chapter Thirteen

At twelve o'clock of the night before his wedding-day, Marese Baskette was galloping, fast as his best thorough-bred could carry him, from Barnham town to The Towers. Barely had he settled himself at his hotel to think over the coming day, than a message summoned him to return. It was a splendid night—warm, still, the sky full of stars, and a faint odour of the hawthorn blossom in the air. The thin mist that Lady Lechester had seen had descended into the hollows, and as Marese rode through it, it reached to his saddle-bow. The horse rushed on, hidden in the cloud that covered the earth; the rider sat above it. Far behind clattered the groom, who had fetched him in hot haste.

"Lady Lechester is lost!" Such was his brief message, and not all Marese's sharp questioning could elicit anything more, for the simple reason that nothing more was known. About eight o'clock she had been seen to leave the house, and the servants took no particular notice of it, expecting her to return in a short time, as she usually did. As she usually did I—this was the first time Marese had heard of the nocturnal walks of his bride. It was a mystery to him: it angered him. A man of plots and stratagems, he was always more or less suspicious of others. An hour had passed, and Lady Lechester did not return. The guests—and they were numerous that night at The Towers—asked for her; the household still kept their mistress's secret, but two ventured out to seek her. They went to the well-known spot, they saw the oak trunk, they heard the roar of the river—but Lady Lechester was not there. An anxious consultation took place; butler, footmen, the upper servants held a whispered discussion. At last the gamekeeper was sent for: if Lady Lechester happened to see him, she would not be annoyed; if she met any of the others, and fancied they had been watching her, it would

243

cost them their places. The guests were put off with various excuses. Time passed: the gamekeeper reported the park clear, and not a trace of Lady Agnes. The truth could no longer be concealed. The alarm and excitement among the wedding guests may easily be imagined. All the gentlemen at once put on their hats, and with lanterns and brandy flasks proceeded to search the park in every direction. A man was despatched post-haste on the swiftest horse for the bridegroom. One gentleman rode with him to Barnham, woke up the police, and instructed them to be on the alert, but, if possible, to keep matters quiet. Especially they were to look out for the dog Dando, who was known to have accompanied Lady Agnes, but had not returned.

Marese reached The Towers about one in the morning. During his ride he had mastered his feelings; he had crushed down the superstitious presentiment which warned him that all was in vain. He had not felt so unusually nervous about this marriage for nothing. But he mastered himself. One of his maxims was never to regret the past, but to apply the mind with iron will to make the best of the present. He called the servants, naturally taking the lead, and made them tell him all they knew. Then for the first time Lady Agnes' strange visits to "The Pot" became known; and at once the gloomiest forebodings filled the minds of the guests. She was drowned; she had fallen down "The Pot." The idea grew and grew, till it became the one belief. Marese himself could not doubt it. It was a strange and solemn conclave they held, at that hour of the night, in the hall at The Towers, Marese standing in the midst, his face pale but composed, the guests crowding round him, the servants coming up one by one to be examined. The great clock at The Towers tolled two, and there stepped silently into the room a stranger, plainly dressed, but remarkably upright, with an air of authority—the Superintendent of police from Barnham. A silence followed his entrance. He marked it, and said that he had brought drags to search the river—was there a boat anywhere to be obtained?

There was no boat. The Ise ran so swift and was so shallow at ordinary times, and lay so deep down between its banks, that no one cared to keep a boat. The nearest known was a little punt four miles down the river, where it enlarged into a small lake. A man was despatched to borrow it, and pole it up the rapid stream; he could not reach "The Pot," work as hard as he might, under three hours. All the gentlemen and not a few of the ladies, too excited to sit quietly within, went with the Superintendent across the park to "The Pot," and watched the drags used. The Superintendent asked them to stand back a moment while he examined the ground round the mouth of the funnel. He did so carefully; the grass had left no mark of a footstep, there was not a trace of a struggle, not a scrap of dress hanging to a twig, or a broken ornament. Then the drags were dropped down the strange funnel into the roaring water, and under the quiet stars the wedding guests gathered in a circle, watching the police as they searched the cave in vain. Neither drag nor pole could detect anything at the bottom; the light of the strongest bull's-eye failed to show any trace that a body had fallen down that narrow crevice; no stones or earth recently dislodged, not a particle of dress or shawl here either.

By this time the ladies were tired, and shivered in the early morning breeze; they retired, but the gentlemen, greatly excited, stayed and assisted to fish the river Ise downwards for miles. The body would surely be carried with the current: but no, not a trace. The bright sun of the glorious May morning found them still at the mournful task. This was the wedding morning. The thrushes burst into song; the cuckoo flew over with his merry cry; dewdrops glittered like gems upon the bushes, and the lovely May bloom scented the breeze. A wedding morn indeed!—but where was the bride? More than one glanced for a moment from the turbid river up to the deep azure of the sky, and the natural thought that followed need not be described. They met the punt at last—but it was useless. The man who poled it up had kept a close look out; nothing had floated by.

"We shall not find it," said the Superintendent, "till the flood subsides."

Even yet there was one hope as they walked sadly back to The Towers: the dog Dando—where was he? It was reasonable to think that if Lady Lechester had fallen into the river, the dog would presently return to The Towers. If he did not return, there was still hope that she had wandered in some other direction, or had met with an accident— sprained her ankle, or broken her leg in the woods, perhaps. This idea had occurred to the Superintendent and to Marese long before, and the gamekeeper, with eight or ten willing assistants, had been searching the woods for hours. As they neared The Towers it was obvious from the group of people talking excitedly before the entrance that something had happened. A policeman came towards them, leading Dando in a leash.

He had but just arrived in a trap from Barnham town. Questions poured out from a hundred lips; it was difficult to get an explanation, but it was understood at last. The Superintendent on leaving Barnham had not omitted to warn the men on their heats in the town to look out for a dog—Lady Lechester's well-known dog—merely as a forlorn hope, never dreaming that Dando would wander thither. But a little after sunrise, perhaps about six o'clock, the dog Dando walked up the high street of Barnham behind a man wearing a grey suit, who knocked at the door of Mr. Broughton's private residence. Before the knock was answered the man in the grey suit was in custody, and the dog secured. The man in the grey suit struggled violently—fought like a wild beast, which still further prejudiced the police against him, and was with difficulty handcuffed, manacled, and conveyed to the station-house on a stretcher. No one to look at his slight figure would have thought him capable of such savage battling. He asked perpetually for Mr.

245

Broughton, declared that he was not mad—which was strange, as no one had accused him of that failing, and refused to give his name—another trait that looked ill. When asked if he had seen Lady Lechester he denied all knowledge of such a person. The dog had followed him just as any other dog might. As to the road he had come he was obstinately silent. The police had not waited to waste further inquiries upon him, but hastened to The Towers with the news for their chief.

His face fell immediately. "I fear," he said, "that Lady Lechester is indeed lost. The dog would never have left her unless. However, we have now got a clue."

Marese gave up all hope; yet with his old cool self-possession before he started with the Superintendent for Barnham, he wrote out a telegram and despatched it to Theodore, briefly acquainting him with what had happened, and asking him to be especially agreeable to that person—meaning Violet, whose value as a second string to the bow had risen at once. This telegram was despatched to a dead man: Theodore had been killed the night before in the Sternhold Hall, but in the confusion and the difficulty of at once identifying bodies, no news had been sent to Marese.

With the Superintendent, Marese went into the cell at the police station, and saw Aymer Malet handcuffed and manacled. Poor Aymer, indeed! His hair was rough over his forehead, his cheeks stained with blood from a scratch received in the struggle, his whole look wild in the extreme. He saw Marese Baskette, the murderer, the man who had confined him. Is it to be wondered at that he grew excited? He said nothing, but his face worked, and his teeth ground together. Marese looked at him steadily, almost with a smile. In that moment, swift as it passed, he debated upon his best course. Truth, or what he called truth, was the safest, although it would save Aymer's life.

"I know this man," he said. "He is a lunatic; he has escaped from my cousin's asylum at Stirmingham. He is very dangerous: without a doubt, this is the guilty party."

Aymer denied it. All his efforts were to make people believe that he was not mad. As yet he had no conception of the darker shadow hanging over him: his one idea was, that he had been pursued and captured—that he should be sent back to the asylum. Therefore he had refused to give his name, or to describe the road by which he had come to Barnham. This very mistake increased the suspicion against him of a knowledge of Lady Lechester's disappearance. It will now be understood why Fulk burnt the paper that Violet might not read it, and why The Place was dark and cheerless when they reached it. These events had happened just before they arrived.

Marese never lost his presence of mind for a moment, not even when he heard of Theodore's awful death. Turn the mind to the present, was his maxim: do the best with it you can. His one concern was the disappearance of Violet: still he felt certain that he should be able to trace her. At present, the one thing needful was to crush Aymer Malet. He held that enemy now in the hollow of his hand: he should "taste his finger," as the Orientals say.

The magistrates on hearing the evidence at once made out a warrant, and Aymer was remanded, while the search went on for the body, which still eluded all search. Upon the third day, however, some important evidence turned up, and it was thought best to take it in the presence of the prisoner. Aymer was in consequence led into the large apartment used for such purposes at the police station, still wearing the handcuffs, for Marese had industriously spread the belief that he was a dangerous lunatic. The general public were not admitted; but a few gentlemen were present, and among these was Mr. Broughton, who at once recognised Aymer, rough as his present appearance wan, and came forward and spoke to him. Aymer asked him to defend him, and Broughton, to his credit, said he would. To his credit, for his interest in the Lechester estates was large.

The magistrates seeing so respectable a solicitor as Mr. Broughton taking an interest in the prisoner, consulted, and to Marese's intense disgust offered to allow the prisoner half an hour to confer with his attorney. In that brief period poor Aymer had to relate his confinement and his escape. Broughton listened attentively; then he said—

"Your story is strange, almost incredible; still you are in a position where nothing will do you much good but public opinion. My usual advice would be to reserve your defence; my present advice to you is to tell the Bench exactly what you have told me, only much more fully. There are no reporters admitted; but I will see that your statement is published. I believe you myself. If the public show any signs of believing you, the prosecutors will withdraw. It is your only chance; for, to be candid, the evidence is terribly against you."

They returned to the justice-room. The first witness called was the policeman who had detected Aymer and the dog in the street. He described Aymer as walking very fast, and dodging from house to house as if trying to escape notice. This was point Number 1 against him. Then came the evidence as to his furious struggle with the police. One constable could barely make himself understood; a blow straight from the shoulder had knocked a tooth out, and his voice sounded hollow and indistinct. Such a violent resistance obviously indicated a guilty conscience. This was point Number 2 against him. Next it was stated, and stated with perfect truth, that the prisoner had refused to give his name, his place of residence, or any information about himself; and that, finally, he had totally denied even so much as knowing that there was such a person as Lady Lechester. He had tried to conceal his identity in every way, and had deliberately told an untruth, for after living so long at World's End, how could he have failed to know Lady

247

Lechester? This was point Number 3. Then he gave a very vague, unsatisfactory account of how the dog had followed him. He declared that the dog was a strange dog to him—that he had never seen it before. Now this must be also a wilful falsehood. Point Number 4. But the darkest evidence of all was reserved to the last. There was brought into the room an "iron-witted" ploughboy, with a shock head of light hair, small eyes, heavy jowl, and low forehead—the very class of witness most to be dreaded, for nothing on earth can make them understand that it is possible for them to be mistaken.

The ploughboy, Andrew Hornblow by name, told his story straightforwardly enough. He said that he had been to the "Shepherd's Bush" that fateful evening, after work; that he had a pint and a half of ale, but was not any the worse for liquor. That at about half-past seven, or a little earlier, he left the "Shepherd's Bush" inn to return to the farmhouse where he slept. He went across the fields and Downs, and his path led him over a section of the park. As he passed a fir copse he heard some one playing on a tin whistle in a most peculiar way. He was curious: to see who it was, and got into the copse. The moment his footsteps were heard the whistle stopped; but pushing aside the boughs, he caught a glimpse of a tallish man, in a grey suit—a dirty-grey suit—who seemed anxious to avoid observation, and plunged into the dark recesses of the copse. He didn't think much of it at the time; but it so happened that the spot where he had seen the man was within a hundred yards of "The Pot;" and talking of the disappearance of Lady Lechester to his master, the fact had got to the knowledge of the police. Had he seen that man since? Not till he had come into the room; and he pointed at the prisoner, who indeed wore a grey suit, somewhat travel-stained and frayed in places, as if from passage through hedges or woods.

Mr. Broughton cross-examined this witness at great length, and with his accustomed shrewdness—but in vain, the ploughboy was certain the prisoner was the man. All that could be got from him was, that he had not distinctly seen the face of the man in the copse, but he was tallish, and wore a dirty-grey suit. This established the fact that the prisoner was near about the spot, where Lady Lechester had disappeared somewhere within half an hour of that mysterious event.

Point Number 6 was still more convincing. Upon the prisoner being searched, there was found upon him a tin whistle. The whistle was produced, and was of a peculiar construction: when blown, it gave a singular sound, more musical than the ordinary whistle. It was covered with sketches—apparently engraved with a sharp tool—of dogs, some of them very spirited and faithful outline representations. It was well known that the prisoner was a good draughtsman. The only point that remained to be established was the death of Lady Lechester. The body had not been found.

Upon this evidence the police very properly asked for a remand till the body was discovered.

Mr. Broughton immediately applied for bail.

The Bench asked upon what grounds, and this gave Aymer an opportunity to tell his tale. Remember, that all this time Marese Baskette was sitting side by side with the magistrates, who naturally felt for his position, and treated him with exceptional courtesy.

When Aymer began, Marese objected on the ground that the prisoner was a lunatic escaped from Stirmingham Asylum, and that these wild statements, if they got into print, would do him harm. The Bench assured him that nothing the prisoner—whose wild appearance proved the condition of his mind—could say would prejudice him in their estimation, and as there were no reporters present nothing could get abroad. It was better to let the prisoner tell his tale; he might inadvertently disclose the fate of poor Lady Lechester. It was true that the prisoner being a lunatic would escape the extreme penalty of the law, but it was very desirable to learn all that could be known of poor Lady Agnes. Marese had to be satisfied, and to listen while Aymer, in clear, forcible language, told his story, hinting broadly at Marese's complicity in the death of Jason Waldron, and describing the manner in which he had been trapped, and his escape. The Bench listened with an incredulous air, as well they might. The man was evidently mad— quite mad. Finally, Aymer came to his arrival at Belthrop late in the afternoon of the day after he had got out of the asylum. Finding Violet was not at Hannah Bond's, and greatly alarmed, he was at a loss what to do. To go back to Stirmingham was extremely dangerous for fear of re-capture, and he hesitated for a while. At last, after partaking of refreshment given to him by old Hannah, he had started for Barnham with the intention of calling on Mr. Broughton and taking his advice. Halfway to Barnham it had occurred to him that perhaps Violet after all was at The Towers, and he diverged from his course and approached the mansion, as he supposed, about one in the morning. He saw a number of people about and in commotion, and afraid of being recognised and captured altered his mind again, and turned to go to Barnham across the Downs. In doing so he admitted that he had passed near "The Pot," but not at the time stated by the ploughboy—half-past seven in the evening—but half-past one in the morning. As he walked through the grass he saw something glistening, and picked up the tin whistle found upon him. He should not have taken the trouble to carry it away had it not been for the curious figures on it, which, being a light night, he could just distinguish. As he came up the side of the Downs, just as he passed The Giant's Ring—i.e., a circle of stones set on edge— some ancient monument—he was overtaken by the dog Dando, who jumped and fawned upon him with delight as an old friend, and followed him to Barnham where he was captured by the police. He had resisted them because he thought they were under orders to return him to the asylum. The dog Dando limped a little, and he had noticed that his back showed signs of a severe recent beating. Hannah Bond could prove that he did not leave Belthrop till nearly or quite eight, and it was impossible for him to get to "The Pot," ten miles, in less than three hours, across a rough country. His dress was dirty and torn because he had walked quite twenty miles when arrested, and passed through several coppices. Upon this Mr. Broughton asked for bail, and offered himself in any sum they might name. But the Bench could not get over the fact of the asylum—the prisoner was a dangerous lunatic; even if his story was true he was a lunatic. No; the prisoner was removed to his cell pending the discovery of the body of Lady Lechester. All that Broughton could do was to order his carriage and set out for Belthrop to find Hannah Bond.

Poor Aymer. It was Violet he thought of still. But events press so quickly, it is impossible to pause and analyse his emotion. The next day about noon, Mr. Broughton came into the cell with a grave look upon his face, and carrying a large parcel in his hand. Aymer begged him to tell him the truth at once. Mr. Broughton told him that first the body of Lady Lechester had been found. A more careful search by boat near "The Pot" had discovered it. Instead of being carried down by the current, an eddy at the cave had thrown it up against the course of the stream a few yards, and lodged it behind a boulder. There were no marks of violence: she had simply been drowned. Secondly, he had been to Belthrop, and found Hannah Bond's cottage shut up, the old lady gone, and not a trace of her to be found, though he had searched the villages for miles round. Thirdly, the book parcel in his hand had been to London to Aymer's address there, and had been returned to him, Aymer having left instructions that his letters should be sent to Mr. Broughton. Upon removing the outer wrapper, there was the name and address of Aymer Malet, Esq, written in the handwriting of the dead Lady Lechester.

Chapter Fourteen

Fulk had a difficult game to play. In the first place, his motions were restricted by the dread of Marese's emissaries: he could only go out at night. He wished to preserve Violet from a knowledge of Aymer's misfortune, and yet to go to work himself to release his friend. The first thing to do was to get Hannah Bond to The Place, for clearly Violet could not remain there alone with him. Knowing the country well, he had no difficulty on the night after their arrival—the very night after the preliminary examination of Aymer Malet—in finding his way to Belthrop. He explained the circumstances to Hannah, who at once packed up a few things, and walked back with him over the Downs to The Place, without awakening one of her neighbours. This was how Hannah Bond disappeared.

Fulk's knowledge of the circumstances under which Aymer had been arrested was very meagre, but on the third day the Barnham Chronicle came out, and Hannah got him a copy. In it was a full, almost verbatim, account of the preliminary examination, furnished, in fact, by Mr. Broughton. Over this paper Fulk spent the greater part of the night thinking. He shut himself up in a room at The Place on the pretence that he had letters to write, and studied the report, line for line and word for word. After an hour or two, his eye became irresistibly attracted by a little paragraph in small type, evidently added at the last moment before going to press. It was but a few lines, announcing that the dog Dando had again disappeared from The Towers. He had been chained up carefully as was supposed, but he had gone in the night. This little paragraph fixed Fulk's attention. He tried to follow the dog's motions. Why, when Lady Lechester fell down "The Pot," did not the dog return to The Towers? Why did he turn up at The Giant's Ring, with a limp in one leg, as if from a kick, and his back bearing marks of a severe beating? How came that odd and peculiar whistle in the grass— how came there to be two men in grey, one at half-past seven, the other at half-past one? The ploughboy had heard a peculiar whistling. By degrees the conviction forced itself into his mind that the other than in grey—the half-past seven man—must have been no other than his cousin Odo. All the facts answered to such a theory. A tallish man, playing upon a tin whistle; the dog—the dog was of the very breed that Odo had such a fancy for. The beating—doubtless the dog had been attracted by Odo, but had refused to obey him, and had been kicked and thrashed till he ran off, and crossed Aymer's path. The Giant's Ring had actually been one of Odo's favourite haunts before he was confined. It was a wild and desolate spot. Fulk saw it all now clearly. Obviously Odo was still lingering about, perhaps trying to find the whistle he had dropped—obviously Odo had stolen the dog Dando from the The Towers a second time. If he could find Dando, he could find Odo; and Odo found, then Aymer's release was a matter of time only. Fulk meditated, and at last resolved upon his course—he would visit the haunts which he knew Odo used to favour. But Odo was a strong and powerful man, endowed with singular physical strength, Fulk was little, and by no means strong. Art must conquer Nature. Fulk prepared a cord with a noose, the use of which he had learnt years and years before in a trip to South America. It was a lasso, in fact.

Then followed an anxious time. Violet grew more and more restless. Although The Place was so retired, yet people began to know that it was again inhabited. Fulk had heard of strangers being seen about, and he at once guessed that Marese had his spies searching for Aymer Malet's companion in the escape. Every night he went out upon his strange errand, hunting the wild man of the woods. Meantime, an inquest was held upon poor Lady Lechester, and a verdict of murder returned against Aymer Malet. Days and nights passed, and hunt and search how he would, still Odo eluded him.

It was a warm, beautiful evening. The same lucent planet that had so often shone upon Lady Lechester during her visit to the fatal "Pot," glittered in the western sky: but its beams were somewhat dimmed by the new moon, whose crescent was on the point of disappearing below the horizon. Fulk, pushing slowly and sadly through the woods and copses, inhaled the fragrance of the pine tree. The rabbits scattered at his approach; now and then a wood pigeon rose into the air, with a tremendous clatter. In the open it was still light; under the trees a dusky shadow brooded. At a distance, he could faintly hear the sound of rushing water, and the fidgety chirping of the restless brook-sparrows and sedge-warblers. Suddenly there rose a shrill, piping sound; and Fulk started, and his heart for a moment stood still. He listened; then came a strange weird music—if music it could be called—for in its indescribable cadences it reminded him of the playing of the savages in far-off shores, visited years ago. But he recognised it in an instant. He had heard Odo play similar notes when they were boys. Gently, gently, he crept through the brushwood, and holding a branch aside, looked down from the bank upon the stream. It rushed along swiftly with a murmuring sound, reflecting upon its surface the image of the bright planet. The sedges and reeds rustled in the light breeze; and there was Odo. Across the stream there was a fallen tree—the very tree Odo had loved in his youth—and astride upon that tree sat the Beast-Man, his feet nearly touching the water, playing upon a tin whistle. Before him was the dog Dando, standing on his hind legs, and moving in grotesque time to the music. Odo reproached the dog, and told him that he was an unworthy son of his father, and could not dance half so well—had he already forgotten his beating? But perhaps it was the fault of his whistle. Ah, he had lost his best whistle— the one he had made with selected tin, and ornamented with pictures of his dogs—among them Dando's father, who danced so much better. Then he muttered incoherent, half-articulate sounds to the dog, sighed deeply, and began to play again. Poor Odo!

Fulk hesitated. There was a large soul in his little body—he pitied the poor fellow before him from the bottom of his heart. All that singular being wanted was the open air, and freedom to play his tin

252

whistle, fondle his dogs, roam in the woods, and tinker up pots and kettles. Had he been permitted to follow these inclinations, it was doubtful if he would ever have committed crime; but civilisation would not permit it. For a whole year he had been roaming from wood to wood, from wilderness to wilderness, whistling, tinkering sometimes, always happy in simple freedom. Probably he had destroyed Lady Agnes to obtain the dog, the progenitor of which appeared to have been a favourite in old times. But Fulk reflected that, while he hesitated, Aymer languished in the cell, Violet was wearing her heart out, and his own liberty was endangered. Moreover, there was a duty to society: such beings must not go wholly at large, or no one would be safe.

The lasso hissed through the air, the noose dropped round Odo's neck, and was drawn tight in an instant. It had taken his neck and one shoulder. He roared aloud with pain and anger, but the cord choked him. His arms struck out, but he had nothing to grasp. He was dragged on shore in a moment. He floundered—leapt up, and fell again, tearing at the rope like a wild beast taken in the toils. With a swift, dexterous turn of the hand, Fulk wound the cord about his arms and legs, much as a spider might its web about a fly, till Odo lay panting on the sward, helpless, but still hoarsely murmuring and grunting. Then Fulk loosened the lasso round his neck, and proceeded to tie the limbs tighten, finally binding him hard and fast to a tree. Odo's frame quivered; and Fulk, in the dim light, fancied that great tears gathered in his eyes. After binding Odo, there was still a piece of the rope left: with this Fulk secured the dog, which, frightened and astonished, had cowered on the earth. Dando evidently had no affection for Odo: he had been wiled away by gipsy arts only. Then, leading Dando, Fulk set off at a run, tearing through wood and hedge, mounting the steep Downs, fast as his strength could carry him, away for Barnham town.

At that very time, late into the night, Mr. Broughton was conferring with the prisoner in his cell. He had been sent for in haste, and went quickly fearing lest Aymer should be ill. The parcel addressed to Aymer Malet in Lady Lechester's handwriting was a large antique Bible, which Aymer recognised in a moment as having belonged to old Jenkins, the gardener at The Place. He had seen it lying about, but had taken no notice of it. It was in fact the very Bible Lady Agnes had purchased of the gardener's wife when left in destitution by her husband's imprisonment. Inside the Bible was a short formal note, dated the very day in the evening of which Lady Agnes was drowned, stating that the writer when she bought the book was unaware to whom it had belonged, and therefore returned it to Aymer's address—not knowing Violet's—as she desired to retain nothing of theirs. She added that she would return the dog Dando if they would receive it, and tell her where to send it. Aymer, having no occupation in his cell but melancholy thoughts and anxious cares about Violet, naturally turned over the leaves of the noble old book, and looking at it closer than before he found at the end, upon one of the spare leaves, a curious inscription which purported to be a copy from a tomb. It was in Latin, English, and Greek—a strange, fantastic mixture—and when translated, read to the effect that Arthur Sibbold Waldron, whilom of Wolf's Glow, born Sibbold, afterwards Sibbold Waldron, was married at Saint S— Church, Middlesex, and was buried at Penge in Kent—with dates, and the usual sentiments. The entry in the Bible simply added: "Copy of ye inscription, now defaced. Mem. To have the same re-cut. B.W." Here was the clue Aymer had searched for in vain, thrown into his hands, by the operation of those strange and mysterious circumstances over which no one has any control. He sent for Mr. Broughton; and so it was that when Fulk found that gentleman it was in the cell. The surprise of Aymer, and his pleasure at seeing Fulk, his still greater joy and relief when Fulk in his first sentence announced that Violet was safe, can easily be imagined. Mr. Broughton had no sooner heard Fulk's explanation than he at once comprehended the importance of securing Odo. He and Fulk with two assistants drove as near the wood as practicable, and after much trouble safely lodged the unfortunate lunatic in the hands of the police. Fulk remained with Broughton, who very considerately went in his carriage in the morning over to The Place, and brought Violet and Hannah Bond to his own private residence in Barnham.

At the inquiry that followed, the first step was the release of Aymer on bail, on the testimony of Hannah Bond, that he had not left the cottage at Belthrop till eight o'clock. The ploughboy, when shown Odo, at once declared that this was the man he had seen—"A' had such mortal big ears—a' minded that, now." And Marese? His position became extremely awkward. It was easy to declare that Aymer was a lunatic; but when Fulk was produced—when the clever escape was related in exactly the same manner by both—when Fulk added what he had overheard about the murder of Jason Waldron, Marese could not but notice that the magistrates and the Court looked coldly upon him. He claimed them both as escaped lunatics. Said the Bench—

"We don't see what right you have to them. The owner of the asylum is dead. We will take it upon ourselves to say, that the lunatics, for lunatics, have a remarkably sane way of talking."

The result was, that Marese withdrew; the more he meddled with the matter, the worse it became for him. To add to the evil complexion of affairs, Odo confessed in his cell to the murder of Jason Waldron. He strenuously denied having touched Lady Agnes; he declared that his sole object was the dog. The dog was the descendant of an old favourite, and he had once followed Miss Merton to Torquay to get it.

But as he stole round from behind the oak trunk to seize the dog, Lady Agnes saw him, started, missed her footing, and fell down "The Pot." He knew her—she was his cousin, and he had no feeling against her. In all probability this story was true, as no marks of violence were found on the body. But he frankly confessed hitting Jason Waldron on the head with the bill-hook; and stated exactly what Fulk had already said—that he was told by Theodore Marese, if he killed that man, and his daughter (Aymer shuddered), he should be always free. He had laid in wait for the daughter; but she was out of his reach at The Towers.

Odo concluded with a cunning wink, and called Mr. Broughton to come near. He whispered to him that he should be the richest man in the world if he would give him liberty. Broughton humoured the miserable creature, and told the rest to leave the cell.

Then Odo disclosed his bribe. He said that years ago the gipsies with whom he consorted had shown him a deed, to which they attached a species of superstitious reverence, and asked him to read it, it being in law characters, and in Latin. It was a deed conferring an entail upon the estate at Wolfs Glow—"the very estate," whispered Odo, "that all the people are trying for."

Odo ascertained that this deed had been stolen by Romy Baskette's elder brother—the man who, with his mother, left the Swamp when old Will Baskette was shot—stolen with the intention of injuring the Sibbolds, his father's murderers. He had watched old Sibbold poring over this deed, therefore thought it valuable, seized his opportunity, and stole it. With the strangest, maddest mixture of shrewdness and lunacy, Odo in his turn stole the deed from the gipsies who had preserved it, and held it, to be used as a bribe in case he should be captured. He now offered it to Broughton, if Broughton would only let him go free.

The lawyer must be forgiven if he told a falsehood, and promised. Odo told him where the deed was hidden; and, as he had described, so they found it. In that tree which had fallen across the stream where he had used to sit astride and whistle, halfway across was a knot. This knot with his tools he had cut out—excavated a cavity, and used the knot to hide it; so that the closest inspection must have failed to find it. They found the tree and the knot. They got the knot out; there was a small tin box—Odo's own workmanship—and in the box was the long-lost deed.

Poor Odo of course never got his freedom; but there were friends who saw that he was as well cared for as under the circumstances was possible. Who could harbour revenge against such a creature? He was but the instrument in the hands of others, and not truly guilty of poor Jason's death. That lay at the door of Marese and Theodore. Theodore was dead. Morally speaking, Fulk slew Marese. He wrote a full account of what he had overheard, and it was published in a great London paper. The asylum was searched, and the holes in the wall found as described. By this letter Fulk secured two objects: first his own liberty in future—for popular opinion rose with irresistible violence in his favour; secondly, he destroyed Marese. Yet it was not the murder of Jason Waldron which did it; it was the Lucca. There were people who had lost heavily over the Lucca, these people pursued Marese Baskette, threatened him with criminal, civil, and every kind of proceedings. He fled, escaping arrest by a few hours only, taking with him five thousand pounds in gold. He is believed to have reached California, but has not been heard of since. Whether the Nemesis of these modern days—"circumstances over which we have no control"—engulfed him in still deadlier ruin, was never known. His fall, as it was, was great indeed.

By the death of Lady Agnes Lechester, Fulk succeeded to her estates, which, added to those already his, made him one of the largest landholders in the county. If he survives Odo, he will be a still more wealthy man. He never left Aymer's side till all was well.

Aymer and Violet were married in the autumn—married in the quietest manner, and, aided pecuniarily by Fulk, left for the south of France, there to try and efface the memory of the awful event that had embittered the path of their love. Fulk joined them with a yacht two months later on. They are very, very happy, but it is in a subdued and quiet manner. It is hardly possible for them yet, even in the sunny south, to feel so abundantly joyous as would be natural to their youth. But as the time rolls on they will gradually supplant the old unhappy memories with fresh and pleasant pictures.

The last letter from Fulk announced that the sea breezes and the fresh air had begun to work wonders with his complexion, and that he hoped ere long to throw off the horrid yellow produced by his confinement, and resume his proper colour. That was natural in Fulk; the proverb says that little men are often conceited. Yellow or rosy, or brown, he will always be the dearest friend of Aymer and Violet.

And the great estate—the city of Stirmingham? To this very hour that Gordian knot remains untied; to this very hour claimants every now and then startle the world with extraordinary statements; and the companies having nothing else to do, have fallen to loggerheads between themselves, and spend their vast incomes in litigation. But aided by Fulk's money, and the influence his family connections possessed, Violet did at last receive a portion of her rights; the chain of evidence proving her descent from Arthur Sibbold was completed down to the smallest link.

The Corporation of Stirmingham, after much law and talk, were finally compelled to acknowledge her claim. By arbitration it was settled that they were to pay her eight thousand pounds per annum for ten years, and at the expiration of that period, ten thousand pounds per annum to herself and heirs, in perpetual ground rent. The companies still hold out, but it is only as to the amount they shall contribute in the same way; and they will have to come to terms. Violet will thus receive a large income without compromising her rights, which are specially reserved. She has not forgotten poor Jenkins, whose Bible gave the clue to the register of Arthur Sibbold's marriage. The old man is at last recompensed for his long-suffering—the imprisonment expired in due time. He and his wife live in the old cottage at The Place, tending the gardens as of yore, being made comfortable with an ample provision from Violet.

Violet and Aymer once a year visit The Place and the tomb of poor Jason. They have taken a mansion at Tunbridge Wells, but spend much time in Aymer's beloved Florence, with Fulk. They love the old house, and yet they do not care to live where everything recalls such gloomy memories as at The Place.

The End